A Hidden
Hope

Novels by Suzanne Woods Fisher

LANCASTER COUNTY SECRETS
The Choice
The Waiting
The Search

SEASONS OF STONEY RIDGE
The Keeper
The Haven
The Lesson

THE INN AT EAGLE HILL
The Letters
The Calling
The Revealing

AMISH BEGINNINGS
Anna's Crossing
The Newcomer
The Return

THE BISHOP'S FAMILY
The Imposter
The Quieting
The Devoted

NANTUCKET LEGACY
Phoebe's Light
Minding the Light
The Light Before Day

THE DEACON'S FAMILY
Mending Fences
Stitches in Time
Two Steps Forward

THREE SISTERS ISLAND
On a Summer Tide
On a Coastal Breeze
At Lighthouse Point

CAPE COD CREAMERY
The Sweet Life
The Secret to Happiness
Love on a Whim

NATIONAL PARK SUMMERS
Capture the Moment

The Moonlight School
A Season on the Wind
Anything but Plain
Lost and Found
A Healing Touch
A Hidden Hope

A Hidden Hope

SUZANNE WOODS FISHER

Revell

a division of Baker Publishing Group
Grand Rapids, Michigan

© 2025 by Suzanne Woods Fisher

Published by Revell
a division of Baker Publishing Group
Grand Rapids, Michigan
RevellBooks.com

Printed in the United States of America

All rights reserved. No part of this publication may be reproduced, stored in a retrieval system, or transmitted in any form or by any means—for example, electronic, photocopy, recording—without the prior written permission of the publisher. The only exception is brief quotations in printed reviews.

Library of Congress Cataloging-in-Publication Data
Names: Fisher, Suzanne Woods, author.
Title: A hidden hope / Suzanne Woods Fisher.
Description: Grand Rapids, Michigan : Revell, a division of Baker Publishing Group, 2025.
Identifiers: LCCN 2024053716 | ISBN 9780800745295 (paper) | ISBN 9780800747435 (casebound) | ISBN 9781493451425 (ebook)
Subjects: LCSH: Amish—Fiction. | LCGFT: Christian fiction. | Novels.
Classification: LCC PS3606.I78 H54 2025 | DDC 813/.6—dc23/eng/20241122
LC record available at https://lccn.loc.gov/2024053716

Some Scripture used in this book, whether quoted or paraphrased by the characters, is taken from the Christian Standard Bible®. Copyright © 2017 by Holman Bible Publishers. Used by permission. Christian Standard Bible® and CSB® are federally registered trademarks of Holman Bible Publishers.

Some Scripture quotations are from the King James Version of the Bible.

Some Scripture used in this book, whether quoted or paraphrased by the characters, is taken from the Holy Bible, New International Version®, NIV®. Copyright © 1973, 1978, 1984, 2011 by Biblica, Inc.® Used by permission of Zondervan. All rights reserved worldwide. www.zondervan.com. The "NIV" and "New International Version" are trademarks registered in the United States Patent and Trademark Office by Biblica, Inc.®

This book is a work of fiction. Names, characters, places, and incidents are the product of the author's imagination or are used fictitiously. Any resemblance to actual events, locales, or persons, living or dead, is coincidental.

Cover design by Laura Klynstra.

Author is represented by Joyce A. Hart.

Baker Publishing Group publications use paper produced from sustainable forestry practices and postconsumer waste whenever possible.

25 26 27 28 29 30 31   7 6 5 4 3 2 1

For all the Charlie Kings out there—
those who persevere against the odds,
who never give up on their dreams.
The world is a better place because of you.

Time is the best doctor.
—Ruth "Dok" Stoltzfus

Meet the Cast

Ruth "Dok" Stoltzfus (age late fifties), the dedicated doctor of Stoney Ridge. She cares for both Amish and non-Amish patients alike and is also the sister of Bishop David Stoltzfus. Once upon a time, young Ruth left her Amish roots to pursue higher education and a medical career—a move that shook things up in her family. Married to police officer Matt Lehman, she somehow juggles it all. (To learn more about Dok's backstory, check out *Anything but Plain*.)

David Stoltzfus (age mid-fifties), the bishop of the Amish church in Stoney Ridge. He's a father to many, both in the literal sense and when it comes to tending his flock. Brother to Dok, husband to **Birdy**, and the kind of man who wears responsibility like a second skin.

Annie Fisher (age 21), office assistant to Dok, daughter of Sally (who can give hypochondriacs a run for their money), and an aspiring EMT. Amish to her core but with ambitions that go beyond the farm.

Evie Miller (age 26), a traveling nurse on a three-month contract with Dok's practice. Her grandparents were Mennonites, so she's got a foot in both worlds. Skilled, dedicated, and figuring out if, where, and with whom she fits in Stoney Ridge.

Charlie King (age 27), a freshly minted med school graduate (though he just squeaked by) and newly arrived resident at Dok's practice. All eyes are on him to see if he can survive Dok's high standards . . . and pass his boards.

Wren Baker (age 27), also a newly arrived resident at Dok's practice, but unlike Charlie, she's got the grades to back up her credentials. Top of her class, sharp as a tack, and eager to prove herself.

Fern Lapp (late sixties), Amish woman and owner of Windmill Farm. Wise, witty, and always ready with a subtle nudge in the right direction.

Gus Troyer (age 25), Amish EMT and smitten with Annie Fisher. Good with a stretcher, bad at hiding his crush.

Sarah Blank (age early twenties), works at the Bent N' Dent. Has a deep interest in others' lives. Some might call it nosiness.

Hank Lapp (ageless), known for his shocking lack of awareness. In *A Healing Touch*, he nearly met his Maker. He's back and louder than ever!

Edith Fisher Lapp (age: classified), Hank's long-suffering wife.

Matt Lehman (late fifties), Dok's husband and the local police officer. Solid as a rock, all-around good guy.

1

She should've known it was too good to be true. Evie Miller had been floating on air . . . until she crashed back down to earth with a thud.

She had landed her top choice as a traveling nurse at the Stoney Ridge Family Practice, with an incredible doctor named Ruth Stoltzfus. Just a few months ago, Evie had seen a television news feature on Dok Stoltzfus—and decided to apply for a traveling job with her rural practice. Imagine having time with a doctor who still made house calls . . . among the Amish!

But then the story got even better.

Charlie King, fresh out of med school, had stopped by her nursing station at Penn State Hershey with news. Big news. After coming up empty on Match Day in March, he'd scrambled to find an unfulfilled residency. And he had. A great one, he said—serving an underserved area, with the added bonus of medical school loan forgiveness. Assuming, of course, he completed the residency, passed his final board exam, and checked all the right boxes.

"Where is it?" Evie had asked.

Charlie leaned over the counter, his eyes lighting up. "Stoney Ridge Family Practice."

Stunned, Evie could only stare at him, suspended in shock. Was this truly happening? Was she dreaming? No words came out of her mouth. She had to just pause at the impossibility of it.

Charlie King was going to Stoney Ridge. To a sleepy little Amish village. To the same medical practice as Evie.

The Charlie King.

And then Wren Baker showed up at the nurse's station, leaning on the counter right next to Charlie. Evie wasn't surprised—Wren always seemed to hover around him, like a shadow that never quite left his side.

But what she said next did surprise Evie. "Did you tell her yet?" Before Charlie could answer, Wren said, "We're both going to be residents at Stoney Ridge Family Practice in Lancaster County."

Thud. Back to reality. Evie plummeted face-first back down to earth.

So many questions. She didn't know where to start.

It didn't make sense! Wren Baker seemed like the type who was destined for a top-notch residency in a sought-after teaching hospital. Hardly one for a farming village.

Then again, Wren Baker had claimed Charlie for herself.

Even more disheartening—Wren did not like Evie.

Wren probably thought Evie was crushing on Charlie.

She wouldn't be wrong.

Ever since Evie first met Charlie at the hospital—his third year as a medical student, her first year as a nursing student—she'd fallen hard for him. It felt like Cupid had struck her with an arrow, and two years later, her feelings hadn't faded one bit. She sensed Charlie might feel something for her as well. They'd had a few "moments" here and there, exchanged smiles, snatches of conversations. Moments that had felt genuine.

Evie sighed, turning to face the half-packed boxes in her bedroom apartment. She needed to keep going, but her heart was no longer in it. Grabbing extra hangers from her closet, she headed to the living room where her best friend and roommate, Darcy, was wrapping the television remote in bubble wrap.

Evie set the spare hangers on the coffee table. "Pretty sure I won't be needing these."

Darcy wrinkled her nose. "Doesn't the old-timey village have closets?"

"Amish village. Well, it has both Amish and non-Amish. More Amish than not, though." Darcy was the reason Evie had become a traveling nurse in the first place. She had talked her into joining her for an adventure. But Darcy was thinking Alaska. When Evie came home and said she'd applied for a contract to go to an Amish village not far from Penn State, Darcy questioned her mental health.

Evie plopped down on the couch. "Apparently Charlie King's residency is going to be the Stoney Ridge practice." She scrunched up her face. "The exact same place!"

"What?!" Darcy gave her a puzzled expression. "But . . . isn't that good news?"

"Yeessss," Evie said slowly. It was, somehow—at the exact same time—both the best and worst news she'd ever heard.

"So you're both off to Stoney Ridge. Why aren't you happy?"

"Because Wren Baker is going to Stoney Ridge for her residency too."

Darcy rocked back on her heels. "Whoaaa. Wren Baker? I would've bet money she'd end up in Beverly Hills doing nose jobs for celebrities . . . not an Amish farm."

"Right? Everyone assumed she'd land a top-tier surgical residency. She wanted one."

"So what happened?"

"She didn't get a match."

"No way! Just like Charlie?"

"Not exactly. Charlie didn't match because . . . well, he probably just didn't stand out enough. Wren, on the other hand, aimed too high. She went for the most competitive programs and didn't get a match. But she never told anyone—Charlie's the one who spilled. Apparently, they both figured, why not apply to Dok Stoltzfus's program? No one else did, so . . . that's where they'll be." Evie groaned, rubbing her cheeks. "How am I supposed to compete with Wren Baker?"

Darcy set down the bubble wrap to give Evie a look. "You're not," she said simply. "Evie, you're an amazing person. You have a huge heart, and you genuinely care about people. If Charlie doesn't see that, then he's the one missing out." She picked up the remote to start wrapping again. "You could always tell him how you feel about him."

No, she couldn't. Whenever Charlie was around, Evie became the most awkward version of herself, and that was saying a lot. The mix of longing, desire, and excitement she experienced when he was near left her completely flustered. She couldn't even say hi to him in an elevator. She'd freeze up, go silent, and end up staring at him, unblinking, like an oddball.

And yet . . . despite how socially awkward she acted around him, she kept getting some kind of undercurrent of attraction between them, like a spark of electricity. She was sure of it.

Or maybe she just imagined it.

And then there was Wren Baker. Ever present, highly territorial. Whenever Evie tried to work up the courage to ask Charlie if he wanted to get a coffee during his break—*boom!*—Wren would appear out of nowhere and whisk him off.

Evie sighed, wrapping her arms around a pillow. "I don't stand a chance. Wren is Velcroed to Charlie."

"But you don't absolutely, positively know they're a couple. No PDA, right?"

"I hardly think two medical students would show public affection in a hospital setting. But everybody talks like they're a couple. Like Wren-and-Charlie is one word."

"Watercooler gossip," Darcy said, rolling her eyes. "Personally, I never have understood what you've seen in Charlie King."

Where to start? Charlie was basically the most kindhearted human on this earth. He had remarkable tenderness and patience with patients, even the worst ones. He had this almost superpower to lighten up a serious moment. Then there was his goofiness, like wearing an enormous stick-on mustache when he was on the pediatric ward. Or his crazy patchwork pants. And his humility—so rare among physicians. Unlike most, Charlie never hesitated to ask for assistance when he was in over his head. That's how Evie had been officially introduced to Charlie—he asked for her help putting an IV into the arm of an elderly woman with nearly invisible veins. What med student ever asked a nurse for help? None!

But Darcy wouldn't know that side of Charlie—she only knew the Charlie-and-Wren-joined-at-the-hip side.

"He does have a good jawline."

Evie sighed. "Doesn't he?"

"Did he really pass *all* his classes?"

"Yes, of course." Just by a whisker. Evie knew that because Charlie was working on her floor at the hospital when the email came in that he had barely squeaked by with a pass in Human Anatomy and Physiology, the class that had him worried. (In his defense, that class was the most repeated one in medical school, because of the crazy amount of detail to be memorized.) He had let out a whoop, picked up Evie (who *happened* to be standing nearby), and twirled her around.

It was the most wonderful moment of her life. So far.

"Well, here's one positive," Darcy said. "If you discover that Wren and Charlie are truly a couple, maybe that will convince you to finally drop your obsession with him."

"Obsession is a bit much. I'm not obsessed."

Darcy squinted at her. "Yeah, pretty obsessed."

"It's not an obsession. Just a regular, all-American crush."

"Call it whatever you want. I think this experience will finally help wash that man out of your hair. He's not *that* cute," Darcy said. "And he's definitely not that smart." Darcy placed a high value on book smarts. The highest.

Evie had a different take on intelligence. She believed in all kinds of smarts, each valuable in its own way. Book smarts opened doors, sure, but fixer smarts—the ability to fix anything—were just as important. And then there were people smarts, which might be the best one of all. That's where she placed Charlie. He just had a way with people. Charming Charlie.

"Look, I get it," Darcy said, returning to her task. "Just don't let Wren Baker get in your head. Focus on why you're a traveling nurse in the first place. The experience, the adventure, the chance to make a difference. And your contract is only for three months in Stoney Ridge, right? When things don't pan out with Charlie, you can pack up and move in with me in Alaska. That's the beauty of our jobs."

Evie gave her a thanks-for-trying smile.

A sly look came over Darcy. "But who knows what's waiting for you there in your old-timey village? Maybe you'll fall madly in love with an Amish farmer."

Evie pretended to laugh, but she didn't think it was funny. Darcy was spot-on about one thing. If something didn't shift in the right direction with Charlie over the next three months, after two solid years of an epic, over-the-top crush on him, then she had to face reality. They weren't destined for each other the way she'd hoped. And prayed.

But what if they were? What if something radical and unexpected did occur in Stoney Ridge? She wasn't trying to break up Charlie and Wren, though she didn't think they were suited for each other. Not at all. But she couldn't extinguish a hope that they might see that for themselves and go their separate ways . . . and she wanted to be there when that happened.

Be careful what you wish for.

Dok Stoltzfus had heard that saying a million times, but she never truly understood it until the Keystone Medical Residency & Service Program finally answered her plea for more doctors. The KMRSP was a prestigious but under-the-radar program based in rural Pennsylvania, designed for medical school graduates willing to serve in underserved communities in exchange for substantial medical school loan forgiveness. Applying to this program had been her husband Matt's brainstorm. He'd been after Dok to find a partner to share her practice with for months now. She had placed ads in medical journals and contacted colleagues, but she'd had no luck. Not a single bite.

Then, late last summer, she and Matt went on vacation to a medical conference in Harrisburg. Bored, Matt wandered through the vendors' booths and picked up a brochure about the KMRSP. Matt became instant BFFs with the woman who ran the program, Stella Penkowski, and that evening in the hotel even helped Dok fill out the application. As in, he did most of it. Dok added her signature.

Dok had agreed with Matt—bringing in a partner to lighten her workload made sense. But supervising a resident? That felt like a whole different skill set, one she wasn't sure she had. She managed her ADHD well enough when it was just her, but adding someone else to the mix? That required structure, consistency—things she still wrestled with. Procrastination might not rule her life anymore, but it hadn't packed up and left either.

On top of her own shortcomings, she was skeptical about mentoring a graduate while the ink was still drying on their degree. Matt reminded her (several times) that there was a national physician shortage in the country, and she really didn't have any other choices.

There was no response from the KMRSP, and before long, Dok completely forgot about it. So much so that when she received an unexpected email—along with a resume—from a nurse inquiring if Dok might consider her for a traveling nurse position and mentioned her Mennonite roots, Dok picked up the phone that same day and offered her the job on the spot. "I'll be there as soon as I graduate," the nurse had said, though Dok couldn't quite remember if her name was Ellie or Eva.

Why couldn't Dok's practice seem to attract anyone with more experience? It was beyond frustrating.

When she arrived at the office this morning, her assistant Annie Fisher reminded her that traveling nurse Evelyn Miller was due to arrive tomorrow.

Seriously? How had that detail slipped off Dok's radar? Somehow, it did.

Then Annie dug out four pink phone messages buried under paperwork on Dok's desk and frowned at her. "This woman called again this morning, Dok. Each time, she asks you to return her call. All she'll tell me is that you'll know what it's about."

Dok had no idea. She didn't even remember who Stella Penkowski was, not until she called her—then it all came back. Stella told her that her application had not only been approved, but that she was getting *two* spanking-new medical school graduates.

Suspicious by nature, Dok immediately wondered what the catch was. "Why two?"

"Well," Stella said, "your application indicated you were doing the work of several doctors."

Dok scowled. That was Matt's version of her job. While it was true that she took her work seriously, she'd hardly say she was doing the work of *several* doctors. Two, maybe.

"And then there was that news story attached to it."

Dok cringed. A few months ago, a local TV news station

had done a feature on her called "The Doctor Who Still Makes House Calls." Apparently, it went viral—whatever that meant. Social media was the last thing on Dok's mind. But one thing she had become aware of after the feature aired: Her practice had been flooded with new patients and, with it, an increased expectation for house calls. At one point, Annie put a cap on the patient load and insisted on a waiting list.

"Of course," Stella said, "I'm sure it will be very tempting to offer one of them a full partnership at the completion of the residency."

That comment snapped Dok right back to the present. "What?!" What all did Matt say in that application?

"Yes. We'll provide a stipend for housing, but it'll be up to you to find living arrangements for all three. There are, of course, some minor expectations required of you. Training, mentorship, supervision. I'll email you a packet of information today."

Minor expectations? This sounded like a full-time job. Dok was no stranger to the demands of being a chief resident. She'd worked in hospitals for two decades until she finally bought Max Finegold's practice in Stoney Ridge. And she really, really didn't think she was cut out to be anyone's supervisor.

"Well, if that's all—"

Not so fast. Dok could sense that Stella was ready to wrap up the phone call, but she had a lot more questions. "Tell me what you know about them. Why did they apply to this program?"

"Well, neither of them matched on Match Day. And they're both deeply in debt."

"What? They didn't match?" Dok saw red flags waving in front of her. Most every resident got a match on Match Day, unless . . . "Did they graduate from a legitimate medical school?"

"Of course."

Dok wanted clarification. "An accredited medical school that is actually *in* the United States."

"Yes. Penn State College of Medicine."

Dok let out a sigh of relief. "But they didn't match? Do you know why?"

"No idea."

Red flag, red flag. "Well, do you know why they want to work in an underserved area? And do they know anything about the Amish? Because cultural sensitivity is very important. The Amish don't view health care in the same way that most Americans do." She hoped Matt had added all that and more in the application. Probably not.

"How's that? What do you mean?"

"Well, one example is that they don't try to deny death is coming. They don't fight beyond a body's biological end."

"Hmm, interesting. Well, honestly, I'm not sure what your two know or don't know." The sound of a phone rang in the distance. "I've got to go. Oh, before I forget, your residents are planning to arrive at the Lancaster train station tomorrow afternoon."

"No car?"

"No car. You'll need to arrange a pickup. And room. Not board."

"Hold it! I have to find housing for them?!" Dok's voice rose an octave.

"Just room. Not board. Part of the program. You'll be reimbursed, of course. Best of luck to you! To all of you!" On that cheery note, Stella hung up.

Luck. Dok leaned back in her chair, holding the phone receiver. Luck? She didn't believe in it. Hard work, determination, resiliency—those were her truths. Growing up Amish, she had seen luck as something devilish, like gambling.

She blew out a puff of air. She didn't even know if these doctors were men or women. Both? How was she supposed to find housing when she didn't even know their gender?

She looked out her window and saw her brother David drive

by in his buggy. She let out a happy sigh. She didn't need luck! Not when she had an Amish bishop for a brother.

David Stoltzfus had barely hitched the buggy reins to the post when his sister Ruth pounced on him. "Are you here as a sister or a doctor?" he asked, their usual greeting.

"Both," she said, as always. And then she added something about new doctors showing up on her doorstep tomorrow, with only one day's notice, and how she had no idea where to put them.

David squinted at her. "Put them?" he said, confused.

"House them," Ruth said. "Apparently, I'm responsible for getting them housing."

"Housing? For how long?"

Ruth shrugged. "I didn't think to ask. This whole thing is Matt's idea." She launched into an overly detailed explanation of the Keystone Medical Residency & Service Program, of the applications sent in to Stella Penkowski, of the phone conversation she'd just had with this Stella woman. His sister grew increasingly exasperated as she described each step of the process. "And now I'm suddenly a supervisor to two first-year residents! They're completely inexperienced. Just interns. And David . . . they didn't get *matched*."

He wasn't entirely clear what that might indicate about these two residents, but from the look on her face, it was inauspicious. "And why are there *two* doctors coming?"

"Matt's doing. He thinks it would take two doctors to replace me."

Good thinking, Matt. Next time David saw his brother-in-law, he would have to remember to compliment him. "But . . . you're not retiring, right?"

"No. Absolutely not. Matt's working on a retirement plan, but I'm not on board. He wants to work another two years to pay off our house, take early retirement, and then he wants us to take some real vacations. All his idea. Not mine." She shrugged, calmer now. "I mean, a real vacation does sound nice." A look of longing came over her.

As David listened to his sister's lengthy rant, it occurred to him how worn-out she looked. Her strawberry-red hair had more white than red in it. Dark circles rimmed her eyes. More wrinkles than he remembered lined her cheeks. He knew she'd been on the search to add a partner to her practice for a while now, but he felt it was a half-hearted hunt. He could see why his brother-in-law had taken the matter into his own hands. "So let me get this straight. You *have* wanted to find a partner. You tried. Yet you haven't had a single bite. So, with Matt's prodding, you applied to this program, but no interest. Until today. And thanks to Matt, you'll be able to choose the best out of two options for a partner."

Her brow furrowed.

"Is that so bad?"

"Yes. No." She frowned. "I don't know."

"Sounds good to me."

"You're missing the point. These two med school grads aren't qualified yet. They still have to pass their final boards to get licensed. Remember, they didn't get *matched*. I wouldn't feel comfortable having them hand out two aspirin without supervision."

David was sympathetic, but this really wasn't his problem. He had a full day of problems waiting for him—half with the store, half with the church. The store's were much easier to solve—delayed shipments, missing boxes, spoiled produce. Annoying but fixable. The church's were the ones that weighed him down. A beloved father of eight, dying of cancer. A young couple having marital difficulties. One of his ministers was thinking of leaving Stoney Ridge to move to a less expensive area. "Ruth, they're educated. Now they need experience. Just observing you will be beneficial to them."

"But how does it help when it means I have to be the one to supervise them? Me! You know how hard it is for me to plan ahead. I thrive on pivoting at a moment's notice. Somehow, I'll have to teach them all the basic skills while still keep on top of my practice. You can't just hand off patients to new residents. Medical students have had very little hands-on experience. They've spent most of their time in a classroom or in a morgue with their cadaver—"

David's eyebrows shot up.

"—or just observing other doctors. I wanted to find a *partner* who can spell me, not brand-new graduates who need constant supervising."

Fair enough. "So maybe at first you might need to do some hand-holding. But I would think it won't be long before you have confidence in them. Start small. Give them duties you know they can handle. Like . . ."

Her eyes squinted, like she was starting to buy in. "Like . . . filling out insurance forms."

David smiled. "Well, um, I guess that's a place to start. And you can go from there. Give them actual patient experience." It was past time for the Bent N' Dent to open, and the graybeards would be arriving for coffee soon, so he gave her a pat on the arm and started to go.

"David, hold on. I need a place for them to live."

He turned, then tilted his head. "Why do I get the feeling that you're asking me to solve that problem?"

"Because you know so many people. And because they arrive tomorrow. Maybe you can find a place for just a short period, until they look for their own living arrangements."

"How long is a short period?"

Ruth let out a puff of air. "I don't know . . . a few weeks? Just until I can figure out how this is all going to work."

Still, David hesitated.

"You must know of someone with a spare room or two.

Someone who'd be willing to offer room. See if they'll include board for a reasonable fee. They'll be paid, of course. The program lady said so. Not really sure how much, but I'll find out."

Ruth made it sound easy, but David knew how busy farming families were, especially during the summer. Providing room and board to an Englisch stranger was not a small ask. Decades ago, it would've been unthinkable. But offering hospitality to non-Amish was a more acceptable practice in the last ten years or so.

"I'd have them stay with us, but Matt just demoed our spare bathroom. He needed a project after baby Gabe was . . . well, you know." Her voice drizzled to a stop.

David filled in the rest. After baby Gabe's birth father gained full custody of him. It had been a painful yet poignant chapter in Ruth and Matt's life as foster care parents. For the first time, his sister had talked about slowing down and working less. About having more time for church work, hobbies, interests. More time for Matt too. All good intentions, but in reality, Ruth seemed to be working harder than ever.

"Can you think of anyone? Please, David? I'm really in a bind. What about the Inn at Eagle Hill?"

"I just bumped into Rose last evening, when I was picking up our mail. She said the inn is booked solid through July."

Ruth let out a tired sigh.

David felt himself caving in, like he always did when his only sister needed his help. "Well, maybe Fern Lapp. Luke and Izzy Schrock had to return to Kentucky to help his cousin for a few more months."

Ruth's eyes went wide. "Would you mind asking Fern for me? And did I mention that they arrive tomorrow?" She started backing up, as if the conversation had concluded.

He knew that particular trick. "Ruth . . ."

She started walking faster, still backward. "You know how that saying goes, David. You can't say no to a bishop." She gave him a five-finger wave and turned around, marching toward her office in that Dok-like way she'd always had, even as a young girl, striding fast like she was being chased.

David blew out a puff of air. Her problem had just become his problem.

This might be the miracle Annie Fisher had been waiting for. She had just finished preparing an exam room for the next patient when she overheard a sort of one-sided whisper-yell conversation drift in through the open crack of Dok's office door. Annie stopped in the hallway, just for a moment, as she heard Dok say something about two new doctors joining the practice tomorrow.

Tomorrow?

Annie wasn't one to eavesdrop. Not like her mother Sally, who had been working at Dok's on Saturdays and reported back everything she overheard in the waiting room, often mixing up names and details. Rumors started. When Sally had been "overcome" with a vague illness in mid-May and had to stop working to recover her health, Dok didn't ask if she planned to return.

Annie was *nothing* like her mother. Complete opposites.

Anyway, so Annie wasn't one to eavesdrop, but Dok's voice had risen quite a few decibels, in that staccato way she had that meant she was not happy. It didn't take long to figure out that Dok was talking to her husband Matt and that he was responsible for the arrival of the nurse and doctors.

If so, Annie wanted to give Matt Lehman a big pat on the back. She knew firsthand how tirelessly Dok worked. The practice had been inundated with patients ever since that TV news story ran. Every single day, Annie had to respond to phone calls of people who begged, literally begged, to see Dok. She had to tell them that Dok couldn't take on any new patients right now, then apologize profusely, and finally offer to add their names to a long waiting list.

That list felt like a lie. There'd only been one new patient accepted and that was because old Simon Miller had died. Annie felt bad turning prospective patients away, but she had no choice. There was only one Dok to go around.

Until tomorrow. Then there would be two additional doctors in Stoney Ridge. *And* a nurse.

Annie smiled.

Then her smile faded.

How would it work to add two new doctors and a nurse? The office was already cramped. There was only one exam room. Dok had one office. The waiting room was tiny and always full. How could they possibly accommodate more doctors and more patients?

Even though Annie felt a bit anxious, she couldn't ignore the flicker of excitement at the thought of Dok getting some much-needed help. With Annie's final EMT exam to occur in August, she had felt increasingly unsettled to leave Dok's practice. She loved working here. She loved being around Dok. Leaving the practice weighed on her like an overstuffed suitcase she'd been lugging around for weeks. She kept trying—and failing—to find the *perfect* moment to tell Dok. In her mind, she'd have enough time to find the right replacement, help train them, and then start looking for an EMT job. But so far, that perfect moment was playing hard to get. Or maybe she just didn't have the nerve to seize it.

Her very special friend Gus Troyer was eager for her to hand in her resignation and start interviewing—at his fire station. "Tell Dok!" he said often. "She'll understand. She's had plenty of assistants come and go."

That was exactly why it was so hard for Annie to tell her. Dok invested so much in people, and some assistants took an enormous amount of effort to properly train—the bishop's daughter Lydie Stoltzfus, for example. Annie had replaced Lydie and spent months reorganizing her confusing work system. Sometimes, she thought that Dok did more for Lydie during her tenure than Lydie did for Dok.

But she did appreciate Gus's consistent enthusiasm for her becoming an EMT, especially as her mother kept trying to change Annie's mind.

Annie knew that Gus had more on his mind than the finishing of the EMT course. He was eager to start courting Annie. And she was just as eager. But they had an agreement to remain "just friends" until she finished her EMT course, to avoid becoming distracted. Gus had not only respected her request to remain "just friends" but even offered to tutor her in the EMT classes. It was no wonder she thought of him as Mr. Wonderful.

Becoming an EMT was extremely important to Annie. She had felt a calling from the Lord to the work, but that didn't mean it was easy. Dok had to step in—not only to get the bishop on board but also to convince her parents.

Dok's voice on the telephone grew so loud that Annie didn't need to feel guilty about overhearing the private phone conversation. Everyone in the waiting room could hear her. Dok asked Matt how he'd like it if she came down to the police station and gave everyone advice about how to do their job?

Poor Matt. He might have meant well, but he was in the doghouse. Husband-wise.

Quietly, Annie returned to her desk in the waiting room. When she'd prayed for a way to resign without leaving Dok in a bind, she never imagined Heaven's answer would be sending not one but two doctors and a nurse.

A big smile spread across her face. *Ask and ye shall receive*, right?

2

Dok stood at the Lancaster train station, waiting for her three aspirants. She needed a better name for them, although she did think of them as aspirants. Temporary until proven to be competent.

How should she refer to them? Protégés sounded too Mozartish. Mentees sounded too young. Apprentices sounded like something out of the Middle Ages. Contenders had a competitive ring to it. She settled on candidates. Yes, that had the right ring to it—modern and respectful, without implying too much hierarchy. She glanced at her watch, anticipating their arrival any minute now. The train's whistle blew in the distance, and Dok felt a surge of fresh nervousness. This could be the beginning of what she had hoped to find—a true partner for her work. Someone who shared her philosophy—the importance of house calls and of offering alternative options of treatments while still providing all that western medicine had to offer. And, as Matt pointed out last night, she had not one doctor to choose from but two. And a nurse to boot!

She should be happy, Matt told her. Fern Lapp had agreed to provide room, for a fee, of course. Dok needed the extra help, he reminded her.

Thanks to Matt's interference, Dok might be facing an ideal solution to the ongoing problem of being perpetually overworked. After receiving the information on the aspirants—um, candidates—from Stella Penkowski via email and reading through it last night, she felt a little better and a little worse. Both.

Far down the tracks, she saw the lights of the approaching train and tried not to think of all the concerns that had kept her tossing and turning most of the night.

Wren Baker, female, age twenty-seven, graduated at the top of her class.

So why would someone as qualified as Wren Baker want to come to Stoney Ridge? Why not Massachusetts General or Dartmouth-Hitchcock or some other prestigious hospital? Why not a fellowship? Or a specialty? Why hadn't she had a match? Dok frowned. What could be wrong with her?

Then there was Charlie King, male, age twenty-seven. He graduated at the bottom of his class.

The very same class at Penn State College of Medicine as Wren Baker.

So why was Charlie King here? Perhaps, Dok wondered, a little worried, he had no other options? None.

On the same train today was Evelyn Miller, age twenty-six, fresh out of nursing school. Excellent recommendations. The only downside, from Dok's point of view, was that Evelyn's contract as a traveling nurse was only for three months.

Why did Evelyn choose to come to Stoney Ridge? Why not someplace exotic or exciting? If Dok were her age and had the option of contract work, she'd be off to Morocco or Istanbul. Not a farming town in Pennsylvania.

No matter the reason, Dok was looking forward to meeting Evelyn. Even if she was right out of nursing school, she would have had far more hands-on patient care than the two new med school graduates. They had spent the last four years primarily as student observers. Medical school was divided into two phases: preclinical and clinical. The first two years were in a classroom and laboratory, the second two were spent watching and learning from other doctors at work.

After medical school came the residency programs, and that's where doctors received intensive, supervised training.

And Dok, apparently, was now their supervisor. She let out a huge sigh. How was she going to manage supervising two inexperienced doctors with her packed schedule?

She could practically hear Matt's answer to that question: "It might take a little time at first, Ruth, but soon those two doctors will be able to handle a lot of your workload. Everyone starts somewhere. Think of the doctors who supervised you when you were a new graduate."

That was the problem, right there. Dok's chief resident was a ruthless dictator, determined to break the residents' spirits—through exhaustion and humiliation—and worse. And then, despite how awful he was, Dok ended up having an indiscreet relationship with him. She cringed. It was a low point. A very low point.

Was she really once that person?

She was. Naive, lonely, insecure, cut off from her family because she left the Amish church, looking for love in all the wrong places. It was only for the grace of God that she was a different person now.

Her back stiffened. She refused to be a ruthless dictator to these two candidates. But she couldn't quite figure out what kind of supervisor she should be or could be. She never thought of herself as a teacher. Maybe it had something to do with her own ADHD—diagnosed as an adult—but patience was not her strong suit. She moved on quickly to the next thing, and it was frustrating to not have others keep up.

As the train pulled into the station, brakes squealing, Dok braced herself for this new situation she found herself in. Matt advised her to take it slow with the candidates, and she thought that was good advice. Very, very, very slow.

A striking young woman was the first passenger off the train. Elegant. Dark brown hair, slicked back into a low no-nonsense bun. And her shoes! High, high heels. She looked around and walked straight toward Dok, rolling a suitcase along the platform. She laid a palm on her chest and said, "I'm Dr. Wren Baker," as if that should explain everything. "You must be Dr. Stoltzfus."

"Why, yes. I am. How did you know? Oh! Never mind. I get it. You must have seen the TV show."

Wren Baker tilted her head. "Actually, you're the only one on the platform wearing a white lab coat."

Dok looked down. Oh. Oops. She'd been in such a rush this afternoon that she'd forgotten to take it off when she left the practice. When she looked back up, she noticed another woman approaching, this one pulling a larger suitcase. She was on the smaller side of average, with a heart-shaped face and a mass of sandy hair that teetered between curly and frizzy, all held back in a ponytail. There was something effortlessly pretty and approachable about her—friendly, in that girl-next-door kind of way. "Evelyn Miller?"

"That's me. I go by Evie." She smiled. "I'm guessing you are Dr. Stoltzfus?"

"I am. So I believe we have one more?"

Wren spun around. "Charlie. He'll be here in a moment."

But the train was starting to leave the station. Suddenly, one suitcase, then another, came flying out of the train, bursting open and scattering clothing, sundries, and books all over the platform. Then someone leaped off the moving train and ran back to collect the huge, beat-up suitcases.

"Oh, poor Charlie," the nurse said under her breath. She hurried over to help him gather his things. The other doctor did not.

Dok blinked, trying to process what she was seeing. *This disheveled man was the other doctor?* His hair was pulled back in a messy topknot, round tortoiseshell glasses perched on his nose. He wore baggy corduroys, a rumpled button-down shirt, and a pair of running shoes that had clearly seen better days. Energetic, Dok could see, as he scrambled to gather his things. Once everything was jammed back into the suitcases, the young man picked them up as if they weighed nothing. He approached with a big, friendly smile, the nurse trotting behind.

"Dr. Stoltzfus! I'm Charlie King. Sorry to keep you waiting. I got my suitcases stuck trying to get them off the train."

Dok studied him for a while, weighing her first impression. Everything about him screamed that he wasn't a professional. Sure, he was warm and engaging. But he lacked that confident authority most doctors, like Wren Baker, had in spades. And he clearly wasn't the most organized person. "How'd you get the suitcases into the train?"

"Sideways," he said, still grinning. "The conductor encouraged me to hurry it up unless I wanted a ride to Philadelphia."

Oh boy. *Bright red flag, waving high.* "Before we leave the train station," Dok said, "I'd like to go over a few things." Just in case they wanted to turn right around and hop back on that train.

"First off, I'll be honest—I only found out yesterday that I'd be supervising two residents. So if I seem a little unprepared, that's because I am. It's going to take some time to figure out how this will all shake out." She let that sink in, giving them a chance to reconsider.

"Now, maybe you already know this, but over half of my practice is with the Old Order Amish. Most of my patients rely on traditional remedies and alternative treatments"—Wren's eyebrows shot up at that—"and they prefer to handle things their way first. Many are reluctant to even step inside a doctor's office, which is why I prioritize house calls. Gaining their trust takes time." Dok knew that firsthand, even with a brother who was a bishop.

She scanned their faces. Evie looked eager, Charlie looked pleased, and Wren . . . well, Wren was checking her watch.

"So, we're all facing a big adjustment. It'll take a few weeks for me—I mean, us—to get our footing, but in the grand scheme of a residency, that's nothing." Dok offered a wry smile. "With that said, welcome to Stoney Ridge."

"Shall we be off then?" Wren said, already heading toward the parking lot.

Dok watched her go, feeling a bit irritated. She knew she should cut them some slack—they were probably just as anxious and uncertain as she was. But in less than five minutes, she'd already gotten a sense of how these three operated. The only one she thought would be the right fit for her practice was the nurse. And she was the only one who wasn't staying.

Evie turned in a circle to take in the full sight of Windmill Farm. It was the most peaceful setting she could imagine. Rolling hills dotted with sheep and horses, a red windmill turning in the breeze. Different from her grandparents' farm, but much the same.

Being here brought Evie a sense of inner calm—something that had gone missing during the tense train ride. Wren's cold demeanor had seemed even frostier than usual, particularly when Charlie was full of questions about Anabaptist history—a topic Evie knew well, thanks to her grandfather's endless stories. It was hard to focus with Wren's impatient sighs and constant glances at her smartphone. Her thoughts kept drifting—Charlie's defined cheekbones, his soulful brown eyes; those thick, lush lashes. Could he have gotten even more attractive than the last time she saw him? Was that even possible?

"That sour smell! It's awful. What is it?"

Evie turned to see Wren covering her nose. "Manure. Farmers spread it on the fields in the spring."

But Wren wasn't listening to her. Her attention, as always, was on Charlie. "Did you see that farmer we passed on the road? His beard was long enough to braid."

Charlie stroked his chin. "I might have to grow a beard while I'm here."

"Don't even think about it," Wren said, like she was in charge of Charlie's appearance.

Maybe she was.

Behind Wren, Evie saw Dok talking to a small older woman standing on the farmhouse porch. The woman pointed to an outbuilding that they'd passed as they drove up the driveway. Dok had told them to wait for her by the car while she spoke to Fern. Charlie had left the car to wander over to the pasture to pat a horse, and Evie wondered how he happened to be so comfortable around animals. There was so much she didn't know about him. Things she longed to know.

Wren strolled over to where Charlie stood by the pasture, with Evie trailing a few steps behind, her pace unhurried. As Wren reached the fence, she extended her hand confidently to pat the horse, only for the animal to jerk its head back and eye her warily before trotting off.

"What's wrong with him?" Wren asked, frowning.

"Her. He's a mare." Charlie gave her a sideways glance. "You can't just approach an animal like that."

"Like what?"

"Like you're a predator sizing up your next meal."

"I am not!"

"You approach *everything* like you're a predator sizing it up."

Evie let out a snort of laughter. Wren spun around, startled to find her standing there, completely unaware they'd had an audience.

Just then Dok bolted down the porch steps and ran toward

the car, holding a device in the air. "Emergency. You'll need to sort things out with Fern. Suitcases out of the back, please. ASAP."

Charlie rushed to the car and started hefting suitcases out of the trunk. Evie and Wren quickly joined him.

"Dr. Stoltzfus," Wren said, "I'll come too. I'd like to accompany you on the emergency."

Dok was already in the driver's seat. "No. This is a home birth. Too stressful for an Amish mother to have strangers arrive without warning. Go get settled in with Fern. I'll be in touch." In record time, she made a three-point turn and headed down the driveway.

"What does she mean?" Wren said. "Get settled where?"

"Right here."

All three spun around to face the small gray-haired Amish woman with bright, piercing eyes. "I'm Fern Lapp. You'll be rooming here, at Windmill Farm."

Wren's perfectly arched eyebrows shot up. "Here?"

"Except for the boy." Fern pointed in the opposite direction of the farmhouse. "He'll be over at the buggy shop."

Charlie burst out with a laugh as he realized that Fern was referring to him. "A boy in the buggy shop!" he said, delighted. "Sounds like a children's book."

Fern ignored that. "The buggy shop has living quarters in the back. Luke Schrock did the work on it. He and his wife Izzy live here and help me with the farm, but they're away for a while."

Charlie picked up his two beat-up suitcases. "I'll be off, then. Ladies, I bid you farewell." He gave them a bow and then headed off to the buggy shop.

Fern peered at Wren and Evie. "Follow me."

Inside the modest, dimly lit farmhouse, Evie kept glancing at Wren, whose eyes grew increasingly wide as she took in their new living conditions. She was staring at the oil lamps hanging from the ceiling and the woodburning stove.

Fern pointed to the stairwell. "First room on the right is yours."

The pale green room had two twin beds with a braided rug covering most of the linoleum floor. A row of wooden pegs hung on the wall, and a flashlight stood upright on the nightstand between the beds. Also on the nightstand was a small oil lamp.

Wren set down her suitcase and looked around the room, a shocked look on her face. "Don't tell me that she expects us to share a room."

"Um, looks that way."

Wren's perfect nose wrinkled, like she was sniffing something unpleasant.

Was sharing a room with Evie really so awful? The sting of being openly disliked left an uncomfortable knot in her chest. The truth was, she wanted Wren to like her—despite the complicated mess of emotions tied to Charlie. As easy and natural as it would be to feel jealous of Wren, she just refused to feed that green-eyed monster.

The weird thing was that Evie actually admired Wren. She had this way about her—so sure of herself, so confident in every step she took. It was like she had her life all mapped out, and all she needed to do was follow the trail.

Evie, on the other hand, could barely see beyond the next bend in the road. She was always caught up in the here and now, unsure of what lay ahead, and somehow, that made her feel like she was always just trying to catch up. Or keep up.

She hadn't expected to be living in such close proximity to Wren either, but now that it was happening, she couldn't help but wish some of Wren's self-confidence would rub off on her— just a little, like a sprinkling of pixie dust.

Enough, at least, to catch Charlie's eye.

She couldn't deny the flutter of hope that she and Charlie might spend a lot of quality time together in Stoney Ridge.

Quality time alone. But even as the thought crossed her mind, it felt like an impossible dream. Wren had a way of filling up the space, and Evie had a way of shrinking back into the shadows.

Wren pulled her cell phone charger out of her purse and looked around the room for an outlet. "Wait, there's no electricity?" Her voice was tinged with disbelief.

Evie suppressed a smile. "Nope." No air-conditioning either. Not such a big problem now, but she could guarantee it would be in July and August. Best not to bring that up right now.

Wren shot Evie a panicked look. "How am I supposed to charge my phone? And what about Wi-Fi?"

"There's no Wi-Fi either, Wren."

"But Dr. Stoltzfus received a phone call."

"Pager." Evie couldn't help but find Wren's panic a bit amusing. "Welcome to Amish country. You'll get used to it." She would've thought Wren knew what she was walking into, but what did she really know about Wren? The train trip today was the most time she'd ever spent with her outside the hospital, and when she wasn't sending disdainful looks at Evie, she had kept her nose in a medical textbook. Preparing for boards, she said.

From their window, Evie could see Charlie out in front of the buggy shop. Here he'd been banished to an outbuilding, and he looked like he was a kid in a candy store. He was wandering around an assortment of buggies and wagons, in different levels of repair.

Something else to add to her ever-growing list of what she loved about Charlie. The guy could find a silver lining in just about anything. Cheerful Charlie. Evie loved uncovering new layers of him, like peeling an onion—only without the tears. While Wren studied on the train, Charlie told Evie a few stories from med school. Apparently, the first two times he visited the hospital morgue, he fainted when meeting his cadaver.

Evie heard Wren mutter something, so she turned around to see her fumbling with an oil lamp.

"How do you even light this thing?" she said with a grumble.

Evie walked over. "Here, let me show you. It's not as hard as it looks." She struck a match and lit the lamp with practiced ease.

Wren's forehead furrowed. "How do you know how to do that?"

"My grandparents were Mennonites. Not quite like the Old Order Amish around here, but close. I spent my . . ." She wasn't sure how much she wanted to share of her upbringing with Wren. Too messy for someone like her to understand. "I spent a lot of time at my grandparents' farm." She set the lamp on the nightstand. "You'll get the hang of it in no time."

Wren arched one dark eyebrow. "Easy for you to say. I need my phone and Wi-Fi to function."

"You'll adjust," Evie said, unzipping her suitcase. "It's actually kind of nice to unplug for a while."

Wren plopped down on one of the beds, looking defeated. "I don't think I can do this. No Wi-Fi, no electricity . . . It's weird. It's old-fashioned. It's like living in the dark ages."

"On the bright side, Fern has indoor plumbing."

That got Wren's attention. She bolted straight up and leaned forward, squinting at Evie. "You mean . . . not all Amish . . . have . . . ?"

Evie started to laugh, then realized Wren was serious. "Some do, some don't. It depends on how progressive or how conservative they are." She sat on the bed across from her. "The Amish aren't one-size-fits-all. Each church is self-standing, so even though they share a lot in common, there's quite a bit of variation from one Amish community to the next."

Wren let out a groan-laugh. "I had no idea that indoor plumbing was optional." She looked almost . . . distressed.

This was a side of Wren she'd never seen. "I'm sure there will be Wi-Fi at Dok Stoltzfus's office. And as for living here, I think you'll be surprised to see how many ways the Amish get things done. It might be different than you're used to, but it's not like the dark ages." Evie shrugged. "And if you really can't adjust, then you can always look for an apartment to rent in town."

"I signed an agreement to let the program reimburse the landlord instead of taking a stipend. I thought I'd save more money that way."

This, too, was a side of Wren that Evie didn't expect. She wouldn't have thought money was a problem for her, but maybe that's why she chose the loan forgiveness program in the first place.

Wren lifted her head. "What about transportation? How are we supposed to get around? I assumed a car would be provided. It certainly should be. We're out in the boonies."

"Lots of extra scooters over at the buggy shop. You're welcome to them." Fern stood at the door, arms crossed against her chest. How long had she been there? Evie hadn't heard her come up the stairs.

"Is it always this hot?" Wren said.

"Just wait a month for the real heat to show up," Fern said. "This is downright winter weather." She disappeared down the stairs.

Wren stood and turned in a slow circle. "Where's the closet?"

Evie pointed to two boards on the wall, each with a row of pegs. "There."

Wren stared. "That's not a closet. That's a couple of sticks."

"Like I said before, welcome to the world of the Amish," Evie said. "You'll get used to it."

Wren shot her a look. "I wouldn't bet on that." She pulled out a blouse, hung it on one peg. Then a pair of pants. Another blouse.

Evie watched as Wren took over all the pegs without a second thought. *Okay . . . it's fine*, she told herself. Living out of a suitcase wasn't the worst thing. A tiny compromise to keep the peace, and Evie was good at making those.

39

3

Early the next morning, Annie Fisher checked the message machine in the shanty, as she always did before doing anything else. Sure enough, there was a message waiting from Dok. "I'll be late to the office today," Dok's voice crackled. "Still waiting on the Glick baby, who's apparently taking his sweet time making an appearance. Move my appointments to later in the day." A pause, long enough for Annie to glance at the clock. "And, Annie, until I get there, you'll be responsible for the three new . . . candidates." Another pause, as if Dok had needed a moment to swallow that last word.

Unfair! First, Annie was still overcoming a crippling shyness, and talking to strangers made her stomach churn. She gave herself a pep talk as she scootered her way to the office, telling herself to act like Gus, Mr. Wonderful—warm and friendly and welcoming. She reminded herself of what good practice this would be for her. As a soon-to-be EMT, she'd be thrust into all kinds of uncomfortable situations. This was an excellent opportunity to work on her social skills. Consider it, she told herself, to be like building a muscle. As she veered around the last curve in the road, she tried to make herself smile. Inside, she was shaking like a leaf.

Ten minutes later, Fern drove her buggy into the Bent N' Dent parking lot and the three climbed out. What was it Dok called them? Something like . . . candidates? Which sounded like politicians. Annie preferred to think of them as medical professionals, just like EMTs. She watched from the window as they left the buggy to approach the practice.

The young man veered off to give the horse a pat. Annie noted his dark hair in a lady's topknot. A woman marched across the parking lot in a determined way. She looked like she belonged on the cover of one of Dok's magazines for the waiting room. Fancy.

The other woman, more friendly looking, kept glancing back at the young man, slowing, waiting for him to catch up.

Annie watched them with a detached curiosity, wondering how these three would fit into Dok Stoltzfus's practice.

Then her nerves kicked in and she remembered that she was responsible for them. Gus would love connecting with three medical professionals, because he was one himself as an EMT. She wished he were here right now. She found herself wishing that more and more and more.

So, she thought, do what he would do. *Pretend I'm Gus.*

She opened the door for them. "Welcome," she said, smiling. "I'm Annie Fisher. I'm Dok's office assistant."

She took them on a complete tour of the office building, which took less than three minutes. And then she ran out of things to show them or to talk about. Her act-like-Gus show had quickly fizzled out. Not knowing what else to do or say, she walked them over to the Bent N' Dent. Sarah Blank, blessed with the gift of conversation, was working the register.

"So you're Dok's new right hands!" Sarah said. "We are so glad you're here because poor Dok works herself to the bone. Well, let me get you some coffee and we can get to know each other! David Stoltzfus isn't here right now, which is too bad, but that'll give us time to chat." She winked at them. "Wann die Katz fatt is, schpiele die Meis." *When the cat's away, the mice will play.*

The two doctors exchanged a look of confusion, but the nurse, Evie, had a look on her face like she was swallowing a smile. Annie probably should have stayed, but as soon as she saw Sarah pour coffee into mugs, she slipped out the door to head back over to the office. She needed to make phone calls to a long list of patients and rearrange the morning's appointments. To her delight, she noticed Dok's car had arrived in the parking lot, and she took off running.

She found Dok in her office rummaging through the pharmaceutical cupboard. "Dok! I thought you weren't coming in at all this morning."

Dok didn't even turn to look at her. "Pretend I'm not here. I'm heading right back out. Another house call. Shelley Yoder is either out of meds or she did something with them, like threw them out. Either way, I want to get her a fresh supply."

"But your three . . . medical professionals . . . they're . . ."

Dok stopped what she was doing and turned to Annie. "Where are they?"

"I took them over to the store."

"Oh, good!" Relieved, she closed the pharmaceutical cupboard and locked it. Then she picked up her medical bag. "I'll try to return by lunchtime."

"Can't they go with you?"

Dok shook her head. "Not to an Amish home with mental illness. Dave Yoder would send me packing."

"But . . . what do I do with the three of them until you get back?"

Dok frowned. "There must be something they can do."

"Maybe . . . they could see patients."

"No! No unsupervised interaction with patients. Be sure to tell them."

Annie's eyebrows shot up. "Me?" It came out like the squeak of a mouse.

If Dok heard, she didn't pay her any mind. At the door, she stopped and spun around. "Actually, now that I think about it, the nurse can see patients. Have Evie handle the patients who are in for a recheck." With one hand, she brushed a lock of fallen hair out of her face. "Did I tell you she has relatives who are Mennonites?"

Twice, Annie thought, nodding.

"Sadly, she's only here for a few months. The other two . . . will be staying on."

Annie couldn't quite figure out how Dok felt about Charlie and Wren. The look on her face was inscrutable. Did she think they didn't want to be here? Or did *she* not want them to stay? Something felt off to Annie.

Not one minute after, Dok's car disappeared up the narrow road and the medical professionals returned to the office. Two of them, anyway.

Wren Baker was first through the door. "That woman doesn't stop talking."

Sarah, she meant. Annie bit her lip. Just wait until Wren met Hank Lapp. As her father always said about Hank: Viel gschwetzt, awwer wennich gsaat. *He talked much but said little.*

Evie came in next. "Did I see Dr. Stoltzfus's car drive up the road?"

"Yes," Annie said. "She was just here for a quick resupply and then she had some house calls. She mentioned that you could see her morning patients, assuming it's all right with them. Patients will start arriving soon."

"Excellent," Wren said, clasping her hands together. "I'm more than ready to get to work."

"Dok meant just Evie," Annie said, eyes on the tops of her shoes.

"What?" Wren said, taking a step closer. "What did you say?"

Annie repeated herself, a tiny bit louder.

"Me?" Evie said, looking pleased. "I'd love to."

Wren's chin dropped. "Why not a doctor? That makes no sense."

Terrible! This was a terrible situation that Dok put Annie in. Eyes still on her shoes, she whispered, "She said something about the doctors needing supervision."

Wren huffed at that.

The door opened again and in walked Charlie, with Sarah beside him. "I noticed Sarah has a bit of gravelly sound to her voice."

"Annie!" Sarah said, sounding distressed. "He said I have polyps!"

"Actually," Charlie said, "I said that it's possible you might have a polyp." He turned to Annie. "Does Dr. Stoltzfus happen to have a laryngoscope? I can take a look."

"Apparently, Charlie," Wren said in a *try-to-keep-up* tone, "we are not permitted to treat patients without the doctor's supervision."

"Ah," Charlie said. "Oh well. Maybe later, then, Sarah."

Sarah's eyes went wide. "But what if I'm dying?"

"No, no," Charlie said. "You're not dying. Polyps are usually benign. Harmless."

Sarah didn't look convinced.

"The nurse could examine her," Annie said quietly.

"You see, Charlie," Wren said, giving him a look, "Dr. Stoltzfus has given Evie carte blanche to treat patients, but not us."

Charlie didn't seem concerned. "Well, that'll work. Evie, let's get Sarah in an exam room and see about that polyp. I'll help."

Wren stepped in front of them. "Not necessary. She has inflammation of the throat, not a polyp."

"I do?" Sarah's eyes went wide. "From what?"

"Allergies, I suspect," Wren said. "You sneezed several times in the store."

Sarah looked surprised. "Did I?"

"Either way, I think we'd better have a look," Charlie said. "Evie, follow me."

"But," Evie said, "I've never been trained to use a laryngoscope."

"Not to worry!" Charlie said. "I'm sure Dok has a medical textbook or two in her office. If not, there's always the internet. I can talk you through." He took Sarah by the elbow and headed back to the exam room.

Evie looked at Annie with a question in her eyes.

Annie was pretty sure that Dok would not approve of this, but she wasn't here, and patients would be arriving soon, and . . . well, quite frankly . . . she was at a loss to know what to do. She didn't even know what Gus would do in this situation.

Evie turned and headed to the exam room.

Wren paced up and down the small hallway, making Annie anxious. "Where are we supposed to work? To . . . be?"

Annie shrugged. The office was already too small for Dok. Then Wren stopped at a door. "Where does this door lead?"

"To the basement," Annie said. "Dok uses it for storage." She hated going down into the basement. Musty, dank, full of spiders. Who knew what else was down there?

Wren opened the door and disappeared down the steps. Fifteen minutes later, Charlie and Sarah came out of the exam room.

"Annie," Sarah said, eyes wide, "call Dok. Tell her it's an emergency. This doctor says I have a polyp on my vocal cords that needs to be removed."

"Not immediately," Charlie said. "Eventually, I said. Very minor procedure." He turned to Annie. "Evie asked me to tell you that she's getting the exam room ready for the next patient."

The door in the hallway opened wide, and Wren emerged. "It's a treasure trove down there!" she said, beaming.

A treasure trove? Annie thought of the basement as more of a cluttered nightmare—a place where old files and forgotten junk went to die. She raised an eyebrow. "Really? All I've ever found down there are mice and musty old boxes."

Wren laughed, brushing some dust off her sleeves. "Oh, there's plenty of that too. Old medical equipment, and even an antique scale for weighing babies. It's like stepping back in time." She turned to Charlie, eyes gleaming. "I think we might have struck gold by coming here."

Sie waar ganz unverhofft. *That was entirely unexpected.* Of the three medical professionals, Wren Baker would be the last one Annie'd expect to be happy about ending up in Stoney Ridge. Turning back to work, she smiled. People could surprise you.

4

Sarah Blank left work at the Bent N' Dent to go home for the day. Something about a sore throat or allergies or . . . David Stoltzfus wasn't quite sure what. All he knew for sure was he'd be managing the Bent N' Dent alone on the busiest afternoon of the week—when the tourist buses came through. For now, the store was quiet. Sally Fisher was the lone customer, so David asked if she needed any help before he went to his office to finish up some paperwork.

Peering at the jars of spaghetti sauces, she waved him off. "I'm just looking for a good sauce for supper. Until the tomatoes start ripening, I need to rely on canned sauce. But I do need dried oregano. I noticed you're all out."

David had noticed too. More than just oregano. Most of the stock for herbs and spices was picked over. He'd asked Sarah to restock them this morning to prepare for the tourist buses, but apparently she'd forgotten. Spices and herbs were sought-after purchases by the Englisch. David bought them in bulk and could offer bargain prices.

"I'll need to go in the storeroom for more oregano. Back in a minute."

"Take your time, David. I'm in no hurry."

He went into the storeroom where extra stock was kept and filled an empty box with sacks of herbs and spices. Coming back into the store, he heard the jingle of the bells on the door and looked over to see Hank Lapp come in, talking to someone he didn't recognize. A young man, with his hair pulled back in one of those... what did his daughters call them? A man bun. It was hard for David to understand why a man would want to bother himself with long hair.

"DAVID! Have you met this fella? He's one of DOK'S new students."

"Um, actually," the young man said, holding a finger in the air, "no longer a student. A med school graduate. In fact, actually, I'm a resident."

"A RESIDENT? So you moved to Stoney Ridge, permanent-like?"

"A resident doctor," he said. "Dr. Stoltzfus is my supervisor."

"A DOCTOR?" Hank's bushy white eyebrows shot up. "David, did you HEAR that?" He leaned in. "Is Dok RETIRING? She's not thinking of LEAVING us, is she? Eddy will be BESIDE herself."

David shook his head. "No, Hank. Dok just needs a little help." He stuck out his hand to shake the young man's. "I'm David Stoltzfus. I run the Bent N' Dent."

"Charlie King."

"DAVID is the BISHOP," Hank said. "PLUS, his sister is the Dok."

A confused look covered Charlie's face. "But... she couldn't be Amish and be a doctor, right?"

"That's correct. My sister was raised Plain, then left before she was baptized to pursue higher education."

"KING?" Hank said. "That's a PLAIN name."

Charlie's eyes went wide in confusion, then he burst out with a laugh. "You're right! It is both plain and Plain. Good one, Hank!"

A loud crash came from a nearby aisle. Charlie was first to it, beating David to the source of the crash. Sally Fisher had dropped a jar of spaghetti sauce, and it splattered.

"Ma'am," Charlie said, "did you cut yourself?"

"I don't think so," she said. She looked at David. "I'm sorry, David. It just slipped right out of my hand." She started to bend down to pick up the pieces, but Charlie had already crouched down, picking up shards of glass.

"Sally," David said. "Just leave it. You too, Charlie. I'll get a mop and clean it up."

Charlie's eyes were on Sally's hands, which were trembling noticeably. "Do you often have trouble with your hands shaking?"

"I do!" Sally said. "Quite often. Shooting pains along my wrists."

"Have you been feeling more tired than usual? Any dizziness?" Charlie asked, his tone serious but kind.

Sally looked taken aback by the questions but nodded slowly. "Yes, actually. I've been very tired and sometimes dizzy, especially when I stand up too quickly."

"Let me help you sit down." Charlie helped her gently sit on the floor, away from the splattered sauce, her back against the wall.

David left to get a mop and bucket out of the broom closet. Everyone knew that Sally Fisher was a raging hypochondriac. Everyone except Charlie King. This young doctor's intentions were good, but he was feeding her imagined symptoms. In the bathroom, David filled up the bucket with hot water, wondering if he should intervene or stay out of it.

He was still pondering his role in this scene as he returned to the splattered sauce and started to mop. The bells on the door rang, and David paused to see a young Englisch woman stand at the open door with a shocked look on her face. "Who's been shot?"

49

Charlie popped up his head. "It's not a crime scene, Wren. This is just spaghetti sauce."

The young woman marched straight over to Sally Fisher. "What symptoms are you experiencing?"

"Wren," Charlie said, "I've got things covered."

"WREN?" Hank said. "Like the BIRD?"

Wren ignored both Charlie and Hank. She took Sally's wrist to check her pulse. "Your heart is racing."

"Is it?" Sally said, worried. "What could that mean?"

"Several potential causes," Wren said. "Arrythmia, heart failure, a sudden surge of adrenaline—"

"Or it could mean you're nervous," Charlie said, interrupting. "My heart starts pounding when I feel anxious."

David watched the exchange of the young doctors with a mixture of curiosity and concern. They were certainly eager, but eagerness didn't always translate to helpfulness. Especially with Sally Fisher.

"Follow my finger," Wren said, rapidly moving one finger in the air from left to right. "Did you hit your head when you fell?"

"But she didn't fall," Charlie said. "She dropped the jar of sauce."

"She's having trouble tracking my finger," Wren said, "which can indicate a stroke."

"Does it?" Sally's head swiveled from Wren to Charlie, back to Wren.

"I'll call an ambulance," Wren said, pulling her cell phone out of her pocket. "Better safe than sorry."

At this point, David jumped in. "Slow down. Nothing happens to Sally Fisher without Dok's permission."

"But if it's a stroke," Wren said, "then time is imperative." She punched some numbers on her cell phone, then looked up, startled. "There's no cell service!"

"Not in here," David said, calmly mopping up the spaghetti

sauce. "Like I said, when it comes to Sally Fisher, you'll have to get permission from Dok. Annie is Sally's daughter."

"Charlie," Wren said, "run and get Annie."

"No!" Sally said. "Annie never thinks anything is wrong with me."

"THAT'S because nothing EVER IS WRONG with you," Hank said. He twirled his finger around his ear, like she was crazy.

Sally scowled at him.

"Sally," David said, "when Dok gets back to the office, you can talk to her then."

Wren shook her head. "That might be too late!"

Sally gasped. "Too late for what?"

"Treatment for a stroke," Wren said.

Charlie huffed. "She *dropped* a jar of spaghetti sauce."

"The question is *why*," Wren said, a tad disdainfully.

"Maybe because it's a HUGE JAR," Hank said. "You should listen to the BISHOP."

Wren's head jolted up. "Who's the bishop?"

"I am," David said.

Wren exchanged a look with Charlie before she rose to stand. "I'm Dr. Wren Baker."

"BAKER!" Hank roared. "Another PLAIN NAME."

"Plain *and* plain. Sharp, Hank," Charlie said, tapping his head. "Very funny."

"But I didn't MEAN it like—"

A small tourist bus rolled into the parking lot. David needed to finish cleaning the floor and dry it off before he had any more accidents in the store. "Charlie and Wren, I think it's best if you both take Sally over to see Annie at Dok's office."

"But . . . but . . ." Sally sputtered. "I need the spaghetti sauce for supper."

David set the mop in the bucket and took a fresh jar of sauce off the shelf. "For you, Sally. My gift." He handed it to Charlie to carry for her.

Charlie needed both hands to hold it. "Whoa, it *is* a big jar."

Wren helped Sally to her feet, encouraging her to lean heavily on her as they made their way to the door. Fifteen minutes ago, Sally had been shopping in the store, quite contented. Now, thanks to those two young doctors, she was a frail, weak woman, needing to be escorted.

David watched the scene with a mix of amusement and exasperation. It wasn't funny, but in a way, it was. As Wren and Sally and Charlie disappeared through the door, David could already imagine his sister's reaction when she heard about this. Dok had little confidence in the abilities of the two residents, and this episode with Sally Fisher would only cement that skepticism.

After returning the mop to the broom closet, David glanced at Hank, who was shaking his head with a knowing smile. "Things JUST got a LOT MORE interesting around here."

"True," David said.

"Those two are just CUTTING their TEETH," Hank said. "WET behind the EARS."

"Can't disagree with that, Hank."

"JUST out of the NEST." Hank laughed out loud, the sound echoing in the small store. "FRESH off the BOAT."

Hank was on a roll, so David lifted a hand to stop him. "Let's hope they learn quickly," he said, more to himself than to Hank. "Or we're in for a bumpy ride."

"Not US." Rocking back and forth in his chair, Hank hacked a laugh. "Poor DOK!"

Returning to the office, Dok was met with a story so absurd it was almost unbelievable: Sally Fisher, a jar of spaghetti sauce, and two overly eager residents who had escalated the situation into a full-blown crisis. As she listened, she was torn between disgust and alarm. She issued a stern reminder that diagnosing patients was her job, not theirs. As she tackled the patient queue, she let Evie assist her while Wren and Charlie took turns observing. On a chair. In the corner. Silently.

Late in the day, after the last patient had been seen and Annie had gone home, Charlie asked Dok to follow him down the interior staircase that led to the basement. Once there, he tugged on the light fixture's pull chain and gestured animatedly around the room as he explained his vision. "This space has so much potential. It's big, it's dry, there's good lighting and ventilation. You could easily divide it up into several rooms for your practice. Framing, drywall, run a few wires for electricity—it's not expensive construction."

Charlie's plans for the basement took Dok by surprise. Her curiosity was piqued. She'd always wanted to expand the building and create more usable space, but she thought she'd have to push out with an addition. Matt had even gone so far as to sketch some ideas to take to contractors for bidding. However, their never-finished house remodel took precedence, and the office redo slipped to the back of the shelf. Or maybe fell off it.

But they *had* talked about it. They'd even set money aside for it.

She and Matt had never considered doing something with the basement. It was a very good idea and much simpler than the plans for the addition. Use what was already here. Such an obvious solution to Dok's growing lack-of-space crunch. How had this never occurred to them?

Probably because no one went into the basement unless it was absolutely necessary. Dok didn't even like to put supplies down there. Too dank, too moldy, too much evidence of mice. Yes, this might be the way to go.

"I can do all the labor for free," Charlie said.

Dok found *that* very appealing. "Do you actually have any experience with construction?"

"Tons of it," Charlie said, waving his hand in an I've-got-it-covered way. "Basic construction, I mean. My dad worked in construction, so every summer of my life since I was fourteen was spent on a jobsite. We'd get someone with experience in for plumbing and electricity, but I can frame and drywall in my sleep." His gaze swept the room. "Besides, this project is pretty simple."

"Simple?" Dok said.

"Not easy, but simple." He walked to a small door. "Like, there's already plumbing down here. Even the makings of a very small bathroom." That was a generous term for a tiny closet of a bathroom, studiously avoided by Dok.

She walked around the large room, then stopped as she faced the stairs. "Charlie, I have to admit I like what you're proposing. But I'm worried it would still feel like a basement. For example, I can't ask patients to go down these steep steps."

Charlie held up a finger in the air. "I have a solution for that. It wouldn't take much to reconfigure the cellar door into a full-sized exterior door. There'd still be a few steps to walk down to reach the office, but no one would have to duck to enter like they do now. I admit that it wouldn't work for a wheelchair, but you have a ramp upstairs for patients in wheelchairs."

Interesting. Quite interesting. But Charlie acting as the contractor? Maybe she should talk to Matt and see about finding an experienced contractor to do it. She frowned. And that would probably mean it would get added to the list of things they didn't have time to do.

"And here's something else we thought of."

Dok spun around to see Wren standing halfway down the steps. So this brainstorm belonged to them both?

"Anyone who is actively ill," Wren said, "could be seen down here, so your waiting room isn't a petri dish of germs like it is now."

Dok tried not to take offense at that. "Seems the two of you have put a lot of thought into this project."

"Well," Wren said, walking down the rest of the steps to join them, "it seems the two of us might end up having a surfeit of spare time. Especially if you aren't letting us accompany you on house calls." There was an odd pause as the attention in the room swung in Wren's direction.

Dok knew what was behind her sharp comment. In the middle of the afternoon, she'd been called out again on a house call to an Amish farm. Wren and Charlie were left at the office with nothing much to do but twiddle their thumbs. "Yesterday, on the way to Fern's from the train station, I thought you mentioned something about needing time to study for the boards. They're at the end of August, right?"

Wren frowned.

Dok had her there. She turned around in a slow circle. Converting the basement into usable space was quite appealing to her, for all the right reasons. Plus, it could buy her some time, keeping Wren and Charlie occupied, while she figured out how she was going to be able to supervise them, because right now she had absolutely no idea how to fit them into her schedule. She was so accustomed to being a lone ranger, she just didn't know how to accommodate two residents. And then there was *this*—they both hadn't matched. She couldn't get that out of her head. She had no confidence in them. She needed time.

A smile started. This was starting to all click into place. Two birds, one stone. Dok turned to Charlie. "Go for it."

"Go for it?" Charlie said.

"Go for it. Everything you talked about. Draw up the plans, get the permits, and get started."

"All of it?" Charlie raised his eyebrows. "Including the redo of the front door, the creation of an exam room, and updating the bathroom?"

"All of it. But I don't want to know anything about it until it's completed. You act as the general contractor. All decisions are your responsibility." She clapped her hands together. "And once it's done, the residency program can get underway."

"What?" Wren stared at Dok. "That could take weeks!"

Which was what Dok hoped for. She lifted her palms. "It'll give you all the time you need to study for your boards. And when it's completed, there will be plenty of space for everyone to work. We'll be ready to roll forward with your residency." She took a few steps up the basement steps, then stopped and looked at Charlie. "You can give the bills to Annie for reimbursement." She started up the stairs again.

"Dok! Just one more thing," Charlie said. "No budget?"

Dok stopped and spun around, her expression firm but amused. "Yes. Always."

⁓

By day's end, Evie felt exhausted. She was relieved when Dok offered to give them a ride back to Windmill Farm. "Scooters in the back," she said, lifting the back door of her SUV.

"Thank goodness," Wren said, under her breath. She was not a fan of scooters as the means of transportation. Buggies either. She claimed the front passenger seat.

Evie and Charlie buckled up in the back seat, so close their elbows touched. It was like the air around them was vibrating.

"So, day one is done," he said. "It was a good day. A great day."

Evie looked at him in wonder. From her point of view, she thought he'd had a terrible day. She had heard Dok snap harshly at Charlie and Wren for overstepping their bounds with Sarah Blank, then with Annie's mother, and now he'd offered to renovate the basement because Dok wasn't quite prepared to start the residency program. Nothing much happened today that had anything to do with being supervised as a resident doctor. And yet he considered his first day as a great day. This guy was like Teflon. Nothing seemed to faze him. Nothing ruffled him. Consistent Charlie.

As soon as Dok hit an open stretch, she floored the gas, sending the car flying down the country road. Charlie had his window down, while Evie kept hers up, but it didn't matter—her ponytail was still whipping around like it had a mind of its own. The wind roared so loudly that Wren's endless stream of medical questions to Dok was mercifully drowned out. At one point, Charlie shot Evie a grin and leaned in to whisper, "Doctor by day, race car driver by night." A laugh burst out of Evie. Spot-on.

Dok's drive from Lancaster Train Station had been a blur of highways and tailgating, matching the flow of traffic. But country roads? Dok's speed jumped from fast to hold-on-to-your-hat fast. She took every curve with the kind of precision that suggested she knew these roads like the back of her hand.

As the car swerved and jolted, each sharp turn sent Evie bumping into Charlie—or Charlie into her. Not that she minded. Nope. Not one bit.

5

It was a shame, Annie thought, that Wren and Charlie couldn't wait for Dok to ask their opinions before blurting them out. It seemed that Dok already had doubts about them, and their competing diagnoses weren't helping. Just yesterday, an elderly man came in with an inflamed toe. Wren took a look and suggested gout. Charlie countered with arthritis. Meanwhile, the patient sat there, nodding politely, probably wondering if either of them had a clue. Dok examined his toe, picked up tweezers, and, without a word, pulled out a deep splinter.

Afterwards, Dok reminded Annie to let them know, every single day, that they weren't to interact with patients in any way, not even if Evie were present. Not without Dok's permission and supervision.

As if Annie could tell such a thing to Wren and Charlie. She would never!

Instead, she thrust into their hands a pile of insurance forms to fill out. Normally, Annie handled claims, but she had no problem relinquishing that tedious task. Anything to keep the two of them busy and away from patients when Dok was out of the office. Wren filled out her pile of paperwork in record time, then took Charlie's pile. Meanwhile, Charlie was completely preoccupied with the initial phases of the basement remodel. As in, cleaning it out.

To Annie's amazement, Wren dove right in to supervise the cleanout. Her enthusiasm was impressive, especially since Dok and Annie rarely ventured down to the basement. Spiders, mice, boxes of musty old patient files from Dok's predecessor, odds and ends—who knew what else lurked in that basement? Annie would've thought Wren was too fancy for such a messy task, but no! She masterminded the entire job. She even hired Hank Lapp and his donkey cart to haul everything off.

Annie would've thought Wren might steer clear of Hank after the spaghetti jar incident with her mother, but she was surprisingly tolerant of him. She kept him on task, even when he got distracted by old curiosities like outdated medical equipment. Wren didn't seem bothered by Hank's loud storytelling, which went on nonstop as she and Charlie emptied out the basement. Hank's voice carried like the wind—it went everywhere.

And so, during that first week, a routine emerged: Each morning, Fern would drop Charlie, Wren, and Evie off at Dok's office in the buggy and leave three scooters for them to return home at the end of the day. Charlie would head straight to the basement, Evie would go to the exam room to start preparing for the first patient, but Wren would stand next to Annie's desk and ask to see the day's patient list.

Dok typically arrived a bit later, often stopping by the hospital to see a patient or making a house call along the way. So Annie would hem and haw and hand Wren some paperwork to do. She'd do it immediately, thoroughly, return it to Annie, and ask again to see the patient list. If Annie knew Dok was due in to the office soon, she'd point to the window that overlooked the parking lot. "Any minute now, you'll see her car drive up."

Annie excelled at sidestepping conflict.

If Dok had been delayed, Wren would head down to the basement to supervise the cleanout. After barking out a few orders to Charlie and Hank, she'd swap her high heels for sneakers and scooter home to Windmill Farm. "Might as well use the time to study for my board exams," she told Annie as she left.

Annie didn't blame Dok for holding off on bringing Wren and Charlie along for house calls. She had spent years earning the trust of the Amish, and Wren and Charlie couldn't just assume they had it too. She explained as much to them: Practicing medicine here was as much about relationships as treatment.

Charlie didn't seem to mind—he was perfectly content banging away in the basement. But Wren's frustration was obvious. Annie could tell that she wasn't really taking Dok's advice to heart.

On the other hand, Dok seemed more than happy to give plenty of patient-care responsibilities to Evie the nurse, including taking her on house calls.

This was heading in the wrong direction.

Annie was weeks away from completing her EMT course. She should've, could've finished after spring quarter, but her mother had a bout of something or other. The true cause of the something or other—Annie's older brothers had forgotten to remember Mom on Mother's Day. Not a card, not a call. Devastated, resentful, Mom took to her bed. She conjured up an imagined disease, possibly terminal, to punish those errant sons.

As usual, Annie had dropped everything. She couldn't leave her dad to manage the dairy cows alone. She couldn't leave Dok without help at the office on Saturday mornings. Her mom had been covering for her so she could take the EMT course, but eventually, something had to give. Annie ended up with an incomplete in the course. Mom, who had never fully accepted the notion of her daughter as an EMT, was delighted. The closer Annie had been getting to finishing the coursework, the more her mother ramped up attempts to dissuade her.

Yet, despite Annie's disappointment at postponing the completion of the EMT course, she didn't mind postponing the end of her tenure at Dok's office. She loved the work, loved being around Dok. She'd been dreading the moment when she would need to leave the practice. Dreaded the thought of actually telling Dok the time had come to find a replacement.

And that time was coming soon. Annie was going to finish what she started. Last week, she had started an evening course again for the summer quarter. Her eagerness to be an EMT hadn't diminished one little bit, even with dropping out. God had called her to this important work, very specifically and clearly, and opened the door to training to be an EMT, despite her mother's doubts and objections.

Last evening, Gus was over helping Annie study—something he did rather a lot of. That, too, was one reason Annie didn't object to postponing the end of her EMT course work. It meant more time with Gus. Mr. Wonderful.

They were sitting at the kitchen table, and her parents had just gone out to check on the dairy cows for the night. A pencil had slipped out of Annie's hands, and as she and Gus bent down at the same time to get it, their faces were only inches apart. They stilled, and he whispered, "Annie, there's something I want to ask you." He leaned a little closer, so close that she held her breath—and then the door opened, and in burst her mother.

"It's getting dark out there!" Mom said. "No moon tonight. I need a flashlight so I don't trip and fall. My cousin Gloria told me about her neighbor who tripped and fell and broke her hip and had to have surgery and then an infection set in and she died a grueling, horrible death."

Gus straightened in his chair. "Sally, I know that neighbor. She was one hundred and two years old." He happened to live next door to Sally's cousin Gloria and knew of her delight in repeating tales of woe. Often, those stories began with Gus! He liked to talk about events in his EMT work. No names or identifying details, of course, but they weren't needed. The stories were gruesome enough.

A bit later that evening, Gus lingered outside the front door, slow to say goodbye. "Annie, have you talked to Dok about resigning?"

"Not yet. First, I need to pass the final exam."

"No problem there."

She smiled. He was always rooting for her. "I can't seem to find time to talk to her alone since the new . . . um . . . medical professionals have arrived." She glanced up at him. "You said you had something to ask me?"

"I do," Gus said, clearing his throat. "There's going to be an opening at my station." He leaned in slightly, his eyes shining with excitement. "What would you think about us working together?"

What would she think? It would be like living in a constant state of spring, where even the most routine tasks felt thrilling.

What would she think? Every day would be an adventure, and she'd be counting down the hours until she could start each morning with him.

But all she could manage to say was, "Ich kann vun wunners net saage." *I don't know what to say.*

"Say yes." Gus took a step closer, his voice full of hope. "I can talk to the captain and see about setting up an interview for you."

At this, Annie hesitated. "That's kind of you, Gus, but I really would like to talk to Dok before I start interviewing. I wouldn't want her to hear about it from someone else. I have been trying to talk to her—I just need to figure out the right time."

Gus closed the gap between them, his gaze intense. "And then there's . . . us. We need to figure that out too."

The door opened wide. "Gus!" Mom said. "Are you still here?"

"Just leaving now, Sally." Under his breath, he whispered, "Your mother's timing is impeccable." He gave Annie a wink and headed to his buggy.

Even this morning, as she scootered to work, Annie couldn't keep the grin off her face. Not even when the waiting room filled with patients and there was still no sign of Dok. Not even when the phone rang and she picked it up. "Dok Stoltzfus's office," she said with a little bounce in her voice. She couldn't help it!

"Annie, it's Dok. I'm going to be a little delayed."

Annie's happiness burst like a balloon. "Delayed? Dok, how late will you be?"

Murmurs all around—not happy ones—as patients cued into Annie's call and realized their wait just got longer.

"An hour. Two, tops."

That meant three hours. Annie scanned the waiting room, then shifted to a whisper. "Dok, you have a schedule crammed with appointments. The waiting room is already full."

"I know, I know. I picked up Evie at Windmill Farm early this morning to go on the house call with me, otherwise I'd let her see to them."

"Dok, why not let Charlie and Wren see some of these patients? A lot of them are just return checks. Like, Billy Yoder needs his stitches out in his knee. And Edith Lapp wants a refill prescription for her eczema. Honestly, I think I could even take care of half of today's patients." Did Annie really say that? She felt shocked by her own boldness. Where did it come from? Gus's influence, she thought. He was always encouraging her to speak up, to have confidence in her own opinion.

But there was only silence on the other end. Long enough that Annie wondered if she'd crossed a line with Dok.

"That sounds shockingly insolent, Annie Fisher."

Oh no. She *had* crossed a line.

But then Dok surprised her with an enormous laugh. "Keep it up," she said.

Annie let out a sigh. She hadn't realized she'd been holding her breath.

"What have the two candidates been doing?"

Dok, Annie noticed, never called them doctors. "Charlie is always down in the basement. Lots of construction noise. There's already been a truck delivery of something or other this morning. I put some of those bills on your desk."

"I don't mind the bills. The basement keeps Charlie busy."

Right. Annie had a hunch that Dok had an ulterior motive with that basement renovation. She sure wasn't paying attention to the basement, or to the two young doctors.

"What's the other one been doing?"

"She always asks for things to do and I try to keep her busy. But she's quick. It's hard to find things for her to do. So when she finishes up, she returns to Windmill Farm to study for the board exams."

"Charlie's supposed to be taking the boards too, isn't he?"

"I think so. He doesn't seem nearly as concerned about them as Wren."

Dok huffed. "Too bad I can't put Charlie and Wren in a paper bag and shake it up." She laughed. "Actually, if I did, the result would be Evie. She's a dream come true."

After reassuring Annie that she'd be in the office by noon—one o'clock, tops—Dok hung up, conveniently sidestepping Annie's question about letting Charlie and Wren handle patient visits.

Annie slowly spun her chair around to face the sea of unhappy patients, preparing to explain why their morning appointments needed to be rescheduled. *This* task, she wouldn't miss.

This last week had already taught Evie something she never would've learned had she stayed in a hospital setting—the value of house calls.

There was something special about racing in Dok's car through the countryside (and that woman had a lead foot), meeting patients where they lived. It made the practice of medicine feel deeply personal, like it was meant to be.

On Monday, they had stopped at an Amish farm to treat a farmer whose hand had gotten caught in a hay baler, and he wanted Dok to sew up what was left so he could get back to work. He held a bloody rag around his hand—half of one finger hung on a hinge of skin. Evie was impressed with how Dok had managed him. A gentle but tough insistence that some things were beyond a quick fix. Dok had him in the car and on the way to the hospital before he could object.

On Tuesday, they got a call to come to the Stoney Ridge Elementary School. When they arrived, they were led to a little boy sitting in the nurse's office. The boy had decided to see if chewed gum would stick to the inside of his ear, and, of course, it did. When he couldn't get it out, another child had tried to help, but his efforts only made it worse. Dok, with a steady hand and a warm smile, carefully removed the sticky mess. As soon as the gum was free, the boy, without missing a beat, popped it right back into his mouth. *Ew.*

On Wednesday, they visited the Sisters' House to check on how an elderly woman was mending after a fall. To Evie's surprise, it was called the Sisters' House because a handful of elderly Amish sisters lived together, and they all appeared with a list of ailments for Dok. They were trying to save money by treating their ailments in one visit. Dok patiently worked through the list, treating each concern as if it were the only one, never rushing or dismissing the women's worries. It was a reminder to Evie of what was often missing in the fast-paced hospital environment—time, care, and genuine connection.

Perhaps the best part of the week was Evie's discovery that she understood more Penn Dutch than she'd expected, considering it had been a few years since she'd lived with her grandparents. Still rusty enough that she didn't want Dok to know she could follow along, but it was nice to listen quietly and feel that familiar connection to her grandparents.

The only downside to the week? She hadn't seen much of Charlie. She found herself hoping that would change soon.

Today, Friday, after the last house call for the day, Dok told Evie she'd drop her off at Windmill Farm. "It's right on the way," she said, even though Evie was pretty sure it wasn't.

As Dok's car flew down the road, she said, "Annie said Wren spends a lot of time studying for the boards. I wondered why Charlie doesn't seem too concerned about them."

"No doubt it's because he wants to finish up this basement project for you first. Charlie's conscientious like that."

"Is he?" Dok was quiet for a moment. "Seems like Charlie might enjoy working with his hands more than doctoring."

Evie turned to her, surprised. A little defensive too. She didn't want Dok to get the wrong impression of her beloved Charlie. "He is a *wonderful* doctor. Exceptional."

Dok raised an eyebrow. "Really?"

"Definitely. The best of the best."

"How so, exactly?"

"Well, for one thing, he notices things that other doctors miss."

"Such as . . ."

"Once, a little boy had been admitted to the hospital with persistent stomach pain. They had run countless tests, but everything came back normal. Charlie spent some time with the boy and noticed his discomfort whenever he drank milk or had a bowl of ice cream. He figured out there was a history of lactose intolerance in the family that no one had mentioned."

"Good call," Dok said, rocking her head slightly back and forth. "But hardly rocket science."

"Apparently it was for the chief resident. He had already scheduled the boy for exploratory surgery."

Dok burst out with a laugh. "Sounds like a couple of chief residents I've known." She mimed scissors with her fingers. "Always eager to cut."

Evie tried to smile, but her stomach tightened. It bothered her that Dok might be underestimating Charlie. He was, after all, extraordinary—even if no one else seemed to think so. Other than Wren Baker.

David gave it some time before he stopped by Fern's to check on how Dok's helpers were settling in at Windmill Farm. He was actually quite pleased that his sister was getting much-needed help, much more pleased than she seemed to be about the arrangement.

The afternoon sunlight filtered through the kitchen windows, casting a warm glow over the wooden table. The air was thick with the scent of fresh pine from Fern's recent mopping, which made David hesitate at the open door.

"Come in, come in!" Fern called from the kitchen, her voice as brisk as the snap in her step.

David stepped inside, immediately noticing the gleaming floor. "I hate to mess up your hard work," he said, glancing at the prints his boots left behind.

Fern waved off his concern, though she kept an eye on the trail of dirt. "I'll just happily wash the floor again and think about our visit," she said, meaning it.

He couldn't help but smile. If it were anyone but the bishop, Fern would have kept them standing on the porch, at least until the floor was dry. But she had too much respect for the church leadership to do anything of the sort.

As he settled into a chair, Fern set a plate of thick, chewy gingersnap cookies between them.

"My favorite," David said.

With a slight grin, she shook her head. "You say that about all my cookies."

"Because it's true." He took a bite and chewed, savoring the spicy, sweet flavor. Fern's cooking was second to none in their church—though he kept that opinion to himself, for his wife Birdy's sake.

They sat in comfortable silence for a moment, the sound of the clock ticking softly in the background. Then Fern, never one to beat around the bush, spoke up. "The last time you showed up at my door, it was to talk me into taking on those young folk. So I figure you're here now to see how it's going with them."

David swallowed, appreciating her directness. "Exactly right." He studied her face for any sign of frustration. "I asked you to house them for just a few weeks. Dok said she'd look for something more permanent, but I don't think she's had much luck yet." He had a hunch his sister was dragging her feet in hopes that the two residents might give up and go away.

"I don't mind them so much, if they want to stay on here. With Luke and Izzy gone, it's nice to have folks around the farm. Hank Lapp keeps showing up with his mule and cart with boxes from Dok."

"Hank? Bringing things here?"

"Says he's helping to clear out Dok's basement."

"According to Sarah Blank, who seems to know everything in this town, Charlie is doing some kind of update at the office. I haven't seen Dok to ask." He gazed out the window at the buggy shop. "But why are boxes coming here?"

"Hank says they're full of old medical equipment that Wren wants. Antiques and the sort, he said." Fern shrugged. "As long as the boxes don't stay longer than those two young doctors, it's fine with me." She raised an eyebrow. "Which reminds me, I have yet to hear anything more about recompense for boarding them."

David sighed, rubbing the back of his neck. "I'll speak to Dok today about that."

"And," Fern said, lifting a finger in the air, "I take them to

Dok's office each morning. They're on their own to get back in the afternoon, unless there's a rainstorm with thunder and lightning. Then I told them I'd come and fetch them. Seems like that should be counted in too."

"I hadn't given any thought to their transportation. I'll mention it to Dok." His mental list of things to do was growing by the minute. He should leave soon, because he had a full afternoon of work ahead of him. And he needed to chase down his sister. But for now, he was content to sit a while longer, enjoying Fern's company and the simple pleasure of a perfect gingersnap cookie. "So, all things considered, they're working out for you?"

"They're settling in," Fern replied, leaning back in her chair, her fingers drumming lightly on the table. "The boy, Charlie, is a big help to me. He volunteered to feed the animals each morning. Gets up extra early for it. He has a nice way about him. Takes care of himself. Doesn't even come for supper. I offer, so long as he shows up at suppertime . . . but he never does."

"Maybe he's trying to save money."

"I wouldn't charge him much. Evie and I worked out an arrangement. I offered the same to Wren, but she said she prefers to make her own meals. Says she has special eating needs." She lifted her thin shoulders in a shrug. "I don't know what that boy is eating."

David nodded, a small smile tugging at his lips. Charlie King was hardly a boy. "That's good to hear. He seems to be pretty absorbed in Dok's basement remodel." He reached out for another cookie. Just one more couldn't hurt. "And the women? They're working out well?"

"Evie, the nurse, is no trouble at all," Fern said, her tone softening. "Very thoughtful. She's good company. Did you know her grandparents were Mennonites?"

David nodded. "Dok mentioned it."

The arch of her eyebrow deepened. "Evie does need a bit of a backbone."

"And the other woman? Wren Baker." For some reason, David braced himself for the answer.

Fern frowned, the lines on her forehead etching a clear message. "She keeps herself scarce. When I do see her, it's quick."

David waited.

"She has plenty of opinions."

He waited.

"And then there's moments like this morning. Wren came downstairs with a bundle of laundry in her arms, handed it to me, then walked right out the door. Assumed me doing her wash was part of her room and board." She lifted her chin. "And it's not."

He had a hunch something else was nettling Fern. "So how'd you handle it?"

"Evie jumped in and offered to do the laundry for them both. I told her no and put the bundle of dirty laundry right back on Wren's bed." Fern frowned. "You can see what I mean when I say that Evie needs a backbone."

David waited.

"Evie likes to give, and Wren likes to take."

David smiled into his iced tea. Es is so! Der Brennesel. *There it is. The nettle.*

6

Annie was at her desk, going over some paperwork, when she heard the front door creak open. She looked up and saw Gus standing in the doorway, and her heart flip-flopped. It always did when she saw him. She stood up to greet him, then stopped. Something was wrong. "Gus, what's happened?"

His face was pale as a ghost, and his usually steady hands trembled as he clutched the brim of his straw hat. He didn't answer right away but cast a glance at the patients in the waiting room, whose eyes were on him. "Could we talk outside?"

Annie followed him out and closed the door behind her.

He took in a deep breath, his shoulders sagging as he let it out. "I just came from a run," he said, his voice barely above a whisper. "It was . . . it was a bad one."

She waited for him to continue.

Gus swallowed hard, his Adam's apple bobbing visibly. "There was a car accident out by the old bridge. A mom and her little girl. The car went off the road, down into the ravine. We got there as fast as we could, but . . ." His voice trailed off, and he shook his head, the words too painful to voice.

Annie moved closer, gently placing a hand on his arm. "But?"

she prompted softly, steeling herself for whatever he was about to reveal.

Gus took a shaky breath, his eyes clouded with the weight of the memory. "The accident happened because the little girl . . . she had crawled out of her car seat. The mom had turned around to get her when the car went off the road." His voice cracked, and he closed his eyes, as if trying to block out the image. "We tried everything, Annie. Whenever a child's involved, we always keep trying, no matter what. We kept trying and trying . . . but it was too late. The mom—she kept begging us to help, to save her baby. But there was nothing we could do."

Annie felt her heart twist. She knew how deeply Gus cared about his work, how much he invested himself in every call he made. "I'm so sorry," she said.

When he opened his eyes, the haunted look in them sent a shiver down Annie's spine.

"I'll never forget the sound that mother made when we had to stop. It was . . . like a wounded animal, like a howl."

Annie's breath caught in her throat. All her EMT training had focused on the rescue, on the saving of lives. She hadn't once considered how it would feel if a rescue wasn't possible. Gus had been an EMT for over two years now, and today's call had clearly shaken him to his core.

"I've been at the scene of plenty of accidents. It's always hard, but you find a way to keep going. My partner once warned me there'd be a call one day that would buckle me at my knees. The one that haunts your dreams, making you doubt yourself. Did I do everything I could? Did I miss anything?" He wiped his eyes with the back of his sleeve. "I guess today was that call."

He didn't need to spell it out: Sometimes, no matter how strong or skilled an EMT was, there would be situations where they just couldn't help—where the loss was inevitable, and the harm couldn't be undone.

Gus tipped his head. "Speaking of my partner, I'd better get going."

Looking past him, she saw the ambulance in the parking lot. "Our bishop David Stoltzfus, he would tell you that the little girl's life was complete."

Gus nodded, managing a faint smile. That was how the Amish made sense of the unimaginable: They leaned on humility and trusted in God's plan. They believed that, no matter how difficult life could get, there was a purpose. That God was good, all the time, even in the midst of painful circumstances. She squeezed his arm before he left, trying to reassure him—and maybe herself too.

⁂

Dok glanced at her watch. She had promised Matt she'd be home by seven tonight so they could make it to their church's small group, but she needed to drop by Clara Zook's and pick up Evie, drop her off at Windmill Farm, then stop by the office to see if some test results had come in. She was already way behind schedule. She pressed on the gas to speed up.

Joining this small group had been Matt's idea. He wanted to get better connected at church, and he thought they needed more friends. Matt was getting increasingly focused on relationship building as he neared retirement. Dok felt she had plenty of people in her life, but he pointed out that she had many acquaintances, not deep friendships. "There's a big difference, Ruth."

Dok let out a sigh. Her social needs were much lower than her husband's. Matt supported her in so many ways; joining the church group was the least she could do for him. It was only fair. And she enjoyed it too. But mostly because Bee Bennett and Damon Harding had joined the group. They were both full of questions about what a life of faith looked like, adding a nice element to the mix. She had a hope that Bee might turn into that kind of deep friendship that Matt wanted for her. Having a best friend sounded rather lovely.

Still, it had been a long day and she would really prefer to enjoy this summer evening by relaxing at home with a good book and a glass of wine. She sighed again. Not gonna happen.

As she veered onto the road that led to the Zook farm, she spotted Jacob Zook mowing hay in a distant field. He'd been at it all day, working hard to get that second cutting of hay done. He was a dedicated farmer, no doubt about that. But he left care of the house and children to Clara.

The Zook farm had always stood out in sharp contrast to the other homes in Stoney Ridge. Most Amish farms were the picture of neatness, with tidy houses, blooming gardens, and freshly painted barns. But the Zook place had an air of neglect. The paint on the house was peeling, and the porch sagged as if it had long ago given up hope of ever being repaired. Even the barn looked tired, its roof bowed and weary.

As Dok's car rolled up to the house, her thoughts drifted to Clara. Barely twenty-two, Clara was delicate in both body and spirit, and Dok worried about her. The young woman had always looked a little overwhelmed, but now, with two babies to care for, that fragility had only deepened. It seemed as if the babies sensed it. For such small infants, they had an impressive set of lungs and were not shy about using them. Their constant crying filled the house with an uneasy energy, making it hard for anyone to find a moment's peace.

Earlier today, after Dok had gently examined both babies and reassured Clara they were healthy, she could see that her words didn't have much of an effect. There was a desperate look in Clara's eyes, so Dok had made a quick decision. "Evie, would you mind staying with Clara for a few hours?"

She knew that Clara was in good hands and that Evie's gentle presence would help ease the young mother's mind. But as she rolled up the driveway, Evie burst out of the front door, as if she'd been watching for her by the window.

She plopped into the passenger seat, relieved. "My ears are ringing."

Dok laughed. "From the babies' cries?"

Evie nodded. "They have the lungs of opera singers. We'd get one settled down and the other would start up. All afternoon. One up, one down. The other up, the other down."

As Dok turned from the driveway onto the road and stepped on the gas pedal, she noticed Evie grip the car's handle, her knuckles white. Matt was always telling her she drove too fast, but that was just him being the overly cautious cop that he was. After all, she knew these roads well. The sooner she got to where she was going, the better. But seeing Evie brace herself, she slowed down a bit. "All in all, did Clara seem a little more confident by the end of your visit?"

"Hard to say." Evie's face scrunched up. "I get the impression that she hides her feelings."

Good observation, Dok thought. "Did Jacob ever come to the house? Did you meet him?"

"Briefly. He came into the house for a glass of water and left again."

"He didn't help with the babies? Didn't hold them?"

"I'm not sure if he gave more than a quick glance at them." Evie shook her head. "He reminds me of my grandfather. A good man but stern. My grandfather's favorite saying was"—she lowered her voice to a growl—"wer sei Kinner liebt, zichdicht sic." *Love a child, chastise it.*

Dok shot a glance at her. Evie hadn't even realized she had spoken Penn Dutch. So she had a grasp of the dialect! There were moments when Dok felt as if Evie could read her mind, anticipating what she needed next for a patient. She'd chalked it up to hospital experience, but now she realized Evie had understood the conversation. She wondered why she kept that skill to herself, and why she didn't speak the language. Sometime, when she wasn't in a hurry, she'd like to know more about Evie's background. She sighed. She should try to get to know Wren and Charlie too.

"Is that typical around here? In the Amish church, I mean. The men, acting all patriarchal?"

"Some," Dok said, turning up the long driveway that led to Windmill Farm, "but most of the men are hands-on dads."

"That's good to hear. Jacob seems . . . quite a bit older than Clara."

Dok nodded. "Yes. Second marriage for Jacob. He and his first wife had four children, including a set of twins. They're grown and gone. I suppose he thinks Clara should be up for the task. His first wife handled them easily," she said with a shrug, "so, in his mind, why can't Clara?" She stopped at the top of the driveway to let Evie out.

Evie put a hand on the door handle. "Where is Clara's mother? Or mother-in-law?"

"Jacob's mother is long gone. And Clara came from a much more conservative church to marry Jacob, so her family has shunned her." Dok sighed. "Compared to what I've heard of her church, Jacob might've seemed like a prize." She glanced at the clock on her dashboard. "I'd better get going. But before I do, I'd like you to carry this with you." She handed her a pager.

Giving Evie a pager had been Matt's idea. Not only would it save time, but he liked the idea of Dok having someone with her for house calls during the night. There hadn't been many night calls lately, but they were part of her work and always seemed to come when she least expected them. "It's the newest model. It can deliver text messages—but with a limited character count, so I apologize in advance for abrupt-sounding messages. So I'll see you tomorrow, unless the pager goes off tonight."

That girl didn't even flinch.

Evie was, Dok thought, sent straight from Heaven.

Evie tucked the pager from Dok into her pocket after setting it on vibration mode. Partly so it wouldn't wake Wren in the night if it went off, but mostly to hide that Dok had entrusted her with a pager. Knowing would only irk Wren.

Everything Evie did seemed to irk Wren. She was an exceptionally persnickety roommate, to say the least. Wren had a laundry list of strict rules—no lights on after she went to bed, not even a tiny flashlight for reading. And regardless of how hot and stuffy the room became, Wren insisted on keeping the windows tightly closed, claiming the air stunk with manure.

The funny thing was, Wren fell asleep almost instantly and slept like a log, complete with loud, rumbling snores. Once that familiar heavy breathing filled the room, Evie would quietly tiptoe over to open the window, welcoming a much-needed breeze that swept away the stale air. She'd then slip back into bed, switch on her concealed flashlight, and read to her heart's content. Early in the morning, before Wren stirred, she carefully closed the window. So far, Wren hadn't caught on.

Wren had never really liked Evie, and Dok's acceptance of Evie's nursing skills only seemed to fuel that feeling. It was a bit of a tangled situation, but Evie couldn't stand the thought of anyone disliking her—even if that someone had staked a claim on her darling Charlie.

Still, Evie was determined to keep being kind, hoping that eventually, she'd break through Wren's wall and they'd become friends.

Someday, it would happen.

Opening the kitchen door of Windmill Farm, Evie sniffed the air. It was filled with the comforting smells of supper in the making. "I'll run up and change my clothes," she told Fern, who was scrubbing the dirt off carrots in the kitchen sink, "and come down to help."

A few minutes later, as Evie returned to the kitchen, she said, "In your church do you see many new mothers who struggle with postpartum depression?"

Fern stopped chopping carrots to look at her in surprise. "Depression? No. None. Babies are a blessing."

"Yes, they are. But a woman can love her baby and still feel overwhelmed by the demands of motherhood."

Fern considered that, then shook her head and went back to chopping. "Not among our people."

"But what if someone did? Would she feel the need to hide her depression?"

"Why would she hide it?"

"Maybe because . . . she feels judged. Sounds like most of the Amish women don't struggle with feelings of loneliness or depression."

"Of course not. No one is lonely here."

"But that's exactly what I mean. What if someone doesn't know how to ask for what she needs? Or wants?"

Fern set down her knife. "Well, I would say that person might need to swallow her pride and take the first step."

Could Evie give that kind of advice to Clara Zook? She seemed so reluctant to accept help, even from Dok and Evie.

"Some folks just need a little more confidence in themselves," Fern said, locking eyes with Evie. "They need to have a little backbone."

Hold it. Did Fern think Evie was talking about herself? *Me?* She slapped a palm against her chest. "You think *I'm* lacking a backbone?"

"You washed Wren's laundry."

"Well, yes . . . but I was doing mine anyway. Wren is studying for her boards. And I'm sure she appreciates it." Evie hoped so. Wren never said.

Fern held a finger in the air. "She leaves her dishes in the sink each night for you to wash and dry."

Evie flushed. How did Fern know that? A couple of times, Wren had come in late from studying for her boards in the buggy shop and made herself something to eat in the kitchen. Fern went to bed early, so Evie would tiptoe downstairs, after Wren had fallen asleep, to wash dishes. She didn't want Fern to face a sinkful of dishes first thing in the morning.

Another finger in the air. "You've given her all the pegs in your room to hang her clothes. Yours are in your suitcase, under the bed. I happen to have noticed when I was dusting under the beds yesterday."

What dust? There was no dust in this house!

Fern's sparse eyebrows lifted. "You need a backbone. Self-confidence."

Wait, what? This conversation had veered off course! Evie scrambled to steer it back on track. "I was just wondering what someone in your church would do if she were lonely."

"The Amish aren't lonely," Fern said. With that, she turned and headed to the garden for a forgotten item, leaving Evie standing there, more puzzled than before. Well, that chat took a turn she didn't see coming—like opening a door expecting a closet and finding a whole new room instead.

⁓

Dok stopped by the office after dropping Evie at Windmill Farm and promised herself she'd only stay fifteen minutes, twenty minutes, tops. The waiting room was empty, Annie had gone home, Charlie was doing something that involved a lot of noise in the basement, Wren was studying for her boards in the buggy shop. Savoring the time alone, Dok closed her eyes and leaned back in her chair. Just resting her eyes, she told herself, before heading home in time for tonight's small group meeting.

She'd hardly seen much of Matt this week. They'd tried so hard to get a handle on balance, and they'd been making progress, and even started planning a big RV trip next summer to some of the national parks . . . but it all unraveled after that feature TV news story came out on her. She never should have agreed to it.

Those thoughts flitted through her mind, circling slower and slower. She must have dozed off when a knocking sound jolted her awake. Her brother stood at the open door.

"David!"

"You were sound asleep."

"I wasn't!" She sighed. "Not *sound* asleep, anyway." She rubbed her face. "It's been a busy day." A busy couple of months.

David came in and sat down across from her. "This won't take long."

Her eyebrows knit together. "Are you here as a brother or a bishop?"

"Bishop."

Dok groaned.

David ignored her. "I spoke to Fern today and she gave me a not-so-gentle nudge about getting reimbursed for her three boarders."

Dok took in a breath of air. "I meant to follow up on that." She scribbled on a yellow Post-it note: FERN—*follow up on $$$.*

"She said something about getting paid to drive them into your office each morning."

Dok nodded. "Fair enough." That whole transportation dilemma had taken her by surprise. She would've thought one of them would have a car.

"Ruth, since we're talking about the boarders—"

Were they?

"—I can't help but feel you could be doing more for those two young doctors."

"I plan to." Dok busied herself with straightening paperwork on her desk. "I just haven't quite figured out how to do it. My day is so full with patients and emergencies . . . and paperwork . . . it's difficult to find a way to fit them in."

"You heard about what happened to Hank Lapp at the store today?"

"No." She froze. "What?"

"Wren Baker told him that he suffered from hearing loss and that's why he shouted all the time."

Dok cringed. "How did Hank take that?"

"Better than you might think. He told her that his mother said he'd been blessed since birth with a voice that could wake the dead."

Dok let out a deep huff. "David, I have been so caught off guard by Charlie and Wren. I'm thoroughly unprepared for them. They need so much supervision." She leaned her elbows on the desk and rested her chin in her palms.

"They're eager." He made it sound like a selling point.

"Yes, eager. I'll grant you that. Very eager. But also culturally insensitive to the Amish." Wren, she meant. She leaned back in her chair. "And did I tell you they didn't *match* on Match Day?" That was still hard for her to swallow.

"You did." David folded his arms against his chest. "But the nurse is working out well for you?"

"Evie? She's a big help. She's had a lot of direct patient care experience, unlike Wren and Charlie. And she's very intuitive. She knows what I need before I ask for it. I told you that her grandparents were Mennonites, right?" She dropped her shoulders in a sigh. "It's unfortunate that Evie's only here for a couple of months."

"So, you say that the residents need supervision, and they need a little work with cultural sensitivity. Since Evie is familiar with Plain ways, maybe she could do some supervising of them when you're called out of the office?"

Interesting. Dok tilted her head. "It's not typical . . . but I suppose Evie could provide guidance. Maybe on some basic patient concerns." She gave him a thumbs-up. "Good thinking, David."

"Why can't you take one or both of them on house calls?"

"Most of my house calls are to the Amish. I guess I just . . . feel protective of them. It took a very long time for them to accept me. Evie is one thing. I don't have to worry about how she handles herself around the Amish. But the residents are a different matter."

"But people do accept you, and if you were to explain to them about the resident doctors, and how they're gaining experience under your supervision, then I think you might be surprised by the acceptance. Your word carries a lot of weight around here. You've earned people's trust."

"And I've worked very hard for that trust. Earning trust doesn't seem to be on the residents' radar. Honestly, they haven't earned *my* trust either."

His brow furrowed. "You're going to have to let them interact with your patients. All of them. Englisch and Plain."

"I'm working on it."

David stroked his beard in a thoughtful way. "King Solomon once said, 'Give instruction to a wise man, and he will be yet wiser; teach a just man, and he will increase in learning.'"

Dok frowned. "It sounds like King Solomon started with someone who was wise to begin with. I'm not sure about these two."

"And then there's Paul's words in the book of Titus, encouraging older women to teach what is good—"

Dok slapped a hand on her chest, coughing a laugh. "Older women?"

"You're missing the forest for the trees, Ruth. Sharing knowledge and experience with the younger generation is pleasing to the Lord."

Dok swallowed a sigh. Once David started quoting Scripture, she knew she was beaten. How does one argue with the Word of God? "Fine. I read you loud and clear."

His face softened, and he pulled at his beard. "Listen, I do understand. Training a store employee isn't the same thing as training a doctor, but I can appreciate the time and investment it takes, especially at first."

Dok grinned. "And you have a revolving door of store employees."

He winced. "I know. As soon as they're trained, they seem to find better-paying jobs. Still, I like to think I've been a building block in their life's journey."

Only her brother. Dok gazed at him, impressed by his ability to try to squeeze out the good to be found in any and all situations. "Okay, okay. I get your message." A yawn escaped. "I'd better get home before Matt wonders if he still has a wife." As soon as she said it, she wished it back. "Don't! I already know what you're going to say. That's why these candidates are here in the first place."

Amused, David rose to his feet. "Maybe you should start by calling them what they've trained to be—doctors."

Overly enthusiastic, socially oblivious, thoroughly inexperienced, green-as-grass doctors.

Nope. Dok just wasn't ready for them.

7

Dok had offered to give Annie a lift home on Saturday afternoon, since she was heading out that way to stop by her friend Bee Bennett's house. As Annie hoisted her scooter into the back of the SUV, Dok watched her with a thoughtful look on her face. "Odd. It just dawned on me that I don't think I've ever given you a ride before."

Not so odd. Dok lived in the opposite direction from Fishers' dairy farm and worked crazy hours. Annie kept strict office hours and enjoyed the independence of riding her scooter. If the weather was bad, either her mom or dad would drop her off or pick her up.

Annie climbed into the plush leather passenger seat, a change from the hard buggy bench she was used to. Eyes wide, she looked over the sleek dashboard, the elegant clock. She hadn't been in a car in years and years, and never ever in one so fancy as Dok's.

"Buckle up," Dok said, and they were off.

Down the tree-lined road that ended at the Bent N' Dent, left at the stop sign, right at the old gray barn. And then they reached a long, open stretch of road, and to Annie's surprise, Dok stepped hard on the gas pedal. The car lurched forward.

Annie gripped the armrest, trying to steady herself, but Dok's speed caught her completely off guard. Everything felt off-kilter. She grew dizzy, her stomach twisted and turned, and she had to squeeze her eyes shut. The sickening churn in her gut intensified, and she fought the urge to gag. The thought of throwing up in front of Dok, in her SUV, was terrifying. *Please, God, no!* Dok made a sharp right turn, jolting Annie into more misery. She opened one eye like a pirate. Home was just a few hundred yards away. *Hold on, hold on*, she told herself. *Nearly there.* As soon as Dok came to a stop at the top of the hill, Annie bolted from the car to hurry toward the house. She needed to get to a bathroom! "Thanks!" she called over her shoulder.

"Wait! Your scooter!" Dok called after her.

Annie rushed back to the SUV and grabbed her scooter from the back.

Dok twisted in her seat, peering at her with concern. "Are you okay? You look pale."

"Yes," Annie said, forcing a strained smile. "I'm just fine." She wasn't fine at all.

Dok hesitated. "Are your folks at home?"

Oh, I really, really hope not. "You know what it's like for dairy farmers," Annie said, backing up. "They're around here somewhere!" She turned around and walked fast toward the house.

As soon as Dok's car disappeared down the road, Annie stumbled to the bushes and threw up. Afterward, she collapsed on the porch steps, her head buried between her knees. The cool, solid feel of the steps beneath her was a small comfort, but her stomach continued to churn with that all-too-familiar, terrible sensation.

It was strange how a problem from so long ago could return so forcefully. Motion sickness had plagued her childhood, but she'd thought she would've outgrown it. As time went on, it was forgotten. She realized now *why* she hadn't been in a car for years—she'd suffered from motion sickness profoundly as a child, so much so that her parents didn't take her along on bus trips to visit her brothers. A horse and buggy traveled slow, less than fifteen miles an hour.

The sudden jolt of being back in a car had revived it with a vengeance. Full force. Annie took deep, steadying breaths, waiting for the nausea and dizziness to pass.

Her eyes flew open. EMT! How could she possibly become an EMT and ride in an ambulance if she suffered from motion sickness? Dok drove fast, but an ambulance? That thing would be like a rocket. Her heart began to pound. What if she couldn't?

Oh, how her mother would love this turn of events! Annie could hear her now, declaring that it must be the Lord's will to keep Annie from pursuing EMT work. Probably a direct answer to her prayers.

"Calm down, Annie," she told herself. "You're just making a big deal out of nothing. Dok's just a wild driver, that's all." She took a deep breath, slowly inhaling through her nose for a count of four, holding it for seven, and then exhaling through her mouth for eight. She repeated the breathing exercise four times, and by the end, she felt a bit more grounded. A tiny less nauseous.

Hold on.

Her head snapped up. Last winter, she had ridden in an ambulance without any major issues. Once. She had gone with Sarah Blank to the hospital after Sarah had fallen through ice into Blue Lake Pond. It had been fine. So it was definitely possible to be in a fast-moving vehicle without succumbing to motion sickness. She let out a big sigh of relief.

But what was the difference? She closed her eyes, thinking back. When she'd been riding in that ambulance to accompany Sarah, she'd been completely, thoroughly mesmerized by watching Gus at work. Mr. Wonderful. Her entire being was so focused on him, there was no room left for her stomach to react to the fast ride in the ambulance.

She squeezed her eyes shut and dropped her head between her knees again. If she could control it once, she could do it again. She refused to let this derail her dream to be an EMT. With Gus.

May turned to June. As another week in Stoney Ridge got underway, Evie had barely seen Charlie. He left at dawn to get to Dok's office and stayed until late each evening. One day after work, she went down to the basement to see what kind of progress he was making. At the bottom of the steps, she waited until he had finished framing a wall with the nail gun. She could have interrupted him, but the opportunity to just gaze at him was too appealing to skip.

What was it about Charlie? Why did he have such an effect on her? She'd spent so much time trying to figure it out, but she still didn't know for sure.

It had to be subjective. Darcy might be right that he wasn't *that* handsome. His nose was a little crooked, like it had been broken once and not reset properly. And there was a thin scar running down one cheek that she'd always wondered about. He wasn't perfect. He should be nothing special at all.

But he just was.

He was endlessly good natured and well-intentioned. He was all in. Thoroughly committed to whatever he was doing. Like . . . this basement remodel. Committed Charlie.

She could have stared at him all day.

Too soon, he set down the nail gun and turned toward her, like he sensed she was there. The expression on his face when he looked at her, like it was the best moment of his day—it just melted her. Did everybody get that look from him?

"What do you think?"

Evie slowly turned in a circle, taking in the bare walls and scattered tools. "There's so much more light in here with that enlarged door space."

"Yeah, that's made a big difference." He'd carved out the space for the new entryway and was just using a piece of plywood as a door for now. The plywood rested on the wall, and light streamed in from the outside.

"I can see the possibilities down here," she said with a smile. "But I've got a pretty vivid imagination."

"Yeah? What else do you see?" Charlie said, crossing his arms, clearly interested.

"Well, off the top of my head, right where you're standing could be more than a waiting room." She moved toward the center of the room where Charlie stood.

"Like what?"

"Like, it's big enough that it could be a gathering place for a group. And given the lighting situation down here, the walls should be a light color, maybe a pale blue, with a little gray in it."

"Don't stop."

Not a problem! She was just getting started. "On the walls, I can imagine some framed pictures of local landscapes. A covered bridge, or some of those beautiful Amish barns. Or quilts! I could look in some downtown shops for them."

Taking a step toward her, Charlie grinned. "Keep going. I like your ideas."

Evie felt a surge of excitement. "We could put down a rug to make it cozy. A durable rug. As in . . . washable." Just yesterday, a little four-year-old boy threw up all over the floor of Dok's small waiting room. "Definitely washable."

He stepped even closer. "You've got a knack for this."

Their faces were just inches apart.

Eyes locking, they both grew very still.

Evie should step back. *Too close, too close!* She didn't trust herself to not throw her arms around him and cover his face with kisses.

Step back, step back! Right now, before it was too late. But she didn't. She couldn't make herself.

Just then, Wren came down the cellar stairs. "Charlie, you won't believe what I've found—" She stopped short at the exposed threshold when she saw Evie, her expression shifting to one of dry disgust.

On the far side of the basement, Dok's voice rang down the steps. "Evie? We've got a house call to make."

"Oh, okay, Dok. I'll be right up."

Wren let out an annoyed sigh. "House calls are a colossal waste of time. You need modern equipment to properly evaluate a patient, and that requires a doctor's office."

Evie couldn't disagree more. So much more about a patient was revealed in their home—like the elderly man who promised Dok that he was taking his medication, only for her to spot the full bottles on his kitchen windowsill. In their homes, patients often revealed things they didn't even realize themselves. Like the woman who insisted she had asthma and needed an inhaler. Each time her cat climbed into her lap, she started having trouble breathing—turned out she was allergic to it.

What was the point of disagreeing with Wren? It was never really a conversation with her. She told you what she thought, with a tone in her voice that you should think that way too. Even if you didn't. Evie glanced up at Charlie. "Guess I'd better go."

Charlie shot her an apologetic look. "No problem. We can talk more later."

Upstairs, Dok was waiting for her by Annie's desk, medical bag in one hand. "Is any progress happening down there?"

"I think so. Definitely." But Evie wasn't talking about the basement.

A Hidden Hope

David finally had a quiet moment at the end of the day. His two little boys were asleep, and he sank into his favorite chair, a book in hand, soaking in the peacefulness. But that peace was short-lived. His wife Birdy appeared from the kitchen with a look that instantly made him squirm.

Hands on her hips, she asked, "Did you really quote Scripture to Dok?"

David grimaced. Apparently, after what he thought was a meaningful talk with his sister about the importance of training others, she'd stopped by to complain to Birdy about him. "I was just trying to make a point."

Birdy raised an eyebrow. "David, you're her brother, not her bishop."

"I just think she's missing an opportunity to share her knowledge and get some help." He explained his suggestion that Dok should start bringing the resident doctors along on her house calls, even to the Amish. "If people see that Dok trusts them, they'll accept the new doctors."

Birdy didn't look sold.

"Go ahead," he said, bracing himself. "Say it."

"I've heard a few stories about those resident doctors . . ."

"If they're from Sarah Blank or Hank Lapp, I'll pass."

"No, from Dok herself," Birdy said, crossing her arms. "She's wrestling with *how* to bring them into her practice, especially with her Amish patients."

"But—"

"David, she's spent years building relationships with the Amish. She listens to them, not just about their ailments, but their lives."

"But—"

"And I know you hate hearing this, but a lot of women in our church don't feel heard. Not by their husbands, definitely not by authority figures like you, the bishop, or the ministers. Sometimes even by older women with narrow views."

He had a "but" loaded up, but it just sat there.

"Dok is very protective of her patients. All of them. She's doing the best she can under the circumstances. Why, it was just a week ago that she first learned she was suddenly supervising not one but two residents! Give her time, David."

David could see where this was going. One of the many things he loved about Birdy was how she made him see what he was missing. And, as always, it left him feeling grateful and humbled. Often, very humbled. "Birdy," he said, "I hope you know that I think what you say is important. I'm listening."

Her face softened into a smile.

He patted his lap. She sat down, resting her head against his neck. "I don't know what I'd do without you," he said.

"Happily," she murmured, "you don't have to."

Early the next morning, Evie came from the bathroom into the bedroom she shared with Wren to find her holding up the pager Dok had given to her. She froze.

"I heard something vibrate and found *this* in your suitcase." Wren held it up in the air. "Dr. Stoltzfus gave it to you, didn't she?"

Slowly, Evie nodded.

"That really takes the cake." Wren shook her head like she'd just bitten into a sour lemon, her lips tight with distaste. "Unbelievable."

"Um, can I have the pager? I need to know what Dok said."

"She's coming to get you in five minutes." Wren glanced at her watch. "Four."

Evie grabbed the pager out of Wren's hand and started scrambling to get dressed for the day, pulling clothes out of her suitcase. While brushing her hair with one hand and applying mascara with the other, she could feel Wren's eyes on her. "Something on your mind?"

"I just don't get why Dok has more faith in you than in me," Wren said, clearly annoyed.

Honestly, Evie had no good response because, well, she kind of agreed. Wren radiated confidence and competence in everything she did. Even in pajamas, she appeared commanding, sophisticated, elegant.

Evie? Not so much. A thousand other words came to mind: average, ordinary, dependable. "Elegant" was definitely not one of them.

She hurried downstairs, bolted out the door, and made her way down the driveway to wait for Dok. Halfway down, she glanced back at the farmhouse and caught sight of Wren at the bedroom window, watching her. What could be going through her mind? Nah, on second thought, Evie didn't want to know.

Every once in a while—especially in moments like this—Evie wondered if she'd made a big mistake coming to Stoney Ridge instead of going to Alaska with Darcy. She was sharing a room with someone who clearly didn't like her. Charlie? Hardly saw him, other than Fern's morning buggy rides to Dok's office. He was holed up in Dok's basement most days, hammering away at something or other. At least, Evie thought with a wistful sigh, he wasn't spending time with Wren.

Wren spent all her spare time in the buggy shop, studying for her boards—just in case, she said, Dok ever let her treat a patient. A bit of an exaggeration, but not much.

On the other hand, Evie was definitely getting varied and unique experiences with patients. She loved the peace and quiet of Windmill Farm. But the best perk of all was Fern Lapp.

In so many ways, Fern reminded Evie of her grandmother. A woman who brooked no nonsense, who did the work of two in the time of one, and somehow kept an eye on everyone. Most mornings, sharing a love of rising early, Evie and Fern would chat over coffee as the sun rose. At the end of the day, Evie fell into a pattern of helping Fern weed or water her big vegetable garden. Those moments meant so much to Evie—she felt as if she was reliving happy memories, before her grandmother's health started to fail. Time with Fern was special.

But that didn't mean Evie had stopped hoping for an aha moment with Charlie, a romantic breakthrough where he'd suddenly stop, take a second look at her, and say, "Why, Evie, you and I are meant for each other!"

So far, that moment had yet to come.

___

David was at the register at the Bent N' Dent when Hank Lapp's booming voice filled the store. "Clara Zook! LOOK at those BABIES!" Hank spoke with his usual enthusiasm, his voice echoing through the aisles. Clara had just stepped in with her infant twins in a stroller and looked a bit worn around the edges.

As soon as Hank's greeting rang out, both babies startled awake. The first let out a sharp, piercing cry, and within seconds, the other followed suit, their combined wails reverberating off the shelves. The noise seemed to paralyze the store. Shoppers paused mid-aisle, glancing around uncomfortably. A woman who had been examining a jar of pickles set it down with a sigh and said, "I'll just come back later." Eli Fisher, Annie's dad, halfway through his shopping, put his items back on the shelf and made a quiet exit behind the pickle jar woman.

David watched the scene unfold, feeling a mix of concern and helplessness. Clara, looking flustered, tried her best to soothe the babies, gently rocking the stroller and murmuring soft words. But their cries only grew louder, drowning out the usual hum of the store. He wasn't sure how to help, as Sarah Blank had called in sick today and he was managing the store alone. Two customers were in line, looking like they wanted to leave as fast as possible.

The jingles on the door rang again, and in marched Wren

Baker. She cast a frown in Clara's direction but didn't break stride. Instead, she headed straight for the refrigerated cooler of drinks.

Hank Lapp had settled back into his rocking chair, oblivious to the commotion he'd created. The babies' cries ratcheted up a few notches. David couldn't even hear the ping as the cash register opened. Clara, her face red with frustration and embarrassment, with both babies still screaming, turned and pushed the stroller out of the store, her head lowered to avoid the stares of the graybeards—covering their ears—in their rocking chairs. The door swung shut behind her, muffling the cries that had dominated the store just moments before.

As the noise died down, Wren stood in line, waiting her turn. When she reached the counter, she handed over a five-dollar bill for a bottle of iced tea. "If I had to hear that racket every day, I think I'd lose it," she said with a half smile, making a downward motion with her hand to emphasize her point. She leaned in a bit closer. "Any chance you've got a discount for impoverished medical staff?"

David handed back the five-dollar bill. "How about a 'Welcome to Stoney Ridge' discount instead?"

Wren gave him a playful wave, raised her iced tea in a mock toast. "Thanks," she said, striding out the door.

As she left, a wave of unease settled over him.

He could practically hear Birdy's voice in his head, asking: *What made you think it was a good idea to give Dok advice on supervising her residents when you don't even know them at all?*

He really didn't have an answer to give her. He winced. Humbled again.

8

Annie had been dodging Gus for a couple of days now, and her excuses were getting flimsier by the minute. When he called her at work today, she barely let him finish his question. "Can I come over tonight and help you study?"

"I can't," she said. "My mom needs help with pie making. I promised."

Which wasn't a lie. The pie making was real. But it wasn't the whole truth either.

It wasn't that she didn't want to see Gus. She did—more than she cared to admit. But her mind flashed back to that stomach-churning ride in Dok's car—the blur of trees, the sharp turns, and her insides flipping over like a pancake. She'd barely managed to keep it together until Dok drove away, and then promptly lost it all in the hydrangea bushes.

That little incident had planted a nagging fear in her gut, one she couldn't shake: What if she never could get a grip on this motion sickness?

"Annie," Gus said, his voice dropping to a softer tone, "I was wondering if maybe I shouldn't have told you about that car accident—you know, the little girl who didn't make it."

"No," she said. "Not at all. I'm glad you shared it with me."

He hesitated, clearly not buying it. "You know, most of the calls are easy fixes, right? We get tons of false alarms. It's hardly ever like that one call was." Somebody called his name in the background. "I gotta go. But I hope to see you soon, okay?"

After hanging up, Annie sat back with a sigh, feeling the full weight of the irony. She could handle the chaos, the blood, the pressure of an emergency. But the very idea of riding in an ambulance, speeding down a road, left her stomach doing somersaults.

She had to get a handle on this terrible motion sickness before Gus found out. And definitely before he got the wrong message from her.

This morning, while Wren took her customary marathon shower, Evie swapped out the old sheets on the twin beds for the fresh sets Fern had left. As she bundled up the dirty linens, Fern appeared in the doorway, arms crossed against her chest. "Now you're changing her sheets?"

"I did mine first, and then, since Wren's still using the bathroom, I figured I might as well tackle hers too."

Fern grabbed the bundle with a resigned sigh. "Evie, you need a backbone." With a quick turn, she banged on the bathroom door and shouted, "Time's up!" and then was off down the stairs as swiftly as she'd come. The shower turned off.

Did Evie really lack backbone with Wren? Throughout the day, Fern's words replayed over and over in her mind, her frustration building with each repetition.

That evening, Dok dropped Evie off at Windmill Farm after making a house call to Annie Fisher's home. While vaccinating his dairy cows, Annie's father had accidentally stabbed himself in the leg with the needle. Dok instructed him to try to remain absolutely still until she arrived—the less he moved, the lower the risk of the vaccine spreading through his system. Once there, she carefully cut around the injection site to remove any contaminated tissue and then stitched up the wound. Fascinating! Evie realized she would never have witnessed such a treatment in a hospital. This was the kind of experience she wanted to get as a traveling nurse, and why she didn't choose an urban teaching hospital.

It was interesting to have met Annie's father—a man who took pain in stride, shrugging off a self-inflicted stab wound with the same ease as if it were a splinter. In stark contrast was Annie's mother, who spoke with acute awareness of every little body ache, treating each minor discomfort as a significant ailment.

As Dok's car zoomed down the driveway, Evie looked over at the buggy shop before she headed to the farmhouse, hoping to see Charlie tinkering with the buggies. She would love to tell him about Annie's father and the cow vaccine. He enjoyed hearing about the house calls she made with Dok, and she enjoyed telling him about them. But there was no sign of him, which probably meant he was still at work in Dok's basement. So diligent! Another reason Evie adored him. Conscientious Charlie.

She walked up the steps to the kitchen door, assuming Fern was inside, but there was Wren at the kitchen counter, slicing a stalk of celery. So she did eat, after all.

Wren glanced at Evie. "Fern's gone to some kind of a quilt party for the evening, so I thought I'd make a salad. Fern's cooking is . . . well . . . it can be . . ."

"Plain," Evie said.

Wren looked up at Evie in surprise, unfurling a radiant smile. "Bingo."

It was such a surprise to be on the receiving end of Wren's smile that Evie felt a giggle of delight slowly erupt from her rib cage. She tried to suppress it, but it slipped out, and to her surprise, Wren laughed. Just once, but it was a definite laugh.

"So plain," Wren said. "So very, very plain."

It dawned on Evie that she had misunderstood her. The same word meant different things to them. Plain to Evie meant lavish, Amish-style food. Plain to Wren meant boring.

But the drawbridge had lowered with Wren! She had smiled at Evie, sort of, and laughed—once—and her voice had softened. "I think you'd enjoy Fern if you spent some time with her. She's a wonderful person. There's so much to learn from her. I could ask her if she'd give us a cooking lesson."

Too much, too soon.

"The only one I need to learn from is Dr. Stoltzfus." Wren's eyes flickered with something Evie couldn't quite read, and her tone of voice changed from soft to sharp. "But it seems as if you've got that role sewed up."

Evie crossed her arms, studying Wren. The look on Fern's face this morning popped into her head, and the words: *"Evie, you need a backbone."*

Okay, then. Okay. Evie squared her shoulders, determination bubbling up inside her. "I haven't sewed anything up. Not intentionally." Which took her right back to thinking about the cow vaccine and Annie's father. It was too bad that she couldn't talk to Wren about the house calls like she could to Charlie. But she was pretty sure Wren would look at her the way she was looking at her now, like Evie had stolen something from her. "There's plenty of work to go around."

Wren's eyes flashed with irritation. "Doesn't seem that way. Especially when it comes to house calls."

Self-confidence! Backbone! "That's not fair, Wren. Dok needs to see that you're making an effort to understand the needs of the Amish. They make up half of Dok's practice. Maybe more. Hiding away in a buggy shop isn't going to accomplish anything."

"I'm not *hiding*. I'm studying." Wren's expression tightened. "I shouldn't have to prove myself to anyone. And I don't understand why she's always getting pulled out of the office for house calls. It's a terrible way to run a practice."

"House calls are very important to Dok, for lots of reasons." It was one of the reasons Evie wanted to work for her.

Wren pointed the tip of her knife at her. "Most all of those house calls could be handled by sending patients to the ER. Or to urgent care."

"There is no urgent care in Stoney Ridge. And don't forget the Amish pay out-of-pocket for their medical bills. No health insurance. Going to the hospital is usually a last resort." Which Wren would know if she bothered to learn more about them.

Wren went back to chopping carrots on the diagonal, with remarkable precision.

Watching her, an odd thought darted through Evie's mind. Wren would make an excellent surgeon. A precise skill was required, yet it also meant minimal people interaction. Wren wasn't much of a people person.

"Did you ever consider surgery?"

Wren turned toward her with an expression that fell somewhere between disbelief and offense. "Did Charlie say something to you?"

"No! I was just watching you, and the thought came to me. I wondered if you'd ever considered it. Seems like you'd make a very good surgeon."

"Are you giving me advice about *my* future?"

"Um . . ." *Backbone, backbone!* "No, not at all. It's just that . . . I know Dok's schedule is sporadic, but Charlie leaves the basement to observe Dok whenever she has time. She was looking for you today, but you'd left to study for boards."

"She was hardly in the office today! Besides, she's the one who told me to use spare time to study until she had a plan for us. We haven't been here very long." She lifted the knife in the air. "And I spent most of that first week cleaning out the basement."

Hardly! Charlie and Hank cleaned it out. Wren supervised.

"Still, Dok's trying to make a choice for partner. She needs to see you make an effort to accommodate the unique needs of her patients."

"What? What did you say?" The frown seeped from Wren's face. "Is Dr. Stoltzfus looking for a partner? Is that why she applied for two residents? Is she choosing *between* us?" She set down her knife. "Does Charlie know about this?"

Oh. Oops.

Evie figured everyone already knew. She thought it was common knowledge. But now that she thought about it, Dok had never actually told her the news. She'd heard it from Sarah Blank, who always sounded like she knew everything. But now it occurred to her that Sarah might not be the most reliable source of information. "Actually . . . I don't know."

"What don't you know? If it's a contest? Or if Charlie knows about it?"

Oh no. Why did Evie start this? She shouldn't have said anything. "Neither. I know nothing. I don't know why I even said that. In fact, forget I said anything." *Backbone, backbone!*

"Well, not everything," Evie said. "I meant it when I said you're going to have to show Dok how much you want this job. You need to become indispensable to her." Charlie, too, but he'd already found a way to become indispensable as Dok's construction guy.

Wren stood silently for a moment, then seemed to have an idea. She straightened up, her expression resolute. "You're right, Evie. I'll find a way to prove myself. Become indispensable. Thank you for this little pep talk." She tipped her head, squinting at Evie. "You look positively worn-out. Here." She pushed the bowl toward Evie on the counter. "Help yourself to this salad. I just remembered something I need to do." Without another word, Wren turned and left the kitchen to head over to the buggy shop.

The drawbridge was pulled up. Evie watched her go, disappointed that the moment of intimacy they'd shared had been so brief, so fleeting, but kind of proud of herself for being clear and direct. She'd had a backbone with Wren!

And then she turned around to see the sink full of dirty dishes.

9

Annie Fisher glanced around the crowded waiting room. The workday had just started and it was already one of those mornings where everyone needed Dok's attention, all at once, right now. Three mothers with fussy children, an elderly man with a walking cane, and two noisy teenagers filled the small space. Hank and Edith Lapp had just walked in the door, asking if Dok could squeeze them in.

If only! Dok was running late and hadn't arrived yet. Annie sighed, sensing it was going to be a long day.

The basement door swung open and Charlie appeared at the top, soaking wet, dripping water. "Annie, I wonder if you might know of a plumber?"

Annie followed him back down to the basement. She hadn't been down there since Charlie had finished carting away all the things that had been stored in the basement. Now, wall studs were up, and an actual door to the exterior had been installed, replacing the slanting cellar door that you had to duck under. Impressive! Everything except the large puddle of water that was spreading across the floor, gushing from a geyser in the small bathroom. "What happened?"

"I was branching in a new pipe with a fitting," Charlie said, brushing wet hair from his forehead, "and, unfortunately, the original pipe broke at the shut-off valve."

Eyeing the mess, Annie sighed. *Oh no.* Squinting, she put her hands on her hips. "Does that mean there's no running water in the entire office?"

Charlie's face scrunched up in an apology. "Not until we get a plumber here."

With that, the door creaked open, and Hank Lapp hollered down the stairwell. "ANNIE! What's this about needing a PLUMBER?"

That man! He could hear like an owl when he wanted to. Annie waded over to the bottom of the stairs and looked up at Hank. "Charlie said a pipe broke."

"Old pipes," Charlie said, wringing water out of the ends of his shirt. "I should've known."

"I'll have a LOOK," Hank said, in the way that men do, assuming they can fix everything.

Annie started up the stairs. "I think I'll just make some calls and try to find a plumber."

Hank chuckled, shaking his head. "NO NEED! I've got PLENTY of experience with plumbing. I know JUST how to fix this."

Oh dear. Dok wouldn't like this. "I think I'd better call a real plumber."

Hank looked hurt. "I've run into more BROKEN PIPES in this town than any REAL plumber. Ask EDDY! She'll tell you."

No way was Annie going to ask Edith Lapp anything, not if she didn't have to. That woman terrified her. She bit her lip, glancing over at the rapidly spreading water. They were in a bind, and Hank sounded like he knew what to do to fix it. On the other hand, Hank always sounded like he knew what to do and he rarely did.

"You need WATER to keep the office open, RIGHT?"

"Right."

"THEN I'll fix this in the BLINK OF AN EYE."

It wasn't like Annie had many options at the moment. Maybe she could let him fiddle around with it while she called around for a plumber. "All right, Hank. If you think you might be able to fix it, give it a shot. But please be careful. Do no damage."

"Don't you WORRY, Annie. THIS BOY and I will have running water for you in no time."

Annie stepped aside to let Hank pass on the stairs, watching as he approached the problem with a determined look. She leaned over the railing to see him crouch down to examine the pipes, muttering to himself in a voice loud enough for all to hear. After a few moments, he started tinkering with the fittings, his hands moving with surprising deftness.

Annie's skepticism slowly gave way to hope. Maybe Hank really did know what he was doing. She doubted it, but she might be wrong.

Back upstairs, she found Wren had arrived at the office. The last couple of days, she hadn't been coming in with Charlie and Evie in the mornings. Dok didn't even seem to notice.

"Annie," Wren said, "I'd like a few minutes to talk to Dok."

"You could if Dok were here—" Before Annie could finish the sentence, a commotion erupted from the corner of the waiting room.

Mary Yoder, an elderly woman with a kind face, was clutching her chest, struggling to breathe. Her wheezing filled the room, causing everyone to turn and look.

Annie rushed over to Mary.

Wren was right behind her. "Everyone, please step back and give her some space." She knelt beside Mary Yoder. "I'm Dr. Baker. I'm here to help."

Mary Yoder nodded weakly, her eyes wide with fear. "Asthma," she said, patting her chest.

"I'll call Dok," Annie said.

"I need a nebulizer," Wren said, calm but authoritative, as she took charge of the situation. "Do you know what that is?"

"Of course." Of course Annie knew what a nebulizer was. "But I'll call Dok."

"No time. She needs it now."

This was exactly the kind of situation that Annie had hoped to avoid with the residents. The thing was, Wren was right that Mary needed treatment, fast. She blew out a puff of air. "Which med should I bring?"

Wren's eyes flicked at her, impressed. "Albuterol. It's fast-acting and will help open up her airways right away."

Annie quickly fetched the nebulizer while Wren prepared the medication. She attached the albuterol to the nebulizer and placed the mask over Mary's face, instructing her to breathe deeply. The room fell silent, everyone watching intently as Wren worked to stabilize Mary's breathing.

"Just breathe slowly and deeply," Wren coached gently, holding the mask in place. "You're doing great."

Gradually, Mary's breathing steadied, and the color began to return to her face. The waiting room of patients, watching the drama, relaxed.

"Thank you," Mary Yoder whispered, relief evident in her eyes.

Wren smiled warmly. "You're very welcome. We'll keep an eye on you for a bit, just to make sure you're feeling better."

The door opened and in walked a pharmaceutical representative. Annie recognized him—the reps made the rounds to doctors' offices on a regular basis to drop off product samples or brochures. Annie would squeeze them in between patients to talk to Dok for a few minutes. Not today, though. She was just about to tell him that Dok wasn't in the office when Wren stepped in.

"I'm Dr. Baker," she said, shaking his hand. "I'm new to the practice. Dr. Stoltzfus isn't here right now."

"Nice to meet you, Dr. Baker," he said. "I'm with Pharmogen."

Wren stilled. "Call me Wren. I'd love to hear about your company's products." She pointed to the hallway. "Let's go to Dok's office." And away she went, the pharm rep eagerly following like a golden retriever, wagging his tail.

Annie watched them go, wondering how Dok might feel about Wren Baker stepping into her shoes. With a patient, with a pharm rep.

But Dok wasn't here. And, fortunately for Mary Yoder, Wren Baker was.

Annie heard some clanking from below. She hurried down the basement stairs. "How's it looking?"

Charlie peered around the bathroom door. "Not too bad."

"NOT BAD AT ALL," Hank said, tightening one last fitting. "Just ONE more twist here . . . and it's good as NEW!" He stood up, wiping his hands on a rag. The water had stopped, and the puddle on the floor was no longer growing.

In the tiny bathroom, Annie stepped around Hank to turn on a sink faucet. It worked! She let out a sigh of relief. Who would've thought it? Hank Lapp saved the day.

Dok pulled into the parking lot, trying not to count how many cars and buggies filled the lot. "Evie, would you mind running into the Bent N' Dent and getting us both a cup of Sarah's coffee? I'll meet you in the office."

As Evie disappeared into the store, Dok remained in the car for just a moment to brace herself, resting her hands on the steering wheel and taking a deep breath. She and Evie had been on an early morning house call that took longer than expected, and she was certain she'd be facing a waiting room full of cranky patients.

As Dok stepped inside, she was hit in the face not by cranky patients but by the smell of freshly brewed coffee. By the sight of her patients chatting and laughing, doughnuts in hand. Edith Lapp, who usually had a bone to pick over the smallest delay, was smiling, dunking her doughnut in her coffee mug. It was like walking into a cozy café rather than a clinic. Dok blinked a few times, convinced she must be imagining things.

What was going on? Dok stood there, nonplussed, trying to reconcile the cheerful scene before her with what she had anticipated. "Annie?"

Seated at her desk, Annie watched her with wide, concerned eyes, as if she wasn't sure how Dok would react to this scene. Frankly, Dok wasn't sure how she felt about it.

"Wren Baker ordered the doughnut delivery. She made everyone coffee too. She said the patients should be compensated for having to wait." Annie handed Dok a fistful of pink phone messages. "And there was a plumbing problem. But that's been taken care of." Annie took in a deep breath. "And then there was a . . ."

Dok had been glancing through the messages, but there was something in Annie's pause that made her freeze. "A what?"

"Mary Yoder . . ."

Dok turned to see Mary Yoder, seated next to Edith Lapp, stuffing half a doughnut into her mouth.

"Elderly patient started to have trouble breathing," Wren said, walking in from the door that led to the exam room. "I administered a nebulizer treatment, and she responded well."

"You did *what*?" Dok said, in a low, none-too-pleased voice. "You're not licensed to treat a patient without supervision."

At first, Wren's eyes went wide, and for a split second, Dok thought she was going to apologize. But then something shifted. Wren's lips twisted and her back stiffened. "It was a situation, Dr. Stoltzfus, that required immediate attention."

And you weren't here. Dok sensed the accusation behind her words. And it was the truth. She couldn't be in two places at once. This kind of morning was the reason she had wanted a partner in the first place. She studied Wren for a moment, then lifted her eyebrows, just a bit, in admiration. "Good work, Wren." She lifted a hand in the direction of the hallway. "Mary, you get to jump the queue today. Head on back to the exam room."

After letting Mary pass by her, Dok turned back to add, "Wren, why don't you come too?"

Wren's mouth curled up at the edges. "Yes, yes. Why don't I?" she said, a little louder than necessary, Dok noted, as she hurried to join them.

David stood behind the counter, realizing that he had just sold the last bottle of Pepto-Bismol. He glanced at the empty shelf where, two days ago, rows of the bright pink medicine used to be.

Sarah came from the stockroom. "I can't find any more boxes."

"I'll call in an express order. Seems like a flu bug is making its way through town."

"That's what Dok told Annie who told Sally who told me," Sarah said. "But I have a theory. No, better than a theory—practically a solid gold fact. Swimming in Blue Lake Pond is making everyone sick."

Sarah liked to be the authority on just about everything.

Over the last year, David had come to the conclusion that God had sent Sarah Blank to the Bent N' Dent to work on his patience. That, plus learning to relinquish into God's hands the things he couldn't control. Sarah told the customers so much gossip about so many people that he couldn't keep track of it all. When she first started to work at the store, he had tried, without fail, to put a lid on it. Not a chance.

"I'm only sharing prayer requests," she would tell David. "Not gossip!"

Birdy had reminded him that Sarah was a good and reliable employee, and that maybe he needed to focus on being her boss instead of being her bishop. It was good advice. "Why would Blue Lake Pond be making people sick?"

"Think about it. The weather's turned beastly hot this week. Everyone's been out at the pond, wading or swimming to cool off. The youth group had a picnic there just yesterday afternoon. The pond is probably crawling with bacteria. Or algae. Or both." Sarah's eyes went wide with concern. "I've heard about this kind of thing. Entire towns, wiped out like the bubonic plague." She swept her arm in a wide arc. "Gone. Just like that."

David frowned. "More likely, it's just a couple of people with upset stomachs."

Sarah, never one to miss an opportunity to be the town crier, leaned forward. "I think I should run over and let Dok know about the algae in Blue Lake Pond. I'm just sure I'm right."

Before David could stop her, she was out the door and halfway to Dok's office. Not two minutes later, she returned, a glum look on her round face.

"Well?" David said.

"Dok told me to get back to work." Sarah returned to the cash register, then looked up. "Oh! She also asked if the Bent N' Dent has any Imodium to spare. She's run out."

Annie was sorting through a stack of patient files when she heard the door to Dok's office open. Looking up, she saw Gus standing there with a grin on his face. Her heart did a flip-flop.

"We had a nearby call," Gus said, stepping inside. "Someone with a flu bug. Nothing too serious."

"It certainly seems to be going around." She tried to keep her wits about her. Gus's unexpected appearances at the office always caused her to come unraveled. Here he was, Mr. Wonderful, looking incredibly handsome in his EMT uniform. So manly, so capable. So . . . wonderful.

"As long as we were in the area," Gus said, "I reminded my partner of the free and delicious coffee they serve at the Bent N' Dent." He leaned forward, now only six inches away from her. "I haven't seen you in a while. And . . . I've got some exciting news to tell you."

He grinned, and then she grinned, and then she got that weird sense that all the patients in the waiting room were watching them. And they were! "Let's, um, go outside for a moment."

After she closed the door behind her, she turned to Gus and tried to keep a casual look on her face, though she felt anything but casual. Her whole body was humming with excitement. Gus had come to see her! "What's up?" she asked, striving for nonchalance but barely concealing her delight.

"I talked to my partner, and he agreed to let you go on a ride-along in the ambulance. It would be a huge bonus for you to observe emergency procedures before taking your final exam." He was beaming.

Annie froze the smile on her face, hoping it wouldn't look as fake as her enthusiasm for this offer. "That's . . . that's so kind."

"I knew you'd be thrilled," Gus said. "It's the perfect opportunity to get some real hands-on experience. You'll see what it's like out there in the field, and you'll be so much better prepared for your final." He lowered his voice. "And this will give my partner time to observe you. It'll give you a leg up to get hired. Think of it as a pre-interview."

Annie swallowed hard, her mind racing. She wasn't ready for this. She needed time to get a handle on her motion sickness scare.

"I talked you up. I let him know that you're a big deal."

But she wasn't a big deal. She wasn't even a little deal.

"I reminded him of how you rescued Sarah after she fell through the ice into the water."

"But I didn't! You did."

"You knew what to do. You kept a cool head. You got someone to call the fire department. You held on to Sarah until help came."

"Gus, you do that kind of thing every day."

"But I'm trained for it. You had no training. It was just instinctive. You're a natural."

She swallowed, feeling tears prick her eyes. No wonder she thought of him as Mr. Wonderful. The things she was good at—he saw them.

And he was being modest about his own instincts. She would never forget the story of why he had become an EMT. He had started out as a volunteer firefighter but soon realized firehouses respond to more medical emergencies than actual fires. "In my first few weeks of volunteering," he had told her, "I watched firefighters bring a child back to life after drowning in a backyard pool, reset broken bones, and save a teenager from an overdose."

"So is it the excitement that you like?" she asked. "The thrill?"

He gave a little head shake. "It's more than the thrill. It's the sense of making a real difference. There's something incredibly fulfilling about stepping into those hard life-and-death moments by trying to make things better. I was hooked. And the firehouse needed EMTs. My bishop was all for it, which was a good thing. Because I can't imagine doing anything else with my life. I'm grateful I didn't have to choose between my church and my life work."

She had felt the same way. She loved the world of medicine. She also loved being Amish.

He put his hands on her shoulders and gently squeezed, jolting her back to the present. "Annie, this ride-along is an incredible opportunity for you. It's worth doing whatever you need to do to make it happen."

Annie nodded, her mind already spinning with excuses to avoid it. She needed time! She needed to test herself before she went on an ambulance ride-along with Gus. "Can I think about it?" she said, trying to keep her voice steady.

"Think about it?" He had a look in his eyes like he was trying to read her. "Why would you need to think about it?"

"It's just . . . this flu bug is running through the town and everyone wants to get in to see Dok and . . . oh! Look! There's your partner. Let's . . . talk about this another time."

"Sure. Of course." But a look of confusion and disappointment flickered through his eyes. "But . . . let's nail down a date sooner rather than later, okay?" he said, as he turned to meet his partner at the ambulance.

Maybe later rather than sooner. Annie sighed in relief as the ambulance drove off, but the lump in her stomach remained.

10

Annie sat at her desk during lunch, tapping her pen against a stack of invoices that needed Dok's attention.

Taking a deep breath, she pulled out the brochure of the bus schedule. She noted the departure and return times, calculating that she could make it back just in time to finish her lunch and get back to work. She needed to know if her childhood plague of motion sickness was back to stay, or if it was just due to a onetime-Dok's-crazy-driving event.

"Okay, Annie Fisher, you can do this," she reassured herself, trying to muster up some courage. She packed up her lunch. "It's just a bus ride. Not a big deal. People ride buses every day."

With one last glance at the clock, as if it held the answer, Annie headed out the door.

Ten minutes later, she took a deep breath as she stepped onto the bus bound for Lancaster, her heart pounding in her chest.

This was it—the moment of truth. Today, Annie reassured herself, was the day she'd leave her motion sickness behind and finally reclaim her future.

As the bus pulled away, she fixed her eyes on a distant tree, mentally coaching herself into calmness. *Breathe in, breathe out. You can do this, Annie Fisher.*

Then the bus hit a bump. Her stomach did a little flip—nothing too bad, just a mild queasiness. But as the bus sped up, that queasiness turned into a full-on churn. A clammy sweat broke out all over her body. *Stay calm,* she told herself, closing her eyes and focusing on breathing. *Slow, steady, in through the nose, out through the mouth.*

Another bump, another sway, and her nausea rose like an unwelcome tide. She tried everything she could think of—counting her breaths, staring at the horizon, even willing her stomach to behave—but it was no use. The scenery whizzing by only made things worse.

She gripped the seat in front of her, her knuckles white. *Please, not now.* The bus lurched again, and she pressed a hand to her mouth, desperately hoping to hold back the inevitable.

Too late.

She grabbed the paper bag she'd packed just in time, retching into it. She yanked the overhead cord, and the driver stopped the bus and opened the door. She stumbled off, her legs wobbling like jelly, and collapsed on the side of the road, head in hands.

It took a long time for her stomach to settle. When she finally stood, her body felt shaky, but she managed to head toward Dok's office. Her heart sank a little lower with each step. How was she supposed to handle being an EMT if she couldn't even handle a bus ride?

She was walking up the steps to Dok's office when Evie opened the door. "Annie, are you okay?"

Annie put a hand to her brow, trying to hide the well of tears in her eyes. "Just a bit of a headache. Don't mind me."

"Oh no." Evie moved closer, placing a comforting hand on Annie's shoulder. "I wouldn't be surprised if you've caught that flu bug that's been going around Stoney Ridge. A lot of people have been coming down with it." She squeezed her shoulder gently. "Why don't you sit down and rest for a bit? You look a little green around the gills."

Green. Gills. An image of a swampy pond filled with rotting fish swam through Annie's head, making her feel even more nauseous. Was that possible? She sank into her desk chair, her head in her hands. "I just need a moment."

"Don't worry, you'll feel better soon," Evie said softly. "This bug seems fairly short-lived."

Annie took a deep breath. Not *this* bug.

⁓

Dok hung up the phone and leaned back in her chair. A knock at the door interrupted her thoughts. "Come in."

David opened the door, his brow furrowed with concern.

"Are you here as a brother or a bishop?"

"Both," he said. "Maybe also as a patient."

"Don't tell me you're sick too."

"No, I'm fine. But I do wonder, Is something going through the town? There's been a run on Pepto-Bismol and Imodium in the store."

Dok sighed, leaning back in her chair. "I've been seeing patients for the last two days with GI symptoms."

"Anyone seriously ill?"

She shook her head. "So far, the symptoms seem to be pretty mild. Nausea and diarrhea."

"What's causing it? Food poisoning? Or could Sarah's theory about Blue Lake Pond hold a possibility?"

"Those who are sick are a variety of ages and genders, which rules out something like bacteria in the pond. And as for food poisoning, people usually recover within a day." She brushed a lock of hair behind her ear. "I ran some tests and found shigella."

David raised an eyebrow. "Shigella?"

"It's a bacteria. It can be a nasty one."

"Where's the source?"

"That's what I haven't figured out."

"Well, what do the patients have in common?"

"Just *that*." Dok rolled a pen back and forth under her hand. "They're all my patients, and they were all seen in the office this week, but not for stomach problems."

David scratched his head. "So . . . the link is . . . your medical office?"

Oh no. Dok's eyes widened as a thought struck her. "Wait a minute. Annie mentioned a plumbing problem earlier this week." She went to the door and called Annie's name.

A moment later, Annie appeared, hovering in the doorway. As soon as her eyes landed on the bishop seated inside, she visibly shrank back.

"Did I do something wrong?" Annie's voice wavered, her posture already retreating.

"No, no," Dok said, trying to ease her tension. David was such a kind man, but he often had this kind of effect on others. Especially someone as shy as Annie. "Just a quick question. A few days ago, you mentioned something about the plumbing?"

Annie blinked, looking even more uneasy. "Plumbing?"

"Yes, the plumbing issue. Something about Charlie working in the basement?"

"Oh." Annie's hands fidgeted with the hem of her apron. "Charlie was working downstairs and asked me to call a plumber. The water wasn't working anywhere in the building, so I was going to . . . but . . ."

"But?" Dok said, watching Annie's gaze drop to the tops of her shoes. Not a good sign. The poor girl looked like she wanted to melt into the floor. She felt a hitch in her gut.

Annie swallowed hard. Her voice lowered a few notches. "Someone in the waiting room volunteered to help."

Dok and David exchanged a look. "Who?" they said in unison.

"Hank Lapp." Her voice was small and whispery.

"Oh boy," David muttered.

Dok dropped her chin to her chest. Of all people! Hank meant well, but disasters followed him.

"Hank said he had experience," Annie said. "And . . . the water came back on before you returned to the office."

David crossed his arms over his chest. "How long was the water off?"

"Just about an hour."

He frowned, clearly puzzled. "But why aren't you sick, Ruth? And you, Annie?"

Dok thought back to that afternoon. She'd returned to the office, expecting to face angry patients who'd been kept waiting. Instead, they were eating doughnuts and drinking coffee. Her eyebrows shot up. "Coffee!"

"Coffee?" David said.

"They all drank coffee. Those are the patients who are now sick. It's the water." Dok squeezed her eyes shut. "I wonder if Hank mixed up the pipes."

"Oh boy," David said.

"Annie," Dok said, folding her arms, "why was everyone drinking coffee in the first place?"

Annie shifted uneasily. "Wren said she wanted the patients to know their time was valuable," she said. "She apologized to all of them for you running late. And then she . . ." Annie's gaze quickly dropped to the tops of her shoes again.

"Go on," Dok said, her brow furrowing slightly.

"She said that the practice clearly needs more doctors," Annie said, her voice smaller now, "and that she was looking forward to providing health care for everyone. But that . . ."

"Go on," Dok said, feeling her patience wear thin.

"But that Dr. Stoltzfus had trouble relinquishing patient care." Annie's voice was barely above a whisper now. "And she hoped the patients would all encourage you to allow the residents more direct contact with them." She paused, biting her lip. "And then she served coffee and doughnuts to everyone."

Dok's frown deepened. *Great. A coffee strategy.*

"I'm sorry," Annie said, her voice shrinking with each word.

"Annie," David said, his tone warm, "you were in a tough spot. You were trying to solve a lot of problems at once." He gave her a kind smile. "I think that's all we need to know." Then his face suddenly shifted, eyes wide. "But don't let anyone drink the water until we get a plumber in here."

After Annie left, Dok let out a long puff of air. "Thankfully, those patients are Amish. At least they won't sue me when they find out my coffee got them sick."

David lifted an eyebrow. "Setting aside the water pipe problem, Wren Baker had an excellent point."

Dok reached for the phone. "Right now, I need a plumber more than I need a resident." A loud bang came from the basement. "Make that two residents. Both of whom think they know what they're doing and they don't."

David rose. "They don't know because they don't have experience. They don't know because they don't have anyone supervising them. They don't know because they aren't learning anything." He gave her a look.

Dok frowned again. She didn't need her brother telling her how to run the practice. "Since you're such an expert on life," she said, with a cranky edge in her voice, "I'll let you be the one to tell Hank Lapp that his plumbing days are over."

11

The summer heat had settled over Stoney Ridge like an unwelcome guest who had no plans to leave anytime soon. Humidity clung to the air so thick you could practically wring it out of your shirt. David Stoltzfus wiped his brow, knowing the only thing that could chase this swelter away was a good rainstorm. And unless the skies decided to be merciful, it looked like the heat was here to stay—hanging over the town like a damp quilt.

David walked into the Bent N' Dent and stopped short when he saw a line of customers at the register. Where was Sarah Blank? His gaze swept the store. No sign of her. He hurried toward his office. "I'll just put my mail on my desk," he said to the first customer in line, "and be right with you."

Opening the door of his office, the first thing that caught his eye was the backside of Sarah as she leaned out the open window. "Sarah," he said, in a tone that clearly conveyed *What in the world are you doing?*

She whipped around, guilt in her eyes. "Just trying to catch a breeze." She waved her hand in front of her face. "So hot in here!"

"Good idea," David said, "but there are customers in the store."

Sarah quickly crossed the room and through the door to return to the cash register.

David tried to dismiss a familiar wave of annoyance. Every time he stepped out of the store, Sarah seemed to take it as a green light to stop working. Boxes that should have been unpacked stayed untouched, and the peanuts scattered on the floor by the graybeards never got swept up.

But opening a window was an excellent idea. David's office in the back of the store could get stifling hot. He set down the mail on his desk and opened another window to get a cross breeze. As he did, voices floated up, carried by the air. Peering out, he spotted Wren Baker sitting at a picnic bench outside, sharing iced tea with a sharply dressed pharmaceutical representative— one whom David recognized. He came around frequently to fill Dok in on his company's latest products and usually stopped at the Bent N' Dent for a cup of coffee or cool drink.

Abgharicht. *Eavesdropping.* So that's what Sarah had been up to when David interrupted her, why she looked like she'd been caught red-handed. He frowned.

And yet . . . he couldn't pull himself away. There was something about the scene that made him uneasy. He couldn't quite catch their conversation, but it was very clear that Wren was peppering the rep with questions. The man was lapping up the attention, answering questions with a touch of bravado. It was hard not to notice how the rep puffed up under Wren's focused attention, clearly enjoying the back-and-forth.

David's chat with Fern at Windmill Farm had only confirmed his impression that Wren Baker had a strong sense of her own importance. This rep, to David, had always seemed eager to impress. Not a good combination.

He wondered if he should mention this to Dok, but then he realized how silly he seemed, as bad as Sarah Blank with her nosy ways. *Wunnernasse un Schneckeschwenz. Nosy and curious.* The very thought made him cringe. His sister didn't need another wild tale-teller to dismiss, like Sarah's algae in Blue Lake Pond theory. What was it his sister said about Sarah? *Sie spricht als wenn sie heissen Brei im Munde hatte. She talks as though she has mush in her mouth.*

A little harsh, but true.

He decided to close the window and stay out of it. Better to focus on his own work, even in a breezeless office, and leave the gossip to the experts. Like Sarah.

⁂

During her lunch breaks, Annie hopped on the bus to Lancaster, each time convinced that *this* ride would be different. She'd sit in the first seat, on the right side so she had a wide-open view in front of her. She had read articles about motion sickness in Dok's medical journals and tried out different strategies. She rode the bus on a completely empty stomach. Didn't work. She tried nibbling on saltine crackers. No help. She sipped ginger tea. It didn't even stay down. She dabbed peppermint essential oil on her wrists. No help at all. Wristbands with pressure points? Useless.

Day after day, she ended up yanking the cord, desperate to get off the bus before her stomach turned inside out. She barely got off before vomiting on the side of the road.

Her motion sickness was more stubborn than she was. It was relentless.

As Annie scootered home after work that afternoon, she barely noticed the breeze rustling through the trees. Her mind was caught up in a whirlwind of worry about her job, her future with Gus, and how they were all tangled together. Everything about her relationship with Gus revolved around becoming an EMT. It was how they met, how she learned about being an EMT, how they spent time together. He'd helped her study, cheered her on, and made plans for their future as soon as she finished the course.

But what if she couldn't get past her motion sickness? If that didn't change, she'd never be able to become an EMT. And if she couldn't be an EMT, what might happen to her and Gus? That worry left her just as unsettled as the fear of failing her own dream to be an EMT.

Was she going to lose them both?

No!

Determined to find a solution, Annie buried herself in Dok's textbooks, searching for any remedy that didn't involve medication. But time and again, the answer was the same—pills. Unwilling to rely on those, she focused on non-drug alternatives, mostly trying to condition herself through sheer will and practice. The bus driver, now recognizing her routine, offered suggestions. He told her to lie down on the back bench of the bus and close her eyes. That only made things worse.

If "worse" was even possible, it found Annie. Today, her queasiness started up immediately as the bus pulled out of Stoney Ridge. One mere half mile down the road, she had to pull the cord, alerting the driver to stop. With a long-suffering sigh, he let her out, and she barely made it before she doubled over by the side of the road, heaving. When she finally straightened up, wiping her mouth, she turned around—only to see Sarah Blank standing there, watching her with wide, concerned eyes.

⁓

Self-doubt was practically Evie's middle name. She had chosen not to go to college after high school, and the main reason, she convinced herself, was because her grandfather suffered his first stroke and her parents were missionaries in Belize. Somebody needed to be there to help her grandmother care for her grandfather. Evie chose to forgo college and remain with them. She never regretted it. Not for a minute.

But if Evie were being honest with herself, she was relieved to have an excuse not to apply to college. The truth was, she was certain she wouldn't get in anywhere. Her schooling had been all over the place—years spent bouncing around mission schools in Central America, twice dropped into boarding schools, then jerked back to the US during her parents' furlough, only to head back out again. It was her grandmother who worried about the toll of being a missionary kid. Her parents were deeply committed to their mission work, fervently pursuing their careers with a divine purpose in mind. The constant upheaval had left Evie withdrawn, introverted, riddled with insecurities. Her grandparents finally insisted she live with them to finish high school instead of starting over in yet another country. That's where she met Darcy, her pushy, well-meaning best friend.

And it was Darcy, now a nurse, who kept nudging her to go to college. After Evie's grandmother passed away, Darcy's nudges turned into full-on shoves. "Apply! Just apply," Darcy would say. "What's the worst that could happen?"

So, Evie applied. And when she got accepted—with a full scholarship—she had never been so astonished in her life. Suddenly, she was out of excuses and off to college with dreams of becoming a nurse. She loved it from day one. The satisfaction of making even a small difference in someone's life gave her a sense of purpose.

But the self-doubt? That didn't magically disappear. Surrounded by nurses and doctors, younger than many of them, Evie constantly felt like the odd one out. They acted confident in all they did, while she was busy second-guessing everything she did, convinced she'd never measure up.

This last spring, the hospital offered her a job after graduation. But Darcy had other plans for them—she was ready for an adventure and she thought Evie was too. "You spent years taking care of your grandparents, then nursing school," she had told Evie. "But now it's *your* time. This is why nursing is such a great career. We can do all kinds of things as a nurse and go all kinds of places."

Darcy's relentless drumbeat convinced Evie to join her as a traveling nurse. She'd chosen for them to spend the summer in Alaska. One of the best perks for the long distance, she stressed, was that it would help Evie get over her ridiculous crush on Charlie King.

In the meantime, Evie happened to see the TV news story on Dok Stoltzfus, and she changed her mind. Not about the adventure-as-a-traveling-nurse part and not about the end-her-obsession-with-Charlie part, but the Alaska part. She applied to go to Stoney Ridge, to the Amish.

At that, Darcy seriously questioned Evie's mental health.

Normally, Evie could be swayed by Darcy, but not this time. Somehow, she just knew she had to work for Dok Stoltzfus, in Stoney Ridge. Among the Amish. At least for three months. This, she tried to explain to Darcy, would help her build her self-confidence. Darcy shook her head, slow and low, in a way that suggested this was a terrible turn of events.

She might've been right. Because, as it turned out, living and working with Wren Baker caused Evie to slip right back in that mental whirlpool of inferiority.

Wren was everything Evie wasn't—tall, willowy, polished, and not a hair out of place, even in summer's humidity. She was memorable. Meanwhile, Evie was short, a little rounder than she wanted to be, definitely not polished, and had frizzy hair that refused to stay down, *especially* in summer's humidity. She was forgettable.

Darcy had told Evie, again and again, that all this self-doubt was just in her head, that she was her own worst enemy. Maybe so, but that didn't change how Evie felt. She wished she could silence the doubts that constantly hissed in her ear. Doubts about her nursing ability, doubts about her lovability. She wasn't good enough. She wasn't *enough*.

This afternoon, Evie stood at the kitchen sink, her gaze fixed on Charlie working in front of the buggy shop, tools spread out around him. Watching him, she could tell that he was thoroughly absorbed in his task. *So all in.* She admired that quality about him. Everything he did, he did with his whole heart. Committed Charlie. She sighed, lost in her thoughts about him, when a sudden voice behind her broke through her reverie.

"Evie, you're staring so hard I'm surprised you haven't burned a hole through the window."

Startled, Evie spun around. "Fern!" Where did she come from? How long had she been there? "I . . . I was just . . . admiring your, um, flowers."

"It's the only place shady enough on the farm for hydrangeas."

Hydrangeas? Evie turned back to the window, squinting. *Oh yes! Right.* Big blue blossoms lined the buggy shop.

Fern joined Evie to peer out the window. "You know, if you're thinking so much about him, chances are he's thinking about you."

"Who?" The burn of embarrassment crept into Evie's cheeks. "Charlie? No, it's not like that. We're . . . not like that. I mean, we're just friends."

"I had to be a little bold with my Amos."

Amos? Fern's late husband? "You've got it all wrong." Evie's face grew even warmer. "Charlie and Wren . . . they're, well, sort of together."

Fern's sparse eyebrows lifted skeptically. "Is that so?" she said, as if she knew everything there was to know. Which she kind of did.

She handed forks to Evie and left the kitchen, heading out the door.

Evie, flustered, set the forks on the table. Most embarrassing of all was that her feelings about Charlie were so obvious to Fern. She seemed to know what Evie was trying so hard not to show.

As she was finishing up, she heard the kitchen door swing open again. Fern came in with Charlie, who stopped to sniff the air, like a dog at dinnertime. "What is that heavenly smell?"

"Roast chicken and potatoes," Fern said, making a beeline for an upper cupboard. "There it is, Charlie. I need that big platter."

Charlie stepped forward and reached easily into the cupboard for the platter. "I think you or Evie could've reached it."

Fern ignored that. "Say, why don't you stay for supper and join us?"

"Really?" Charlie's face lit up with genuine delight. "I'd love to! Honestly, my diet's been a bit of a joke since I arrived. Peanut butter and jelly sandwiches for breakfast, lunch, and dinner, and cold cereal on the side. Macaroni and cheese on Sunday, as a treat."

Evie's eyes widened in surprise. "Peanut butter and jelly for every meal? I thought there was a kitchen in the buggy shop."

He shrugged. "Yeah, but I don't know how to cook. And I'm on a string-bean budget."

"Still," Evie said, "that's quite a . . . limited menu."

"Standard fare for a med student." He was practically salivating over Fern's roast chicken as she lifted the pan out of the oven and set it near the platter.

Fern glanced toward the buggy shop. "Go fetch the other one to let her know supper's almost ready."

Charlie flicked a glance out the window. "That's nice of you, but I'm 99 percent sure Wren would say no. She's kind of a particular eater."

A laugh burst out of Evie, the sound escaping as a snort. Charlie caught her eye. A slow smile began, his eyes crinkled at the corners in amusement, and for an instant, she felt one of those jolts of electricity run between them. A spark. Then it was gone. Or maybe she imagined it.

Probably.

Charlie sat at the table and watched Fern and Evie work together in the kitchen, his eyes wide as if the whole concept of making dinner was a revelation. Fern sat down at the table and tucked her chin. Evie shot a side glance at Charlie, wondering how he would handle the moment of offering a silent grace. It was a habit of Plain life, one that Evie was familiar with. Was he?

To her surprise, his head was already bent in silent prayer. Evie followed suit, thanking God for this moment, for Fern's boldness, for Charlie being here. *Oh!* And for the food.

And then Fern's head lifted and she picked up the platter of chicken and potatoes to pass the food around. Evie had made a salad with freshly picked greens and cucumbers from Fern's garden. Charlie chewed and swallowed with such enthusiasm, like he'd forgotten the delight of a home-cooked meal. He helped himself to seconds, wolfing an entire plate of food down in, like, thirty seconds.

"This is incredible," he kept saying between bites, his eyes lighting up with every forkful. "Absolutely amazing."

Evie couldn't help but smile at Charlie's delight. She'd never seen anyone so genuinely excited about dinner.

Even Fern seemed pleased. "You should start showing up at suppertime. Consider it an even swap for the farm chores you've been doing. You've been a big help to me."

Charlie's eyes went wide. "Don't tell me you eat like this every day?"

Fern tried to hold back a grin, waving her hand dismissively. "This is nothing special."

"You're pulling my leg," Charlie said, turning to Evie. "Isn't she?"

"She's not," Evie said, laughing. "Fern is a wonder." For so many reasons.

Fern left the table and returned with a tin of thick, chewy cookies, dotted with M&M's.

Charlie's eyes grew even bigger. "Are those . . . ?"

"Monster cookies," Fern said with a smile.

Charlie dramatically covered his heart with his hands. "Fern Lapp, you're never going to get rid of me."

If Evie wasn't mistaken, she heard a giggle slip out of Fern.

And it wasn't just good food that fascinated Charlie. After supper, he asked her for a garden tour and took quite an interest in it, wandering through the rows of vegetables and fruits. A late afternoon storm had blown through Stoney Ridge, cooling off the air and chasing away the humidity. The large garden looked especially green and lush and inviting. "What's this?" Charlie'd ask, pointing to a squash or a pepper bush, genuinely curious about everything he saw. He offered to help stake some tomato plants. Fern hurried off and returned with a hammer and stakes and twine, handing them to him.

How could anyone resist him? Charlie was helpful, eager, grateful—and just plain fun to be around. Convivial Charlie. By the end of the garden tour, even Fern seemed a little smitten.

Annie was halfway through setting the dinner table when she spotted Gus in his buggy, trotting up the driveway. Why was he here? What did he want? She quickly assessed her chances of slipping out the side door unnoticed.

Too late. Her mother had already spotted him. Sally Fisher, crossing the yard from the barn, practically sprinted to greet him. She adored Gus—mostly because she could pepper him with questions about her latest imagined ailments. And Gus, with extreme patience, would humor her every time, gently explaining how none of her carefully curated symptoms fit the profile of any disease. Medicine, he'd say in that calm, level tone of his, was like detective work. Symptoms were clues, pieces of a puzzle. Sally's clues, however, never quite belonged to any known puzzle. Not even close.

Gus was a saint.

As her mom bustled into the house with Gus in tow, she shot Annie an eyebrow-wiggling grin. "Look who the cat dragged in for supper!" she said with an exaggerated wink that made Annie cringe.

"Hi, Annie," Gus said, lifting a brown paper bag slightly, his tone a little uncertain. "I was passing by and thought I'd bring some books that might help with your studies."

"Thanks." It came out sounding awkward and shy. Annie never felt that way around Gus. Only around everyone else.

Both her parents seemed oblivious to the odd tension between Annie and Gus. Dad never said much, anyway. He left the talking to his wife. Tonight, throughout supper, Annie didn't mind how much her mother talked—she was grateful, actually. Anything to keep the conversation far away from the EMT class, the upcoming final exam, or the dreaded ride-along in the ambulance. She couldn't commit to it until she could figure out how to stop her motion sickness.

As supper ended, her mom announced she was heading over to Windmill Farm to pick up some extra canning jar lids from Fern, and before Annie could even blink, Gus jumped in. "Annie and I can go for you, Sally," he said.

Her mother shot her a wink, and Annie winced. *Perfect.*

As they walked toward the buggy, the awkwardness trailed along behind them like an unwanted shadow. Not a word was spoken. Gus opened the buggy door for her with a polite nod, then paused. "Let's walk instead," he said, as if the thought just struck him. "It'll give us more time together without—" He stopped mid-sentence, catching himself.

"My mother," Annie finished for him, a smile tugging at her lips despite herself.

Gus smiled back, and just like that, the tension between them began to crack, the way ice splinters under the warmth of the sun. Before long, the awkwardness melted entirely, and they slipped back into the easy rhythm they used to share—him talking about his EMT work, and her sharing stories of patients at Dok's.

They walked along the road but soon decided to take a more scenic route, cutting through farms. Climbing over a wooden fence, they crossed through a horse pasture, the ground still soft and damp from the afternoon rainstorm. The cool air gusted around them, carrying the clean scent of rain-soaked grass. They passed Edith Lapp's clothesline, where forgotten clothes hung heavy, still dripping from the storm. A few cows at Jimmy Fisher's farm grazed nearby, eyeing them with mild curiosity. They skirted around a bright red barn, its paint vivid against the lush green fields. When they reached the creek that ran along the edge of Beacon Hill, they rejoined the road, the field too mushy from the rain to continue.

"So, Annie, when do you want to go on the ride-along? My partner's been asking."

She looked away so he wouldn't catch her cringing. "I'm sorry, Gus. I haven't thought about it."

"You haven't *thought* about it?"

She glanced at him. "It's just . . . the office has been so busy."

"What about this Saturday afternoon? Dok's office is closed."

"Well, you see, Saturday afternoon is my catch-up time."

His brow furrowed. "Catching up with what? What's more important right now than becoming an EMT?"

Getting over motion sickness, that's what.

When she took too long to answer, he said, "You'd tell me, wouldn't you, if you've changed your mind about becoming an EMT?"

She stopped abruptly, shaking her head, hard. "I haven't."

"If you're waffling, I hope you know it's okay. I get it." His obvious concern for her was touching. "A lot of people can't handle it. There's dark stuff out there."

"No, that's not it." She wasn't afraid of dark stuff! It wasn't the thought of becoming an EMT that had her second-guessing everything. It was the queasy, sickening, dizzying feeling that overcame her whenever she was in any vehicle going faster than fifteen miles an hour. Such a small thing, and yet it was everything. This simple issue had the power to turn all her big plans upside down—and worse, it threatened to steal them away completely.

She couldn't tell him, not yet, not while she was still figuring out how to manage it. She just needed a little more time, a chance to get this under control.

Instead, she shifted the conversation to a different topic. One that would hook him, fast. "Gus, what is it you like most about being an EMT?"

"What do I like most?" He tipped his head. "It's kind of a long story."

Oh, perfect! A lengthy distraction. "I'd like to hear it."

He pushed his hands down into his pockets, gathering his thoughts. "When I was six or seven years old, I was helping my dad gather firewood and kindling out in the woods behind our house. I heard a crack, and suddenly a huge dead tree branch fell right on my dad, pinning him to the ground. He was knocked out cold. The branch was too heavy for me to lift to free Dad, but I remembered seeing him use wood as a lever once. I found a big stick and was able to move the branch off him."

"Was he hurt badly?"

"Pretty bad. A concussion, plus a broken shoulder. Could've been worse, though." He shrugged. "Don't get me wrong. It was scary, seeing Dad like that, but I remember this total calm filling my mind so I could think clearly. And when I got older,

I realized that it was, well, kind of a gift. Most people shrink away from emergencies, but I like to enter into the chaos and confusion. Sometimes, staying calm, offering help . . . it seems like a way to bring God's presence into a person's pain." He glanced at her. "I think you have the same gift, Annie. And God gives us gifts to use them." A buggy was approaching, so he took her elbow to steer her over to the side of the road. "A few minutes ago you said the dark stuff wasn't *it*. So what is *it*? What's making you so reluctant to finish the EMT training? To even agree to go on the ride-along? Because I know there's something that's bothering you."

The look on Gus's face nearly broke her. He was so eager for her to finish the EMT program. So eager for her to work with him at the fire station. He'd been waiting patiently to start courting, always cheering her on. Always rooting for her. How could she tell him the truth? She couldn't. This was her problem, and she had to find a solution. Somehow, some way, she wasn't going to disappoint Gus. "Like I said, it's just been busy."

Just then, the horse and buggy reached them, slowing down to pass. Hank Lapp's voice boomed from the driver's seat, through the open buggy window. "ANNIE! Sarah Blank told me all about your TERRIBLE CAR SICKNESS! How're you ever gonna MANAGE running around in an ambulance ALL THE DAY LONG?"

Gus's head whipped around. "Car sickness?" His eyes opened wide. "Annie, is that the *it*?"

12

Sharing supper with Evie and Fern in the cozy kitchen at Windmill Farm had quickly become a routine for Charlie. Even the basement remodel didn't keep him away, though after supper he'd scooter back to Dok's to work on it a few more hours. Nearly done, he would say when Fern asked about it. Fern's eyebrows would lift high, as if to say, *That seems hard to believe.* Evie wondered, too, if he was being overly optimistic. The month of June wasn't even over yet.

Fern always invited Wren to supper, but she begged off, saying that she needed to stay focused on studying for the boards, and everything was spread out in the buggy shop. She said she had stocked Charlie's small refrigerator with food. Evie had never been invited inside, but she sometimes wondered if Wren ate much at all; her slender figure suggested she didn't.

Nevertheless, Fern would always set a place at the table to include Wren, and always send Charlie over to the buggy shop to invite her to supper. That was just Fern's way.

Today, Evie could see Charlie from the kitchen window of the farmhouse. He was tinkering with something out in front of the buggy shop. As Fern took a savory-smelling meatloaf out of the oven, she nodded in the direction of the shop. "Why don't you go on over and tell those two that supper is about ready? I'll finish setting the table."

Evie set down the forks and walked outside, passing by Fern's garden and the horse pasture, to reach the buggy shop. As she drew near, about fifteen feet away, she could see what Charlie was fiddling with—adding an electric motor to a scooter. She stopped for a moment to watch him, his hands covered in grease, his intense focus, and she couldn't hold back a smile. She knew the backstory to this scene.

Yesterday morning, Wren had asked Dok if she'd given any more thought to providing a car for them. Dok had been vague in her response—kind of a "we'll see if you stick around" kind of answer. Evie knew Dok well enough by now to know that was her way of saying no, that she'd never given it a moment's consideration. But Wren didn't seem to catch Dok's meaning, so she persisted: "It seems like a reasonable expectation to have a car, don't you think? After all, in a rural area like this, a country mile can feel more like two or three city miles."

Half-focused on the conversation, Dok skimmed through the day's patient list. "Why don't you just buy a used car if you need one so badly?"

Right then, Charlie came up from the basement, catching enough of the exchange to laugh. "Because she's broker than broke," he said, grinning. Wren shot him a frown, but he didn't notice. He was already moving on to something else. "Dok, how do the Amish feel about motors?"

"How do you mean?" Dok had said.

"I've seen Amish farms with gas lawn mowers," Charlie said. "Weed eaters. Lots of diesel generators. Batteries for electric fences. But I haven't seen any bicycles, so I'm guessing those aren't kosher. I thought I might try to add a small motor to one of Fern's spare scooters."

Dok gave that some thought. "That could probably work. It's the dependence on the public utility grid that the Amish want to avoid. As for bicycles, the Lancaster Amish just prefer scooters to bikes. Lots of other Plain communities permit bicycles." She lifted a finger in the air. "Say, Wren, I've got an old ten-speed bicycle at home. I can bring it in for you to use." A look of alarm came over Wren. "Thank you, no." A snort-laugh burst out of Charlie. "She doesn't know how to ride a bike! I've tried to teach her and it's hopeless." He started laughing again, and it only got worse when Wren jabbed him with her elbow. He tried to pull it together, tried to swallow his smile, but he just couldn't. Still chuckling, he turned and went down the basement steps.

Grinning at the memory of Wren's embarrassment—so rare! so delicious!—Evie took another step but froze when the door to the buggy shop flew open and Wren charged out. She headed straight for Charlie, who was hunched over the scooter, a small motor in one hand and a screwdriver in the other. They had their backs to Evie and didn't notice her. For reasons she couldn't explain, Evie tiptoed to the side of the buggy shop to eavesdrop. She pressed against the wall, holding her breath, standing there like a silly middle school girl who should know better. She did know better! But she couldn't help herself.

"I've finally found them!" Wren said. "It took all this time to figure out his system. It's a terrible system."

"Oh yeah?" Charlie didn't even look up from his work. He seemed only mildly interested in what Wren had to say.

"I'm pretty sure," she said, her voice filled with excitement, "that it won't be long until we're ready for the next step."

At this, Charlie gave her his full attention. "Slow down, Wren. There's a lot to consider."

"But this is what we've been planning for. This is why we're here."

"There's no need to rush into anything. I'm nearly done with the basement. Just waiting on a few things to get delivered.

That's why I had time to make you a motorized scooter this afternoon."

"I don't need a scooter. I need a car. I need a residency that's actually letting me practice medicine. Look, Charlie, things going faster than we expected might be a blessing in disguise."

"Yeah, but we want to do things right. I don't want to leave here—"

"Why not?" Wren interrupted.

Leave here? Evie wondered. *Why? Why would you leave?*

"Charlie," Wren said, "this was always just a stepping stone to somewhere else."

He scoffed. "Maybe for you."

"Don't worry. I'll always make sure you've got a good opportunity. Always. I promised you that years ago, and I've never let you down, have I?"

"No, of course not. You've been incredible, Wren. But I've got a good opportunity here. I think I can really learn from Dok."

Now it was Wren's turn to scoff. "We hardly see her to learn anything, Charlie."

"That's why I'm trying to get that basement done as fast as I can. You heard Dok. She said she'd start our residency in full mode when there was space for us."

A long pause. So long that Evie inched forward to better hear them.

"I suppose," Wren said, "I could keep digging." She let out a sigh. "And keep studying for the boards." Her voice tightened. "They're not far off, you know. You might try cracking open a book."

"I will, I will. As soon as I get the basement finished."

"Charlie, I know there's another reason you want to stay here."

Evie held very still. *What? What could it be?*

Charlie's voice dropped to an indistinct murmur, and Evie

could only hear a scrap of a sentence. She edged closer to get a better listen.

"Oh yeah?" Wren said. "Try living with Merry Sunshine every day—"

Unfortunately, as she inched forward, Evie neglected to notice a bucket on the ground in front of her. When her foot kicked it, the clattering sound startled both Wren and Charlie. They spun around to see Evie right at the corner of the buggy shop.

Wren's eyebrows knitted together. "Were you eavesdropping on us?"

"No! Absolutely not." *Busted.* "Fern just sent me to let you know supper's ready."

Wren folded her arms, a skeptical look settling on her face. "And you just happened to end up on the *side* of the buggy shop?"

"I was, uh, admiring Fern's hydrangeas." *Brilliant.* That sounded so convincing.

"Thanks, Evie," Charlie said. "I'll be right over."

What was that expression on Charlie's face? Kind of a forced smile. Was he embarrassed? Guilty? As Evie turned to walk back to the farmhouse, feeling as foolish and immature as she had sounded, she couldn't shake the uneasy feeling that continued to gnaw at her—there was definitely something going on between Wren and Charlie, far more than she'd realized.

A few days later, after the office had closed, Dok was wrapping up her usual end-of-day routine—planning for the next day's appointments, reviewing patient histories, and ordering lab tests. It was a habit she'd picked up to make the next day run more smoothly, and it really paid off.

After her ADHD diagnosis, Dok had learned to rely on every organizational trick in the book to keep her days on track, and those tricks made a world of difference. She'd gotten better at managing her ADHD, but it still had her by the heel. Juggling her own chaotic schedule was one thing—she thrived on the adrenaline—but structuring a plan for Charlie and Wren required a different kind of focus. And once again, she pushed it to another day.

Seated at her desk, she looked up when she heard a knock at her open door. "Charlie? You're still here? I thought everyone had gone home."

He had a funny look on his face, like he was trying to keep a grin at bay. "If you have a minute to spare, I'd like to show you something in the basement. Go out the front door and I'll meet you there."

Curious, but hoping this wouldn't take long, Dok set her computer in sleep mode and went out the front door. The afternoon sun cast long shadows over the parking lot. It was later than she thought, and Matt had asked her to get home early tonight. He was making his world-famous lasagna. Famous in their world, anyway.

Charlie stood at the top of the cellar steps, a look of satisfaction plastered across his face. The once scruffy, overgrown path to the cellar now boasted a tidy path of decomposed granite leading from the parking lot to the steps. "Welcome to your new and improved office space," he said, gesturing grandly as he descended the steps and swung open the door.

Dok followed him, her footsteps faltering as she reached the threshold. "Charlie!" Her eyes widened in amazement. What had once been a dark, damp cellar crammed with forgotten junk had been transformed into a bright, welcoming space.

"This is your new waiting room," Charlie said, motioning to chairs arranged neatly against the wall. "Large enough for groups to meet. Credit Evie with that. I thought it was a pretty cool idea."

Dok thought so too, though she knew of no groups that

would want to meet in a doctor's waiting room. It was large, though, bigger than she had envisioned. She strolled around the space, her expression a mix of astonishment and delight. "This is fantastic, Charlie. I never imagined it could look like this." She took in the framed photographs on the walls and the fresh paint color. "The pictures on the walls, the paint—it's absolutely perfect."

"All Evie's doing," Charlie said, a hint of pride in his voice. "She picked out those photos in a local store. She chose the paint colors too." He led her to another door, opening it to reveal a small windowless room painted a soft, buttery yellow. On one wall, a framed photograph of a field of sunflowers added a splash of cheer. "We thought this could be an exam room."

Dok stepped inside, impressed. "This is a great setup." No window was actually a plus for an exam room.

Charlie guided her to yet another door. "And here's a usable bathroom," he said, flinging open the door to reveal a clean tiled space. "With certifiably correct plumbing." His grin grew even bigger.

Dok peeked into the small room, noting its compact but efficient design.

"And finally," Charlie said, opening a door to reveal a rather large closet with a desk against the wall, "a small office in the back."

"Calling it an office is generous, but I like using every inch of spare space," Dok said. Walking back toward the waiting room, seeing everything for a second time, she felt almost overwhelmed with delight. He had turned her humble office into a full-fledged clinic. "You really outdid yourself. This place looks fantastic, Charlie."

"I still have some paint touch-ups to finish tonight." Charlie shrugged modestly, his hands stuffed in his pockets. "But it's been a fun project."

Dok raised an eyebrow. "I heard from Fern that you've been

helping her out around the farm. You're pretty handy, aren't you?"

"I like fixing things. Learned a lot from my dad."

Dok tilted her head, curious. "Do you like fixing people as much as you like fixing things?"

"I think so." He wiggled his eyebrows. "Only time will tell . . . and passing the boards."

Not exactly a vote of confidence.

An hour later, Dok sat at the dinner table with Matt. The table was set with a large casserole pan of steaming lasagna, a fresh garden salad, and a round loaf of freshly baked sourdough bread. "You just won't believe it when you see it," she said, tearing off a piece of bread to dip into olive oil. "Charlie did a fantastic job. Not only with carpentry skill but also with how he used the space. It's so much bigger than it seemed. To think I've been sitting on that basement all this time, never giving it a thought. I feel almost embarrassed by it."

Matt nodded thoughtfully as he scooped a large serving of lasagna onto their plates. "I've been telling you to expand that building for years."

Yeah, sure, but you never thought of using the basement. Dok held that thought back.

"Sounds like Charlie brought a lot to the project," Matt said, passing the salad to her.

"He's a very good guy," Dok said, dipping another piece of bread in olive oil.

"But . . . ?" Matt said, sensing more to her thoughts.

Dok glanced at him. "No but. He's a truly great guy."

"What about as a doctor?"

She looked down at the pool of olive oil, noting that the color reminded her of the yellow paint in the new exam room. "Yet to be seen."

"So, then, you're ready to get started."

Dok looked up. "What?"

"Now that the basement is finished, you can officially kick off the residency program. Isn't that what you promised Charlie and Wren?"

Dok felt her stomach tighten. She had conveniently shoved that promise to the back of her mind, never thinking Charlie would finish so quickly. "I might have mentioned something along those lines . . ."

"Ruth, you've got a golden opportunity here. In fact, it seems to me like you've got your potential partner right under your nose, to train just the way you want him trained."

Her eyebrows shot up. "Charlie?"

"Yep. I have a good feeling about him."

She sighed, her shoulders slumping a little. "It's not that simple, Matt."

Matt leaned back, eyeing her with curiosity. "Okay. Enlighten me."

"Charlie's a great guy—no doubt about it. But Wren . . . she's the one who shows real promise."

Matt raised a bushy eyebrow. "How so?"

"She's more knowledgeable, decisive, quick. She's just . . . super smart. And guess what? I found out the reason Wren didn't match on Match Day was because she had wanted the most competitive surgical residencies in the entire country. She didn't get chosen."

"She told you that?"

"No. Charlie did. And he didn't match because . . . well, for just what I'd thought. Bottom of his graduating class."

"Isn't Wren the one who poisoned your patients with her coffee?"

"She didn't know the water was bad," Dok shot back, frowning. It always amazed her how Matt could recall the most random details while forgetting half the things on the grocery list. "Lately, whenever I'm in the office, Wren's been at my side like a shadow. I don't deny that she oversteps sometimes, but that's only because she's eager to put her knowledge into practice. And I happen to know that she spends every spare minute prepping for her boards."

Matt frowned. "You need to give Charlie a chance. He's been remodeling your basement for you."

"Don't get me wrong. I'm grateful for what he's done down there. But he doesn't seem overly concerned about treating patients, not like Wren. And he has boards coming up too. I'm pretty sure he hasn't even begun to study for them."

"What makes you think that?"

"Because I've overheard Wren nagging him to make time to study. Honestly, I'm not sure how he's going to pass."

"You know, Ruth," Matt said, setting down his fork and leaning in, "this reminds me of when I used to train new recruits. At first, I thought the best ones were always the smartest. But after a while, I learned to look for something else. I'd take someone teachable with passion over a know-it-all any day. Those so-called geniuses often burn out fast."

Dok lifted a shoulder in a half shrug. "Wren's got that brainy edge that could really make a difference, especially in a rural practice. She's the one I'm eyeing for a partnership." She couldn't believe she said that out loud. She hadn't even realized she'd been thinking it.

She felt an odd affinity for Wren, something she hadn't quite put into words. Almost a conviction: that Wren Baker had been sent to her for a purpose.

"That's only because she reminds you of you," Matt said with a chuckle. "If you'd had a daughter, she'd be Wren."

Dok opened her mouth to protest, but the words never came. *Wren? Like a daughter?* The remark was so unexpected, she couldn't even process it. She blinked, caught off guard, her brow knitting as Matt's words bounced around in her head. *"If you'd had a daughter, she'd be Wren?"*

Matt noticed her squirming and grinned. "It's like looking

in a mirror. The smart, headstrong doctor with something to prove. Sounds a whole lot like you. She's a mini-you."

Dok wasn't sure whether to laugh or cringe. *Wren . . . a mini-me?* The thought unsettled her, yes, but at the same time, it pleased her.

"And what," she said at last, a smile tugging at her lips, "would be so bad about that?"

Fern had already gone to bed. Evie had been reading a book on the couch when she felt her pager vibrate and hurried outside to read Dok's message: "*Office @ 7:30 a.m. Bring Charlie and Wren.*"

Hmm. Abrupt but significant. Evie wondered what Dok had in mind for Charlie and Wren, because, so far, they weren't on Dok's mind much at all. A horse nickered in the pasture, so she wandered over to pat it. She loved being here—the peace and quiet, the open spaces, the natural beauty.

"Velvet nose."

Evie spun around. Charlie was about two yards away from her, holding on to the handles of a scooter. "Charlie! I thought you were still at Dok's."

"I was. Stayed late to finish things up." He grinned. "It's done."

So that's why he didn't come to Fern's for supper. "Done? You mean, the basement is completely done?"

He grinned. "Yeah. I showed it to Dok, and she seemed pretty pleased."

"In less than a month?"

"It really wasn't that complicated a project. Nothing load bearing was getting moved, so city planning green-lighted the permits. And then everything kind of fell into place."

He was being modest. "I hope Dok expressed appreciation to you."

"She did. And she liked your pictures and paint color. Liked 'em a lot." He looked up at the sky. "Strawberry moon tonight."

"What's that?"

"The moon is full and low in the horizon, and the light gives off a reddish hue."

"So it's called a strawberry moon because it's red?"

"I think Native Americans gave it that name because this is the time of year when strawberries are harvested."

"Fern's been making strawberry jam all day! The kitchen smells like a sweet bakery."

He smiled, and she couldn't help but smile back. She noticed his eyes, how they crinkled at the corners. Those lashes! Why did guys always get the thick eyelashes?

"Evie," he said, "I noticed that last Sunday you looked like you were heading out to church."

He had noticed? She felt her cheeks grow warm. "I did. But I think I'll try another one this Sunday."

"Not the right fit?"

"I was the only person under one hundred years old and without an oxygen tank."

He chuckled, then it grew into a full belly laugh. Soon, his body shook.

She heard the squeaky sound of a door opening. "Charlie?" Wren called out. "Is that you? I've been waiting for you. There's something I want to show you."

His laughter died down pretty fast. "I'd better go see what she wants." He started walking his scooter toward the buggy shop.

"Charlie!"

He turned back to Evie.

"Dok wants to see all of us in her office at seven thirty in the morning."

"Gotcha." He tipped his head. "I was thinking that maybe, on Sunday, we could church shop. You know, together."

Are you kidding? Yes, yes, yes! Is this a date? Close to a date? Could going to church be considered a date?

But what came out of her mouth was a nonchalant, "Sure. I guess so."

He gave her a thumbs-up and headed off toward the buggy shop.

She was never going to sleep tonight.

13

Dok stood at the entrance to the newly renovated basement, the warm morning air already hinting at the heat to come. She'd left the cellar door open, airing out the fresh paint smell and hoping to catch a little breeze, though she knew it wouldn't last long. It was only 7:30 a.m., and the day was already starting to press in on her, both from the heat and the thoughts swirling in her mind.

The conversation with Matt last night had cost her a good bit of sleep. He'd been right—she knew it as much as she hated to admit it. David had said the same thing, many times. Wren, and maybe Charlie, had provided a golden opportunity to her. They deserved more than what she was giving them. They deserved a proper residency program. But that meant Dok had to step up her game too.

Planning ahead had never come naturally. Her ADHD made sure of that. She could handle pressure, think on her feet, and adapt in the moment, but laying out a structured plan was her Achilles' heel. It took a Herculean effort—and that was the very reason she kept putting it off. This last month had exposed her shortcomings in an embarrassing way.

But that was going to change. It was time to face this residency program, head on.

Dok glanced around the bright freshly painted space, still amazed at the transformation. Basement didn't seem like the right word for it anymore. She needed a better term. Lower level? Ground floor? *Bleh.* Too industrial sounding. Maybe . . . garden level?

She sighed and shook her head. Naming the place wasn't the priority right now. She wanted to talk to Wren, Charlie, and Evie before Annie arrived at eight o'clock and the day whooshed away. She wanted to get everyone on the same page. It was time to give Wren and Charlie the structure and guidance they needed, and Evie . . . well, Evie was an unexpected short-term bonus.

Dok heard a horse's loud, nose-clearing snort, then the familiar rhythmic clip-clopping. She made her way up the steps to see a horse and buggy pull up outside. Fern sat confidently at the reins, while Wren and Evie climbed down from the buggy. Charlie was already on the ground, efficiently unloading three scooters from the back with a practiced ease.

Dok walked along the path and gave Fern a friendly wave. "Want to see what Charlie's been up to?"

Fern shook her head with a smile. "Another time, maybe. I've got a full day ahead of me."

Dok nodded, not surprised. "Of course you do. Thanks for bringing them in early."

As Fern shook the harness reins to head off, Dok turned to Wren and Evie. "I'll let Charlie take the lead for the grand unveiling."

Charlie, grinning with pride, led the way down the steps. As they stepped into the newly remodeled space, Evie's eyes lit up. "Wow, this is incredible!" she said, spinning around to take it all in.

For a split second, Dok thought she saw something more

than just admiration in Evie's gaze when it rested on Charlie. Hmm. Was she missing something?

Wren stayed silent, but Dok caught the appreciative glint in her eyes as she surveyed the room. It was clear she was impressed. It would've been nice, though, if she had offered Charlie a compliment.

Once the tour was over, Dok gathered them in the waiting area. "Now that we've got the space ready, it's time to talk about how we're going to start your training here." As they settled into the chairs, Dok continued. "When I'm in the office, I want to let you both start handling basic patient care, like annual physicals and rechecks. But if I'm out on a house call, Evie will supervise."

Charlie's head bobbed once or twice. "Sounds good to me."

Dok turned her attention to Wren, who was shifting uncomfortably in her seat, her hands clasped tightly together. "What about you?"

Wren met Dok's gaze with an unexpected intensity. "Nothing personal," she said, flicking a glance in Evie's direction, which meant it was very personal, "but nurses don't supervise doctors. I graduated at the top of my class, and it's only right that you supervise me. That's why I'm here."

An awkward silence fell. Dok had anticipated some pushback from Wren, though not in front of Evie. "I assure you, Evie is more than capable of supervising you, especially for routine tasks."

Charlie nodded in agreement. "Absolutely."

But Wren wasn't backing down. "I'm sure Evie's skills are . . . proficient . . . but I came here for direct guidance from you, an experienced physician. Not from a recent graduate of nursing school."

Dok cast a glance at Evie, whose chin was tucked, as if embarrassed. She raised an eyebrow. "If you want direct patient care, then this is how it's going to work. More often than not, half my time is spent on house calls."

Wren's response was quick. "I've been ready to join you on those house calls since day one. You were the one who thought patients wouldn't be comfortable with anyone else. Yet Evie goes out with you every day." She glanced at Charlie. "If you're not willing to supervise a resident, maybe you should've thought twice about taking one—or two."

Dok had the distinct feeling she'd just been outmaneuvered by a rookie. Exasperating, but she couldn't help feeling a grudging admiration for Wren. Matt had seen it first—Wren reminded Dok of herself as a resident. Gutsy. Bold. Audacious. *She's a mini-me.* "All right," she said, her tone firm but laced with a fake sigh of resignation. "Wren, you're now on house calls with me. But in the office, you respect Evie's role as supervisor. Got it? And remember, until you both pass your boards and are licensed, no treating patients without supervision."

Wren gave a quick, no-nonsense nod. She extended her palm out toward Evie. "Pager, please."

Slowly, Evie took the pager from her pocket and handed it to Wren.

Seriously? Dok barely resisted an eye roll at that power play. She turned her full attention to Charlie and Evie. "And you two? Ready to jump into this new setup?"

Charlie looked at Evie and grinned. "Absolutely."

Evie's face lit up, cheeks turning a bright shade of pink—enough confirmation for Dok that there was definitely something brewing here. But she didn't have time for that. "All right then," Dok said, shifting into "let's get to work" mode. "Charlie and Evie, you've got the morning patients. Annie should be here soon with the day's list. Wren, after that, you're with me on a house call."

Fifteen minutes later, Dok and Wren were in the car. "We're heading to Simon Esh's," Dok said, "to help him change out his colostomy bag. Apparently, it's leaking." She forced herself to keep her eyes on the road, resisting the urge to grin at Wren's mortified reaction.

If this young doctor was going to give Dok a run for her money, she might as well make it a lesson worth learning.

⁓

Annie shut the basement door and spun around to find Gus standing at the top of the cellar steps. His hair was tousled by the breeze, and that easy, winsome grin of his sent a little jolt straight through her. Every time he popped up unexpectedly, her heart did the same little stutter step. Nerves fluttered in her belly, leaving her slightly lightheaded. If sunshine could be bottled, it would look like him. Mr. Wonderful. "Gus! What are you doing here?"

"It's my day off. I had a few things to do in town, so I thought I'd start at the Bent N' Dent." He tipped his head toward the store. "You know, for Sarah's good coffee."

Gus didn't drink coffee. He'd come to see *her*. A slow smile escaped. After Hank Lapp had spilled the beans about Annie's car sickness, Gus had been very empathetic. Turned out, he'd struggled with it once or twice too. He understood! When she told him she was working on some remedies and was confident she could manage it, his only response was, "I know you'll overcome it, Annie."

She'd felt such a sweep of relief that she'd even slept well that night, something that hadn't happened for a while. She'd had to ask the Lord for forgiveness for telling Gus she was confident she could manage it. That was a lie. Annie never lied. She promised the Lord she wouldn't do it again.

And here he was, this morning, on his day off, just to see her! She felt a little shiver of delight and nervously smoothed her apron.

Gus glanced at the path that led to the basement. "How's the remodel coming along?"

"It's done! Charlie did a wonderful job." A giggle escaped. "The first patient arrived this morning—Hank Lapp, with a rooster under one arm."

"A rooster?" Gus blinked.

"Hank headed straight to the basement, calling for Dok. He told Dok he was here to 'inspect the new coop.' He held out the rooster and said that 'this one's been a bit off his crow.'"

Gus laughed. "How did Dok handle that?"

"She just gave him that *look* she has," Annie said, furrowing her brows and pointing at Gus. "'Hank Lapp, this basement is no coop. It is the . . . garden level . . . for a medical practice for *human beings*. You and your crowless rooster can turn around and head back home. And tell Edith to put that rooster in tonight's supper pot.' Hank sputtered away, deeply offended." She giggled again. "One thing for sure—that man never quits. If there's a door, he'll find a way through it."

"Speaking of persistence," Gus said, a probing look on his face, "I thought I'd come to your office and take you to lunch. If you're free, that is."

A little thrill ran through her, knowing their special friendship had returned to the way it used to be—easy, comfortable—before her motion sickness got in the way. "I am free, in fact."

Then his mouth broke into a wide smile. "Good. We're going on a bus ride."

Annie's good mood popped like a balloon.

⁓

A spark of adrenaline had shot through Evie when Dok Stoltzfus decided to pair her with Charlie for patient care. She never saw this coming—Wren's insistence on being supervised exclusively by Dok meant Evie was left in charge of Charlie. Every day! It felt a bit odd being his supervisor, but the silver lining was that she got Charlie all to herself. While she'd miss the house calls with Dok, the idea of spending so much time with Charlie—without Wren lurking around—was more than enough to make up for it. This was precisely what she'd hoped for during her three months in Stoney Ridge: a chance to connect with him on a whole new level. It was finally happening!

After Annie handed Evie the patient list for the day and Dok and Wren left for a house call, Evie went into the exam room to get it prepped for the first patient. Charlie came in and watched her, taking in everything with a mix of curiosity and eagerness. "Should I go get Lena Johnson?" he asked, glancing at the patient list.

"Actually, Annie said Lena Johnson called in to say she's running late. It's just as well, because there's been an emergency."

Charlie's head snapped up. "An emergency?"

"Just a minor one. Timmy Kauffman got hit by a baseball on his way to school this morning and needs some stitches to his eyebrow." Evie set out the necessary instruments.

Charlie grinned. "Ah, the classic childhood injury." Then his grin faded. "I haven't, um, stitched up an eyebrow before. Or anything else either."

"You've . . . never given anyone stitches?"

"Never."

Oh my. Evie's first instinct was to say she'd do the stitching and he could watch, but that wasn't what Charlie needed. He needed experience. "Well, I guess you're going to start today."

Timmy, a freckle-faced seven-year-old, entered the room holding an ice pack to his forehead. He looked more curious than scared, but his mom was clearly anxious.

"Hi, Timmy," Evie said warmly. "This is Dr. King. We're going to fix your cut."

Charlie crouched down to Timmy's eye level. "Hey, buddy. How did a baseball manage to hit you in the head this morning?"

Timmy shrugged and glanced at his mom. "It just came flying out of nowhere."

Charlie nodded, his expression serious. "Yeah, that can happen sometimes."

He had such a way with kids! It was a talent Evie had always admired in Charlie—his knack for connecting with patients. But now wasn't the time to add to her Charlie list. "Okay, Timmy, I need to clean the area first. And then Dr. King is going to give you a local anesthetic so you won't even feel the stitches."

As Evie cleaned the wound, Charlie observed closely. Quietly, he said, "What's the best technique for stitching up an eyebrow?"

A gasp. "Hold it a minute," Timmy's mother said, reaching out to clasp her son's shoulder. "I assumed you had experience stitching people up. Maybe we should wait for Dok Stoltzfus."

"I was just testing Nurse Miller on her knowledge," Charlie said. He spun on his stool, his knees bump-bumping with Evie as he cast a plea at her.

"We test each other a lot around here," Evie said. "Keeps us all on our toes. Let's see, eyebrows." She looked up at the ceiling, as if reading from a textbook. "Eyebrows are tricky because they have a natural curve. Make sure the edges are perfectly aligned. Timmy doesn't want a crooked scar."

"But I do!" Timmy said. "Like Harry Potter."

"Oh, right!" Charlie said. His finger made a large jagged lightning stroke in the air. "Gotcha."

"No, no!" his mother said. "I really think we should wait for Dok."

"Not to worry," Evie said. "This cut's not as big as Harry Potter's, but Timmy definitely needs a couple of stitches." She made a point to telegraph how many stitches Charlie should make on the eyebrow, just in case he got carried away.

Charlie nodded, absorbing the information. He rolled his shoulders as if preparing for the challenge. "Okay, Harry"—he cleared his throat—"I mean, Timmy. Here we go." He held the syringe of local anesthesia in the air. "This will just be a little pinch."

As soon as the anesthesia took effect, Charlie picked up the needle and thread to begin stitching. Evie kept a close eye, offering tips. "The tension should be even . . . There you go. Perfect." One stitch down.

Charlie was so inexperienced, his skills so . . . amateurish. But he was so teachable too. So earnest.

Three stitches took much longer than they should have, but Charlie took great care to finesse each one. Finally, he tied off the thread and leaned back to admire his handiwork. "Impressive, if I do say so myself, Harry." He cleared his throat and added, with a wink, "I mean, Timmy." He held up a mirror for Timmy to admire his new scar.

Timmy peered at it, frowning. "I can't even *see* the stitches."

Charlie beamed. "Music to my ears."

Timmy's mom had been hovering anxiously but relaxed when she saw how tiny the stitches were. Charlie applied a Band-Aid over Timmy's eyebrow. "Dab some Neosporin on the stitches each day. The stitches will dissolve on their own. Just call the office if you're concerned about anything."

At the door, Timmy's mom turned and said, "I'm sorry I doubted you, Dr. King. I can tell this isn't your first rodeo."

As the door closed, Charlie swiveled on the chair to look at Evie. "Ah, but it was."

Chuckling, Evie took away the tray of used tools and set it on the small counter. "You're a natural with kids, Charlie."

He shrugged modestly. "Wren would probably argue that's because I'm still a big kid myself."

Evie tried to ignore the Wren reference as she finished changing the paper on the examining table. "I'll go see if Lena Johnson has arrived for her blood pressure check."

"I'll go," Charlie volunteered.

Another win for Charlie, Evie noted. Most doctors wouldn't dream of fetching a patient themselves.

Lena Johnson, a jolly woman in her seventies, bustled into the room, her face flushed from her hurried pace. "Hello, dear," she said, puffing, catching her breath. "Sorry I'm late. It's been one of those mornings."

"Worked out just as well," Evie said. "A little boy needed stitches, and we were able to fit him in." She handed the blood pressure cuff to Charlie. "So you've met Dr. King."

With that, Charlie took the reins. "Let's see how your blood pressure is doing today, Mrs. Johnson." He wrapped the cuff around her arm.

As he fumbled with the cuff, Evie almost stepped in to stop him but decided to let Charlie handle it. Another opportunity for him to learn something new.

As Charlie checked her blood pressure, his brow furrowed. "Quite high," he said, glancing at her chart on the computer. "Higher than usual."

"Oh dear!" Lena said anxiously. "I've been cutting back on salt like Dok told me."

"And you're taking the meds every day?" Charlie said.

"Every single day!"

"Sometimes," Evie said, "just coming into a doctor's office can spike a patient's blood pressure, especially if they're running late. Dok Stoltzfus likes to wait at least five minutes before taking it."

Charlie gave her a thoughtful nod. "Good tip." He took the cuff off. "Let's wait a couple of minutes and try again." He asked Lena about her busy morning, and she launched into a lively tale about discovering a tomato hornworm in her garden that looked like a prehistoric monster and nearly gave her a heart attack. As she chatted and laughed, Charlie prepared the blood pressure cuff for another try.

"All right, let's see how we're doing now." After a moment, he read the results. "120 over 80. Perfect!"

Lena Johnson's face lit up with relief and joy. As Charlie opened the door to escort Lena to the front of the office, he waited a moment for her to go through the threshold, then leaned back to whisper in Evie's ear, "Thanks for that, oh wise one."

Evie felt fluttery from his closeness, from his clean, warm scent, from the sweetness of his breath. When the door closed behind him, she leaned against it, nearly swooning.

She had found another characteristic to add to Charlie's list of virtues. His ease with correction and lack of defensiveness was incredibly unique in the world of medicine. Correctable Charlie.

Dok adjusted the rearview mirror as the farmhouse dwindled in the distance, the dusty road behind them giving way to open fields. The tension in the car was palpable, with Wren's dissatisfaction simmering just below the surface.

House calls had been so easy with Evie. She was thoroughly comfortable with the Amish. Wren kept looking around Mona Beiler's kitchen as if she was in a foreign country. Dok cringed when she asked Mona why the calendar hanging on the wall was ten years old.

"I like the pictures," Mona said.

"But how," Wren said, "do you keep track of the days?"

Mona tapped her wristwatch. "This tells me all I need to know. The Lord is always reminding me to stay in the present."

The look on Wren's face! Like she was trying to make sense of that.

As Dok came to a stop to let a farmer send his cows across the road, she said, "I get the impression that there's something you want to say."

"The bulging disc in Mona Beiler's back isn't going to heal with acupuncture," Wren said, her voice clipped. "She's going to need surgery."

Dok's gaze remained steady on the cows in front of her. Jersey cows, she noted. Good milkers. "Maybe, maybe not. I like my patients to be part of their own healing journey. If a patient chooses to pursue alternative treatments, I'm willing to support them."

Wren's eyes narrowed. "You can't be serious."

"I'm completely serious. Alternative treatments can offer support and comfort, and often complement traditional methods."

"Complement?" Wren scoffed. "Sounds to me like you're just indulging patients' whims. Mona's back pain is only going to get worse."

Dok's patience was fraying. "Nothing will be lost for Mona by trying a few alternative treatments before surgery. Acupuncture could help alleviate her pain. Look, Wren, I've seen unexplained recoveries that make me believe in the possibility of healing beyond the conventional. More than a few times, I've observed how hope and patience can play a significant role in recovery. Prayer too. Especially prayer. I think of those unexplained answers as my Miracle Box."

Skeptical, Wren rolled her eyes. "Well, I'm a believer in the miracle of modern medicine. Not hokeypokey stuff. And I think waiting could put Mona Beiler in a worse situation than she's in now."

Dok's tone grew softer. "Sometimes, Wren, time is the best doctor."

At that, Wren went silent. The farmer hurried the last cow across the road and waved to Dok to cross. The road stretched out ahead, and the silence in the car grew heavier with every mile.

They'd had only two house calls so far. Dok hoped the rest of the morning wasn't going to be just as contentious.

"*What you focus on, you find.*" That was Fern's frequent advice to Dok.

Okay, focus on the good. Wren didn't contradict Dok in front of the patients. And her assessment of Mona's back pain was spot-on. Dok was pretty sure that she'd end up needing surgery, so Wren's assessment was correct.

Dok's thoughts drifted to her brother David. She could almost hear his voice in her head, calmly advising her, even if she didn't want his advice. He would say that these house calls were Dok's chance to shape and form Wren's thinking, to build confidence in her strengths and help overcome her weaknesses.

Thank you, Fern. Thank you, David.

"So what's next?" Wren said.

"This will be quick. We're stopping in at Sally Fisher's. Annie's mom. She thinks she has a case of shingles."

Wren's head jerked to face Dok. "Isn't she . . ."

"Yes. A raging hypochondriac. Sally had been doing much better, but something happened recently that's caused her to slide right back into her pattern of imagined illnesses. I have found that when she feels listened to, her symptoms lessen." She glanced at Wren. "An imaginary illness is worse than a real one."

Wren let out a long-suffering sigh.

14

David sat at the kitchen table, hands wrapped around a mug of lukewarm coffee, staring out the window. Birdy was busy at the stove, stirring a pot of stew, but her mind wasn't on dinner. He could tell by the way she'd glance over her shoulder every few minutes, lips pressed into a thin line, that she had something on her mind.

Finally, she turned to him, her voice gentle but firm. "David, don't you think you should have a little talk with Jacob Zook?"

"Jacob Zook?" David raised an eyebrow. Jacob wasn't exactly chatty—unless the topic was about the weather. He was a farmer through and through. "Why would I do that?"

Birdy sighed, as if wondering about her husband's perceptiveness. "Clara's twins are a handful. Our buggies passed each other yesterday, and we stopped to talk, but with those babies hollering, we barely exchanged hellos."

Yes, David remembered the lung power of those two babies echoing through the store. "I'm still not seeing why I need to talk to Jacob."

"It just seems Clara could use a little help with the babies."

David set his mug down, getting a sense of where Birdy was headed with this. Jacob Zook wasn't just frugal; the man was tighter than the lid on a jar of pickles. And Birdy? Well, she was about to suggest David "encourage" Jacob to hire a mother's helper. He could already imagine the conversation going nowhere fast. "Jacob's not exactly fond of parting with his money," he said, leaning back in his chair.

Birdy frowned. "If that's the case, then he should help with those babies himself."

"Maybe *you* could—"

Birdy cut him off with a raised hand. "I offered. Clara turned me down. She's not easy to help."

David stroked his graying beard, feeling a familiar sense of weariness. "And you think I should have a word with him?"

Birdy turned off the stove and faced him, her look determined. "I do. He's a good man, David, but he's stuck in his ways. Clara's struggling, and he's too focused on getting the hay in to notice."

David sighed deeply, leaning forward. "Jacob's not much for taking advice."

"Tell him you had twins yourself," Birdy said, her tone softer but firm. "Remind him how it's double the work, and that Clara needs some help."

David let out a dry chuckle. "You want me to say all that to Jacob? Birdy, he's not going to listen. He's had twins in his first marriage. He knows how much work they are. All that's on his mind is timing the drying of his hay so he can cut it."

Birdy came over and sat beside him, placing her hand gently on his arm. "You're the bishop, David. That still counts for something—even with Jacob Zook. If anyone can get through to him, it's you."

David shook his head. "Being the bishop doesn't always mean people listen. Sometimes it's just a label."

Birdy wasn't giving up. "It's a label that carries weight. You don't need to come down hard. Just give him a nudge. Help him see things from Clara's side. She's doing the best she can, but . . . she's not . . ."

"She's not like his first wife."

"Exactly."

"I'll think about it," David said, though the idea of tackling a conversation with Jacob was about as appealing as . . . well, helping cut hay. He was no farmer.

Birdy gave his arm a squeeze. "You'll say the right thing, David. You always do."

Did he? He smiled faintly but wasn't so sure himself.

The next day, Annie watched the bus approach with the same enthusiasm she had for getting a cavity filled at the dentist. Without novocaine.

Gus noticed. "It's all about getting used to the movement," he said, after he complimented her on the wisdom of choosing a bus to practice overcoming her motion sickness. "It's the perfect way to simulate the motion of an ambulance or fire truck, minus the sirens."

Annie wasn't at all convinced; after days of increasingly queasy lunch breaks, her stomach was less "eager for the challenge" and more "already regretting it." But the last time—the only time—she'd ridden in an ambulance, she hadn't gotten sick. Gus had been there . . . and he was here today.

Maybe this could work.

They made their way to the back of the bus—he insisted the back was more realistic to an ambulance—and sat down. As the bus pulled away from the stop, she felt her hands grow clammy and moist. She curled her hands into fists and wrapped them up in her apron.

He noticed.

He took her hands in his, their warmth and solid grip a stark contrast to her own sweaty, wet, pathetic ones. "Annie," he said, looking at her in that intense way of his. "Just look at me."

That wasn't hard.

As close as they were, she couldn't help but notice things she'd missed before. Like the tiny scar just above his eyebrow—when had that happened? There was a little bit of stubble on his neck, like he'd missed it when shaving. And he smelled so good! Clean and crisp, like fresh laundry dried in sunshine. Amber flecks in his eyes seemed to shimmer with a depth she hadn't noticed until now.

What was it about eye contact that was so intimate? She didn't know.

On the upside, every time they hit a bump, they ended up closer and closer together, until their shoulders and thighs were touching. Downside: As captivating as it was to be in such close proximity to Mr. Wonderful, her stomach had other ideas. Dizziness came first, a sudden chill followed by a hot flush washing over her, then a queasy, unsettled sensation—all warning signs from her body that something wasn't quite right. *Not now!* she thought, willing herself to overcome her wooziness. *Go away!* she pleaded with her nausea. She squeezed her eyes closed, but that only made it worse. The churning in her stomach had begun in earnest. Motion sickness was winning the battle. She gripped her elbows, hugging herself to stifle what she knew was coming.

"Are you okay?" Gus asked.

"I'm not okay."

"You don't look well." His eyes stayed on her face. "You look really pale."

A swell of nausea rose up. "I need to get off this bus. Now." She yanked on the cord and saw the driver glance in the rearview mirror, let out a dramatically long-suffering sigh, and pull the bus over. She practically pushed Gus off the bench to get to the aisle and run down to the open door. She jumped off the steps and rushed over to the side of the road, sat down, and put her head between her knees. *Please God, please God, please God, help me not throw up in front of Gus.*

A moment later, Gus put a hand on her back. "We're going

to breathe together, and you're going to start to feel better." In a quiet voice, he counted five counts to breathe in, and then back out for four. Then again, and then again. They breathed in together and out together, in sync, as she slowly started to recover. He seemed to sense that she was too nauseated to speak because he didn't say anything.

She tried to stand up, which was foolish because she was still woozy.

"Hold tight for a while longer," he said, his hand lightly brushing over her prayer cap. "Your color's just starting to pink up."

Really? She felt like she'd gone from green to blushing furiously. "I'm sorry," she said, closing her eyes.

He tenderly tucked a strand of hair behind her ear. "Is it always this bad?"

She sucked in a tight breath and said, "Worse."

"We barely made it down the road."

Yes, she was aware of that.

He rubbed her back in gentle circles, and she felt the tight knot in her stomach gradually loosen as the nausea subsided. "Annie, when did you first know about this?"

With those horrible symptoms bearable now, she pushed her cap strings behind her shoulders and straightened her back to answer him. "When I was just a little girl, our family took a bus ride to visit relatives in Ohio one summer, and I remember feeling sick all the way there and all the way back. My parents said never again."

"What about cars?"

"Same thing, though I hadn't been in a car in a very long time. Like, years. With a dairy farm, there's never much of an opportunity to go anywhere."

"Why didn't you tell me?" His voice was heartbreakingly soft.

"Mainly," she said, "because I have a mortal fear of embarrassment."

He gave that some consideration. "What if I told you something embarrassing about myself?"

"Doubtful you could top this," she said with an eye roll.

"Ah, you have no idea. I've got a treasure trove of embarrassing stories." He paused, feigning deep thought. "It's just a matter of picking the right one."

Despite herself, a smile tugged at her lips. "I don't believe you."

"Okay, got it," he said then. "Have I told you about my first encounter with firefighters?"

"Yes. You were a volunteer firefighter."

"No, that's how I became involved with the firehouse. This predates that by a long shot."

By now her breathing was steady and the dizziness had faded, leaving her with a sense of stability and relief. Lots of relief. "I'm listening."

"Picture this. An adorable, adventurous five-year-old climbs a tree in his yard. He goes up and up and up, until he reaches the top. He forgets about the getting-down part. When he looks down, he panics. Freezes. Calls for help. Of course, no one can hear him. He's up in the clouds. Finally, around suppertime, his mom realizes that no one has seen him for a while. The family goes outside and calls for him. At last, someone hears his now weak cry for help. His father calls the fire department. The siren can be heard in three counties. The boy has climbed so high that they need to call in to a second fire station. Another loud siren comes bellowing to the house. And then a third. At this point, the entire town has arrived, curiously watching, as the boy held on to the tree for dear life. Finally, a hook and ladder truck was dispatched to get the boy down out of the tree."

"And that was you?"

He grinned. "Some of those guys are still at the fire station.

Not a week goes by that one or the other doesn't remind me of the story."

Annie heard a church bell in the distance. She needed to get back to the office soon.

Gus didn't seem to be in much of a hurry. "Annie, how can you be an EMT when you suffer from such severe motion sickness?"

"I . . . I'm not sure."

Gus looked up into the sky at a hawk circling overhead. She wondered what was running through his mind. Was he thinking the same worry that had been keeping her up at night? That she wasn't suited to be an EMT after all? And did that mean they weren't suited for each other either?

He dropped his chin and turned to her. "You know what? We're going to cure you."

15

Evie's friend Darcy had this theory: Spending time with Charlie every day would eventually extinguish her crush, like tossing water on a flame. Daily exposure, Darcy said, would douse it for sure.

Darcy couldn't have been more wrong. Instead of fizzling out, Evie's feelings burned brighter and hotter with each passing day. The more time she spent with Charlie, the longer grew her list of his virtues. Daily exposure wasn't squashing her crush—it was feeding it.

She kept hoping Charlie might drop a hint that he felt even a smidge of what she did. Aside from an occasional fleeting moment, a shared laugh, Evie's hope was still a distant dream. But for now, things were moving in a lovely direction. Whenever Dok and Wren went out on house calls, Evie and Charlie worked in tandem to see the patients who came to the office—a routine that suited her quite nicely. Sheer heaven.

This morning, when Evie recognized the name on the patient list, she hesitated, glancing over at Charlie. "Our next patient is Clara Zook, an Amish woman. She had twins a few months ago. She's . . ."

Evie faltered, searching for the right word. Guarded? Passive?

No, those didn't quite capture the full picture. She settled on, "She's trying very hard to be a good mother."

"Twins?" Charlie's expression instantly sobered. "She's probably exhausted."

Evie gave a small smile. "No doubt. But she's coming in today with a possible case of mastitis."

"Got it," Charlie said.

Clara entered the room, her face pale and drawn, dark circles rimming her eyes.

"Hello, Clara," Evie said. "Do you remember me? I'm Evie Miller. I came to your house a few weeks ago with Dok Stoltzfus. And this is Dr. King."

Charlie stood from his stool, offering a warm smile. "Hi, Clara."

Clara's eyes darted around the room, anxiety rolling off her in waves. "Isn't Dok here?"

Evie shook her head gently. "She's been called out of the office. But Dr. King and I can help you."

Clara's hesitation was palpable as she took a step back toward the door. "Maybe I'll just wait until Dok is free."

Evie moved forward instinctively, not wanting to let Clara slip away. "Annie mentioned you might have mastitis, Clara. You really can't wait. We need to get you on antibiotics before it gets any worse."

Clara's resistance faltered as tears welled up in her eyes. "I've just been a little . . . sore."

Evie took a step closer, her voice soft and soothing. "I think we can help." She gently guided Clara to the exam table and helped her unpin her top. The sight of Clara's inflamed, rock-hard breast made Evie wince. "Oh, Clara. That must be so painful."

"Just a bit," Clara admitted, her voice barely above a whisper.

"How long have you been in pain?" Evie asked, placing a

hand on Clara's forehead, noting the heat there. "Feels like you've got a fever." She turned to grab a thermometer as Clara hastily pinned her dress back up.

"Started a few days ago," Clara said in a mumble.

Charlie pulled up a chair, making sure to hold Clara's gaze. "I hear twins are more than double the work."

Almost on cue, a wail echoed from the waiting room, where Annie was watching the twins while Clara was in the exam room. One baby's cry was soon joined by the other's, creating a chorus of distress.

"Clara," Charlie said, his tone laced with concern. "Are you able to get much sleep?"

Clara hesitated, waiting for the thermometer to beep before Evie pulled it out and read the display, showing it to Charlie—one hundred and one degrees. "I do the best I can," she said.

"Does your husband help out?" Charlie asked.

"He's a farmer," Clara replied, as if that explained everything.

"When I was at your house that day," Evie said, "we talked about finding a mother's helper to come for a few hours a day."

Clara shook her head sharply. "Jacob wouldn't hear of it. Costs too much."

Charlie leaned forward slightly, his voice filled with quiet determination. "Not getting enough sleep can take a toll."

"I'm fine. No different than any other new mother," Clara said, though the dark circles under her eyes betrayed her. She looked exhausted.

"Lack of sleep is a concern for all new mothers," Charlie said. "It can have a profound effect on a person's well-being. What about naps? Are you able to get any rest during the day?"

"Sometimes, there's a place on the farm that I like to go," Clara said, her voice softening. "It's real nice. Dark and cool and quiet."

"That's good to hear," Charlie said, nodding encouragingly.

"It's important to take care of yourself, Clara. For the babies' sake as well as your own." Evie's heart melted as she watched Charlie, his concern and compassion so evident in his every word and gesture. He scribbled something on a prescription pad and handed it to Clara. "This is for some medicine that will help you feel better soon. Be sure to finish the bottle. A lot of people stop taking antibiotics too soon."

Evie cleared her throat, drawing Charlie's attention. "I think we might have some samples."

Charlie caught on quickly. "Yes, yes, we do. More than we can use. Evie, would you mind getting those samples for Clara? And maybe some pain meds." He took the prescription from Clara and handed it to Evie.

Stepping into the hallway, Evie was startled by the intensity of the babies' cries. So loud. So demanding. Poor Clara, she thought as she took samples out of their packages to fill a small bottle. She returned just in time to hear Charlie ask Clara a question, speaking in a gentle voice. "Have you had any moments where you felt completely overwhelmed? Or times when you felt like you just couldn't cope?"

The room grew quiet, and Evie and Charlie watched as Clara seemed to gather her thoughts, the pause stretching longer than they expected. Just as she opened her mouth to answer, the door flew open, and in came Annie, struggling with the double stroller and two wailing babies, screeching at the top of their lungs. "They won't stop crying! I've tried everything—I don't know what else to do!"

"Neither do I," Clara said with a sigh, rising from the exam table to take the stroller from Annie's hands.

"Clara, wait," Evie said, gently touching Clara's arm. "Here are the meds you need. Take them as soon as you get home. In fact, Annie will get you a glass of water and you can start the meds now. You'll feel so much better by this time tomorrow."

Clara took the amber-colored container from Evie, managing a weak smile before following Annie back to the waiting room, the sound of the babies' cries echoing down the hallway.

Evie turned to Charlie. "I think I'll ask Dok to follow up with her."

"Good idea," Charlie agreed, his brow furrowed with concern. "She seems pretty fragile."

Fragile! Just the word Evie'd been looking for to describe Clara Zook.

Annie was in the middle of her lunch break, nibbling on a sandwich, when she heard the familiar creak of the office door. Gus stepped inside, a big grin on his face and a brown paper bag in hand.

"Hey, Annie," he said, walking to her desk. "I brought you something."

She set her sandwich down and eyed the bag curiously. "Gus, you didn't have to do that."

"Oh, but I did," he said, his grin widening as he started pulling out a variety of over-the-counter remedies. "Look, I've got motion sickness bands, ginger chews, peppermint oil, even some of those acupressure wristbands. I figured we could try a few different things, see what helps."

Annie felt touched by his thoughtfulness . . . and pressured by it. "Gus, this is so sweet of you, really. But I've tried all of these before and, well, none of them worked."

Gus's face fell just a bit. "You've tried them all?"

She nodded, giving him a small, apologetic smile. "Nothing helped."

For a moment, he was quiet, his brow furrowed in thought. "What about drugs? I could go get some over-the-counter meds."

She shook her head.

"If they won't work, I'm sure Dok could prescribe something."

She shook her head hard. "No drugs."

"Why not? Why would you say no to something that could help?"

"I don't want to take any drugs."

"Okay. Hold off on drugs for now."

Not for now, Annie thought. *For good. No drugs.*

He rubbed his chin. "Have you spoken to Dok about this?"

"No."

"Would you?"

Annie rocked her hand back and forth. "She's so busy right now."

"She's never too busy for you, Annie." He frowned, and then a determined look came into his eyes. "Well, don't you worry. I'm not giving up. Something out there will help. I'll keep working on it until we find the right remedy."

Annie appreciated how earnest he was, but it also spiked up her anxiety. "Gus, you don't have to go through all this trouble. It's my problem to solve."

Gus shook his head, his voice firm. "No way, Annie. We're in this together. If this is what's holding you back from our working together, then I'm going to do everything I can to solve it."

Through the window, she watched him head across the parking lot to join his partner. What if this was a problem that couldn't be solved? *What then, Gus?*

The next morning, Dok asked Wren and Charlie into her office to test their medical knowledge. All Matt's idea. Last evening, during dinner, she had been complaining to him that she felt like she was constantly answering questions for Wren and Charlie. "I know it's part of the supervising gig, but sometimes I feel like I'm their personal Google."

"So turn the tables," he said. "Ask them questions."

Of course! Why hadn't she thought of doing that? There was one patient, in particular, whose symptoms were stumping her. It might be interesting to hear what the two residents might come up with.

"Arthur Roberts, age seventy-one," Dok said, "had complaints of muscle weakness, fatigue, swelling, and difficulty breathing. I need both of you to take a look at his case and see if you can come up with some possible causes."

"Evie and I saw Mr. Roberts just the other day," Charlie said. "He stopped in to get his blood pressure taken. After he mentioned those other symptoms, we thought it best if you checked him out."

That same day, Dok had seen Arthur Roberts and ran a standard blood panel to rule out obvious causes. Nothing showed up.

"Mr. Roberts is a widower, isn't he?" Charlie nudged his glasses up the bridge of his nose. "I think he said his wife died five or six weeks ago."

Dok nodded. "That's right."

"I wonder," Wren said, "if something changed with his diet when she died."

Dok's eyes cut to Wren. She hadn't considered diet. "Go on."

Wren leaned forward. "What if it's something as simple as a vitamin deficiency?"

Charlie turned to her. "How so?"

"Scurvy!" Wren's arms lifted in the air, like she was getting excited. "Sailors used to get scurvy on long whaling trips because they had no vitamin C. It's possible that Mr. Roberts has been eating heavily processed foods since his wife died. No fresh fruits or vegetables."

"Interesting thought," Dok said, "but symptoms of scurvy take longer to present."

Wren's arms fell to her lap before she straightened abruptly. "Beriberi! It presents quickly."

Dok raised an eyebrow. "Beriberi?" She almost laughed out loud. Almost. "Highly unlikely. Quite rare in this day and age."

"But it does fit his symptoms," Wren said. "Beriberi is caused by a deficiency in vitamin B1, also known as thiamine. If Mr. Roberts has been eating a diet lacking in fresh foods rich in thiamine, it's entirely possible."

Wren spoke with such confidence! She was most likely wrong in her diagnosis, but she was definitely confident. Dok, trying to be a good supervisor, decided to test the theory. "Let's rule it out. Wren, ask Annie to call Mr. Roberts. We're going to need a specific blood test to check his thiamine levels."

As they stood to leave, Dok jolted, momentarily startled. She'd completely forgotten Charlie was still there! He'd gone so quiet during Wren's lively monologue, it was as if he'd faded into the background. And, truthfully, Dok blamed him for that. She'd asked for input, but Charlie had brought almost nothing to the table. Not exactly a confidence booster.

The next day, Arthur Roberts's blood test results arrived, and Dok reviewed them carefully. Her jaw nearly hit the floor. Severe thiamine deficiency. Beriberi—practically unheard of!

Wren had nailed the diagnosis. Smart, sharp, intuitive—and that girl had opinions. Charlie had none.

Wren continued to impress Dok as a potential partner. Charlie, not so much.

16

During the lunch break the following day, Evie found Charlie in the garden level's tiny office, looking rumpled and adorable, with textbooks sprawled across the desk. "Sorry to interrupt, but I can't make out your handwriting on this script for Silas Yoder. He called in about needing something for a rash."

Charlie immediately stood up, squinting at the note he'd written. "Ah, sorry about that. It's supposed to be 2.5% hydrocortisone. One refill."

She glanced at the barely legible cursive and raised an eyebrow. "Maybe . . . you might want to write in all caps."

He sat back in his chair. "Noted," he said, sounding genuinely appreciative of the suggestion, as if the thought had never dawned on him before. It was one of the things she liked about him. He was so open to new ideas that improved things. No. Ideas that improved *him*. Coachable Charlie.

She looked past him at the stack of books on the top of the desk. "What's all this?"

"Cram time," he said, lifting one of the books. "Wren keeps reminding me that board exams are right around the corner."

"When's the exam?"

"End of August. Too soon for me, not soon enough for Wren." He shot Evie a wry grin. "I've never been much of a test-taker. Frankly, I've never been one of those guys who loves school. Or books, for that matter. Takes me too long to read."

"But you're a med school grad. You must've done something right."

"Well, just barely. I have Wren to thank for that. She basically tutored me through medical school."

Another Wren reference. A significant one.

Those were the moments when Evie felt confused, to say the least. Obviously, Charlie and Wren had history. But were they a couple?

She could just ask. But she couldn't make herself.

Probably because she didn't want to know the answer.

"I really just scraped by," he said with a smirk. "I'm living proof that miracles happen."

Evie crossed her arms, leaning against the doorjamb. "You know, most people don't even get this far."

He looked at her, a hint of appreciation in his eyes. "True. But there's always another mountain, and right now, it's called the final board exam."

"I thought the pass rate was pretty high—96 to 98 percent?"

Charlie sighed, rubbing the back of his neck. "Yeah, and I seem to always be in that 2 to 4 percent that gives statisticians something to talk about. Wren's been reminding me of that too."

Evie's heart softened at the sight of him, hunched over the cluttered desk, struggling to focus. He looked so scruffy, so earnest, and yet so defeated. She hesitated, then offered, "Maybe . . . I could help?"

His head snapped up, eyes bright with hope. "Really? You'd do that? Be my study partner?"

Was he kidding? She was practically doing cartwheels—though only in her head, of course. She shrugged, playing it cool. "Sure. It'd be good for me too. You know, lifelong learning and all that."

He leaped up and dashed past her, returning with a chair from the waiting room. With an exaggerated flourish, he set it down. "Your throne awaits, m'lady," he said.

She couldn't help but laugh as she took the seat next to him. Their shoulders brushed as he shifted the book to rest between them, and she suddenly wished she'd taken the time to wash her hair this morning instead of just throwing it into a ponytail.

At the end of their lunch hour, he closed the book and looked at her with such genuine admiration that she felt a sudden warmth creeping up her neck. "You're really something, you know?"

But she wasn't.

And yet he made her feel so special. It was new to her, having someone view her as extraordinary. A man someone, especially.

So another routine started to take shape, where Evie and Charlie would have lunch together when the office closed for a break—which only happened when Dok and Wren were out on calls. Evie'd quiz him on whatever he was studying that day—whether it was the cardiac cycle, pharmacology, or pathophysiology—and found herself enjoying it more than she expected.

It wasn't just about being around Charlie, though that was definitely part of it. Most of it. But she was soaking up knowledge too, and what he was expected to know went way beyond what she'd learned for her nursing school exams. It was fascinating, even if it was all theory and not the hands-on patient care she was used to.

Still, there was so much to be learned through hands-on experience, beyond what a textbook could teach, or even observing another doctor. You just had to do things to get the feel of them, even something as simple as giving a flu shot. The first time she'd handed an injection needle to Charlie, she assumed he knew how to hold it. Not so! She stopped him right away. "Hold the needle at a ninety-degree angle, and make sure to inject quickly and smoothly," she had said. "That creates the least discomfort to the patient."

Like always, Charlie was quick to listen and make adjustments—then he'd thank her for pointing out the needed correction. It never failed to surprise her how open he was to being taught, especially when she thought about how Wren usually reacted to Evie's suggestions—so eye rolly.

After every lunch study session, Charlie would shower Evie with gratitude, telling her how much he appreciated their time together. She loved spending that time with him, but the more she did, the harder it was to keep her feelings in check. And whenever he tossed out a significant Wren reference, which he did quite often, she just wasn't sure that this was good for her.

Late in the day, instead of heading home when the last patient left, Annie knocked on Dok's office door. She'd been dreading this conversation for months, but now she was dreading it for a different reason. Ich wees net wu mir der Kopp schteht. *I am at a loss to know what to do.*

Dok glanced up, immediately noticing Annie's discomfort. "What's up? You look a little pale. Are you sick?"

Annie shook her head. "My EMT final exam is coming up."

"Oh, right!" Dok leaned back in her chair. "Oh . . . right." She rubbed her forehead. "You're here to give me your leave of notice, aren't you?"

Not exactly. Annie took a shaky breath. "There's a tiny glitch."

"Come in and sit down."

Annie sat down in the chair, fidgeting with the edges of her apron. "As a child, I suffered from severe motion sickness. I thought I had outgrown it, until . . . that day with you . . . when you drove me home after work on a Saturday . . ."

Dok gasped. "I remember. I *knew* something was wrong with you!"

"I thought it was just your wild driving—"

"I don't drive wild."

But she did. Everyone knew that about Dok. Annie kept her eyes on her hands, wrapped up in her apron. "So I did some tests. I've been taking bus rides during lunch . . . and now . . . it seems that it wasn't just because of your wi—uh, your driving. It just keeps getting worse." She glanced up at Dok and suddenly felt she may not be able to control her tears. She'd tried to be stoic through this ordeal, but in the face of Dok's obvious concern, she could barely keep herself from falling apart. This must be what it felt like to be Dok's patient. Her eyes were on Annie with such a focused intensity, full of empathy, like nothing was more important in the world right now than this conversation. "I don't know how I can be an EMT with this"—she patted her abdomen—"problem."

Dok's brow furrowed. "Are the symptoms mild?"

Annie shook her head.

"How bad?"

"Really, really bad," she whispered, clamping a hand against her mouth to stop a sob from escaping.

Dok cleared her throat. "What *are* the symptoms?"

Annie took a moment to shove down her emotions. She rubbed her sweaty palms on her apron and took in a deep breath before answering Dok's question. "Dizziness, nausea, fainting, vomiting. As long as I'm in a moving vehicle that goes faster than a horse and buggy, I can't even function."

"What about afterward?"

"I've had to sit down on the side of the road for a long time. Usually, I've—" Annie started to feel her face grow warm. "I've gotten sick."

"How long does it take to recover?"

"At least an hour, but usually a couple of hours. Sometimes, it's taken the rest of the day before I feel completely steady again. And I always end up with a headache."

"Oh Annie," Dok said, her voice full of empathy. "I'd hoped you were going to say ten or fifteen minutes."

"That," Annie said, "would be lovely."

"What have you tried?"

"All kinds of treatments—wrist pressure points, breathing exercises, ginger. Nothing's helped."

Dok nodded thoughtfully. "When is it worse? In the morning or afternoon? Any specific triggers?"

Annie shook her head. "I can't pinpoint any triggers. It just . . . happens whenever the bus or car gets going, speeding up, then my stomach starts churning. Then I get hot or cold or both, and woozy . . . and then . . ." She imitated yanking on the cord for the bus driver to pull over.

Dok considered this for a moment. "What happens when you use Dramamine?"

"I haven't. I don't want to rely on medication."

"It's available over the counter."

Annie shook her head firmly. "Not over the counter. Not under the counter. No drugs."

"But why? I could provide a letter for your future employer. I can explain your situation."

"Thank you, but I prefer not to depend on medication." Her voice sounded surprisingly firm, even to her own ears.

Dok tapped her fingers thoughtfully on the desk. "And this happens every single time?"

"There was one time when I didn't feel sick," Annie said. "Last winter, when Sarah Blank fell through the ice and had to be taken to the hospital by ambulance."

"And you didn't feel sick on that drive? Why do you think that was?"

"The ambulance wasn't speeding, but . . ." Annie hesitated, her cheeks flushing as she focused on the tops of her shoes. "There was a very nice EMT in the ambulance with Sarah."

One of Dok's eyebrows arched. "Is this the same very nice EMT who frequently visits the office?"

Annie nodded slowly, surprised by how much Dok noticed around the office, considering she was always moving fast, so busy. "I thought . . . maybe that's a good sign. With the right mental conditioning, I could overcome this."

Dok sighed. "Annie, that was a onetime experience where your feelings for someone were strong enough to overshadow everything else. But how long do you think that could really last? Love can be very exciting at first—"

Who said anything about love?

"—but love changes with familiarity. In a good way, of course. You can't live on new love's high alert all the time. Nothing else would get done in this world." Dok sighed, her tone softening. "I'll be honest with you, Annie. The kind of motion sickness you're describing is often linked to issues with the inner ear, vision, and balance."

Annie didn't need Dok to say anything more. She'd read about those circumstances. All issues that couldn't be fixed. "If I can't get over this, then I can't be an EMT." Her voice betrayed her with a tremble.

"Let me mull this over, Annie. There could be other ways to tackle it."

The phone at Annie's desk rang, so she rose from her chair to go answer it.

"We'll figure this out," Dok said, offering a reassuring thumbs-up.

Annie managed a small smile, but she had a gut feeling that she already knew the answer.

Suppers with Charlie and Fern had become a *thing*, something Evie looked forward to all day, almost as much as the other *thing*—study lunch sessions with Charlie. After supper, they'd linger around the table, swapping stories about the little moments that made up their days. It was sharing the everyday with Charlie that she savored most. You really got to know someone when you spent that much time together. The more she knew him, the more her feelings for him steadily grew.

Today had been one of those sticky, humid days. After work, when Evie climbed off the scooter at Windmill Farm, she was dripping with sweat. She took a quick shower, changed, combed her hair out, and then gave herself a once-over in the mirror. Hearing Charlie's voice float up from the kitchen, she decided to add just a touch of mascara and lipstick—enough to look better without looking like she was trying too hard.

She came down the narrow stairs, and just as she reached the last step, Charlie looked up from the table where he was pouring water into glasses. His gaze lingered a moment too long, until water was spilling over the edge of the glass, flooding the table.

"Charlie, the water!" Evie grabbed a dish towel from the counter and rushed over to help mop up the spill.

He fumbled with the pitcher, his cheeks flushing. "Sorry about that."

Fern turned from the counter, looking like she was trying to swallow a smile. "Supper's off to an exciting start."

Once the table was patted dry, they sat down to bowls of Fern's garden gazpacho, the summer heat making the cold soup a perfect choice. Fern bowed her head, and Charlie and Evie took her lead. After a long moment, Fern lifted her head.

"Amen," Charlie said, like he meant it.

Fern gave him an approving look and handed him the breadbasket. "So, how did you two first meet?"

Evie nearly choked on her spoonful of soup. What was Fern up to? "I don't remember."

"You don't remember?" Charlie sounded kind of disappointed.

Fern's eyes were fixed on him. "Do you remember meeting Evie?"

"I sure do," he said. "It was my first week at the hospital, and I was completely lost. Not literally, I mean, but in every other way. My supervisor needed to get an IV started on an elderly patient, but then he got called away so he told me to do it and disappeared. I'd never done an IV on a real person before. I couldn't find a vein in this poor woman's arm."

Actually, Evie did remember. Charlie had been completely flustered.

"And then," Charlie said, "Evie came into the patient's room, like she just knew I was in over my head. She had this calm, confident way about her. I asked if she could help me and she walked me through the whole thing."

Their eyes met and held, and Evie felt both shy and pleased. "Doctors don't usually ask for help."

Charlie rolled his eyes. "Most doctors don't need help."

"Not true," Evie said. "Most of them do. You were just the first I'd ever worked with who was willing to ask. And now that I remember that moment, you did great."

Charlie shook his head. "Only because of how you helped me. You didn't make me feel stupid for not knowing how to do it properly."

"Sounds to me," Fern said, "like a pretty memorable way to meet someone."

It was, but it wasn't the first time Evie had met Charlie. That had happened a few days prior to the IV incident. And *that* was far more memorable.

It was one of those perfect days of autumn. Evie was on her lunch break at the hospital, sitting outside under a tree, reading a book. Suddenly a dog dashed past her at full speed. She only noticed because the dog was wearing a white jacket.

A minute later, Charlie ran by, then stopped abruptly and approached her, panting hard, asking if she'd seen a golden retriever in a doctor's coat. Apparently, he was a therapy dog gone rogue, he said. "It's my first day on the pediatric ward and I thought the kids would relax around me if I brought him with me. Or maybe I thought I'd relax more." He bent over to catch his breath, hands on his knees. "Either way, it was a terrible idea. Wren warned me not to do it, but I didn't listen. She's always right. That dog doesn't want to be a therapy dog. He wants to be a greyhound. Before I could even start rounds, he broke free of his leash and flew down the hallway. All the nurses are mad at me."

That was a lot of information to convey, most of it not necessary, but somehow endearing. Evie pointed in the direction the golden retriever had run.

"Thanks!" And Charlie took off running.

That was how they had first met. And just now, Evie realized it had included the first significant Wren reference. It kind of spoiled its memory for her.

"Did you ever think of becoming a doctor?" Fern said.

Evie's thoughts jolted back to the table. "Who, me?" She shook her head. "Never. Too much schooling, too much money, too much everything."

"You'd be a great doctor," Charlie said. "You're an incredible nurse."

Blushing, she had to look away. *Stop being so wonderful*, she thought. *Stop making me feel so special.*

Afterward, Charlie went to feed the animals and Evie offered to do the dishes so Fern could finish up a patch for a comfort quilt. Tomorrow, she was hosting a group of women to sew all the patches together. The comfort quilt was going to be raffled away in a fundraiser for a family who lost their barn to a fire. Of course, they had no insurance because they didn't believe in relying on that. They relied on their community to help in times of need. Just one of the many things Evie admired about the Plain people: They had each other's back.

Through the window, Evie watched Charlie push a wheelbarrow full of hay toward the horse pasture. Just then, Wren appeared from the buggy shop, something clutched in her hand. Evie squinted—folders, maybe? Charlie parked the wheelbarrow as Wren reached him, and whatever they were discussing must have been pretty important, because Wren's hands were doing that wild dance they did when she got really worked up. Charlie stood there, still as a statue, but you could tell he was locked in, listening like his life depended on it. Evie couldn't help but wonder—what on earth were they talking about?

Fern came up behind her to gaze out the window. "You got quiet during supper."

"Did I? It's the heat, I suppose. Kind of takes a toll."

Fern folded her thin arms over her chest. "When are you and that boy going to stop stealing glances and just tell each other how you feel?"

Evie nearly dropped the plate she was washing. "Fern, just look at those two!" Couldn't she see? Charlie and Wren were so obviously . . . enmeshed . . . with each other.

Fern peered out the window, unimpressed. "The only thing I can see is that he looks for every opportunity to be around you. He shows up at the crack of dawn for coffee. He helps prepare dinner. He cleans up afterward."

Evie shook her head. "It's your good food that he wants, Fern."

Fern sighed. "It's not my cooking he's after."

Later that night, Evie tossed and turned in bed. The upstairs bedroom was like an oven. No breeze, even with the windows open. Just thick, stifling heat. She finally gave up on sleep. Wren was zonked out cold, so Evie slipped into her bathrobe and slippers and padded downstairs, desperate for some fresh air. The full moon bathed the farm in silver light, and stepping outside felt like a tonic. She heard a horse nicker and wandered over to the pasture. The horse trotted up to the fence, as if just as restless. "Can't sleep either, huh?" she murmured, stroking his soft nose. "Too hot for us both."

"And the poor horse has a fur coat on." Evie turned to see Charlie approaching. "I came out hoping for a breeze, but the air is so still."

"Yeah. The buggy shop is an oven. These are the moments when air-conditioning doesn't sound so bad."

"I'd settle for a fan." Suddenly aware of her robe, she cinched the belt a little tighter.

"Wren's asleep?"

"Like a baby."

He burst out with a laugh. "She's always been a champion sleeper."

True, but it was another Wren reference. It bothered Evie that he knew such an intimate detail about Wren. Why was that? She wondered again what they'd been talking about this evening. "What are you doing up?"

"I'm not so much up but out. I've been studying for the boards and needed a break before I call it a night. I always go outside before I hit the sack. It's like nature calls to me, reminding me of its awe." He craned his neck to look up. "So many stars. It's always soothing to be in the presence of things greater than myself."

Evie nearly swooned at that. How many guys did she know who had such deep thoughts? None. Charlie was one of a kind. A question popped out of her mouth, unfiltered. "Why did you become a doctor?"

He snapped his head back, caught off guard. "You think I'm not cut out for it?"

"No, that's not—"

"It's fine, Evie. You wouldn't be the first to say it."

"Seriously! That's not what I meant." She hunted for the

right words. "It's just . . . sometimes I get the sense you'd be just as happy as a forest ranger or construction worker, or—"

"A clown."

"A clown?"

"That's what I wanted to be when I was six."

She grinned. "I was thinking more like outdoorsy, hands-on work."

"I like that too." He lifted a foot onto the bottom plank of the fence, leaning his forearms on the top. "But I'd always had this secret longing to be a doctor, ever since I was a kid." He wiggled his eyebrows. "After the clown stage, I mean."

"So why a doctor?"

"Same reason I like construction work. I like fixing things. Making things better." He turned to face her. "This might sound a little cheesy, but I felt called to it. Called by God. Being a doctor just seems like a way to be God's hands, to help him do his best work—healing people. Helping them when they suffer, or hurt, or grieve."

He shifted his gaze back to the pasture. "The thing is, school was always a struggle for me. Like, 'barely scraping by' kind of tough. Holding my breath at the end of each school year to see if I'd get promoted to the next grade. I learned early on to set my expectations low to avoid disappointment. Like, basement low." He coughed a laugh. "Then Wren showed up halfway through high school. When she found out I wanted to be a doctor, she practically made it her mission to make sure it happened—whatever it took. Honestly, I'm not even sure if she wanted to be a doctor herself as much as she wanted to see me become one. If it weren't for her, I'm not sure I would've made it through college or med school. Determined is an understatement when it comes to her. I'm guessing you've already picked up on that."

"I have," Evie said. Boy, had she noticed.

"Maybe relentless is a better word. She's like a force of nature. Smart, beautiful, and always in charge." He flashed a grin. "And amazingly, here I am."

Evie had to look away. So Wren was the reason Charlie had become the remarkable man he was today. Knowing that loosened up the tight knot of frustration with Wren. Just a little. How could she wish away the very person who had helped him fulfill his dream?

But it still stung. A lot. He seemed so dependent on Wren, and hearing him describe her as smart, beautiful, and always in charge? *Ouch.* Even if it was true . . . and it was.

The bigger question jabbed at her: Would Wren always hold the reins in Charlie's life? And more importantly, would Charlie always want her to?

But Charlie, gently stroking the horse between its ears in a way that practically made it purr like a contented cat, had no clue the swirl of thoughts running through Evie's mind. "I love being a doctor," he said. "Being here, seeing the kind of work that Dok does, only makes me love it more. Every single day, I'm doing what I love. It's the best job in the world. It's all about helping people."

Evie squeezed her eyes shut for a moment. If only he'd stop being so giving . . . so caring. Charitable Charlie.

"But it's still not easy for me. I have to work twice as hard as everyone else. Probably always will. Helps me to 'stay humble and stay hungry.'" Charlie sighed, long and deep, and pushed the bridge of his glasses up. "And that's assuming I can actually pass the boards so I can get licensed and practice medicine someday." He turned to her. "So what about you? Why are you a nurse?"

She cast her mind back, to long before nursing school, all the way back to the first moment she remembered loving being a caregiver. "My grandparents needed help. Their bodies were, well, they were wilting. Withering. I ended up as their caretaker through their last years. I felt as if . . . I made a difference."

"Must've been hard. To watch the decline of people you love."

"It was. But a good kind of hard. I'd promised myself that I would never turn away from someone's pain, no matter how much I wanted to."

He turned to her. "I believe that. I see that in you. I see your strength. You were born to be a nurse." It seemed like he wanted to say something else, then decided not to. He pushed off the fence. "It's late. Try to get some sleep, Evie. Morning will be here soon."

She was still catching up with the idea that Wren was the reason he had made it through med school when she suddenly called out, "Charlie!"

He turned back, eyebrows raised.

"I think you're a good doctor. A really good doctor."

"Yeah?"

"Yeah. Definitely."

A slow smile spread across his face. "Good thing God doesn't give up on us, huh?" Then he pivoted and continued on his way back to the buggy shop.

Evie watched him go, her thoughts returning to what he'd revealed about Wren. So she was the reason he was a doctor. There was a history between the two of them that Evie didn't fully know, and it just made her feel . . . defeated.

Wren and Charlie were so much more connected than she'd realized. Who was she to interfere? How dare she even want to?

17

David Stoltzfus sat at his old wooden desk in the back of the Bent N' Dent, tapping the end of his pen against the worn surface. The store was quiet, a rare moment. The kind of quiet that seemed to settle in like an old friend when no one else was around. David appreciated these moments, when chatty Sarah Blank wasn't here, and no customers were in the store, and the only sound was the occasional creak of the building settling or the rustle of a mouse somewhere. He wasn't fond of mice in his shop, but they were God's creatures too.

He was finishing up a talk he'd be giving on Saturday to a youth gathering, made up of young people from a variety of Amish churches. Some parents had asked if he'd offer encouragement to their teens to consider baptism sooner rather than later. Most young people waited until they were eying marriage before they chose to get baptized, some as late as mid-twenties.

When he mentioned the talk to his wife, Birdy gave him *that* look. "Hmm. So the parents want you to convince their youth to get baptized. Do they have any idea what you're actually going to say?"

Ah, she knew him too well.

Not only would he avoid pushing anyone toward baptism, but he'd probably end up planting the seeds of a healthy fear of it. He cleared his throat, shuffled the papers in front of him, and tried to picture the group of wide-eyed youth he'd soon be addressing—blissfully unaware of the long, bumpy road that adulthood had in store for them.

"When it comes to baptism, don't take it lightly. This isn't about making your parents happy or following the crowd. It's not about checking a box or doing what's expected. Baptism is about making a real commitment—one that comes from the heart, fully and completely."

David paused, and then scratched out the last line. He could hear Birdy's voice editing him. "Too formal," she would say. "Too stiff. They're young, David. You need to make this real for them, something they can grab onto with both hands. Something that will stick."

He tried again. "There's no good that comes from being half a Christian. If you're only halfway in, you're just living burdened by rules, and you're missing out on the blessings that faith brings. It's like trying to drive a buggy with only two wheels."

David smiled at that. Birdy would like that analogy. These young people had grown up around buggies, and most of the boys had been given a courting buggy. They all knew what it meant when a wheel went bad—a lopsided, bumpy, and downright miserable ride.

He read the line back to himself, this time louder, with a few adjustments. "Don't be half a Christian!" His voice rang through the empty store, bouncing off the walls and echoing back to him. It sounded better this time, more convincing, more real. But it needed a bit more punch.

"Don't be half a Christian!" he repeated, raising his voice even more. "You'd live a life burdened by rules and miss all of the Lord's blessings that comes with faith."

David nodded, satisfied. That was better. He scratched out a few more words, changing them to better fit the rhythm he was after. "You can't pick and choose which parts of Jesus Christ you want to follow. It doesn't work like that. You can't accept his teachings and ignore his lordship. You can't say you believe God is sovereign over the whole earth and then doubt he's sovereign over your own life. Halfway belief won't get you the peace that comes from truly knowing God. You'll miss the chance to see how he brings good out of even the toughest situations. So, if you choose to be baptized, do it because you're ready to live your faith all in, not halfway. Just don't be half a Christian!"

David leaned back in his chair, closing his eyes for a moment, and let out a long breath. He could almost see the doubts in the teenagers' eyes. He had been their age once, after all. He knew how easy it was to think you could manage on your own, that you didn't need to be all in. But half a Christian? He knew that was a road to nowhere.

He sat up again, ready to give it one more try, when the sound of the bells jingling on the door up front startled him. He hadn't heard anyone come in or go out, but then again, he'd been so focused on his talk, maybe he missed the telltale jingle. He stood up, the old chair creaking beneath him, and made his way out of the office and into the store.

"Hello?" he called, his voice carrying through the aisles of canned goods and cereal boxes. No response. The store was just as empty as it had been five minutes ago. David frowned, glancing around, then walked toward the door.

As he peered out the window, he caught sight of a woman hurrying across the gravel driveway toward Dok's office. Even from behind, he recognized Evie, the traveling nurse who worked for his sister.

David's frown deepened. Had Evie been in the store? Had she heard him practicing his talk? The thought made him feel strangely self-conscious. Preaching to a group of youths was one thing, but being overheard in mid-preparation was another. He thought of how he had repeated phrases, practicing how he emphasized the words. Almost shouting at times.

Embarrassing. It was like being caught with your suspenders down—just a bit too unbuttoned for comfort.

He shook his head, dismissing the thought. Evie was moving fast across the parking lot. Surely she hadn't had time to spare to stand around listening to him. With one last glance at the door, he turned back toward his office. But as he made his way back, a small voice nagged at the back of his mind: What if she had heard him?

Then, a chuckle of relief escaped him. He'd been speaking in Penn Dutch—it would've sounded like gibberish to her!

David sat back down at his desk, picked up his pen, and let the last of his grin linger as he continued to practice his talk to an empty store.

―――

Evie hadn't meant to eavesdrop. Fern had wanted her to pick up a spice pack of chili powder at the Bent N' Dent for tonight's supper. At first, she'd thought the store was empty, but then she heard David Stoltzfus's voice, ringing out loud and clear, sailing throughout the store from the open door to his office. Was this how he preached at Sunday church? Evie felt startled by the disconnect. Normally, the bishop spoke in low, calm tones. Not this time. His words echoed as loudly as Hank Lapp's. Curious, she had stilled to listen.

Even though her grasp of the language wasn't perfect, she understood him, and the message cut straight to her heart. "Don't be half a Christian!" David had said—over and over, and with every repetition, it felt like he was talking directly to her. Shouting, really.

She wasn't sure why those words stung so much, but they did, so much so that she fled from the store. Throughout the rest of the afternoon, she couldn't shake them. Something about that phrase—*half a Christian*—shook her, like it had lodged itself somewhere deep, unsettling her in a way she hadn't expected. It was a new concept, something she'd never even considered. And it didn't help that Charlie's comment from the other night kept resurfacing—that she was *born to be a nurse*. She'd never viewed herself like that, never thought of her role as a calling. She was just filling in where her grandparents needed her. Then Darcy had come along, sweeping her into nursing almost by accident.

It was starting to feel like her whole sense of self was off-kilter, out of focus, like she'd been seeing herself all wrong from the start. Maybe she didn't know herself as well as she thought.

Late in the day, after the last patient had been seen, Evie made her way down the stairs to the garden level. Dok had offered a ride back to Windmill Farm, so she went to fetch Wren and Charlie. She knew Wren would be overjoyed to not have to ride a scooter home—even the motorized scooter was bothersome to her. She wanted a car, but Dok wasn't budging on that for now, and apparently Wren didn't have the money for one.

Just as Evie reached the final step, voices—heated ones—drifted out from the little office, with its door left slightly ajar. Charlie and Wren. Quietly, she tiptoed closer. Then she stopped short, ashamed, squeezed her eyes shut, spun around, and started to head back, disgusted with herself. She was becoming a full-time eavesdropper!

But she caught little snatches of their conversation and curiosity tugged at her. She slowed, hesitating.

"But I'm *not* wobbling," Charlie said, his voice firm but edged with frustration.

"You are too," Wren shot back, her tone sharp and unyielding. "I knew this would happen. We had a deal. Everything is ready to roll forward, and now you're backing down."

Maybe just one little, tiny listen. Evie turned around and tiptoed back.

"I know you, Charlie," Wren said. "I've warned you about this before, back in med school. You're sooo close. But if you wobble now, you'll never pass the boards."

Evie heard Charlie let out a heavy sigh, then say, "All I said was that I'd like to finish out my residency here. I just don't want to jeopardize what we have."

"Look." Wren's voice softened just a bit. "I can see that you love it here. And it's obvious this place loves you back. Or rather, she does."

Evie's heart skipped a beat. She? She clasped a hand on her chest. *Me?*

Was Evie that obvious? Did everyone know how she felt about Charlie? Leaning closer, she strained to hear more, her pulse quickening.

"You can't have it both ways," Wren said. "There's too much at stake. Think of how this could help us! We've been through too much together to let it go now. You can't afford to let yourself get distracted."

"That's not what I meant *at all*," Charlie said, his voice dropping slightly. "Evie and I are just friends. Pals, really. That's all. She's been a big help to me." He let out a small, forced laugh. "And you know better than anyone that I need all the help I can get."

Evie froze. Her throat closed off, her chest tightened up. *Just friends? Pals?*

So that's all she was to Charlie? Just a big help. Just a stupidly naive big help. She felt her heart freezing over, with icy tendrils creeping toward its core. Her foolish hopes, that tiny glimmer she'd been holding on to, believing that she and Charlie were meant for each other, shattered into razor-edged shards.

Darcy had called it out. She should've listened to her. Evie should never have allowed herself to be in this position of pathetic hopefulness. Charlie didn't care about her the way she cared about him. What an idiot she was, letting herself believe there might be something more between them. He'd already chosen Wren.

She blinked away the tears that pricked her eyes, refusing to let them fall. Not now. Not here. She wiped her hands across her face and made herself breathe normally.

She hurried back up the stairs, her head spinning. Wren and Charlie would figure out Dok was looking for them when they heard the car horn honk impatiently.

Evie left a Post-it note on Dok's office that she had an errand to run in town so she'd scooter home by herself. Right now, she needed to be anywhere but here, before the tears finally broke free.

Minutes later, as she scootered down the tree-lined road, she could already feel that familiar heaviness settle in, like dark clouds gathering overhead. She knew it well—the aching emptiness of second place. It was how she'd been raised. Mission work was always more important to her parents than anything or anyone else, including their own daughter. How could Evie compete with God? She couldn't. It was impossible.

And it felt nearly as impossible to compete with Wren.

Dok sat behind her desk, wondering what this meeting was about. The day had ended early with the last patient canceling his appointment, so Dok had offered to give Charlie and Wren and Evie a ride back to Windmill Farm. Evie left on her own to head into town, Charlie had scootered off to Windmill Farm, and only Wren remained. Instead of accepting a ride home from Dok, she asked for a private meeting.

"So, you've got my full attention." Dok glanced at her watch. "For exactly five minutes."

Wren took a deep breath. "When we were clearing out the

basement to remodel, I found these old patient files." She patted some folders on her lap. "And I took them to Windmill Farm."

Dok gave her a *look*. "You took files from the office?"

"Yes. Old files. They were all part of Dr. Max Finegold's practice. Nothing was current."

"Still, I'm surprised that you would take them off-site without asking me first."

"Well, no doubt you will recall that you said the basement was full of junk. You gave Charlie the all clear to renovate it. Everything in the basement had to go somewhere."

"Wren, those files are confidential." Or were, anyway. Or should've been. Dok grimaced. Why hadn't she shredded them? She'd meant to.

"Actually, that's exactly what I want to talk to you about. I've been going through them, and I've uncovered something troubling."

Dok's eyebrows furrowed. "Troubling? Like what?"

"During a specific period from 1975 to 1976, I found files of three Amish women who were treated with a new medication in a clinical trial by a pharmaceutical company named Pharmogen." Wren paused and glanced at Dok. "From the look on your face, I see that you're familiar with Pharmogen."

"Of course. Their rep comes through quite regularly."

"He does. In fact, I've met him a few times. Quite a chatty guy."

"So what was this medication used to treat?"

"It was called Serofem. Used for PPD. Postpartum depression."

"Yes, Wren. I'm familiar with PPD." Dok tried, without much success, to keep the annoyance out of her voice. But then her mind bounced off in another direction—how was Clara Zook doing lately? Dok didn't think she'd come in for a follow-up check on her mastitis. She wrote down Clara's name on a Post-it note before she forgot.

Wren, sensing Dok was distracted, cleared her throat quite pointedly. "I'm confident that Dr. Finegold didn't disclose to these women that the drug was not yet approved by the FDA. And that tells me that, most likely, he never let them know about the risks of side effects."

Those were two giant leaps of assumptions. But first things first. "What kind of side effects?"

"Worsening depression. And possible infertility. None of these women had children after that clinical trial. I suspect all three suffered from reproductive complications."

So many skeptical thoughts were running through Dok's head that she didn't know where to begin. "And you've discovered all this in those files? Including that Dr. Finegold didn't inform the women that they were taking part in a trial. Including that he didn't warn them of side effects."

"I'm making that assumption based on . . ." Wren hesitated. Then she lifted her head. "Based on the lack of any informed consent forms in their files." She handed one file to Dok.

Dok opened it and skimmed through a few patient details, written in Dr. Finegold's familiar cursive handwriting. During that first year or so after Dok had bought the practice, she had referred often to his files for patient history and knew what to expect: patient's name and date of birth, medical history, visit notes. All handwritten, all information stored on paper. One of Dok's first office tasks was to transfer all patient files online. Matt helped her with that big job during winter evenings. And after it was done, they moved all of Finegold's files to the basement. Dok wanted to keep them for a year, just to make sure she hadn't missed anything. Then she would shred them. Unfortunately, out of sight meant out of mind. She forgot all about them.

She skimmed through the pages to find Finegold's notes on prescriptions. There it was: *Serofem, prescribed after patient complained of PPD.* She glanced through a few more pages to see if there was any disclosure notice. None. "You're sure the drug was in clinical trial?"

"Absolutely sure. Confirmed by the rep just the other day, in fact."

Dok closed the file. "You do realize that Dr. Finegold has passed, don't you?"

"I do. I mean, I didn't until I went through the files. Then I googled him and found out he had died in Florida."

"Right. I bought his practice when he retired. Then he moved to Florida." And then he died. Dok folded her hands on her desk. "So let me get this straight. You went through an enormous stack of old patient files and discovered this concern about three patients. Only these three. And all three are—were—Amish."

"Yes."

A text message went off on Dok's phone. She glanced at it and saw it was from Matt, wondering why she wasn't home yet. She'd texted him thirty minutes ago that she was on her way. "Okay. I'll go through these files myself."

"How long will that take?"

Dok leaned back in her chair, holding Wren's gaze. "They've been sitting in the basement for years. What's the hurry?"

Wren dropped her eyes. "I'd like to finish this conversation, that's all."

"Well, I do have a practice to run. I won't have time to read through them until the weekend. So in the meantime, I'd prefer you not share this information with anyone. Not even Charlie and Evie."

"How do I know you won't tamper with the files?"

Dok's head snapped up. She couldn't believe how audacious that remark was. "May I remind you that those files belong to this practice?"

That flash of irritation in Dok's voice seemed to give Wren permission, suddenly, to be irritated too. "And may I remind you that they've been sitting in your basement, neglected, since you took over this practice?"

They stared at each other for a tense moment, but Wren blinked first. She set the files on the desk and left. Dok leaned back in her chair, resting a hand on top of the stack. An uneasy feeling crept over her, so much so that she yanked her hand away.

Silly, she thought, as she got ready to go home. She was about to take the three files home with her but decided to leave them here. She took enough problems home to Matt. Why add this one? It could wait.

18

The next day, midmorning, Dok turned onto the long, winding driveway of Windmill Farm, her car tires crunching over the gravel. The familiar sight of the weathered red windmill came into view, its blades creaking in the slight breeze. Before Dok had left the office, Annie had just finished organizing a line of patients down in the clinic's garden level for their flu and Covid shots. With Evie in charge of supervising—not just the process but mostly keeping an eye on Charlie and Wren—Dok felt confident the team could handle it. That left her with a perfect window to slip away for a quiet chat with Fern.

As soon as she opened the car door, she knew what task Fern was busy with: canning peaches. As she inhaled the sweet aroma of Fern's freshly canned peaches, a flood of memories washed over her. She was transported back to her own childhood, standing in her family's hot, cramped kitchen, helping her mother can fruit. She could never seem to do it quite right. Her mother would hover over her shoulder, criticizing the way she held a knife, the way she sliced a peach.

Not the kind of memories the majority of Amish women had of their mothers. Most of Dok's friends adored their mothers and wished only for more of their attention. Not Dok.

When Dok was fifteen or sixteen, on a sweltering August day of peach canning, she'd worked up the courage to talk to her mother about something that had been gnawing at her for months. "I've been thinking," she had said, her voice a bit shaky, "that I want to get my GED."

Her mother spun around from the hot stove. "Why?"

"I miss school, Mom. I want to learn more. I want to keep learning."

Her mother's reaction was immediate and fierce. "Du bist so dumm as Backholz," she snapped, eyes blazing. *You're as thick as a stick.* "You can't even cut a peach in half properly, and you think you're smart enough for more schooling?" The words cut deep.

Dok never ate another peach.

Now, decades later, she had a better understanding of what was behind her mother's harsh anger—fear of change, fear of losing her daughter to a world she couldn't understand. But back then, all Dok felt was hurt and a burning determination to prove her mother wrong.

From that moment on, Dok had stopped sharing her dreams with her mother. She kept her plans secret, quietly studying whenever she had a spare moment, preparing herself for the GED. The day she passed the exam felt like a triumph, but it was a victory she couldn't share with her family. Not even her brother David, and he was a stellar secret keeper, even back then. She didn't want to put him in a difficult position.

And then, one day, she just left. She packed a small bag, took a deep breath, and walked away from the only life she had ever known.

And oddly enough—as her gaze swept over Windmill Farm— she had returned to that former life. But in her own way.

She followed the sweet aroma of peaches into Fern's kitchen. "Wie geht's?" Dok said, stepping inside. *How goes it?*

Fern turned from the stove, her face red from the boiling

water, her glasses steamed up. "Dok! I made a batch of sun tea. It's in the refrigerator, if you don't mind helping yourself."

Dok shook her head, smiling. "I'm fine, thanks. I just wanted to have a chat, see how things are going with your boarders."

Fern continued her work, not missing a beat as she sliced peaches and packed them into jars. "It's going nicely. Evie and Charlie are good company."

"And Wren? How's she settling into life on a farm?" Dok asked, leaning against the counter.

Fern shrugged, her hands never stopping. "Don't see much of her. Always studying or working."

"She's very diligent."

Fern nodded. "Seems like it."

Dok watched Fern for a moment, then asked, "So what else do you think of Wren?"

Fern didn't look up. "Doesn't eat much."

Dok raised an eyebrow. That didn't surprise her. Wren was quite slender, quite disciplined, and Amish food was carb-laden. Designed to provide energy to farmers. "Anything else?"

"She has plenty of opinions."

"Yes." Dok smiled. "Yes, she does." All this, she knew. "What else?"

"She bosses Evie around. But Evie lets her."

Yes, Dok had noticed that too. Then again, Wren bossed everyone around. Most doctors did, Dok had to admit.

She waited, sensing there was something Fern was reluctant to say. "What do you really think of her, Fern? I'd like to know. I need to know. I trust your instincts about people." Fern could be surprisingly savvy. Plus, she had no patience for drama or disingenuousness.

"What do I really think?" Fern paused, knife held midair. Then she pivoted on her heels to look straight at Dok. For a moment she said nothing, and her mouth kept that tight, stern look. "I think that girl is up to something." She turned back to her task.

Dok stilled. Fern had just answered a question that Dok didn't even know she was asking. *That girl is up to something.* A long moment passed before she straightened up, having gotten what she came for. "Thanks, Fern. That's helpful."

As Dok put a hand on the door, she turned. "Do you go into the buggy shop much?"

"Once or twice. Nothing in there but books and boxes." She lifted her knife in the air. "I've told Wren and Charlie that those boxes need to go when they go."

"Would you mind if I just popped into the buggy shop? Wren said she left some files in there."

"Go right ahead."

A few minutes later, Dok opened the door to the shop. It was just like Fern had described. Banker boxes of Finegold's old files, neatly stacked against the wall. Textbooks laid out on every horizontal surface, with study notes for each topic. Inside, she turned in a circle. Wren had pretty much claimed the small living space. There wasn't much sign that Charlie lived here, other than an unmade bed and an open suitcase left on the floor, full of wrinkled clothes. No wonder he always looked so rumpled.

As Dok walked back to her car, Fern hurried down the porch steps to hand her a jar of canned peaches. "Save that for a cold winter day. It'll remind you of summer."

"Thanks, Fern. I'll do that." Dok took the jar, feeling the warmth of the liquid through the glass. She just might try another peach.

All day, Evie did her best to keep her distance from Charlie. She asked Annie to assist him with the patients who came for flu shots so she could work side by side with Wren. Not enjoyable, not at all, but definitely easier that way—safer. If she didn't have to interact with him, she could try to ignore the heavy ache in her chest.

Charlie, however, seemed to catch on quickly that she was avoiding him.

During the lunch break, he caught her refilling the supply closet—something Annie always did. "There you are. I was hoping you could run through some study cards with me."

"Can't today." Or any other day. Ever again. She got back to business, stacking boxes of gauze pads. "Try asking Annie." It came out more snappish than she intended to sound. Then, softer, she added, "Annie's got her EMT exam coming up. I'm sure it would be helpful for her to work with you."

He held up a tin. "Fern gave me a whole bunch of brownies. Plenty to share." He opened the tin to reveal Fern's thick, dark, chocolatey, fudgy brownies. Indulgent, decadent, crave-worthy.

"Nope."

His brows lifted in surprise. "Really?" he said, like she sounded odd.

No, of course not really. She loved Fern's brownies. Loved them. But her emotions felt so fragile that she couldn't trust herself around Charlie. Too much interaction and out would spill her big tangled mess of feelings, which would only make everything worse. She was sad, disappointed, heartsick . . . but mostly she was mad. At herself. It was her own fault for falling for a guy who was already involved with someone else.

Hadn't Darcy warned her? Yes! She'd even wondered if Evie was self-sabotaging by setting her sights on a guy who was unattainable.

"One of the patients this morning told me about his church. Meets in a gym. I thought we could try it out on Sunday."

She stopped, holding a box of gauze pads in her hand. "Sorry. I've already made plans."

Swaying from foot to foot, he studied her for a few seconds. "Evie, have I done something wrong?"

"No," she said, her voice clipped. She knew she wasn't being honest, but she couldn't help it. It was the best way she could think of to protect herself, to keep from crumbling. If he considered her as a friend, then she would try to see him in the same light. Pals. Chums.

Charlie's puzzled expression deepened. "You've been acting weird all day. You've barely said two words to me."

Evie shrugged, forcing herself to meet his gaze. "The office has been super busy," she said flatly, hoping he'd drop it.

But he didn't. "Busy avoiding me, it seems."

"Avoiding you?" She coughed a laugh. "Why, I've hardly given you a thought." *Lie, lie, lie.* Plus, the words sounded way too harsh again. She was never harsh to anyone, not even to Wren, who often deserved it. The look on his face made her regret it immediately, but she couldn't let her guard down. Not now. Not when she was hanging by a thread. She just had to get through the day. She could fall apart later. Not here.

Charlie's shoulders slumped slightly, the hurt in his eyes unmistakable. "Evie, if there's something going on—if I've done something to upset you—you'd tell me, right? I don't want to lose our friendship over a misunderstanding."

So there it was. He said it to her face. Friendship. Pal-zone. Evie took a deep breath, steeling herself. "You're overthinking. There's nothing to talk about, Charlie."

He closed the lid of the brownies and left her to finish stacking gauze pads in the supply closet, and she was equally glad he'd left as she was disappointed.

After all, they were just pals. Just chums. Chummy Charlie.

─────

At noon on Saturday, after Dok finished with patients and was ready to close the office, she told Annie she wanted to give her a ride home. "I want to see for myself how motion affects you."

Annie blanched.

"How about if I promise to not go over the speed limit?"

Annie winced. "How about even slower?"

"We need to go a little faster than a buggy, Annie. Conditioning could be the answer."

Clearly, Annie didn't share her optimism, but Dok had a theory that Annie was suffering from panic attacks, probably brought on from her childhood bus trip. If so, she was confident that slow and steady conditioning was the best way to overcome run-of-the-mill motion sickness.

A few minutes later, in the car, Dok glanced over at Annie, who was buckled in the passenger seat, looking a bit pale but determined. "All right, Annie, today we're going to start the process to get a handle on this."

Annie nodded nervously.

Dok's eyes flicked to Annie's hands—trembling. If this was a panic attack, the anticipation was the worst part. The symptoms might feel all too real, but they could be managed. She felt a glimmer of hope. "Concentrate on something else, Annie. Anything that makes you happy. Like, how good it's going to feel when you pass that EMT exam."

Annie gave her a weak smile.

Dok started off slowly. For the first few minutes, as she eased down the lane and stopped at a sign, Annie seemed to be holding it together. Left at the stop sign, right at the old gray barn—so far, so good. But as soon as Dok turned onto a road that stretched out in front of them, she picked up speed and saw the color drain right out of Annie's face. With every sideways glance, Dok noticed something new—sweat beading on her forehead, her hands shaking even more. The change was as swift as the road opening up before them. That brief acceleration had triggered Annie's discomfort.

Dok slowed the car way, way down. "Annie, you okay?"

Annie moaned softly, clutching her stomach. "It's really bad."

"Let's try some breathing exercises. Deep breaths, in and out." She took a loud breath in and blew it out. "In, out."

"Please, Dok, I've tried breathing." She squeezed her eyes shut.

"Don't close your eyes, Annie. Focus on a spot on the horizon."

"Dok, please, I've tried that too. I can't . . . I can't do this," Annie pleaded, her voice trembling. "Stop the car. Please!"

Dok swerved to the side of the road and slammed to a stop. Annie barely waited for the car to halt before she bolted out, rushing to the grass, her head dropping between her knees as she retched everything in her stomach.

Dok quickly followed, coming around to where Annie was hunched over, gulping in deep breaths of fresh air. She placed a steadying hand on Annie's shoulder, offering feeble silent support. It took a very long time before Annie's breathing calmed, the blood finally returning to her face, bringing a hint of color with it. An unsettlingly long time.

At last, Annie managed to sit up. Dok handed her some tissues, and she wiped the sweat from her brow, then covered her face with her hands. "How can I ever be an EMT," she whispered, her voice filled with frustration, "when I can't even stay upright in a moving car?"

Dok put an arm around her shoulders. "I know it seems hopeless right now, but we'll keep looking for a solution. Don't give up yet. I'll do more research on this and see if there are other treatments we can try."

Annie managed a weak smile. "I'll just get my scooter from your car and head home."

Dok helped get the scooter out of the back of the car and watched Annie head down the road. The sight made her sad. Annie's chin was tucked and she scootered slowly, as if defeated.

After this brief car ride, Dok's optimism was fading. Over the years, she'd seen a few cases of severe motion sickness and they were always linked to an inner ear imbalance. Tough to treat, often persistent.

Her heart sank. This was no ordinary run-of-the-mill motion sickness.

It was kind of Dok to say "we" when, in reality, Annie was the one who had just been throwing up on the side of the road. As she scootered along toward home, keeping her pace slow—mostly because she still felt queasy—she tried to stave off a creeping sense of despair. She was convinced God had called her to be an EMT. That belief had carried her this far, and she had to trust he wouldn't let her down now. Not when she was so close.

As she passed the Jacob Zook farm, she thought of Clara. If she weren't still feeling so woozy, she might've popped in to check on her. Hopefully, Dok had remembered to call and see if Clara's mastitis had cleared up. Annie had seen the Post-it note Dok left on her desk to remind herself, but that didn't always mean she got to it. It would've been best if Dok had asked Annie to make the call—at least then it would've gotten done. Annie handled most of the patient reminder calls. A lot of patients skipped their rechecks, trying to dodge a second doctor's fee.

She slowed as she neared the Zook driveway, feeling a pinch of guilt about Clara—who seemed to ask so little of anyone—and debated whether she should stop in. But then she heard the ear-piercing wails of Clara's babies—loud enough to reach her down on the road—and quickly decided against it.

Nope, she just couldn't handle those babies today. In fact, she could barely manage keeping the scooter in a straight line as she wobbled her way down the road.

Evie wiped her cheek with the back of her hand, smudging away tears as she bent down to try and reach a hand into a nest to collect eggs for Fern. An ornery hen kept eyeing her, feathers fluffed like she was gearing up for a fight.

Fern appeared in the small doorway of the henhouse. "You took so long to get eggs that I worried you'd been cornered." Her sharp eyes taking in everything—the lone egg in Evie's basket, the suspicious hen, and the telltale wet streaks on Evie's face. Fern didn't miss a thing. "What's happened?"

Evie quickly ducked her head, brushing away another tear. "Oh, it's nothing. Just that hen over there. She keeps pecking at me and it hurts." She lifted a hand to show some small bloody marks left by that horrible hen. She sniffed back her tears, but that just let more out.

Fern's gaze didn't waver. Without a word, she walked over to the hen, who squawked in protest as she scooped her up, holding her close to her chest. "This one will end up in the chicken pot tonight," she said, as if it was the most natural thing in the world.

Evie's eyes widened in alarm. "I didn't mean you had to kill her!"

Fern looked down at the hen, stroking her feathers with a tenderness that didn't quite match her words. "She's not laying anymore. It's time for her." Then she turned to Evie, fixing her with a steady gaze. "Es is en Zeit fer alles."

There's a time for everything.

Evie swallowed hard, feeling the weight of those words settle over her. Just an hour ago, she had asked God to give her some idea of what she should do. It was new to her, this asking, but she was really trying not to be half a Christian. She hadn't expected such a speedy response. *There's a time for everything.*

It was probably what she needed to hear. Darcy had already delivered her same old advice in a slightly different package: "It's easier to accept Charlie and Wren now," she'd said during a quick phone call today, "before it has a chance to hurt."

But it already hurt.

A Hidden Hope

Thirty minutes later, Evie stepped down the farmhouse's porch steps, clutching a single letter. As she crossed the grass to head toward the mailbox, she spotted Charlie in the pasture, patting one of the horses. She faltered, her steps slowing to a stop. Charlie turned and saw her, then did a double take. He walked toward her, but when he reached her, there was a long silence, as if both of them expected the other to speak up first.

He broke the silence. "I was just heading out for a run." He noticed the letter in her hand. "Want me to put that in the mailbox for you?"

"Sure, thanks." As she handed it to him, her fingers brushed against his as he took it, and she felt a tiny tingle. How was that possible? Her heart kept ignoring her head.

As he took the envelope, he glanced at the address. "Who do you know in Alaska?"

"Only one person. Another traveling nurse." Evie hesitated to say more, then decided it was fortuitous. "But that'll change soon." She wanted him to feel a sting.

Weirdly, it worked.

Charlie's eyebrows shot up. "What do you mean?"

"That's my application for my next traveling nurse assignment," she said, watching his reaction closely.

He lifted the envelope a few inches in the air. "Alaska?"

"Yes."

"An application?"

"Yes. They're old school in this part of Alaska. Everything has to be in paper. Sounds like their Wi-Fi can be unreliable."

"You're leaving?" Charlie sounded a little stunned, as if trying to make sense of her words.

"Assuming they offer me a traveling nurse contract. I think they will." Darcy said they were desperate for nurses.

"You're just . . . done here?"

"Yep," she said. Really, really done with pining after him. In her head, anyway. Her heart hadn't caught up yet. Even being this close to him was causing her heart to start pounding.

"But why?"

"For one thing, my contract will be up soon," she said, trying to sound casual despite the mix of emotions swirling inside her.

He regarded her with inquiring eyes, his head slightly tilted. "So you want to go to Alaska . . . for the winter?"

Evie hesitated. Wintering in Alaska hadn't really occurred to her. "That's the plan," she said, trying to keep her voice steady. "It'll be an adventure." That's what Darcy kept advising her—pursue adventure! Like it was a thing to be captured.

Charlie started to say something, but then he noticed the mail truck coming down the road. "Let me take care of this for you," he said, and jogged down the driveway with the letter in hand. She saw him chatting with the mailman, so she turned and made her way back to the farmhouse, feeling a little deflated. He could've tried a little harder to stop her.

She let out a sigh. It only confirmed to her that it was the right decision to go.

Es is en Zeit fer alles. *There's a time for everything.*

Time for her to leave Stoney Ridge and Charlie behind. Clueless Charlie.

19

On Sunday morning, David Stoltzfus sat on the hard backless bench, breathing in the familiar scent of horses, cows, and hay filling the barn. His eyes wandered over the sea of white and black prayer caps on the women's side, while straw hats lay tucked under the benches of the men's side—each one a quiet testament to the life he cherished. It wasn't that he sensed God more here than anywhere else—God was with him always. But in these moments, surrounded by his family and friends, he felt especially attuned to God's presence. For David, simply being here was an act of worship.

Still, he couldn't deny that his mind was wandering a bit during the sermon.

He was fond of Menno Yoder, trusted in his unwavering faith, and secretly admired his long fluffy beard—something David had never quite managed to achieve on his own. Still, he couldn't help wishing the minister would shorten his sermons by at least half. Menno had a reputation for being long-winded. Why use five words when ten would do? That was Menno's style, every time. Plus, his low voice had a tendency to flatten into a soothing, almost somnific rumble. Combine that with the heavy, thick air, the rising heat, and it was a perfect recipe for nodding off. David, sitting at the front with the other men, was near the open door, but an occasional breeze wasn't enough to keep the sweat from trickling down his back. His gaze wandered upward. Not even the barn swallows had the energy to swoop through the rafters today.

With effort, he refocused on Menno's sermon—the story of their ancestors, many martyred for their beliefs, who had kept the faith alive and brought it with them across the perilous ocean. David wondered how he would've responded to such persecution if he'd lived in another time. He liked to think he would've stood firm, but without having faced true hardship, he wasn't sure. Still, the strength of those who had suffered for their faith cast a long shadow, one that gave strength to those who followed. He glanced up again toward the rafters. "Wherefore seeing we also are compassed about with so great a cloud of witnesses," as the writer of Hebrews said. David offered a silent thank-you to them.

A high-pitched wail jolted David back to reality. Clara Zook, sitting at the back on the women's side, was wrestling with her twin babies. Just as she soothed one, the other would start fussing. It was evident she was having a tough time, the tension etched on her face as she tried to keep the little ones from disrupting the service. A few worshipers shifted uncomfortably on the hard benches, clearly distracted.

Birdy, David's wife, caught Clara's eye and motioned that she'd take one of the babies. Clara shook her head. She was trying to manage on her own, though it seemed more than she could handle. David thought back to his own twin daughters as infants, Emily and Lydie, to the sleepless nights, the exhausting days.

When both babies started wailing at once, and Menno stopped his sermon to stare her down, Clara quickly stood and hurried out of the barn, chin tucked in embarrassment.

David could hear the babies continue to cry outside the barn.

Across the room, Birdy was giving him the eye. *Clara needs help*, she was telegraphing, as clear as a bell. David leaned slightly back to glance at Clara's husband, assuming Jacob would follow her out, but he remained in his seat, staring straight ahead, statue-like. The only sign he was aware of his wife's situation was a deep flush spreading up his neck and over his cheeks. David felt a pang of concern. This was exactly why Birdy had wanted him to have a talk with Jacob—but he'd completely forgotten. Jacob might not realize how overwhelmed Clara was or, more likely, he expected her to handle the babies like his first wife had done.

Frankly, David wasn't quite sure what to do. The babies' cries hit a new octave—if that was even possible—nearly drowning out the sermon. Not to be outdone, Menno cranked up his volume to a full-on shout, which, naturally, woke up yet another sleeping baby. David could practically hear the collective squirm of bodies on the benches as people shifted, clearly trying to pretend they weren't counting the minutes until the service ended.

Birdy's eyebrows kept dropping and lifting at David, as if to say, *Do something!* David was closer to the door than anyone else, so he quietly slipped out the open door. Blinking against the sudden wash of sunlight, he first saw the buggies and wagons lined up in the yard like pigs at a feeding trough. Beyond them, grazing in the pasture, were the unhitched buggy horses. Then he turned and saw Clara standing under the shade of a tree, not too far from the barn, trying to calm the wailing babies.

"Clara," David said gently as he approached. "My first wife Anna and I had twins. Emily and Lydie. Grown now, with families of their own, but I remember what it was like at first. I used to have a knack at calming a baby down. Let me hold one of them for you and see if I still have the talent."

Clara looked up at him, her face flushing with embarrassment. The idea that the bishop would offer to help hold one of her babies, during a church service, clearly mortified her. He'd only made things worse for her. "Thank you," she whispered, "but I'll just go inside the house to feed them."

David watched Clara hurry toward the house, her slight frame and youthful appearance making her seem almost like a child herself. Concerned, he offered a silent prayer for both her and the babies. Soon, he would stop by the Zook farm to talk to Jacob.

As he pulled a handkerchief from his pocket to wipe the sweat from his brow, he noted how the day's heat was pressing down hard. He should return to the barn. With him set to preach next and the temperature creeping higher, brevity would be welcomed. Most of the church had been toiling under the summer sun to bring in the harvest, and they were feeling the strain. Still, no Plain family would ever miss a church Sunday if they could help it, not even during harvest.

By now, since Menno had dropped his voice back to a rumble, half of them had drifted off, even on those unforgiving wooden benches. David smiled to himself. He was confident the Creator of all must have a soft spot for farmers. After all, he'd started everything in a garden, hadn't he?

On Sunday afternoon, Annie sat on the shaded porch steps of her house, arms crossed, watching a cloud float across the sun as Gus paced back and forth in front of her. He looked like a man on a mission—determined but also undeniably frustrated.

"We've tried everything else," Gus said, listing them off on his fingers like a checklist. "Conditioning, wrist pressure points, ginger tea, breathing techniques. Everything but . . ." He stopped short and turned to face her. "Everything but over-the-counter meds like Dramamine or Bonine. You could take the meds right before your shift starts at the fire station."

"Assuming I get hired."

"Yes, assuming you get hired. And of course you will."

"And what about if they don't work? Or what happens if they stop working?"

"For long-term management, you can use scopolamine patches. I'm sure Dok would prescribe them if you asked."

She shook her head, the gesture small but firm, and her cap strings tickled her shoulders.

The broad brim of his straw hat lifted to reveal his face. "Annie, why won't you just consider medication?" Gus stood with his legs sprawled, hands on his hips. "It could solve your tendency to get motion sickness."

"More than just a tendency, Gus." Couldn't he see? Why didn't he understand that? But her annoyance faded when she saw the anguished look in his eyes. "I just can't function if I'm in a fast-moving vehicle."

He took off his straw hat and slapped it on his knee. She watched his Adam's apple bob above his open shirt collar. "You're being so stubborn about this, Annie! And you're usually the most reasonable person I know."

"I won't take drugs. I just can't." Annie stared at the worn wood of the porch step, rubbed smooth by all the mornings her father and brothers—and plenty of times, she and her mother—had trudged to the barn for milking. Like clockwork, 4:00 a.m. and 4:00 p.m., every single day of the year. Whether Dad had a cold, was dog-tired from a long day, or just plain sick and tired of cows, he never missed a milking. That worn step was somehow precious and dear to her.

Gus sat down beside her, exhaling a deep sigh of frustration. "Can you at least give me a reason?"

Annie took a deep breath, steeling herself. "I don't want to end up like my mother."

Gus's brow furrowed, confusion flickering across his face. "What do you mean?"

She looked away, her voice barely above a whisper. "You know as well as I do that she's a hypochondriac, Gus. She's tried every medication under the sun for illnesses that weren't even real." She glanced at him, seeing his expression soften instantly, concern replacing the frustration in his eyes.

"Annie, you're not her." The sound of his voice, so full of comfort and tenderness, nearly undid her, and she had to blink back tears. "You're nothing like her. Just because that's her path doesn't mean it's yours. You get to make your own choices."

"But it starts somewhere, doesn't it?" Her voice wavered, the fear slipping through. "Whether it's genetic or just circumstances, the results are the same. First, it's one pill for this, then another to fix that. And before you know it, you're juggling a dozen prescriptions just to get through the day. I don't want that, Gus. I can't let that be my future. The only way I know how to avoid it is to not start relying on medication just so I can work." She paused, swallowing the lump in her throat, her heart aching. Even if it cost her a dream job. Even if it cost her a dream man.

Gus stayed quiet for a long, long time, the tension between them thick enough to slice through. When he finally spoke, his voice was low. "But don't you want us to work together? Isn't it worth a shot?"

Annie's throat tightened. She pressed her lips together and closed her eyes. When she opened them again it was to face him, the words coming out in a painful whisper. "Of course I do." She felt the weight of her decision settle deeper on her shoulders. "But not if it means relying on medication. I've prayed about this, Gus. Prayed and prayed. And I think this is the answer—the Lord's answer to me. I have no peace about taking any drugs, not even over-the-counter ones."

"There's no changing your mind about this?" His expression said it all—disappointment, hurt, defeat.

Annie gave him a small, bittersweet smile, even though her heart felt like it was breaking—no, shattering.

"I'm sure."

Gus reached up to straighten her prayer cap, and he let his fingers slide softly down her cheek. "I was really looking forward to a time when we would do everything together."

So was she.

⁓

Late Sunday afternoon, the sky had finally given up its relentless heat, trading it for the promise of rain as gray clouds rolled in. The kitchen at Windmill Farm felt a little cooler, but Evie barely noticed. She sat at the kitchen table, half-heartedly jabbing at her supper with her fork. The food was fine; she just wasn't in the mood to eat.

"Charlie hasn't joined us in a few days," Fern said, breaking the silence.

"Back to his peanut butter and jelly diet, I suppose."

"I haven't seen much of him." Fern cast a curious glance in Evie's direction. "Where's he been hiding?"

Evie shrugged. "Probably holed up studying for his boards. He seems pretty worried about them."

That much was true. Medical boards weren't exactly a walk in the park, and Charlie had said his test-taking skills were pretty nonexistent. Then again, he'd just started studying for them recently. Heavy-duty cramming. It was his own fault if he didn't pass.

She frowned. That was mean. It wasn't like Evie to be unkind. She didn't like herself this way. Even if Charlie didn't feel the same way about her as she did for him, she should want the best for him.

That mean little voice inside her head reared up again: *Even if the best for him means Wren?*

As if on cue, Wren came bouncing down the stairs, a whirlwind of energy wrapped in Lululemon shorts and a T-shirt that looked as fresh as her mood. Her running shoes made a rhythmic tapping sound on the linoleum floor as she breezed past the kitchen table.

"I'm off for a run before the rain arrives," she said, giving them a five-finger wave. "Toodles."

Fern raised an eyebrow as Wren disappeared outside. "Well, she's in bright spirits."

Now that Fern mentioned it, Wren had been unusually cheerful this weekend, even offering to give Evie a makeover, which she'd politely dodged. She could already picture the outcome. An Evie-shaped version of Wren. An imitation Wren. A Wren wannabe.

Way too weird.

But it wasn't like Wren to be so . . . well, friendly. She usually had a bit more of an edge, a prickliness that Evie had grown accustomed to. These last few days, she'd been all smiles and sunshine, which only meant one thing. Evie stabbed her fork into a piece of lettuce a little harder than necessary as the realization settled in. Wren's good mood likely sprang from that chat with Charlie—the one Evie couldn't resist overhearing. Of course it did. Wren had plans for Charlie—who was neatly wrapped up in her grasp, with a big bow on top.

And where did that leave Evie? Off to the side, a spectator in someone else's happily ever after.

Fern, who seemed to know everything without being told, reached out and put a hand on her forearm. "Don't lose hope."

Tears pricked Evie's eyes. "Holding out hope for too long is one thing . . ."

And then, with her signature wisdom, Fern finished the thought in her Fern-like way. "Giving up too soon is quite another."

※

Dok sat at the kitchen table, surrounded by those three patient files left behind by Dr. Finegold. The house smelled too good for her to think straight—garlic, herbs, something roasting in the oven—and it was all thanks to Matt. Sunday was his day to shine in the kitchen, and oh, did he ever take it seriously. Matt's Sunday cooking wasn't just a meal; it was an event, a ritual, a kitchen takeover.

Every Sunday, after church, lunch, and a nap—in that order—he'd roll up his sleeves, pull out every pot, pan, and utensil, and get to work. It didn't matter that a single dish might take two bowls, a whisk, three knives, and four sauté pans—Matt would use them all, and then some. His Sunday dinners were legendary, but so were the piles of dirty dishes he left in his wake. Over the years, they had crafted a bargain—he cooked, she cleaned up. By the time he was done, the kitchen would look like a war zone—flour dusting the counters, pots bubbling over, and every available surface covered with some kind of kitchen gadget.

But that was Matt's style, and she couldn't complain too much. His Sunday dinners were masterpieces. And while she knew she'd be elbow-deep in suds later, scrubbing away at the aftermath, Dok couldn't help but look forward to the meal that was about to be served. It was a ritual she secretly loved, even if it did require a lot of dish soap.

Wiping his hands on a towel, Matt settled into a chair across from her. "What have you learned so far?" His eyes scanned the files spread out on the table.

Yesterday, at the office, just before taking Annie on that disastrous car ride, Dok had stuffed the files into her briefcase to take home. Ever since Wren had told her about them, they'd kept nagging at her, so she decided to just dig in and see what she might discover about those women. She'd spent the afternoon studying them, piecing together the story of Finegold's actions and the pharmaceutical company's role. It was a mess, one that had left lasting scars on those women's lives.

Matt was waiting for her response.

She looked up at him. "Sadly, Wren was right. These women

didn't seem to know they were part of a clinical trial when they took the drug for postpartum depression. At least, they didn't sign any kind of disclosure. I can see how it all unfolded. The pharmaceutical company approached Finegold with this trial drug. Three of his patients, who'd given birth recently, displayed evidence of PPD. All Amish women. Knowing Finegold, he wouldn't have bothered explaining it was a trial drug because he assumed they wouldn't understand. He was always at odds with the Amish, with how they handled illness and injury, birth and death. And of course, those three women, already ashamed about PPD, wouldn't have asked many questions."

"Why would they feel ashamed?"

"Postpartum depression isn't common among Amish women. They would've felt judged. They probably judged themselves."

Matt's brow furrowed. "So what happened to them? Did the drug help?"

Dok leaned back in her chair, rubbing her temples. "Not at all. Pharmogen pulled the drug—it never made it to market. One woman left the Amish, so I don't know her story. But the other two never had other children. Wren seems to think infertility was a side effect of the drug."

Matt shook his head. "So what now?"

Dok shrugged. "The two who remained Amish have passed away. Finegold too. It's a troubling story. These women were already vulnerable, struggling with postpartum depression in a culture that doesn't really acknowledge or understand it. And then to be used in a trial without proper consent . . ." She sighed again, feeling the weight of the files and the stories they contained. "These women deserved better."

"And Wren Baker just stumbled on this information?"

"That's what she said."

"Sort of remarkable. I mean, what are the odds?" He got up from the chair. "Sounds like something you'd uncover, fresh out of med school. Eager and hungry, just like Wren." Matt leaned over to give her hand a squeeze. "Speaking of hunger, though . . . dinner's almost ready."

"Got it. I'll clear the table and set it for dinner." As Dok closed the file, an unsettling feeling lingered. Something felt off.

Maybe it was because she saw so much of herself in Wren—ambitious and determined. If Dok had come across this kind of information as a resident, she would've pursued it with the same zeal Wren was showing. She understood that drive, that hunger for success. She'd always had an inner compulsion to make a contribution, to have something to offer this broken world.

Something still felt oddly out of place. Like Dok was missing something. What was behind Wren's motive to succeed? She wasn't quite sure.

Over dinner, Matt asked her why she felt so troubled about those files. "You can't be held liable, right?"

"No. I'm not legally responsible . . . but I do feel some concern. The descendants are my patients." *My people.*

Matt forked his salad, thinking it over. "You know what you should do? Talk to David. See what he says."

Kick the can down the road to David, was what he meant. Dok did that a lot.

Dok woke up in the middle of the night with a start. What *were* the odds? Matt was so right! What were the odds of Wren reading through those particular files, among hundreds of files, and stumbling on that information?

She slipped out of bed and padded quietly downstairs to the kitchen. Sitting at the table, she opened each file again, scanning the patient details with fresh eyes. Then, with a deep breath, she powered up her laptop and logged into the portal to review the residents' applications. A little more digging, a few more clicks . . . and there it was. Oh wow. Her eyes widened. Wow. Wow, wow, wow. She should've known.

20

Dok sat at her office desk, the early morning light filtering through the window, casting a soft glow on the scattered patient files. She glanced at the clock. Wren should be here any minute. Taking a deep breath, she closed her eyes and whispered a quick prayer. This conversation had to be handled with care. "Help me, Holy Spirit," she whispered, knowing she needed guidance and wisdom. She couldn't afford to reveal too much, not when she didn't know exactly what Wren planned to do with this information.

She heard the front door open and pushed the files slightly to the side but kept them within reach. She cupped her hands around her mouth to call out. "I'm in my office." When Wren appeared at the door's threshold, she lifted a hand toward a chair. "Thanks for coming in early."

Wren nodded as she took a seat. "Of course. You said to be in your office by seven o'clock." She patted her thighs. "So here I am." Her gaze flickered to the files on the desk, then back to Dok.

"I've had a chance to review the files," Dok said, watching Wren's reaction. "It's clear that these three Amish women didn't know they were part of a clinical trial."

Wren's eyes narrowed slightly, but she remained silent, waiting for Dok to continue.

Dok took another deep breath. "It does seem that Dr. Finegold didn't fully disclose the nature of the treatment to these women. And considering the Amish community's general lack of familiarity with medical trials, it's no surprise they didn't question it."

"So then," Wren said, "my findings were accurate."

"Yes." Silence followed, hanging heavily in the air. "Wren, what do you want to do with this information?"

"It seems to me that the affected women and their families should receive some form of justice."

"In what way?"

"There's a class action lawsuit already underway to sue Pharmogen for negligence."

Dok's eyebrows shot up. She didn't see that coming. "You didn't just stumble on these files, did you?"

Wren looked down at her hands for a long moment.

"Baker is a common name among the German. Common among the Plain people, too, though more common in Ohio than in Lancaster. Still, it didn't take much digging to find a connection." Dok picked up the top file. "This file belongs to your grandmother, doesn't it?"

Wren didn't flinch. It was as if she'd been expecting Dok to figure that out. "Yes. Mary Baker was my father's mother."

"This file is why you applied to my practice for your residency, isn't it?"

Wren met her gaze evenly. "I'd learned about the lawsuit during my last year of med school. I had a pretty good idea that my grandmother might have been in that clinical trial. But I needed proof." She shrugged. "I have to admit that I didn't expect to find the proof just sitting in your basement. It was so easy. Like it was waiting for me."

Dok ignored that. "Tell me about your grandmother."

"She and my grandfather met in Ohio and married, and then came to Stoney Ridge because of some problem in their church. I'm not sure what it was, but I do know they had no relatives here. And then they had twins, a girl and a boy. The boy was my father. From what I know, she ended up suffering from PPD. So, from what I can gather in her patient file, she came to Dr. Finegold for help, and he put her on Serofem. The drug only made everything worse for her. At that point, my grandparents left the Amish and then my grandmother died in her mid-twenties. My dad and his sister were barely two years old when she passed."

"Do you know what caused her death?"

"No one would talk about it, which makes me pretty sure that she took her own life. And I wonder if the drug had something to do with that too."

Dok scrunched up her face. "That's a big leap."

"Clinical trials can create all kinds of dangerous side effects."

"True, there are risks, but they're also crucial. That's how the medical field figures out if new treatments are safe and actually work. And I'm sure you know from med school that the benefits are worth the risks—life-saving medications, better ways to manage diseases, and major advancements in what we know. A clinical trial can be a gamble, but it's the only way to move things forward."

Wren narrowed her eyes. "Yet my grandmother—and those other two women—they weren't informed of the risks."

Dok glanced at the three files spread out on her desk, feeling a knot in her stomach. After reading through them, she couldn't deny that. "You're right, Wren. It looks like they were only told about the benefits. That's not acceptable."

"So you agree?" Wren leaned forward, eyes bright. "There's enough evidence in those files to become eligible plaintiffs in the lawsuit, isn't there? I already spoke to the attorney who's representing the plaintiffs. All the groundwork has already been laid. There's no costs to the plaintiffs. To opt in, I just need to provide evidence that these women participated in the clinical trial and suffered resulting harm." Wren snapped her fingers. "Easy." Her mouth twisted. "But the deadline is approaching soon, so we need to keep this moving forward."

Dok froze, her thoughts swirling. This was one of those moments in which she could sense a bright yellow Sharpie pen highlighting her Plain roots deep in her soul. Her life's work was to help others, not to judge them, especially in a court of law. She took a deep breath, grappling with the conflict inside her, trying to set it aside for now. Dok looked at Wren's face, awed by her composure. She was too calm. *If this were me, if I'd found this information about my grandmother, I would feel angry.* But Wren didn't seem angry. "Why come to me? Why not go straight to the attorney with your grandmother's file?"

Wren put her hands on her knees, her eyes intense. "It would help the case if I could present documentation from all three families. But I need you to speak to those descendants."

"Hold it! I'm not going to get involved in this lawsuit."

"No, no. I don't expect you to. I just want you to ask them if they'll meet with me."

Dok sighed. That was a weighty request. "Wren, that's asking a lot. You've barely settled in here, and these people don't know you. They have no reason to trust you."

"But they do trust *you*. I've seen how much respect your patients have for you. They'll listen to you. If you ask them, they'll say yes."

"They won't agree to a lawsuit," Dok said, shaking her head.

"They might," Wren said. "I've read about how the Amish will allow others to represent them in court."

Dok sighed, leaning back in her chair. "That usually only happens when they are being forced to do something that's against their beliefs or traditions. And even then, it's very rare."

"I'd still like a chance to talk to them," Wren said. She

dropped her chin to her chest, as if gathering her thoughts, then lifted her head. "Look, Dr. Stoltzfus, these three women had no idea they were part of a clinical trial. They sought help and it ended up making their lives worse. They were vulnerable *because* they were Amish."

That was hard to argue. Harder to dismiss. "It's really my brother David who needs to be involved in this. A bishop is a bit of a gatekeeper. He's the one who needs to be convinced that dredging up old history is worth doing. And I'm not at all sure he would agree to anything. This all happened long before David was the bishop in Stoney Ridge."

"Yes, I realize that," Wren said. "I'm hoping you'll be able to get him to see why this is so important. And why time is of the essence."

That statement was like an electric shock to Dok; it clicked into place a full picture in her mind. *This* was why Wren wasn't angry. "Wren, are you hoping to cash in from the lawsuit?"

Wren stiffened in the chair. "This is about justice."

Was that the whole story, though? Dok wasn't quite sold. She knew all too well about the mountain of debts that came with medical school. "But you wouldn't mind a little monetary relief if it came your way, right? And you mentioned the case had a better chance of winning if the other Amish families joined in, didn't you?"

"What I *said* was that someone needs to be held accountable to stop this from happening to vulnerable people, like those poor Amish women."

That wasn't quite how Dok remembered it. "What about Charlie? What's his role in all this?"

Wren hesitated for a moment. "What do you mean?"

"Why is he here?"

Wren's eyes dropped. "Charlie is . . . he's here for his residency."

"Does he have a part in this lawsuit too?"

She wouldn't look at Dok. "You'd have to ask him."

Dok swallowed an apple-sized knot. What had been going on with these two residents, right under her nose? She felt a sinking feeling from her head to her toes. This was a mess, one that she helped to create by being careless with Finegold's files, by giving Wren and Charlie weeks of free time, by being such a reluctant, distracted supervisor. Clearly, she was not cut out for supervising.

"I'll talk to my brother," Dok finally said, "but no promises."

"Thank you," Wren said.

Dok glanced at her watch. "And for now, this topic needs to be set aside. We have a day of work ahead of us."

Wren stood to leave. "Just remember, the deadline to join the lawsuit is just a week away. We need to act fast."

But do we, though? Dok thought as the door clicked shut. *Or rather, do you?* Because it seemed pretty clear Wren had already joined the list of plaintiffs. No doubt about that.

However this rolled out, it was clear to her that Wren was not the partner she'd been hoping to find. She had a bright future in medicine ahead of her, but not as a country doctor, not to the Amish. She was far too cunning, too canny. Dok doubted Wren would even stick around once this lawsuit business was settled.

Dok leaned back in her chair and let out a long sigh. Evie's contract was almost up. Every time Dok had casually mentioned extending it for another three months, Evie had seemed open to the idea. But when Dok brought it up again on Friday, just in passing, Evie dropped a bomb—she'd had a change of heart. Apparently, she needed an adventure.

Dok had blinked, baffled. Medicine *was* an adventure.

Meanwhile, Annie was gearing up for her final EMT exam and would probably be moving on soon—assuming they could figure out how to tackle her ongoing battle with motion sickness.

Dok leaned forward and gently knocked her forehead on the desk a few times. That left her with . . . Charlie.

After work, Annie sat nervously in Dok's office, flanked by Charlie and Wren. This morning, Charlie had administered a bunch of tests to Annie, supervised by Evie. Dok had asked if Annie minded her bringing in the residents to be part of this conversation. "Just to give them experience," Dok said.

Annie said she didn't mind, though she did. She minded Wren, mostly. Being around her made Annie feel as if she was witnessing a bullfight, minus the bull.

"All right, Annie," Dok said, glancing at the patient chart on the computer. "The basic tests Charlie gave you all came back normal."

Wren leaned forward, her brow knit in thought. "Perhaps we should consider more specialized testing? An MRI or CT scan could rule out any structural problems in the brain or inner ear."

Annie's hands fidgeted in her lap, and she felt her heart rate increase. "Is that necessary?" She couldn't afford all those fancy tests.

Dok shot Annie a knowing look. "Wren is just making sure that nothing gets overlooked." She glanced at Charlie, who'd been quiet. "What about you? Any theory that could point to a clear cause?"

Charlie looked up, seemingly surprised to be in the spotlight—not so much like he'd been caught daydreaming but as if he hadn't expected to be asked for his opinion. "Well, I was thinking, maybe, could it be stress? Or anxiety?"

Annie's mind started to race. "What could that mean?"

Wren's voice broke into her thoughts. "It's possible that your response could be psychosomatic."

Annie's anxiety ratcheted up a couple of notches.

"It's possible," Wren said, "deep down, there's self-sabotage involved."

"What?" Annie said. It came out like a squeak.

"Like, maybe you don't believe you deserve to be happy. Maybe you're looking for a reason to fail." Wren folded her arms against her chest. "I could find you a therapist."

Charlie gave Wren a look like *Really?*

Wren lifted her hands in the air. "What?"

Dok raised her eyebrows. "Wren, let's stay focused on practical ways to help Annie with this problem."

"That's exactly what I'm trying to do," Wren said.

Charlie rolled his eyes. Then he turned to Annie to offer reassurance. "I think Wren is trying to say that there's help to be had, Annie. Whatever the cause of this might be."

"Not necessarily," Wren said. "There's all kinds of documented cases of permanent motion sickness."

"We're not at that point quite yet," Dok said, frowning at Wren. "Annie, I'd like to send you to a friend of mine, Dr. Fitzgerald. He's an ENT—ear, nose, and throat—and owes me a favor. He'll be able to do more specific tests to find out exactly what's causing the motion sickness. Then we can figure out how to solve this problem. It'll just take time."

But Annie was running out of time.

And, if Wren was right, she might already be just like her mother.

Dok had saved the end-of-day appointment for Annie, to go over the results of her tests, and wanted Wren and Charlie to sit in on it. That meant Evie could go home early, which was perfectly fine by her. The more space she could keep between her and Charlie—without making it too obvious—the better. Later that afternoon, just before supper, Evie joined Fern for a walk up to the orchard to check on the apples.

They strolled through rows of apple trees, the air rich with the scent of ripening fruit. The summer sun glinted off the apples hanging firm and green on the branches, with just a blush of red starting to show. "Needs a few more weeks," Fern said casually, running her hand along the leaves before she darted away, leaving Evie to wander on her own.

Evie couldn't help but smile as she watched Fern disappear down the row of trees. That woman always seemed to know when to stay and when to go, leaving her with just the right amount of company and solitude. And right now, Evie needed solitude. As much as she tried to push it away, David Stoltzfus's words kept echoing in her mind: *"Don't be half a Christian!"*

She sighed and bent down to pick up a fallen apple, rolling it between her palms. Half a Christian. Was that what she was? The thought gnawed at her. She'd spent her whole life going through the motions, following the rules, doing what was expected. Her parents had swept her up in their faith so fully, so completely, that she never really thought much about it. It was just . . . there. Like the air she breathed. It wasn't a choice; it was a given. Their faith had been so large, so overwhelming, that there wasn't any room left for her to make her own decision about it.

Evie tossed the apple lightly in her hand before letting it drop back to the ground. She was starting to realize, with a bit of a sting, that maybe she had never truly decided anything for herself when it came to God.

She brushed her hands on her skirt and wandered farther into the orchard, feeling the quiet sturdiness of the trees around her.

David's words had cut deep. The more she thought about them, the more she knew he had described her. Half a Christian, caught in the middle between faith and rules. She'd followed the "do unto others" bit to the letter, but when it came to experiencing the blessings of faith—the peace, the assurance that God truly cared about her—she'd come up short. If she only believed halfway, she was missing out on everything that faith had to offer.

No peace. No confidence. No assurance that she mattered much to God.

But then she thought about Charlie's words that she was born to be a nurse. Maybe God had been guiding her, all along, even though she was oblivious to it. A memorized Bible verse from years of Sunday school popped into her head: "If we are faithless, he remains faithful, for he cannot disown himself."

God doesn't give up on us.

Evie glanced down the row where Fern had disappeared. She needed to talk to someone about this. Maybe Fern. She squinted. Probably not. Fern wasn't exactly the type who invited long heart-to-heart chats. Maybe she just needed more time to think. Either way, she knew one thing for sure: She couldn't keep living as half a Christian. If she was going to have faith, it had to be the real thing, or it wasn't worth much at all.

Annie had just locked up for the day and was turning off the light in the exam room when frantic banging rattled the front door, followed by someone shouting for help.

She rushed over and opened the door to find Tina Smucker, barely holding up her husband Abe, who looked ghostly pale and drenched in sweat.

"Annie, help! It's Abe!" Tina's voice wobbled with fear.

"Come in!" Annie helped get Abe into a chair in the waiting room. Then she sprinted to the door leading downstairs, flung it open, and cupped her hands around her mouth. "Charlie!"

Charlie had been in the garden level, studying in the small office, and barreled up the stairs when he heard Annie's shout, sandwich in his hand. His eyes went wide at the sight of Abe.

He dropped the sandwich and rushed over, immediately taking Abe's pulse. "Where's Dok?"

"Dok and Wren left on a house call."

"Evie?"

"She left for Windmill Farm over an hour ago."

A look of panic flitted through Charlie's eyes. "Should I call for an ambulance? This must be, uh . . . a cardiac event, right? Should I get nitroglycerin? Or aspirin?"

Annie's gaze swept over Abe, taking in his flushed face and the sweat rolling down his cheeks, the wisps of straw in his beard. "Tina, what's he been doing all day?"

"He's been out in the fields, cutting hay," Tina said, her voice laced with concern.

Annie turned to Charlie. "I think it's heat exhaustion."

"Heat exhaustion?" Charlie echoed, half question, half statement, as though testing out the words.

"Abe needs cooling down. He needs water." Annie went to the bathroom and grabbed some cloths, soaking them with cool water, then filled a glass and brought it to Abe. While he sipped the water, she pressed the cold cloths on Abe's neck and wrists, her movements deliberately calm.

Charlie ran a hand over his chin, looking increasingly nervous. "Annie," he said, "are you sure he's just overheated?"

"Pretty sure. We'll know soon." A minute later, Annie smiled. "See? He's already starting to look better." Abe's face had lost that bright red color.

"Shouldn't we, uh, be doing . . . more? Something preventative?" Charlie glanced at Abe, then at Annie, still holding his breath like he expected Abe to keel right over.

Tina let out a relieved sigh. She could see that Abe was improving. Annie could see it. Why didn't Charlie? It was as if he wasn't trusting his own eyes.

It wasn't long before Abe felt well enough to go home. Charlie helped him out to the buggy. After Tina and Abe drove off,

Charlie searched out Annie. She was putting the used wet cloths in a laundry bin to wash. "You did really well there, Annie. Calm, cool, collected."

"Thanks." She dipped her head, a little embarrassed by the praise.

"What tipped you off to heat exhaustion?"

It seemed so obvious. "The wisps of straw in his beard."

Charlie looked at her in amazement. "For real? That's all?"

She rattled off the other things she'd noticed: It had been a very hot day. Abe wasn't clutching his chest. His face was bright red, but his skin was cold and clammy. He was sweating profusely, like his body was trying to cool down. "EMT training teaches us to assess a situation before taking action."

He shook his head, clearly impressed. "Is this all just second nature for you? Staying so calm?"

"Well, EMT training teaches us to stay calm, in every situation. Even as an EMT enters an emergency scene, we're told to not run but to walk in, to keep our movements slow and deliberate." She glanced at him. "Wasn't that what you were taught to do in medical school?"

Charlie coughed a laugh. "Not at all. What was taught was to be the fastest draw in class." He whipped out his hands and pointed them like guns. "Sorry." He dropped his hands. "Totally inappropriate thing to say to a pacifist. What I meant was, we were encouraged to make a fast, decisive diagnosis."

"Even if it's wrong?"

He laughed. "Thankfully, I could usually rely on someone else to keep me from shooting from the hip." He smacked his forehead. "Sorry! I did it again."

Annie had to smile at him. Charlie could be funny. She enjoyed being around him, even if he did need a big dose of confidence if he was ever going to win over Dok. She could tell Dok didn't have a lot of faith in him. Whenever she wanted a second opinion on a patient, she always asked Wren first.

Charlie came second, kind of a polite ask. Like "oh, you're here too."

As Annie scootered home, she thought about what she'd told Charlie about EMT training. She wondered if she'd ever get to put her training into action, to walk in calmly on an emergency scene, to assess a situation before acting. Would she ever be an EMT? The very thought made her feel like weeping.

21

David cleared a chair for his sister to sit on, wondering why she'd come to his office. He knew how busy her days were, but she had a look on her face like she had something on her mind. She'd come for a reason.

She sat down and gazed around the room, a contented look on her face. "Your office always feels cozy."

"Messy. Cluttered."

"True. A little too hot in the summer for my liking, a little too cold in the winter." She smiled. "But always nice to see my brother seated behind the desk."

"So you're here as a sister? Not a doctor."

"Both." She took a deep breath. "David, something important has come up, and it involves you, and some of your church members—who have already died—and it involves me. Sort of. But I'm hoping to extricate myself from it and hand it over to you."

Thoroughly confused, he said, "I was following along until you mentioned church members who had died."

"Right."

She set three musty old files on his desk. "You've met Wren Baker, one of my residents, haven't you?"

"I've crossed paths with her once or twice." Never very pleasant experiences for him.

Dok paused and tipped her head. "Does she remind you of me when I was her age?" Then she waved that away. "Never mind. Don't answer that. Anyway, Wren found these old patient files when she and Charlie were emptying out the basement to remodel. They're from the Max Finegold era." She lifted a finger in the air. "To be perfectly accurate, Wren didn't just stumble upon these files. She came to Stoney Ridge specifically to look for evidence about her grandmother from the 1970s. A woman named Mary Baker."

David's eyebrows knit together. He was already confused, but he didn't interrupt.

"Mary Baker was part of a clinical trial for a drug to help postpartum depression. Two other Amish patients were in that same clinical trial. But in all three files, there's no consent form. It appears that these three women weren't aware of the risks of a clinical trial. There should have been signed documentation from every patient. Finegold's mistake, but a catastrophic one for the drug company. They hadn't ensured that every trial participant was fully informed and had given proper consent. And there were serious risks. The drug never made it past the trial phase before Pharmogen took it off the market."

David had an uncomfortable feeling that his sister was about to dump this all into his lap.

"Apparently, there's a civil lawsuit brewing against Pharmogen. Wren Baker has spoken to the attorney who is leading the charge, and now she wants to speak to the descendants of the two Amish families who were involved. Oh, I forgot to mention that Wren's grandmother, Mary Baker, left the Amish long ago. But the other two women remained."

"Do you know their names?"

"One is Fisher and the other is Zook."

David cringed. "Half our church is named Fisher or Zook."

"Right." Dok knew that. "You don't even need to say a word about how you feel about lawsuits, David. How everyone in the church feels about them. But on the other hand, these women were in a vulnerable frame of mind, and they were taken advantage of. Seems like that should be addressed. Maybe it would be good for these families to just listen to Wren."

David gazed at her. "Why would it be good for them to listen to her?"

Dok sighed. "Because . . . there are Amish who struggle with depression, for different reasons, and they're forced to hide it. When it comes to postpartum depression, there's such an assumption that a new mother should feel blessed and happy to have a child. But when she doesn't, she can't find the help she needs."

David felt his stomach clench. It had completely slipped his mind to heed Birdy's warning to talk to Jacob Zook about providing help for Clara.

"So, what do you think? Would you be willing to gather those families sometime this week so Wren could explain what she's discovered? You're welcome to use my new garden-level waiting room."

Despite the seriousness of the topic, David laughed. "Garden level? Ruth, there's no garden down there. It's a basement."

"Maybe not," she said with a smug smile, "but it has a nice ring to it."

He dropped his chin, asking the Lord for guidance. Trusting it would come. Slowly, he lifted his head. "Let me host the meeting at the store. That'll help you stay out of this. In fact, don't even come to it. I'll oversee it. I'll talk to the families and plan for an early morning meeting before the store opens."

"I'd prefer it to be sooner rather than later. Wren can be . . ."

"Determined. Relentless. Tenacious. And yes, she does remind me of you at her age."

Dok scowled at him. "I told you not to answer that question." With a huff, she gathered her musty old files and left his office.

∽

Annie Fisher sat in Dr. Fitzgerald's waiting room, her fingers fidgeting with the hem of her apron. The curious glances at her from other waiting patients only added to her nerves. She kept checking the clock, wishing for a bit speedier passage of time.

When her name was finally called, she was led into a fancy exam room and questioned by the nurse. Then came more waiting, until the ENT finally knocked on the door and came in. He looked as young as Charlie, though he carried himself entirely differently. A tall man with a neatly trimmed beard and glasses that magnified his gaze. "Hello, Annie. I'm Dr. Fitzgerald. I hear you're having a little trouble with car sickness?"

Annie's gaze stayed on the top of her shoes. "More than a little."

The doctor nodded sympathetically. "Let's do some tests and see what's going on."

First up was the hearing test. He handed her a pair of bulky headphones. "Just raise your hand when you hear a sound."

The beeps from the headphones seemed to come from all directions, and Annie tried her best to stay focused. She raised her hand with each beep, feeling like she was participating in an odd exercise routine—each beep a cue to respond.

Next came the VNG system, whatever that meant. The doctor handed her a pair of large goggles and said, "These are to track your eye movements. Follow the lights with your eyes."

The lights moved in a pattern that reminded her of the flickering lanterns used for evening gatherings. Following them felt less like a test and more like an exercise in patience.

Then came the caloric stimulation test. The doctor carefully placed a small device in her ear. "We're going to use warm and cool water to check how your balance system responds."

The warm water trickled in first, followed by the cool. The sensation made her head feel like it was being gently rocked, though not in a pleasant way. She focused on her breathing, determined to stay steady even as she felt wobbly.

When the tests were finished, the doctor removed the equipment. "I'll review the results and send them over to Dr. Stoltzfus. We'll get to the bottom of this."

The problem, Annie thought as she guided the horse and buggy onto the road, merging with cars, was that getting to the bottom of this might signal the end of her dream.

⁂

Dok hung up the phone, having just received the ENT's report on Annie's tests. She exhaled deeply, a hint of worry slipping through. After a moment, she called Annie in.

"Have a seat," Dok said, gesturing to the chair across from her desk, her voice steady but serious.

Annie sat down, hands clasped tightly in her lap, as if she already had an idea of what was coming.

"So, Dr. Fitzgerald called. He is convinced you've got something called vestibular dysfunction. It's a condition with the inner ear, and when there's a mismatch between what your inner ear senses and what your eyes see, it can cause this kind of severe motion sickness."

Annie's shoulders slumped, her disappointment palpable. "I've read about it. It's not something that can be fixed quickly—maybe not at all."

Dok leaned forward, resting her forearms on her desk top. "I realize what this means to your plan to become an EMT."

"Kills it," Annie said, her eyes shiny with tears.

"Maybe . . . postpones it indefinitely. But until then, I've been thinking of an alternative path for you. Similar, but different." She paused, waiting for Annie to meet her eyes. "What would you think about becoming a public safety telecommunicator? You know, a 911 dispatcher?"

Annie blinked back tears, clearly taken aback. "A dispatcher?"

Dok nodded. "You'd still be involved in emergency response work but from a different angle. I looked into it, and you'd make an excellent candidate. You're over eighteen, you have a GED, you're CPR certified, and you have no criminal record, no felonies—"

Annie's eyebrows shot up.

Dok smiled. "I mean, you meet the basic requirements."

"Is it like becoming an EMT? I would think I'd need to take classes."

"Yes and no." Dok felt encouraged that Annie hadn't automatically dismissed the idea. "Once you're hired, there's a state-approved training program. It lasts about six to twelve months, but it's on the job."

"Would it be difficult for me to get hired?" Annie's tone was skeptical but curious.

"Not at all," Dok said firmly. "Your EMT training would give you an edge, and you're exactly the kind of person who's needed in emergencies—calm under pressure, quick on your feet. You don't panic, and you think clearly. Plus, it's less dangerous work, which might sit better with your mother."

"Dok, do you think my mother would agree to this?"

"I'm confident she'd be in favor of this over EMT work." *Fairly confident.* Sally Fisher had a remarkable capacity for catastrophic thinking.

Annie's chin was tucked. Quietly, she said, "I wouldn't be working with Gus."

Dok raised an eyebrow. Gus, of course—that EMT who seemed to drop by the office quite regularly. "No, not directly. But you'd still be a crucial part of the team, making sure help gets where it's needed most." She pushed a file folder full of dispatcher information across the desk to Annie. In it was a job application. Dok was tempted to fill it out for Annie, but she held back. Matt was always accusing her of overhelping.

Annie stared at the file Dok pushed across the desk. She didn't pick it up right away, just looked at it as if the paper itself held answers she wasn't quite ready for. "I just thought . . . I'd be doing something different."

"I know," Dok said. "But this is still important work. You're needed, Annie. You've always had a calling to help people. This is just a different way to answer that call."

Annie finally reached for the folder, her fingers lingering on the edges before she picked it up. "Thanks, Dok. I'll think about it."

"I know you will."

Annie stood, gave Dok a quick nod, and walked out with the file tucked under her arm, her expression thoughtful yet impossible to read.

As the door clicked shut behind her, Dok leaned back in her chair with a knowing smile. Annie Fisher was going to read every last word in that folder—probably twice.

22

David Stoltzfus eased Sally Fisher into one of the old rockers in front of the cold, still woodstove at the Bent N' Dent. It was early—barely seven—and the store wouldn't open for another hour. Over the past few days, he'd reached out to the direct descendants of Laura Zook and Carolyn Fisher, inviting them to Wren Baker's talk about the pharmaceutical company and the trial medication. But turnout was slim; most claimed to be too busy. So far, Sally was here, along with her uncle Pete and his wife Elizabeth. Carolyn Fisher's elderly first cousins, Alice and Ada, had made it and flanked Sally on either side, as if she needed some shoring and bolstering. Maybe she did. Or maybe they just needed to sit close enough to catch what Wren Baker had to say—their hearing was a bit hit or miss.

To David's surprise, Clara Zook had arrived with her babies in a stroller. He hadn't even thought to invite her. Clara wasn't directly related to Laura Zook—her husband was, though the connection was extremely distant.

Two others showed up who weren't related to anyone but always managed to find their way into these sorts of gatherings: Hank Lapp and Sarah Blank. David considered asking them to leave but thought better of it. He didn't want Clara to misunderstand and think he meant her. She was sensitive like that.

Wren stood in front of the small group, holding the files. She looked at each person before she introduced herself. "Thank you for coming today. While clearing out the basement of Dr. Stoltzfus's office, I found these three files. They contain records from two generations ago, documenting a trial medication given to three Amish women suffering from postpartum depression. The drug had severe side effects, and many of these women, including my grandmother, suffered greatly from it."

"WHO'S your grandmother?" That came from Hank.

"Mary Baker."

The Zooks exchanged a look. "Baseball Joe's Mary?" Pete said.

"My grandfather was named Joseph," Wren said, "and he was a baseball player."

"Why, I do remember them," Elizabeth said.

Wren was delighted. "I'm so pleased that you remember my grandparents!"

"That's because we're AMISH," Hank said. "Everybody finds out EVERYTHING."

Sarah, leaning against the checkout counter, giggled.

Elizabeth lifted a hand. "But I believe Mary and Joe left the Amish."

"That's correct," Wren said.

"Joe wanted to become a professional baseball player," Pete Zook said. "Did he ever do it?"

"Well, no," Wren said. "He was a used car salesman."

"OOOOF," Hank said. "Not even close."

"If we could stay focused," Wren said with a frown at Hank, "I wondered if you could think back. Were you aware of your relative taking this medicine? Did it give her any lingering side effects? For example, my grandmother Mary didn't have any other children after twins."

"MAYBE twins were ENOUGH for her. Our Clara might understand THAT!" Hank said. "CAN'T you, Clara? When those babies start hollering, my molars start RATTLING."

Mortified, Clara Zook stood against the wall, pushing the twins' stroller back and forth. She pressed her finger against her mouth to silence Hank, but he'd gone back to cracking open shells to pop peanuts in his mouth, oblivious. David shook his head.

"Oh, that is too bad," Sally Fisher said. "Children are a blessing from the Lord. Though sometimes sons can be rather insensitive. Don't expect much on Mother's Day, I've learned."

Oh boy, David thought.

Wren looked a little panicked. "So I wondered if your relatives might have had a similar result from taking the drug."

"And WHAT drug was this?" Hank said.

Wren sighed. "It was called Serofem and it was taken for postpartum depression."

Hank leaned forward in his rocking chair. "POSTPARTY depression?"

"Close enough," Wren said with a minimal eye roll. "It often hits after a woman delivers a baby. Some experience a lot of difficulty in those first few weeks and months. It should be a happy time for a mother—"

"It is a happy time," Elizabeth said.

"Happy until your children marry," Sally said, "and forget all about you."

Wren put her hands together, as if trying to reel everyone back in. "Let's return to the matter at hand. Some women have hormonal fluctuations that make it quite difficult to care for their baby and for themselves."

"Maybe for the Englisch," Elizabeth said, "but not for us."

Wren sighed. "Maybe not for *most* Amish women, but some do suffer from postpartum depression." She lifted the files. "These three women suffered greatly and they suffered alone.

That's why they went to Dr. Finegold and why he gave them the drug."

"Did it help?" Everyone turned to Clara Zook, pushing her stroller back and forth. Her eyes were on Wren. "Did the medicine fix them?"

"No," Wren said. "It didn't. It only caused more problems."

Clara's chin dropped. Just then, one of the babies began to stir, letting out a few squeaks, then a full cry, and soon enough, the other joined in, wailing in unison. Clara quickly pushed the stroller out of the store. David considered chasing her, thinking he might offer to take the stroller for a spin around the parking lot so she could stay in the meeting, but with both babies now crying at full volume, he knew she wouldn't accept his help. Besides, he recognized that his place was right here in this meeting.

He needed to stop putting it off and go have that talk with Jacob Zook. *Soon.*

When the door closed behind Clara, Wren—looking a bit relieved that the noisy babies were gone—picked up where she left off. "It seems my grandmother's depression only worsened after she'd taken Serofem. Some reports suggest that infertility was one result. Can any of you remember if there might have been side effects for your loved one?"

"Now that you mention it," Pete said, "my father was youngest of two children. My grandmother was Laura Zook. Does seem kind of rare to have such a small family, at least among the Plain people."

"See?" Wren lit up. "That's exactly the kind of information I'm looking for. It's entirely possible that your grandmother was affected by the drug. What about Carolyn Fisher?"

Sally Fisher's arm shot right up in the air. "My husband's father was her only child."

Wren turned to her. "So Carolyn had no other children?"

Sally shook her head.

"Don't you see?" Wren said, her arms flying in the air. "These were such young women! It's entirely possible that they were unable to have more children after they took this drug. It's no wonder their depression deepened."

Ada and Alice, whose hearing wasn't stellar, had been quiet throughout the meeting. But now Ada lifted a finger in the air. "Cousin Carolyn was always a bit . . ."

"Down in the dumps," Alice finished. "Even as a child."

David could see Wren grow increasingly baffled. She wanted people to get excited, to feel indignant, but they remained calm. Other than Sally Fisher. She looked quite distressed.

"These young women," Wren said, her voice earnest, "didn't know the risks they were taking. They weren't told about the potential side effects. Dr. Finegold didn't tell them. That was wrong. The drug company didn't ensure that every trial participant had given consent. That was wrong. The pharmaceutical company should be held accountable for what happened." She clapped her hands together. "We have powerful evidence to proceed."

"PROCEED?" Hank said. "Proceed in WHAT?"

"In a lawsuit against Pharmogen."

David watched as the mood in the room subtly shifted the moment Wren mentioned the lawsuit. Their expressions would be tough for anyone to read, especially for someone unfamiliar with the Plain way of masking emotions, but even Wren seemed to sense the sudden drop in temperature.

She ramped up her pitch, hands waving like she was trying to flag down a passing buggy. "It's already underway! You won't have to do a thing, just submit your relative's file. I'll represent you. You'll never have to step foot in court. I've got it all covered."

Still nothing. The families remained stone-faced. Wren's gaze darted from one expressionless face to another, searching for a flicker of interest. Nothing. Not a spark. Not even from Sally Fisher.

Finally, Pete Zook rose to his feet, his voice gentle but firm. "We thank you for caring about our relatives, and for wanting us to understand the . . . uh . . . situation they were in. We're awfully sorry about Baseball Joe's Mary. That's a real shame, not being able to have any more little ones. But we think it's best to let God be the judge here."

Quietly, he helped Elizabeth to her feet and they made their way to the door. Ada and Alice followed behind. Then Sally and Hank. Sarah made herself scarce and went to the storeroom to look for supplies.

As the store emptied, Wren, bewildered, sank into a rocker, lost in thought. After a long moment, she turned to David, her eyes wide with disbelief. "I don't understand. How could they not want vindication?"

"The Amish believe that revenge is up to God. They trust in his justice and mercy, knowing that retribution isn't their job."

Wren shook her head, still trying to process it. "But they were wronged. Doesn't it matter that their relatives were wronged?"

David nodded. "Of course it matters. But peace doesn't come from trying to fix the wrong. It comes from trusting that God will handle it, in his time."

It was clear Wren wasn't convinced. "True peace can only come with justice."

"I agree with you," David said, "but true justice can only come from God. Only he knows what's in a person's heart." He paused to let that sink in. "Two things can be true at the same time."

From the confused look on her face, he almost wondered if he had spoken in Penn Dutch. He had a habit of doing that—slipping into the dialect at times. He was just about to explain himself when she sprang from the rocking chair and made a quick exit out of the store.

David stared after her in dismay. He was wrong. Wren was nothing like his sister.

Wren Baker was in a mood.

All day, Annie, Evie, and Charlie sensed something was going on with her and they stayed clear. Even Dok. But then Dok sent Evie and Charlie off in her car to deliver insulin to Dan Hostetler, who had a broken leg and couldn't come into the office for supplies, and Dok was busy in her office, so that left Annie to deal with Wren.

She was at her desk, reading through the dispatcher information in the file Dok had given to her, when she happened to look outside the window and see Silas Eicher, an Amish farmer, shuffling up the path into the clinic. He looked unwell, his face pale and his movements sluggish.

"Silas, please have a seat," Annie said, motioning to a chair in the waiting area. "I'll get you in as soon as Dok is free."

Silas nodded weakly, sinking into the chair with a sigh. Annie's eyes darted back to Wren, who was now heading their way from the exam room. She'd been hoping Dok would've been the one to come in, but she was on a phone consult with another doctor.

"Silas Eicher should be seen before the next patient," Annie said.

Wren frowned. "Does he have an appointment?"

"No, he's a walk-in. Dok makes allowances for emergencies."

Wren looked up, her expression sour, like she'd just taken a bite of a lemon. "Because they're never real emergencies."

Annie hesitated. "Silas doesn't look too good. Maybe—"

Wren cut her off with a curt nod. "I'll handle it, Annie. Get him settled in the exam room and I'll be right in."

Annie bit her lip, feeling the familiar rush of intimidation. She helped Silas into the exam room, her concern growing with each step.

Wren came into the room. "So what seems to be the problem today?" Annie noticed that she didn't introduce herself and

249

barely glanced at Silas but spent most of her time looking at his file on the computer monitor.

"Dizzy . . . can't catch my breath," Silas mumbled.

"Probably just too much hard work in the hot sun." Wren's voice was brisk. "I'll need to take your blood pressure and listen to your heart."

Annie's worry grew. She knew Silas well enough to sense something was off.

"Your blood pressure is high," Wren said. "Higher than last time you were in. I'll prescribe you something to manage it. And you need to listen to your body. Pace yourself when the weather is this hot."

"But . . . my chest . . ." Silas's voice was faint.

Annie's heart raced. "I'll go get Dok." This wasn't just sunstroke.

"No need to bother her." Wren didn't even glance up as she wrote on the prescription pad. "Annie, the pharm rep left some samples of lisinopril. If you'll get them for me, we can get Silas feeling better right now."

Annie darted out of the room and went straight to Dok's office, bursting right in. "We need you."

Dok's face tightened with concern. "I'll call you back." She hung up the phone.

Annie followed as Dok entered the exam room. Wren was writing a prescription, her back to Mr. Eicher.

"Wren, what's the situation?" Dok said, her voice calm but firm. She moved closer to Silas, her eyes scanning him quickly.

"It's just a case of high blood pressure. I'm prescribing him medication."

"Chest . . . feels tight . . . can't breathe," Silas gasped. He was grasping his left arm.

"This is more than high blood pressure. He's showing signs of a heart attack." Dok acted swiftly, her voice taking on an authoritative edge. "Annie, call 911. Now. Then bring me aspirin."

Wren froze, her pen hovering over the prescription pad. "But he . . . but I . . . I didn't realize . . ."

In a flash, Annie was in Dok's office to call 911, then to the medicine cabinet and back to the exam room. But in that brief time, Silas had gone into full cardiac arrest. He was flat on his back on the exam table and Dok hovered over him, doing CPR. "Annie," she said, somehow knowing she'd come back into the room, "get the defib."

Annie ran to the hallway and brought back the defibrillator. She set it up in record time and handed the paddles to Dok.

Dok checked the defib monitor. "Stand back."

Annie took a step back, watching for a sign of life returning to Silas. His face was losing color. Three quick shocks, one right after the other, and then Dok was back to CPR.

Annie held her breath, silently praying for him. Ten seconds, thirty seconds, fifty seconds—

"I got it!" Wren's fingers were on Silas's wrist. "I feel a pulse!"

The sound of approaching sirens filled the air and in walked Gus and his paramedic partner. He was all business, hardly acknowledging Annie other than a slight wiggling of his eyebrows. Gus prepared the gurney as Dok provided some staccato-style information about Silas's condition, making sure they knew everything. They whisked Silas on the gurney through the office, past the waiting room full of wide-eyed patients, and out the door into the ambulance. Dok and Annie followed until the doors closed and the ambulance left for the hospital.

The waiting room full of patients was completely silent, watching the scene.

"DOK! Is SILAS gonna MAKE it?" Hank Lapp said. Annie didn't even know when Hank had come in.

Dok turned and pointed at Hank. "Say a prayer for him." She headed back to the exam room but stopped for a quick second. "Annie, come with me." They went into the exam room, where Wren sat ashen faced in a chair. Dok closed the door.

"He had a pulse," Wren said, as if that fixed everything.

Dok nodded. "A weak one. Why did you miss the signs of a heart attack, Wren? Annie spotted them. I saw them as soon I walked into the room."

"Because . . ." Wren sounded flustered. "Silas Eicher has a history of high blood pressure. That was the most logical assumption. Go first to the chart and see a patient's history. That's what I've been taught—"

Dok lifted a hand in the air to stop Wren. She turned to Annie. "Why do you think Wren missed Silas Eicher's heart attack?"

Annie swallowed. Suddenly, she was five years old again, with a doctor asking her to contradict her mother's imagined symptoms. She didn't like being put in that spot then and she didn't like it now.

Dok knew that. "Annie," she said, her voice softening a bit. "This is about helping Wren to be a better doctor."

Annie cleared her throat but kept her eyes fixed on the tops of her shoes. "Wren doesn't really . . ."

When her pause went on too long, Dok said, "Doesn't really what, Annie?"

"She doesn't really look at the patients."

"I do too!"

Dok let out a sigh. "Wren, you have to *see* the patient. Really see them. That's why I believe so strongly in making house calls. I learn more from going into someone's house than I ever could in a twenty-minute appointment in the office."

Wren's eyebrows knit together. "House calls are an incredibly inefficient use of time. Not to mention that half of your patients don't have access to the internet. There's no data on them. Data is what you need to make an accurate diagnosis."

"Medicine is more than data. More than statistics."

"That's not what I've been taught in med school."

Annie's head went from one to the other, like she was watching a tennis match. The tension in the room might have been invisible, but it was thick.

Dok lifted her eyebrows. "And that's the whole reason why medical students are required to have residencies. This is the time to gain experience and learn to rely on more than numbers to tell you what you need to accurately diagnose a patient."

Wren's face was a mixture of determination, defiance, and just a hint of guilt. "Then maybe I need a bona fide residency." She rose and left the room.

Dok exchanged an exasperated look with Annie. "I'll go call Silas's son and let him know what's happened."

Annie cleaned up the exam room to prepare it for the next patient. By the time she returned to her desk, she noticed the door had been left open.

"If you're LOOKING for that lady doctor with the BIRD name," Hank Lapp said, "she's GONE."

Before Annie closed the door, she swept a gaze over the parking lot.

Had Wren left the office? Or the practice?

23

Evie wasn't sure what to expect from Wren when she returned to Windmill Farm that afternoon. Dok had sent Charlie and Evie out to deliver insulin to a patient when, according to Hank Lapp, Wren had stormed out of the office in a snit.

Not a huge surprise. All day, Wren had acted like her knickers were in a twist.

As Evie walked into the farmhouse, she was surprised to be met with utter silence. She found a note from Fern on the kitchen table: *Forgot to tell you. Helping out at a Haystack fundraiser this evening for a family whose baby is in the hospital. Leftovers in the fridge.*

Evie had been around the Plain people long enough to know that a Haystack was a favorite meal. It was really just a pile of toppings—kind of like nachos, or french fries with everything you could think of heaped on top.

"Wren? Are you upstairs?"

When there was no answer, Evie assumed Wren was over at the buggy shop, complaining to Charlie about Dok, about the residency, about the Amish, about Evie. Since she had the house to herself, she decided to take a shower and wash her hair.

She climbed the stairs, a satisfied smile tugging at her lips as she thought about how the visit to Dan Hostetler's house had wrapped up. She hadn't been particularly happy to have been paired with Charlie for the insulin delivery to Dan—but it was nice to get out of the office and even nicer to get away from Wren.

Just a week ago, Evie would've been jumping for joy to be alone with Charlie. Not today. The drive to Dan Hostetler's had been quiet. She and Charlie were cordial, but the warmth and companionship they'd shared was gone. Evie just couldn't pretend that everything was okay between them when it wasn't, and although Charlie did sense things had changed, he didn't seem to have a clue why.

Despite *that* undercurrent, it ended up being one of those visits where everything just clicked. Dan Hostetler needed a lot more help than he'd let on to Dok—the screws on his crutches kept loosening and he'd just been using one to hop around the house. Charlie was able to fix his crutches and then give Dan some tips on how to get around on them. Turned out that Charlie had broken his ankle in high school playing football, and as soon as it healed, he promptly broke the other playing basketball—so he'd had a full school year on crutches and considered himself something of an expert.

Evie showed Dan how to better monitor his blood sugar levels, as the diabetes diagnosis was a recent one. She explained diabetes to him in a way that he hadn't previously understood, and she could see the tension ease from his shoulders. They shared a cup of tea afterward, talked about Dan's huge flower garden, and by the time Evie and Charlie left, it felt more like a visit with an old friend than a house call. The ride back to the office felt like a completely different experience than the trip out to Dan Hostetler's. Most of it, anyway.

"That went well," she said as she buckled her seat belt. "I didn't realize how much I've missed going on house calls with Dok."

"Pretty cool," Charlie said. "Are they all like that?"

"Yes. Different, but the same. It's why I love being a rural nurse. You get to really connect with people, be there when they need more than medical treatment. A lot of people need someone to listen and make them feel cared for."

Charlie slowed at a red light and turned to her. "So why would you want to leave Dok's practice?"

Ugh. She'd forgotten she was supposed to be giving Charlie the silent treatment.

"Dok wants you to stay. Annie does. Fern does." He faced the windshield again, clearing his throat. "I do."

Evie stared out the window. "Wren doesn't."

Charlie shot her a sharp look. "Wren? What does she have to do with anything?"

Everything! Evie wanted to shout. *You've let her mold you, shape you, claim you, and plan your whole life.*

But she didn't say any of that. What would be the point?

"Evie, I know Wren can be . . . a little much. But you shouldn't let her get to you. You shouldn't let her boss you around."

Evie let out a deep, long sigh . . . meant to convey that she considered that remark to be the pot calling the kettle black. Even his man bun was Wren's doing.

Charlie probably didn't pick up on what the sigh was meant to say, but he did seem to catch on that she wasn't interested in talking about Wren or about anything else. The rest of the ride to the office was in silence.

Oh well.

In the bathroom, Evie started the tap on the shower to give the water time to get hot. Fern's water took a long time to warm up, so while she waited, she went to the bedroom to get a fresh set of clothes. As she opened the bedroom door, she stopped. Something seemed funny.

All Wren's clothes were off the wall pegs. Her shoes, usually lined up meticulously along the wall, were gone.

Evie went to the bathroom and pulled open drawers. Everything of Wren's was gone. All her makeup, hair products, combs and brushes, soaps and shampoo.

A cold sense of urgency seized Evie. She turned off the shower faucet, hurried back down the stairs, almost tripping in her haste, and dashed out the door toward the buggy shop. The door was wide open, and even before she got within a few yards of it, she could hear Wren's voice, loud, raised in anger.

"We had a deal, Charlie. Before we got here, we made a deal. I only came because you agreed to that. You promised me."

Evie froze just outside the door, her breath catching in her throat. Wait. Was Wren leaving? Was Charlie?

"So it didn't go the way you wanted, Wren." Charlie's voice was calm, but Evie could hear the frustration beneath the surface. "That doesn't mean you just up and leave."

"There's no reason to stay any longer."

"There's every reason. You've got an opportunity to work with an outstanding doctor. What more could you want?"

"So much more . . . than *this*!"

This. Evie knew Wren well enough by now to know what *this* meant to her. A stinky farm, a run-down buggy shop, a rural doctor who encouraged her patients to try what Wren considered whacky, nontraditional remedies.

Charlie's voice had an edge to it, one that Evie hadn't heard before. "Then . . . just go back and get it."

"Without you?"

"That's right. Go without me."

A long pause. "What about us? What about our plans?"

"Those are your plans, Wren. They've always been yours." Charlie sounded firm. "I'm not leaving."

"Well, *she's* leaving."

"Maybe. Maybe not."

"Charlie, be serious." Wren's tone shifted, the anger slipping away, replaced by a tinge of panic. "You can't make it on your own. You never could. I'm the only reason you got through college and med school. You've got the boards staring you in the face and you've barely started to study! You'll never pass them without my help."

"Quite possibly right. But I'm willing to try. I'm not leaving, Wren."

"Well," Wren said, her voice tight with emotion, "I'm not staying."

"Look, I want you to stay. But if you need to leave, then leave. I think you're making a terrible mistake by going."

There was a tense silence, followed by the sound of something being moved inside. Suddenly, Wren stormed through the door, suitcase in tow. She stopped short when she saw Evie standing there. "Oh, for Pete's sake. You're eavesdropping again."

Eavesdropping was turning into a terrible habit for Evie, but it was not without its benefits. Hearing what she heard, she stood taller, as if it would make her feel braver. "Wren, don't leave."

Wren's eyes blazed with a mix of hurt and fury. "Give me one good reason why I shouldn't go."

"There's only one good reason. Dok Stoltzfus can make you a better doctor."

Wren took a step close to her, until their faces were inches apart. "I don't need Dr. Stoltzfus's help to make me a better doctor. I don't need anyone's help."

Before Evie could even think of how to respond, Charlie joined them at the door. "Man, Wren. You're always pushing good people away. When will that ever change? When are you going to figure it out?"

Wren turned on him, her expression a mix of defiance and something deeper, something raw. "What does that mean?"

"That you need people," Charlie said, his voice quieter now.

Evie could see Wren was taken aback by his words. There

was a flicker of something—doubt, maybe—but it was gone as quickly as it appeared. A honk from the road shattered the moment. Wren's Uber had arrived. She glanced between Evie and Charlie, her face hardening again, before letting out a huff of frustration, turning, and heading toward the waiting car.

Charlie and Evie stood side by side, watching Wren climb into the car. The engine hummed to life, and without a glance back, Wren was down the road, the dust trailing behind her. They watched until the car disappeared around the bend in the road.

"I thought coming here would be good for Wren," Charlie said quietly. "But it didn't work out the way I'd hoped."

A week ago, Evie would've been dying to know what exactly he had hoped for. But now, she wasn't so sure she wanted the answer. Knowing would only add salt to a wound she was trying to let heal. Best to leave it alone.

Charlie turned to Evie, like he wanted to say something. His lips parted, his brow furrowed, but after a moment's hesitation, he closed his mouth and turned back toward the buggy shop.

Evie watched him go, wondering if he might decide to leave Stoney Ridge to join Wren, wherever she'd gone. Just days ago, such a thought would've left her in pieces. But now? She didn't feel as bereft as she would have thought. Things like love, she was starting to learn, might be better left in God's hands.

Maybe that was the strange thing about her newfound faith. It wasn't some earth-shattering, part-the-seas kind of transformation, but it was there, steady and sure. She didn't feel as lost as she once had. Even if Charlie did choose to leave, she'd be okay. And that was saying something. She had spent the last two years thinking he was her everything, but people weren't meant to fill those kinds of gaps.

Evie turned and headed toward the farmhouse. She would be lying if she didn't feel some relief at Wren's sudden departure.

But she felt a sadness too. For Wren's sake. She might be brilliant, but she'd never be half the doctor that Dok was.

It was getting late. The last patient, a blacksmith with a nasty gash on his arm, had just left after Dok finished sewing him up. Annie had stayed to help Dok and was tidying up the room, moving quickly but methodically as she put the supplies back in order.

Dok heard the front door creak open. She frowned, certain she'd locked it after the farmer left. Had she forgotten? Wiping her hands on a towel, she headed to the front of the office. Then she stopped abruptly.

Wren Baker stood at the open door with a woman at her side. Dok had to blink a few times as she realized the woman was Clara Zook, looking completely disoriented. Her tangled hair fell long, she wore no prayer cap, her dress was filthy, and she was barefoot.

"I found Clara walking down the highway," Wren said. "She needs help."

Dok snapped into action. "Where are her babies?"

Wren gasped. "I . . . didn't think to ask. I forgot she had babies. They weren't with her."

Dok's pulse quickened. "Clara, where are your babies?" she asked, stepping closer, trying to keep her voice steady.

Clara's eyes darted around the room but didn't settle on anything. "It's better this way," she said, over and over.

"She keeps repeating that," Wren said. "Nothing else."

Dok turned to Annie, who stood at the doorway, eyes wide. "Annie, call Matt. Tell him to get to Jacob Zook's and do a welfare check on the babies. Tell him it's an emergency. Then go to the Bent N' Dent and find David. Bring him here."

Annie nodded, concern in her eyes, then hurried off.

Wren, still supporting Clara, looked at Dok. "How can I help?"

"Let's get Clara into an exam room."

They guided Clara into the room, where Dok quickly checked her vitals. Each reading was troubling—dilated pupils, a rapid heart rate, and high blood pressure. Clara couldn't follow even the simplest direction. Couldn't make eye contact with Dok. She seemed to be in her own world.

"Clara, your babies need you," Dok said softly, trying to reach her. "Tell us where they are, and we'll go get them."

"It's better this way," Clara mumbled.

Dok felt a chill run down her spine. "What's better, Clara? What's happened?"

But Clara had no answer.

Dok turned to Wren, noticing how pale she looked. Frightened. "Tell me exactly where you found Clara."

"I was in an Uber, and the driver noticed someone far up on the road. A woman was wandering right into the lane, kind of staggering, like she'd had too much to drink. The driver slowed down, and that was when I realized who the woman was. It took both of us, the driver and me, to get her into the car. Then he drove straight here so I could bring her to you."

"But where exactly were you? Do you remember anything specific about the road? Any signage?"

Wren pushed a lock of hair behind her ear, a nervous gesture. "Um, about four or five miles from here. On that two lane road that leads to Route 30. Not far from . . . a covered bridge."

"Did Clara say anything about the babies? Anything at all?"

"No. She just kept repeating that it was better this way."

"Did she have anything else with her?"

"No."

Dok lifted Clara's foot. Amish women went barefoot often, especially in the summer, so they had thickly calloused feet.

Clara's heels were bleeding, which told Dok that she'd been walking a long time on hot asphalt.

Wren noticed. "I let the Uber driver go. But maybe I should try to go back to where I found Clara and look around?"

"Let's wait for Matt's call. I'm hoping the babies are with Jacob."

Oh, she prayed so. The room felt heavy with questions that only Clara held the answers to, and Dok could sense she was slipping out of reach.

⁂

Waiting, waiting, waiting. Es is aryets en Schraub los. *There is something wrong.* Annie could feel it in her bones.

A half hour had passed since Matt had called in to say that Jacob Zook didn't know where the babies were, didn't even know Clara had left, and that they were now searching the house and farm. The Bent N' Dent had closed for the day, so Annie had left a phone message for David Stoltzfus at his shanty, but she wasn't sure when he'd check messages. She jumped from her desk chair when she heard something and looked out the office window to see a police car pulling into the parking lot. "Dok! Matt's here."

Dok hurried to the front room as Matt and Jacob reached the door. "Jacob wants to talk to Clara," Matt said. "He's sure she will tell him where she put the babies."

"Oh Matt," Dok said, "I don't think that's a good idea."

"Wu is sie?" Jacob said, his voice rough. *Where is she?*

From the stern look on his face, Dok couldn't tell if he was frightened or furious. "Slow down, Jacob. Clara's not in any condition to answer questions, especially if you bark at her."

"She's right," Matt said. "Jacob—"

"I will talk to my wife."

Jacob marched back to the exam room and threw open the door. Dok, Matt, and Annie followed closely behind. Wren sat on a stool, her face showing surprise, while Clara quickly jumped off the table, pressing herself against the far wall with her head down, cowering.

"Clara, was fehlt dir denn?" *What's the matter with you?* "Wo sind die Boppli?" *Where are the babies?*

Annie watched as Jacob's harsh voice made Clara shrink into herself, even more withdrawn than before. She didn't respond to his questions, didn't even look at him.

Jacob looked at Dok and Matt. "Sie is en schtarrkeppicher Mensch." *She is a stubborn person.*

No she's not, Annie wanted to shout. *She's broken. Can't you see? She's broken!*

Matt, in a remarkably calm voice, broke the tense silence. "Jacob, maybe it'll help Clara remember if we go over everything again. You said you last saw Clara in the house when you went in for lunch. Were the babies there?"

Jacob shook his head, his beard trembling with the motion. "I don't remember seeing them. They were probably asleep."

"But did you actually see them?" Matt kept his voice low and steady.

Jacob's frown deepened. "I already told you, they were probably asleep." His tone was defensive, clearly agitated.

Matt kept his composure. "What time was that?"

"Two or three o'clock," Jacob said, glancing away. "Then I went back to the field to finish work."

Just then, Matt's phone rang, cutting through the tense atmosphere. He answered quickly and went into the hallway, his voice low and focused. The room fell silent, everyone waiting anxiously. When Matt ended the call, he came back in the room with a serious expression. "I left two officers at the farm to search it. Still no sign of the babies."

Matt resumed questioning Jacob, continuing to piece together the details like a jigsaw puzzle, trying to clarify the timeline.

Jacob, clearly exasperated, snapped at Clara. "Was fehlt dir denn?" *What's wrong with you?*

Clara didn't flinch, didn't meet Jacob's eyes, and seemed to be in her own world, disconnected from the situation.

Was fehlt ihr denn? Annie thought. *What's wrong with her?* Bist du, Jacob. *It's you.*

Wren's voice cut through the heavy silence. "Clara's dress is dry now," she said, "but it was wet and muddy when I found her. I remember that it smelled funny."

Matt's eyes shot to Dok's. "There's a creek that runs along the county road. I'll have the canine unit head out there right away." He glanced at the bundle of baby blankets he had brought with him, his expression grim. "Wren, why don't you come with me and show me exactly where you found her?"

Wren practically jumped from the stool. "I'm ready."

"I'm coming too," Jacob said.

"Okay," Matt said. "Okay, let's go. We've only got a few hours of daylight left. Ruth, why don't you and Annie send out phone messages for neighbors to start a search for Clara's babies. Everyone aged ten and up. They should begin at the Zook farm and spread out from there, in teams of two. Tell them to be quiet as they search so they can listen for the babies' cries. We'll start at the place where Wren found Clara on the road and work backwards. Let's make your office the control center for information."

As soon as the door shut behind them, Dok turned to Annie. "I'm taking Clara to Mountain Vista. I called in while I was waiting for Matt, so they're expecting us. Annie, would you mind staying here to wait for word? Make some calls to start a search?"

"Of course I don't mind." Annie watched them leave. She was right back to waiting. But how could she leave? Es is aryets en schrecklich Schraub los. *Something is terribly wrong.*

24

Word traveled fast through the Amish community of Stoney Ridge about Clara Zook's missing babies. They'd come to the Zook farm by buggy, on horseback, on scooters, all in record time. A dozen had already arrived, and more were on their way: men, women, teens, older children, all with faces drawn tight with concern. In the shade of the Zook barn, Evie swatted a mosquito off her arm and glanced sideways at Charlie, who was staring blankly at David Stoltzfus as he gave out instructions in Penn Dutch to the gathered neighbors.

"I'm not catching a single word of this," Charlie whispered, his brows knitting together.

Evie stifled a smile. "David says to head out in teams of two, to fan out from the farm and head toward the county road where Clara was found. If we see any sign of the babies—a blanket, a bootie, anything at all—get word to Dok's office right away. And to try and stay quiet to hear the sounds of babies crying."

David had looked directly at Hank Lapp as he said that. Hank then shouted out something that was on everyone's mind: "How LONG can those babies LAST without MILK or WATER? That is . . . assuming they're STILL alive."

Everyone froze at that. All eyes were on David, as his troubled look deepened. "The next few hours are critical," he said, his voice heavy with worry.

Teams of two fanned out over the farm, so Charlie and Evie headed to the road, flashlights in hand. The heat of the summer evening wrapped around them like a heavy blanket, and the humidity wasn't helping. "Evie, how do you know Penn Dutch?"

"My grandparents were Mennonites. They spoke to each other in Penn Dutch. To me, they spoke in English. But I picked it up. You'd be surprised how much you can absorb when you're listening to enough conversations." It dawned on her, just now, where the habit of eavesdropping had started for her. And that she'd had that habit most of her life. *Bleh!*

Charlie sounded impressed. "I can barely handle one language, let alone two."

Evie didn't respond, her attention turning back to the search. She tripped over something in the road, and he reached out to steady her.

"Careful," he said. "With the sun setting, it's starting to get dark."

Under the thick canopy of tree limbs, it was already hard to see. He flicked her flashlight on and handed it to her. "Charlie, what if . . ."

"What if we find the babies and return them, safe and sound, to their parents?"

Right. That was a much better frame of mind to have.

"Let's keep going."

His flashlight cut a path through the shadows. The sky had darkened, but there was still enough light to see the outlines of trees and fences, creeks and crevices. Evie and Charlie trudged along, their flashlights sweeping over the ground as they moved, listening carefully to the sounds of the night.

One hour passed, then another. The rising moon cast an eerie glow over the fields, and the soft sound of horses' hooves clopping along the road carried through the warm, still air. Flashlights flickered and lanterns bobbed in the darkness, as people searched and searched, some on horseback, some on foot, some on scooter. Despite the urgency, the night had an almost surreal calm to it.

Evie and Charlie had been walking in near silence, ears straining for any sound that might lead them to the babies. Finally, Evie spoke, almost without thinking. "It's kind of a big deal that Wren's the one who found Clara and brought her in, isn't it?" She wasn't sure why she'd said it—fatigue, maybe. The thought just slipped out before she could stop it.

He glanced at her. "It is. A really big deal. Wren can be bullheaded, but she comes around. I know she can rub people the wrong way, but she's got a good heart."

Did she really? Evie wasn't so sure. Especially now. "While everyone was waiting for the bishop to arrive, I overheard Hank Lapp say something about a lawsuit that Wren's involved in." *Bleh!* Evie was mortified to realize how *much* she eavesdropped. All the time. But she learned so much! And Hank spoke in a shout. It wasn't hard to overhear him as he explained to the people standing around him about Wren's grandmother and the other two Amish women, all suffering terribly from postparty syndrome (Hank's words) and the clinical trial with Dok's predecessor. Evie's stomach had twisted when she heard Hank describe the lawsuit against the pharmaceutical company.

"Yeah. Didn't work out the way she wanted it to."

Evie wanted to know more, a lot more, but now wasn't the time.

Charlie let out a sigh. "Evie, after this is all over, we need to have a long talk."

So Charlie was aware of the lawsuit. Maybe . . . he was in

on it with her? Is that why they both came to Stoney Ridge in the first place?

Even in the heat, Evie felt a chill run through her.

Conniving Charlie.

Wily Wren.

Worse. Evincible Evie.

They turned down a dirt lane, listening for sounds of crying infants. Other than owls hooting to each other in the treetops, they heard nothing. At the end of the lane they turned around to head back to the road.

Exhaustion was starting to set in. But they couldn't stop. Not yet.

After another hour of searching, not far from Dok's office, Charlie suggested they head over to see if there was any news.

As they rounded the corner and approached the office, the sun was just beginning to cast a soft, golden light over the scene. How late was it? Evie couldn't believe it. They'd been searching all night long. No wonder she felt exhausted.

Some Amish women had set up card tables out in front of Dok's office, handing out coffee and food to the searchers. As Charlie and Evie walked toward them, they spotted Dok standing near Matt at his police car and went straight to them.

"Any news?" Charlie said.

"Not yet," Matt said.

Evie searched Dok's face for something positive, but she saw only exhaustion and worry. "Did Clara remember anything?"

"No," Dok said, shaking her head. "Mountain Vista promised to call if there's anything to report."

"As searchers come in," Matt said, "ask them if they can think of any place Clara might have spoken about. Maybe a favorite spot?"

Evie saw Charlie freeze, his expression shifting as if a puzzle piece had just clicked into place. "Wait," he said slowly, a look of realization dawning on his face. "When Evie and I had Clara as a patient, she mentioned a place she found to rest in. Someplace cool and dark and quiet."

Evie's eyes widened. "Do you think . . . ?"

"Yeah." Charlie nodded. "I wonder if she might have left the babies there."

Matt was already moving toward Jacob. "Get over here!" Jacob had been sitting on the porch steps of the Bent N' Dent, head in his hands. His head popped up and he hurried over.

"Charlie, tell Jacob what you just told me."

Charlie repeated it, and a funny look came over Jacob. "All I can think," Jacob said, "is . . . maybe the old root cellar?"

Matt didn't waste a second. "Let's go check it out. Jacob, you come with me." He opened the door to his car and Jacob got in the passenger side.

"Wait for me!" Charlie bolted over to Dok's office.

Evie wanted to go too. She hopped in the back of the police car, and at the last minute, Charlie jumped in with a medical bag on his lap.

When they arrived at the Zook farm, the sun had risen. Jacob led them to an overgrown area that hid the old root cellar. It was covered with old boards and brush, easy to overlook. Jacob easily yanked the boards away, revealing an entrance. Evie's breath caught in her throat as she heard a feeble cry. She and Charlie bolted down into the dark root cellar, each one grabbing a baby and getting back up into the daylight. The babies' skin was pale, lips dry, eyes a little sallow. Charlie ran his hand over each baby's fontanelle, to see if it had sunk.

"Will they live?" Jacob said. "Will they? Tell me!"

"They're dehydrated and weak, cold and hungry," Charlie said.

"Noch lewendich," Evie added.

Jacob stared at her, and then a sob erupted uncontrollably out of him, first one, then another, his shoulders shaking with each gasp of air.

Charlie and Evie quickly set up IVs, working together with precision. As the fluids began to flow into the babies, Evie felt a wave of relief wash over her. Clara, even in her disoriented state, had known enough to protect her children. She had placed them somewhere she thought was safe, even if she couldn't fully explain why.

After the ambulance arrived, Charlie and Evie stepped back to let the paramedics handle the babies, to take them to the hospital for evaluation. Jacob climbed in the ambulance to go along with them.

Watching, Charlie put his hand on Evie's elbow. "What was it you said to Jacob?"

"I told him they're still alive." The babies were safe.

25

A different Wren Baker sat across from Dok than the one who had stormed out of this office just yesterday. The rigid tension was gone, replaced by something quieter, almost humble. Dok observed her closely, noticing the dark circles under her eyes and how she seemed smaller, as if the weight of her experience had physically diminished her.

Wren kept her gaze fixed on the floor, unable to meet Dok's eyes. "Is Clara going to be all right?"

"In time, I think," Dok said. "She's been diagnosed with severe postpartum depression. I knew she was struggling, but I didn't realize how bad it was. None of us did. She wouldn't ask for help, wouldn't accept it. But you saw how unstable she was, how disoriented."

"Clara came in just two days ago. Annie was out on her lunch break, and I was the only one here. She asked to see you, but she didn't have an appointment, and the afternoon was fully booked." Wren's voice trembled. "And her babies were screaming . . ." She cupped her hands over her face, her voice breaking. "I sent her away. I meant to tell you, I really did. But the day got so busy . . . and I just forgot."

Dok was hardly one to point a finger of blame. She understood. She'd done it herself. She'd meant to check up on Clara and hadn't gotten to it. And then she slipped through the cracks. "Wren, this is what acute PPD looks like up close. It's a very serious condition. Very unstable. Very dangerous. You can understand now why women would seek help."

Wren nodded slowly. "I never realized . . . I mean, I knew my grandmother struggled, but seeing Clara like that . . ." Her voice trailed off, and she took a deep breath, trying to steady herself. "So, I guess you're trying to tell me that I shouldn't join the lawsuit?"

Dok leaned forward, her gaze steady as she spoke. "Honestly, I don't really care. Whether you join the lawsuit or not—that's entirely up to you. What truly matters to me is that you start seeing your patients as whole people, not just a collection of symptoms. You have all the tools to be a good doctor, but to be a great one, you need to treat the person, not just the illness. Your patients aren't mere tasks on a to-do list. You need to be attentive to them as human beings."

For a moment, the room was silent. Then Dok spoke again, her voice filled with quiet hope. "I'd like you to stay. Finish your residency."

Wren looked up, her eyes filled with surprise. "You want me to stay?"

"Yes. I think you have enormous potential."

Wren looked down at her hands in her lap. She didn't answer for a long moment. "I appreciate your confidence in me, especially after . . . all that's happened." She lifted her head. "But I can't stay here. I need more than a rural practice. I'm going to do research this year, then apply again for another residency. I'm sorry. I just . . . I need more."

So disappointing. Dok squeezed her eyes shut for a few seconds. "Wren, what made you decide to become a doctor?"

Wren shifted slightly in her chair. "Doctors get respect. People look at them like they're . . . gods. Especially surgeons—

they literally hold someone's life in their hands. I want that kind of respect."

Oh, how badly Dok wanted to say, *That is a terrible reason to be a doctor! Where is your desire to serve others? To be an extension of God's mercy to a broken world? To have the skills to bring healing to those who are suffering, in pain or great need? Because at its core, being a doctor—any kind of doctor—is about being a caregiver.*

But instead, she tucked her hands under her legs, resisting the urge to lecture. "I have a hunch," she said calmly, "there's more to the story."

Wren took her time answering, as if she wasn't comfortable delving into personal territory. "One day my mom went on a bender. As she passed out, she hit her head. The neighbor called the police, and they took us both to the ER. I saw how everyone treated the doctors—like they could fix anything. Make anything better. That's when I knew. That's what I wanted for myself."

"How old were you?"

"I guess . . . the first time, I was five years old."

Oh, ouch. So young. "That must've been a frightening situation for you."

Wren shrugged, almost dismissive. "Actually, it happened a lot with my mom."

"Well, maybe you can use that experience to guide you."

Wren squinted. "How so?"

"Each time you interact with a patient, remember how it felt to be that five-year-old girl."

"Why would I do that?"

"To deepen your compassion for others." Dok let that settle in.

Wren stood up, hesitating for a moment before extending her hand. "Thank you, for everything."

Dok reached out and took her hand, giving it a gentle squeeze. "Take care of yourself, Wren."

With a final nod, Wren turned and walked out of the office. Dok jumped up and ran to meet her before she reached the front door.

"Wren! One more thing."

Wren turned and waited.

"I want to leave you with some hard-earned advice. It took me years and years to get this right."

"I'm listening."

"Ambition can be a leaky bucket."

Wren tipped her head. "What do you mean?"

"You remind me a lot of myself when I was younger. Trying to prove myself to others. To myself." Dok paused, gathering her thoughts. Should she really say it? Why not? At this point, what was there to lose? She thought of the verse from Acts: *"Grant that your servants may speak your word with all confidence."*

So speak up, Ruth.

"I even had something to prove to God. I wonder if that's at the heart of what you're longing for—wanting others to respect you. It took me a long time, way too long, to realize I didn't need to prove my worth to anyone. And definitely not to God. I was loved by him, just as I was. Flaws, weaknesses, sins—my whole messy self. And that belief, that foundation, changed everything. It set the right things in motion instead of always trying to fix the damage from making the wrong choices."

She walked up to Wren and put her hands on her shoulders. "Just think on that, Wren. I hope you can learn this truth a lot sooner than I did. You are deeply loved by God, just as you are." She wrapped her arms around Wren and gave her the kind of hug she'd always longed for from her own mother. When she released her, there was a shiny gleam in Wren's eyes.

But she still left.

How did someone slip through the cracks? Especially an Amish someone. David drove the buggy home from the Bent N' Dent, the late afternoon sun casting a warm glow over the fields. The first hints of autumn were just beginning to touch the edges of the leaves, but summer still held its ground, with lush greenery all around. He hardly noticed.

As he guided the horse along the familiar path, the conversation he'd just had with his sister about Clara Zook, how she'd been struggling in silence, kept replaying in his mind. For all the flaws of the Plain People, and there were many, he'd always thought they did community so well. But, as Dok said, Clara had slipped through the cracks, and she felt as if she'd failed her. Birdy had seen how Clara was struggling. She'd asked David to speak to Jacob about it. Had he? No. He meant to, but other things crowded out that intention. He felt a sting of partial blame. Not the full blame, of course, but he had failed her too.

Still, why hadn't Clara accepted help when offered? Didn't she bear some responsibility?

Ten minutes ago, he had posed that question to Dok and could tell she was barely holding back an eye roll. "David," she had said in that older sister tone, "motherhood is revered among the Amish. It gives a woman purpose and identity. Status, even. How could someone like Clara Zook tell any Amish woman that she didn't feel love for her babies? That she could barely tolerate all the demands she was facing? That her husband didn't lift a finger to help her? Of course she couldn't ask for help. She's been paralyzed in shame."

Shame. He'd been bumping into that a lot lately.

As a bishop, David was well aware of the undercurrents of struggle in his congregation. There was one man he suspected had a drinking problem, another with a fierce temper that his family bore the brunt of. And then there was the farmer who kept a stack of *Playboy* magazines hidden in his barn. When the deacon confronted him, the man denied it flat-out—until his wife pointed out the hiding place herself. Was that shame? Or pride? Probably both, David thought.

Shame mixed with pride was a dangerous combination. It was like a poison that seeped into the soul, keeping people trapped in their sins and secrets. David believed it was the Enemy's work, to keep such things buried in the dark where they couldn't be healed.

For people who eschew pride, he thought, *we can sure be a prideful bunch.*

He pulled gently on the reins, letting the horse slow to a steady pace. Dok had bounced a new idea off him—she suggested the church create a support group for first-time mothers. "We can't let anyone slip through the cracks." She volunteered her garden-level office as a place to meet. "And we need to find someone to lead it," Dok said, "who's got a knack for nurturing others."

David knew just the person. "Birdy! She'd be ideal."

"Nope." Dok had shaken her head firmly. "She's the bishop's wife. No one would say a word."

That was true. David's mantle of responsibility had a tendency to be a conversation killer.

Well, Birdy would know who to ask to lead it.

A slight lift in his spirits brightened David's mood. If the new mothers group worked out, maybe it could open the door to tackling other silent struggles, even the ones men dealt with but rarely talked about.

Noticing the horse had slowed to a crawl, David gave the reins a gentle shake. "Come on now, let's keep moving," he said. The horse picked up the pace, and they continued down the road toward home, the warm breeze rustling the leaves around them. Dok's last words to him had been to remind him to pray for Clara because she had a long road of healing in front of her.

He had put a hand on his sister's shoulder and said, "Count on it." She didn't even have to ask.

Annie sat on the bench outside the fire station, fiddling with the hem of her dress, waiting for Gus to finish his shift. When he finally appeared, his face lit up in a smile that quickly faded as he approached and saw her somber expression.

"Annie, what's wrong?"

She patted the bench. "There's something I need to tell you."

He sat down beside her. "Has something happened? Clara Zook? The babies?" He'd helped with the search last night.

"No update on Clara, but the babies are doing well."

Gus tipped his head. "What's brought you here?"

She took a deep breath. "I'm going to take the EMT exam."

"That's fantastic! I know you'll pass it with flying colors."

She looked at him, her heart melting. He was such a champion for her. She was going to miss his encouragement. She was going to miss *him*. She blew out a puff of air. This part was hard. "But I've decided to try to be a dispatcher instead of applying to work at the fire station."

His smile faded, his disappointment immediate and visible. "Annie, you've worked so hard. There are other treatments for your motion sickness. Don't give up. We can try more things."

Try more things? How could she try *any* harder?

She shook her head, her resolve firm. "No, Gus. I've tried everything that I feel comfortable trying. I won't take medication. This is what I'm going to do."

His jaw muscle flexed as he swallowed. "I know how much you've wanted to be an EMT. You've tried so hard. I'm just . . . disappointed. I was looking forward to all the experiences we would share. We'd make such a good team."

Annie felt a pang of guilt but stood her ground. "Maybe someday it'll happen," she said, though she doubted it. "But for now, this is what I'm going to do. I'm going to be a dispatcher. That is, if I get the job. It's still important work, Gus."

"I know it's important, but . . . I just imagined us out there, together. I had all these plans for us."

They sat there in silence for a long time, the weight of his disappointment hanging in the air. She could feel it, the way you could feel lightning about to strike. She hadn't realized how much of her anxiety about not being able to become an EMT had to do with disappointing him. This was it, then. Their relationship, which had never really gotten started in the way they had hoped, was ending.

Finally, he lifted his head and gave her a gentle smile, though it didn't reach his eyes. "At least," he said, "I'll get to hear your voice over the radio."

She braced herself, willing herself not to cry. *Do not cry, Annie Fisher. Do not cry.*

He reached out and took her hand. He looked down at their enjoined hands, like he was visibly gathering his next words. "There's one good thing out of this. You told me that I couldn't court you until you finished the EMT course. Well, you're done with it."

She looked at him, confused. "You still want to court me?"

"Hold on." He shifted on the bench to face her. "Were you becoming an EMT . . . for me?"

"No. Yes. Both. I wanted to be an EMT for me. But when it became pretty clear it wasn't going to work out, then I wanted to do it for you."

"Annie Fisher . . . my feelings for you wouldn't change no matter what you did." He cleared his throat. "I love you."

He loved her?

Annie didn't know what to say. She stared at him. He loved her?

"This is the part where the fellow hopes the girl might say she loves him too. If she does, that is."

She nodded, her throat too full for words.

"Is that so?" A slow smile crept over Gus's face. "Then,

maybe our courting could start . . . now?" He leaned in slowly, giving her plenty of time to pull away if she wanted to, but she didn't. His kiss was gentle and sweet, filled with the promise of new beginnings. It was their first kiss, and it was everything she had hoped it would be. Maybe even more.

Dok stood in the kitchen, leaning against the counter as she watched Matt chop vegetables for their dinner. The sizzle of onions in the pan filled the room with a comforting aroma. She took a deep breath, exhausted but antsy. So much had happened in the last twenty-four hours—Wren's first departure, Clara's collapse, the search for the babies, Wren's second departure, followed by a very good talk with David, and then another one with Annie. Her mind was spinning.

Matt scooped up the carrots and dropped them into the cast-iron fry pan with the onions, then started chopping celery. "Are you worried about Wren?"

Dok coughed a laugh. "No. Not worried. She will do just fine in life. But I am sorry she left, mostly for her sake but also for my sake. Especially now that Annie's applying for a position as a dispatcher. And I'm sure she'll get the job."

Matt glanced up, his hands still busy with the chopping. "What makes you so sure?"

Dok gave him a smug smile. "Because I've recommended her for it."

Matt put down the knife. He had a frown on his face, as if he sensed where this was headed. "So, you'll lose Annie. Wren's exited stage left. Evie's leaving soon. And you don't think much of Charlie."

"Actually, I'm starting to change my mind about Charlie. He's going to need a lot of supervision to develop his skills, but long term, I believe he could be a good doctor. I like the fact that he tries to make things better."

A smile tugged at the corner of Matt's lips. He'd always been a fan of Charlie's.

"Matt, I know you want me to find a partner. Maybe it'll be Charlie, but that's a long way off. I do want to keep working on more balance in our lives. But I want you to know that I love my life. I love my work. I love you and I love our marriage. I don't want to retire early. I'm not ready yet."

He let out a defeated sigh. "Can't you keep Evie from leaving?"

"I don't know. She seemed pretty determined to leave when I last brought it up."

"Try again. Make it happen. Because I just put a down payment on an RV."

Dok stared at him, stunned. "You put a down payment on an RV without talking to me first?"

Matt chuckled, raising his hands in a placating gesture. "It's refundable, don't worry. But I'm serious about taking time off next summer. I want us to go see all the national parks, starting with the Grand Tetons."

She let out a breath she didn't realize she was holding and smiled. "Only if we get to stay in Jenny Lake Lodge while we're there."

"Okay. But we're taking the whole summer off."

"Two weeks."

"Six weeks."

"One month, tops."

Matt grinned, reaching out to take her hand. "Deal."

She hesitated, then shook his hand firmly. "Deal. I'll work on getting Evie to stay. You work on the trip details."

Matt nodded, satisfied. "Good. Now, let's get dinner on the table. We've got a lot of planning to do. Like how we're going to cram everything into an RV for our trip to the Grand Tetons."

Dok smiled to herself. Or, she mused, how many nice hotels she could book along the way.

26

Evie, feeling restless from all that had happened, decided to take a walk around the farm and wandered up the hill toward the orchard. The sun was starting to set behind the trees, casting a warm, amber glow over the ripening apples. She noticed a few leaves started to change color. Autumn wasn't far off, and the thought brought a pang to her heart. She'd be leaving soon. As soon as that contract arrived from Alaska.

She heard a noise and spun around to see Charlie approaching, his silhouette outlined against the fading light.

"I saw you head up the hill," he said. When he reached her, he jammed his hands in his pants pockets.

"Your hair." The man bun was gone. His hair was cut short, a bit uneven in places where it tufted straight up, but it made him look entirely different. Even more handsome, if that were possible.

He ran a hand over his scalp. "Yeah. Fern's handiwork. She said there's a time for everything and it was time my hair got cut." He rocked back and forth on his sneakers, like he was nervous. "Evie, I was, uh, hoping we could have that talk."

Here it comes. The words hung in the air between them, and for a moment, Evie didn't say anything. "It's okay, Charlie. I know."

He tipped his head. "Know what?"

"I know that you're going to leave to be with Wren. You should go. You should be together."

"Why?"

"Because . . . she's helped you become the person you are. Because . . . she's brilliant and driven and can help you go farther than you could ever imagine. And mostly because"—Evie shrugged—"she's your girlfriend."

But he was frowning. "I don't have a girlfriend."

She froze. "Of course you do."

He shook his head slowly, like he couldn't imagine what she was talking about. "I don't."

"Well, Wren thinks otherwise. Everyone does. She's claimed you. For as long as I've known you, she's claimed you."

His eyes softened, and then crinkled at the edges. "She can't claim me."

"Well, she can and she did."

"That would be weird. Like, illegal in most states." He peered at her, reading her face. "Wren can't claim me because she's my cousin."

"Your cousin?" His *cousin*?! "So . . . you're not . . . a couple?"

"Not a couple. We're first cousins. We share a grandmother. The same one who took part in that clinical trial." He tipped his head, confused. "You thought we were a couple?"

"Everyone did! You were always together. Always."

"That's only because she was sure I'd mess up and flunk out of school."

Evie gave a little head shake, like she couldn't make sense of it all. "Why didn't you ever say you were cousins?"

"It was Wren's idea, back when we were trying to get into medical school. She thought we'd have a better chance getting through med school and residencies together if we kept it a secret. You know what she's like with statistics. Siblings are always separated. She figured it would be the same for cousins."

"You could have said something." He *should* have!

"Yeah. You're right."

"You've told me how Wren helped you get through school. How she was the smart one. You could've mentioned she was your *cousin*!"

He nodded. "I know . . . I even started to . . ." He was fumbling this conversation, like he didn't know how to explain himself. "But I never lied to you, Evie."

"You never told me the truth either!"

"I wanted to." Charlie shifted his weight from one foot to the other, his hands still stuffed into his pockets, a nervous gesture she'd seen him do a hundred times before. "I wanted to tell you on the train, right as we were heading to start the residency, but Wren warned me not to say anything. She thought it could jeopardize her efforts to gather information for the lawsuit if anyone knew we were related." He rubbed the back of his neck. "I have to be honest that she's always scared me a little. A lot, actually."

"Me too. She terrifies me." Evie let out a breath. She was still simmering in indignation, but its intensity was fading. But just a little. "Still, you *should* have told me."

"I didn't mean to deceive you. That was never the intention." He shook his head like he was trying to shake the words out. "To be perfectly honest, it wasn't just all about the lawsuit. You know how she's helped me get through school. I never could have made it without her help. Wren is all about staying focused. She said I'd never pass the boards or make it through the residency if I started . . . well, if I got, um, well, diverted. And I think she's probably right. I get easily distracted."

Evie's mind was spinning, trying to fit this new information into the way she'd viewed Charlie and Wren for the past two years. It was like he'd thrown a filter over a digital photo—everything looked different, but still somehow the same. So *this* was what cognitive dissonance felt like, she thought.

"As long as I'm making one confession, I'd better come clean on another." Out of his back pocket, he pulled an envelope, his expression a mixture of nervousness and resolve. Wordlessly, he handed it to her. "I hope you can forgive me."

Evie stared at it, her eyes widening as she recognized the familiar envelope—the one that should have been on its way to Alaska. "What have you done?"

"It's what I didn't do."

"Why didn't you mail it when you said you would?" she said, her brow furrowing as she searched his face for an explanation. "I saw you talking to the mailman."

Charlie shook his head slowly, his eyes not quite meeting hers. "I didn't mail it because," he said, his voice low, almost a whisper, "because I had to at least talk to you first, and then if you still wanted to go, I planned to mail it."

Evie's breath caught in her throat. She blinked, trying to process his words. "So you didn't mail my application?" Her fingers tightened around the envelope, crinkling the edges slightly.

Charlie finally looked up, his eyes filled with something vulnerable, something raw. "I want you to stay. Here. With me."

The entire orchard seemed to shrink around them, the air thick with unspoken feelings. Evie's mind raced, emotions swirling—surprise, confusion, and something else she wasn't quite ready to name. She opened her mouth to respond, but no words came out. Instead, she just stared at him, her heart pounding in her chest, feeling both touched and bothered by everything he was telling her.

Evie's hand slowly lowered, the envelope now dangling by her side as she struggled to find her voice. "Charlie . . . I don't know what to say."

"Just . . . say you'll think about staying," he said, his voice almost pleading, his eyes locking onto hers. "That's all I'm asking."

Darcy would tell her to walk away. To feel indignant. *Charlie kept things from you! He didn't even send in your application! Don't trust him!*

But Evie did trust him. She couldn't explain it to Darcy, but deep down, she knew she could trust Charlie. And the only feeling that was buzzing through her was a sudden rush of happiness that washed over her, like her insides were suddenly dancing with tiny sparks of joy. She felt giddy, almost like she might burst out laughing. To keep herself from grinning like a goofy girl, she quickly pressed her hand to her mouth.

Too late. He caught the smile in her eyes.

He took another step closer to her. "Evie, why do you think I came to Stoney Ridge in the first place?"

She clasped her hands behind her back. "Because you and Wren are trying to sue the pharmaceutical company to get your medical school debts paid off."

"No." He laughed. "Well, that *is* why Wren came." He looked straight into her eyes. "I'm here only because of you."

"Me?" *Because of me?*

"Only because of you. When you told me you were applying to Dok Stoltzfus's Stoney Ridge practice, I put in my application that very day for a residency."

"But . . . you and Wren came together . . ."

"When I decided to apply to Dok's practice, she had just learned about this lawsuit. It got her wheels turning, so she decided to come too." He looked down at his shoes, trying to figure out how to say something. "Ever since I saw you at the hospital, that very first time . . . Wren warned me. She knew."

Knew what? Knew *what*?

"It's just . . . it's hard to keep it in, you know?" he began, his voice hesitant, like he was choosing each word with care.

Keep *what* in?

"I couldn't stop thinking about you," Charlie said. "At the hospital, in between shifts, all I could think about was when I'd see you again. Then I could barely concentrate if you were anywhere near me on the floor. And when we came to Stoney Ridge and it seemed pretty clear from day one that Dok wasn't too keen on us, I volunteered to tear apart her basement just so I could add value. Just so she'd let me stick around as long as possible."

As Charlie stumbled through his words, Evie felt her heart rate pick up. Was she dreaming? Because it felt like a dream.

"When you see that someone, and it's like a part of your heart just . . . clicks into place, like a piece you didn't even know was missing—it's kind of hard to ignore."

Evie blinked, her breath catching as she tried to follow along. Was this really happening?

"I just knew that you were the one for me. The only one." He stopped and looked down at her, his eyes searching hers for any sign of understanding, of hope. "And I wondered, if there's any chance . . . that I wasn't alone in this? Like, maybe you felt the same feeling?"

Um, yes. A thousand times yes. But she held still.

He leaned forward until they were just inches apart. He looked at her like she held the key to something he'd been hoping for. He cupped her face and angled it up to his. "Like maybe, somehow, miraculously, you might love me like I love you? Even just a little?"

Without overthinking for once, she wrapped her arms behind his neck, pulled him closer, stood on her tiptoes, and kissed him. When their lips met, it was as if everything clicked into place. Charlie's arms wrapped tightly around her waist, pulling her close, and in that moment, it felt like they had finally found where they were meant to be.

Fern Lapp was right. Holding out hope for too long was one thing.

But giving up too soon was quite another.

Epilogue

Evie settled onto a picnic table bench over by the Bent N' Dent, the warm sun filtering through the trees. It was such a beautiful October day, with a lingering hint of summer's warmth. The nights were getting longer and colder, and while she usually dreaded the coming of winter—how on earth had she ever thought she could survive a winter in Alaska?—this year felt different. Instead of dread, she felt excitement about the future. It was a big change for her, and honestly, it felt good. Really, really good.

Just then, she heard a door slam and looked up to see Charlie coming out of Dok's garden-level office, thick books and notes piled under both arms. Halfway across the driveway, one of the books slipped from his hold, and as he bent down to pick it up, the others tumbled to the ground. His notebook opened wide, sending papers scattering everywhere.

As he scrambled to gather his things, Evie couldn't help but smile. *Oh, Charlie.* She loved him so much; he had so many gifts, but organization definitely wasn't one of them. It was like watching a golden retriever puppy try to catch its tail—adorably chaotic.

Regrouping, he approached the picnic table and plopped his books down in front of her. "Take two," he said, his voice light, but Evie caught the double meaning beneath the surface. Charlie's biggest fear had come true—he was part of that 2 to 4 percent of medical school graduates who didn't pass his final board exam on the first try. True to form, he promptly signed up to take them again. Dok, in her usual pragmatic way, said she wasn't worried but subtly reminded him that passing was, well, nonnegotiable. She never dangled the possibility of becoming a partner in front of him like she had with Wren. Maybe that was Dok's way of keeping the pressure low, or maybe it was her way of saying, "Prove it first, then we'll talk."

The silver lining? Dok's confidence in Charlie was steadily increasing. Evie could see it. The more he got his hands on real cases—learning treatments, understanding procedures, diagnosing injuries and diseases—the better doctor he became. It was like a switch flipped when he familiarized himself with the task at hand; everything just clicked into place.

In the meantime, Evie accepted Dok's offer to work at the practice as both nurse and office manager, taking over Annie's job—at least until Dok could find a replacement. That meant she didn't have much time to spare, but when she did, she helped Charlie prep for round two of the boards. But even she could see that traditional study methods weren't cutting it.

One day, during a lunch study session, she put down the anatomical index cards she'd made for him. "Charlie, were you ever tested for a reading disorder? Like dyslexia?"

He looked at her like the thought had never dawned on him. "No."

"No one ever suggested it?"

He shook his head. "I was always told I wasn't that smart. My high school counselor even said I shouldn't bother with college."

"What a terrible thing to say to a teenager!"

Charlie shrugged. "She wasn't trying to discourage me. She

was just trying to guide me toward a vocation. Something I'd be good at."

And yet, here he was—a doctor. A really *good* doctor. Sure, he credited Wren with getting him this far, but Evie knew it was his own sheer, white-knuckled determination that had really done it. "How did Wren help you?"

"Well, mostly, she would talk through the material with me."

"And hearing it out loud made it stick?"

"Pretty much."

Evie's mind started racing. *Brilliant.* Wren was onto something. She wondered if she'd known, or if she just stumbled on it. She crossed her arms, decisively. "Audiobooks."

"Audiobooks?"

"That's how you're going to pass these boards. I'm going to scour the internet for audio versions of the study material. And if I can't find them, I'll record them myself."

Charlie blinked. "You would do that for me?"

"Of course!"

"Why?"

"Because I believe you can be a great doctor. As good as Dok."

Charlie's eyes grew shiny. "No one has ever believed in me the way you do."

Evie raised an eyebrow, clearly curious. "What about Wren?"

"She wanted me alongside her, but I'm not sure she was ever really convinced that I could make it. Certainly not without her help." He leaned forward to give Evie a kiss on the lips. "You're something special, you know that?"

No, she wasn't. But the more time she spent with Charlie, the more she was starting to believe him.

Evie blinked back to the present, the warmth of that kiss lingering in her memory as she watched Charlie shuffle through his scattered notes. He glanced up, pushing his hair back, a little breathless but grinning. She tapped her screen, and the steady drone of the medical textbook filled the space between them. Slowly, Charlie's pen stilled, his frantic energy settling as he listened, his thoughts finding direction. When he looked at her then, gratitude softened his eyes—along with something deeper, something certain. Love.

Evie just smiled.

Six months later, Charlie took the boards again. And six weeks after that—on the very morning of his and Evie's wedding—just before picking up Wren at the train station so she could stand in as his best, um, person (next to Darcy, who was serving as Evie's maid of honor), he got the news: He'd passed.

Just like Evie always knew he would.

Discussion Questions

1. A major theme in this novel is discovering one's calling. Annie Fisher felt God's tap on the shoulder to become an EMT, and Charlie King was equally driven to become a doctor. But neither of their journeys was easy. How do you view the idea of a personal calling from God? What insights do this story offer about the challenges and rewards of following one's calling?

2. Wren Baker appears to have it all—intelligence, beauty, ambition, and plenty of self-confidence. So what is it about Evie Miller that seems to trigger such dislike from Wren?

3. Evie and Charlie both faced confidence challenges, but their reactions were very different. What do you think shaped their unique responses to feeling insecure? How did their life experiences shape the way they handled their self-doubt? And when it comes to their faith, who seemed more grounded, and why?

4. "Don't be half a Christian." What do you think Bishop David Stoltzfus meant by that statement? How did it trigger a "sea change," a transformation, for Evie when she overheard it?

5. Charlie didn't seem like the type of guy headed for a career that required so much schooling. But with Wren's support, he made it through med school, even if he barely scraped by. His teachable attitude really helped, and there were moments when his talents—outside of academics—stood out. Evie noticed those gifts early on. Dok did not. So, what kind of doctor do you think Charlie eventually became?

6. Annie has great concern about taking medication for her motion sickness. "But it starts somewhere, doesn't it?" she said. "First, it's one pill for this, then another to fix that. The only way I know how to avoid it is to not start relying on medication just so I can work." What do you think of Annie's reluctance? Do you understand where she's coming from, or do you think there's another side to the issue?

7. Darcy, Evie's best friend, may not have been front and center in the story, but her influence was clear. Just like Gus helped Annie, Darcy gave Evie the confidence to step into her own. Has a friend ever helped you become more of your best self? How did that change things for you?

8. Wren said, "True peace can only come with justice," and David responded by agreeing, but added that true

justice can only come from God. Two things, he said, can be true at the same time. What are your thoughts on David's perspective?

9. Clara Zook managed to slip through the cracks, even in a tight-knit Amish community. What are your thoughts? Do you think Clara's breakdown could have been avoided? If so, how?

10. Dok opened up to Wren about how she had once scrambled to prove her worth—even to God—before realizing she didn't have to. She was loved just as she was. Can you relate to that feeling of needing to prove yourself? How do you think that pressure affects the choices we make? And how might things shift if we believed we were already enough, already loved?

11. As the book closes, Wren's tangled choices lead her to leave Stoney Ridge. Try to imagine an ending for her. What do you think her future holds?

12. This novel challenged the idea of first impressions. Charlie proved to be a better match for Dok's practice than Wren, despite initial assumptions, and Wren's tough exterior hid a deep vulnerability. And Evie, who appeared very comfortable with religious traditions, discovered that she really had no idea what a life of faith can mean. How often are you surprised by what lies beneath the surface?

13. "Good thing God doesn't give up on us," Charlie said. Later, Evie connected his remark to 2 Timothy 2:13:

"If we are faithless, he remains faithful, for he cannot disown himself" (NIV). Reflecting on this, how have you personally experienced God's faithfulness, even in moments when you've struggled with your own faith? If this is a new thought for you, take time to marinate in it. The answers you'll find might be life changing.

*Read on for a sneak peek
at the next book in the*

NATIONAL PARK SUMMERS
series

available May 2026.

One

> May your trails be crooked, winding, lonesome, dangerous, leading to the most amazing view.
>
> Edward Abbey, environmental activist

Ranger Scout Johnson was the kind of person who loved allowing room for error. Leaving ten minutes early to beat traffic. Double-checking weather before a hike. Carrying an extra water bottle. Never letting her gas tank dip below half. Keeping a spare key hidden outside her cabin. She tried to anticipate any and all "just in case" possibilities. But *this* was something she could not have anticipated.

She stood on the rocky shore of Baker Island, arms crossed as she watched the skiff wobble its way back to the tourist boat—without her. She let out a long sigh. Any second now, Frankie would realize he'd left her behind. Surely, he'd notice.

Patience, Scout reminded herself. Frankie Franklin was barely eighteen. Chief Ranger Tim Rivers had called it a great privilege when he'd asked her to supervise him over the summer. Frankie was the son of the Deputy Director of the National Park Service, and apparently he'd had a little bit of trouble fitting in his father's shoes. "I've been at this job long enough," the chief told her, "to know a true parkie. If anyone can turn Frankie around, it's you." That vote of confidence filled her sails. She promised herself that Frankie Franklin would be the pride of the National Park Service.

One week later, she was just about ready to throw in the towel.

It didn't take long for Scout to understand why Frankie had already been "relieved of duty" from his other youth program opportunities. The Youth Conservation Corps had lasted three days with him. The Summit Stewards . . . only two. Frankie considered his seasonal work for the NPS as his summer break.

Scout squinted, wondering *what* in the world Frankie was doing out there. Here it was low tide, calm seas, yet the skiff was zigzagging so badly it looked like he was playing connect the dots with the waves. She winced. One of the tourists had suffered from seasickness on the boat ride from Bar Harbor. The lady had recovered once she walked around on Baker Island, but this skiff ride would get her stomach churning again.

If Scout was being honest, her doubts about Frankie's capabilities had started the first day he'd accompanied her on the Baker Island NPS tour. She'd wrapped up her carefully memorized script about the lighthouse and capped it off with a joke: "Now, I know y'all don't need me to say this, but it's regulation, so here goes: Don't lick the lighthouse. The paint's got lead in it."

Normally, that got a chuckle out of the tourists. After all, who would ever do such a thing? But minutes later, there was Frankie, tongue out, just inches from the lighthouse wall. A girl on the tour had dared him, he'd told Scout. A pretty girl, of course.

Today might be the worst of the Frankie days. Just thirty minutes ago, Scout had left the group to do what Frankie hadn't done. She'd told Frankie to close up the whale oil house near the lighthouse after the last person left, but halfway down the trail, she had a nagging feeling that he hadn't followed through. A couple of adorable teenage girls, Frankie's kryptonite, had been on the tour.

So she told him she'd be right back, in plenty of time for the last skiff trip. She had backtracked up the path, and sure enough, the door was banging open in the wind. Originally built to store the whale oil needed to keep the lighthouse burning—and positioned at a safe distance to prevent fires—the old brick oil house had since been transformed into a miniature museum of the island. A tiny treasure trove.

Scout stepped inside to check the window. Wide open. She sighed, frustration prickling at her. This was exactly how those priceless old photographs of Baker Island's history could be ruined. Storms had been rolling through nearly every day this June, bringing wind and rain that could seep in and destroy them. Did Frankie think of that? *No sir.*

She had exhaled a sigh of exasperation as she pressed the window sash down. Her knee bumped against the wall, and a brick shifted.

Strange.

She knelt down and jiggled the brick that had moved. To her surprise, it came loose in her hand, revealing a weathered brown envelope wrapped with a string. Her first thought was that she would need to submit a request form to maintenance to repair a loose brick. Her second thought was wondering what might be inside that brown envelope that was worth hiding.

Curiosity won over. Carefully, she brushed off dust, untied the string, and opened it up. She found some papers, fragile but intact, and unfolded them. A yellowed newspaper clipping fell to the ground. She picked it up and read the headline.

Tragedy at Sea: USS North Atlantic Wrecked off Maine Coast—Dozens Feared Lost.

Then her gaze slid to a handwritten note on the top of the clipping.

I did it.

Her pulse quickened. Her eyes went back and forth between the headline on the newspaper and the . . . what could it be? A confession, that's what. It sent a chill from head to toe, and she folded up the papers and tucked them back into the brown envelope, tying it hastily with the string. This was the property of the National Park Service, and she shouldn't be reading it.

But someone should know about it.

She stuffed the envelope into her jacket and zipped it up, then ran down the path to the beach.

And that's where she was now, waiting for Frankie to notice her absence. She squinted again and saw the skiff was tied to the tourist boat as the last group loaded onto it.

Scout waved and waved but no one waved back. She tried her walkie-talkie, but there was no response, which meant Frankie had it turned off. More likely, he'd never turned it on. He said he didn't like it. Too much static.

Surely the tourist boat skipper would realize she had gone missing. Surely he had the good sense to do a head count before leaving for Bar Harbor. Frankie certainly didn't. She had to remind herself that it was a privilege to be given responsibility to shape the character of Frankie, the deputy director's son. It came with the honor of serving the NPS. And Acadia truly was worth it.

Sometimes Scout could hardly believe she was here. This park had always been her goal. Four years patching together seasonal ranger work—summers in one park, winters in another—she'd been working her way sideways, climbing the ladder one park at a time. Landing a permanent status position at a heavily trafficked park like Yellowstone or Yosemite or Acadia was the NPS equivalent of winning the lottery. Each year, Scout had applied to openings in Acadia. So far, her postings had been Petrified Forest in Arizona, Voyageurs in Minnesota, Badlands in South Dakota. Each one special in its way but under-the-radar national parks. That's how things rolled in the NPS.

Then, this year: Acadia National Park. Interpretive ranger. Permanent status. A dream come true! When the email came through, she stared at it for a solid minute, convinced it was sent to her in error. Interps were the most competitive, most sought-after jobs in the NPS. Someone, somewhere, must've said a prayer for her—though definitely not her mother. Mother's prayers were laser-focused on getting her back to Atlanta to meet a Southern boy and "settle down."

No thank you, ma'am.

Scout had never wanted the kind of Southern debutante life that her mother wanted for her. Not her style. It was a constant rub of friction with Mother—one of the reasons Scout kept her applications strictly outside the South. Not Great Smoky, not Shenandoah, definitely not the Everglades. Way too close to Mother's reach.

Scout had been given a love of the great outdoors from her gone-missing father. He's the one who gave her the nickname Scout, a blessed escape from the cringeworthy name her mother had chosen: Magnolia Pearl. *Lord, help me, just no.*

Shielding her eyes from the summer sun, Scout let out a long sigh and plopped onto a smooth granite boulder, its surface warm from the afternoon sun. The rhythmic sound of the tide filled the quiet, interrupted only by the distant cries of gulls. She squinted out at the skiff, still tied to the tourist boat. "Take your time, Frankie," she said aloud to no one. "No rush or anything."

Around Scout, the beach was a patchwork of stone, slick with seaweed and glistening with brine. A soft breeze carried the scent of salt and spruce from the island's edge. Seagulls soared past her. She hardly noticed. The envelope inside her jacket kept poking and prodding—like it was downright begging to be read more thoroughly.

She unzipped her jacket and pulled it free, cradling it in both hands. She really shouldn't open it—it was like snooping through someone's diary, and Scout wasn't raised to be that kind of nosy.

Her fingers drummed against the paper.

But then again . . . one quick skim couldn't hurt, right?

Ten or fifteen minutes later, her heart racing and her brain spinning, someone yelled her name, snapping her out of the pages.

"Scout!" Frankie stood in the beached skiff, hands on his hips. "Where'd you go?"

Quickly, she retied the string around the envelope as Frankie jumped from the skiff and stalked toward her.

"What have you got there?" Frankie's gaze dropped to the envelope.

"Nothing." She tucked the envelope under her arm and stood, brushing sand off her uniform. Before she could stop him, he grabbed it.

He flipped it open, and the newspaper clipping fluttered out. He grabbed it before it hit the ground. His eyes went wide as he read it. "Whoa. Whoa. Whoa."

"Frankie, give it back."

Naturally, he ignored her and started to read the papers. His mouth fell to the ground. "This is epic!"

She put a hand on his wrist and squeezed, then carefully took the papers out of that hand and tucked them back into the envelope, then tied it with the string. "Let's go. We're late. You're late."

"Where'd you find it?"

"Behind a loose brick in the wall of the whale oil house. The door was wide open, Frankie. You told me you latched it."

"Good thing I didn't!"

"Frankie, we have a boatload of people we are responsible for. Let's go."

"I'm serious, Scout. This is, like, history-book-level awesome. You know what this means, right? We'll be famous! We'll be rich!"

Scout shook her head. "Not awesome. Not famous. Not rich. Not for nothin'. This goes straight to the superintendent. No detours."

Frankie scoffed. "The superintendent? She'll turn it into a park fundraiser. And you know how obsessed people get about shipwrecks."

"Actually, I don't."

"Well, they do. Trust me—I know these things."

Scout raised an eyebrow. "Trust you? Frankie, you didn't latch the door to the whale oil house. You didn't close the window. Two things I specifically asked you to do. And then you left me stranded on the island. And you think I should trust you with this?" She held up the envelope in the air.

He grinned sheepishly. "Hey, I came back for you, didn't I?"

"Only because the skipper did a headcount. I've told you and told you. Always do a headcount before you leave the island." She tucked the envelope into her jacket. "Now, let's get back to the boat."

As they walked toward the skiff, Frankie said, "Pretty incredible we found it, huh?"

Scout turned to him with a glare. "We? We found it?"

"Teamwork, Scout. You found it, and I found you."

"I wasn't lost, Frankie. I was *forgotten*." She pointed to the front of the skiff. She wasn't about to let him near the controls. As they approached the tourist boat, Scout caught the curious stares of passengers leaning over the railing. She grabbed the rope the operator tossed her way and secured the skiff to a boat cleat with a sharp, practiced tug.

The skipper raised an eyebrow. "What took you so long?"

"Just tying up a loose end," Scout said.

Frankie snorted. "I'll say."

She spun to face him, her tone dropping to a no-nonsense whisper. "Not one word about that envelope," she said, her eyes narrowing. "Or I'll put you on latrine duty for the rest of the summer."

Frankie's jaw dropped. "Wait—you can do that?"

Scout arched an eyebrow, adding just a flicker of a smirk. "Try me." Her bluff seemed to work, but as she stepped onto the tourist boat, her thoughts remained on the envelope's contents. An odd feeling flickered through her—like the first ripple of a tide about to turn, a quiet pull whispering that something big was on its way.

***

Chase Fletcher stood on the pier, watching boats come in and out of the harbor, wondering how things had gotten to this point. He was the owner and publisher of the *Bar Harbor Gazette*, a newspaper that had been in his family for six generations. It had survived the Great Depression, two world wars, and more economic downturns than he could count. But under his brief watch, it was dying.

The morning's meeting with the bank manager had ended quickly, with a firm no. No loan extension. No lifeline. No room for negotiation. Chase should've gone back to the office, but he couldn't bring himself to face his staff just yet. They were like family. But without that extension, all options were gone. The thought of telling his staff that they were out of a job made him sick to his stomach.

His dad had always said it was easier to hear God's still small voice near the water. Chase had hoped that would be true today. So after leaving the bank, he had wandered down to the waterfront, trying to clear his head. It wasn't working.

His nerves were a mess, jittery, as if he'd overdosed on caffeine. He needed time to think, to pray, to figure out how to salvage everything. His mind swirled with the options suggested by the bank manager: Chapter seven bankruptcy—liquidate everything and walk away. Or chapter thirteen—buy some time to reorganize, though that might only delay the inevitable. What he really wanted, though, was something to keep the paper alive. A reason to keep fighting.

He silently offered up the questions to the Lord, asking for guidance.

And then it happened.

The sound of voices caught his attention. He glanced up and spotted Ranger Scout Johnson stepping off the Baker Island tour boat and onto the pier. Chase smiled faintly. Scout was easy to recognize, even from here. He'd met her at church a couple of months ago, when she'd first arrived in Bar Harbor. He'd asked her out for coffee on that very first Sunday, and they'd gone out several times since. Or had tried to. Seemed like he'd had to cancel about half their dates because of work. But he liked her. A lot. If he weren't drowning in deadlines and the endless crisis at the paper, he'd make more of a consistent effort to get to know her.

He picked up his pace, intending to catch up with her, but something in her body language made him hesitate. Scout had stopped at the end of the pier and was leaning in toward a young guy dressed like a ranger-in-training. Her voice was too low to make out, but the teen's was sharp and excited, his words carrying on the breeze. "But Scout . . . it's a shipwreck . . . with gold . . . we'll be rich!"

Scout's sharp response followed immediately: "Hush your mouth."

Chase froze mid-step. Shipwreck? Gold?

His reporter instincts flared to life. He pivoted, ducking behind a row of stacked lobster traps. Through the nets, he watched them. Scout had one hand awkwardly pressed against her jacket, as if she were hiding something inside. Her expression was guarded, tense.

She held a secret.

Chase's heart kicked into overdrive. He'd been praying for a sign, for something—anything—that might save the newspaper. A shipwreck, buried treasure, a story begging to be told. Mainers *loved* this kind of thing. If he could get the scoop, it might be the lifeline his newspaper desperately needed.

Chase peeked around the lobster traps again. Scout was heading up the road now, walking briskly, clearly on a mission. The kid was trying to keep up.

This could be it—the break he needed. Ranger Scout Johnson might hold the key to a story that could save everything.

He fumbled for his phone and quickly typed out a text message to his editor.

> Following a lead on a story. Won't be back in the office for a while.

Slipping his phone back into his pocket, Chase looked skyward and mouthed a quiet thank-you.

***

To: drjhjohnson@oceandiscoveries.org

Subject: Dad, You Won't Believe This

Dad,

Only a minute to spare. Long story short, on Baker Island today I happened upon a curious old envelope. Inside was a newspaper clipping about an 1852 shipwreck and . . . (brace yourself) . . . a handwritten confession of sabotage from the lighthouse keeper. Here's even more of a shocker: the keeper recovered gold coins from the shipwreck and hid them all over the park, leaving cryptic clues to the caches' whereabouts.

Wow, Dad. This is right up your alley! Or, better yet, right on your ocean floor.

Gotta go. About to tell the Chief. Stay tuned for what happens next.

Love, Scout

And with a decisive click, she sent the email to archives on her phone.

Author's Note

Charlie King's character is inspired by someone very near and dear to me—someone who grew up with an undiagnosed reading disorder and was told by his high school counselor not to bother with college. The advice? "Stick to a vocational path." Well, luckily, he didn't take that to heart. Much like Charlie, he pushed through and not only earned a master's degree but went on to have a successful career and a deeply fulfilling life. Still, there's always been this small part of him that feels he's not quite as quick or sharp as others, leading to this constant need to outwork the next guy.

School years are formative—whether they're helpful, hurtful, or somewhere in between, they leave a mark. Like Charlie, this real-life person has always had a teachable heart. Maybe that's why he's so great with people. He recognizes that everyone brings something unique to the table, and not everything can be measured by academic success. Sure, doing well in school might open doors, but keeping them open? That takes a whole other set of skills. As Evie Miller wisely pointed out, "There are all kinds of smarts. Book smarts, people smarts . . . and people smarts might just be the best kind."

On another note, I feel the need to caution readers that I have no medical training, whatsoever. I am blessed with an overabundance of curiosity (most writers are, I think), which leads me to reading quite a bit of nonfiction books about health and wellness, plus I listen to a variety of health-related podcasts while I go on daily dog walks. Still, this is a work of fiction. Any and all blunders are mine.

Acknowledgments

Thank you to my insightful editors: Andrea Doering, Barb Barnes, Kristin Kornoelje, plus her team of crackerjack proofreaders. The time and care you take to help each manuscript turn into the best possible book it can be—well, it's something most writers can only dream of. A big shout-out to everyone else at Revell for creating such a warm, supportive home for me and my books, including but not limited to Karen Steele, Raela Schoenherr, Brianne Dekker, and Laura Klynstra. You're such an incredible team to collaborate with.

To my readers—you make this whole writing journey such a joy. I cherish the connection we've built through the pages.

And as always, a heartfelt thank-you to the Lord, for giving me this amazing opportunity to tell stories. With each book, I try to find fresh ways to share your love for people. My hope is that these stories might draw someone just a little closer to you—the ultimate Storyteller.

Suzanne Woods Fisher is the award-winning, bestselling author of more than forty books, including *Capture the Moment* and *A Healing Touch*, as well as many beloved contemporary romance and Amish romance series. She is also the author of several nonfiction books about the Amish, including *Amish Peace* and *Amish Proverbs*. She lives in California. Learn more at SuzanneWoodsFisher.com and follow Suzanne on Facebook @SuzanneWoodsFisherAuthor and X @SuzanneWFisher.

Connect with SUZANNE

SuzanneWoodsFisher.com

Be the first to hear about new books from Revell!

Stay up to date with our authors and books by signing up for our newsletters at

RevellBooks.com/SignUp

FOLLOW US ON SOCIAL MEDIA

@RevellFiction

A Note from the Publisher

Dear Reader,

Thank you for selecting a Revell novel! We're so happy to be part of your reading life through this work. Our mission here at Revell is to publish stories that reach the heart. Through friendship, romance, suspense, or a travel back in time, we bring stories that will entertain, inspire, and encourage you. We believe in the power of stories to change our lives and are grateful for the privilege of sharing these stories with you.

We believe in building lasting relationships with readers, and we'd love to get to know you better. If you have any feedback, questions, or just want to chat about your experience reading this book, please email us directly at publisher@revellbooks.com. Your insights are incredibly important to us, and it would be our pleasure to hear how we can better serve you.

We look forward to hearing from you and having the chance to enhance your experience with Revell Books.

The Publishing Team at Revell Books
A Division of Baker Publishing Group
publisher@revellbooks.com

Revell